Praise for

THE SINGULARITIES

summons from Stockholm'

Globe

THE SINGULARITIES

THE
SINGULARITIES

John Banville

Swift

SWIFT PRESS

First published in Great Britain by Swift Press 2023
First published in the United States of America by Alfred A. Knopf 2022

1 3 5 7 9 8 6 4 2

Typeset by Scribe, Philadelphia, Pennsylvania
Designed by Soonyoung Kwon
Offset by Tetragon, London
Printed and bound in Great Britain by CPI Group (UK) Ltd, Croydon, CRO 4YY

A CIP catalogue record for this book is available from the British Library

ISBN: 9781800753365
eISBN: 9781800753372

MIX
Paper | Supporting
responsible forestry
FSC® C171272

In memoriam

Janet Elizabeth Dunham Banville
1944–2021

Singularity */-lar'i-ti/ n* the fact or state of being singular; peculiarity; individuality; oddity; oneness; anything curious or remarkable; a point in space-time at which matter is compressed to an infinitely great density.

The Chambers Dictionary

I

Yes, he has come to the end of his sentence, but does that mean he has nothing more to say? No, indeed, not by a long stretch. Here he is, in the chill brilliance of a breezy April morning, striding out into the world a free man, more or less. Whence came such spiffy raiment? There must be someone who cares for him, someone who cared. Witness the classy if outmoded camel-hair overcoat, its belt not buckled but nonchalantly knotted, the hand-tailored tweed jacket with a double vent at the back, the buffed brogues, the glint of gold at his shirt cuffs. Note in particular the high-crowned hat of dark-brown felt, new as the day, cocked at a dashing angle over his left eye. He bears lightly by its handle a gladstone bag, scuffed and scarred but discreetly good. Oh, yes, he is every inch the gent. The Squire was his nickname, one of his nicknames, inside. Nickname: apt, that. His name in the nick. Words are all that remain, to hold the dark at bay. For his bright morn is my brumous twilight.

Who speaks here? I do, little god, the great ones having absconded.

As a matter of fact, he has decided to change his name. Few will be taken in by this ruse, so why should he bother? But his aim, you see, is nothing less than total transformation, and in that endeavour there was no more radical start he could make than to erase the manufacturer's mark, so to speak, and replace it with another, of his own devising. The notion of an assumed identity excited him, the poor sap; as if a new name could hide old sins. Nevertheless, he spent what turned out to be an exasperating half-hour in his cell squatting cross-legged on the narrow bunk with pencil and paper, like a backward schoolboy toiling over his lessons, collar awry and hair on end, trying to fashion a plausible anagram out of what already he thought of as his former name; but there were too many consonants and not enough vowels, and anyway he wasn't any good at this kind of word game, and so he gave it up, frustrated and annoyed, and sought for a ready-made moniker instead. The choice was bewilderingly wide, from John Smith to Rudolf of Ruritania. In the end, though, he hit on what he believes is just the thing.

The simple pleasure of being free, or at large, anyway, is tempered by a dab of disappointment. He had always foreseen his release in the jet-and-nickel glamour of the gangster films of his youth. There would be a big blank wooden gate in which a much smaller, postern gate would open inwards and he would step briskly out, in double-breasted flannel and a broad tie, with his few belongings wrapped up in a brown-paper parcel under his arm and a tight cold smile notched in place at one corner of his mouth, and walk across a no-man's-land of cobbles and raked shadows to where a flash car awaits, with a toothpick-chewing thug at the wheel, and lolling on the plump back seat a platinum blonde in a white fur stole and seamed stockings, smoking an insolent cigarette. Or something like that, if something can be said to be like something else; the Brahma theory, as we know, puts even self-identity in doubt. But whatever potential there might have been for picturesque drama on the day was dissipated by the fact that the process of being released had been surreptitiously set in train long before the moment came when they shot back the bolts and flung the cell door wide and withdrew to a safe distance, bullwhips and pump-action sawn-offs at the ready—I exaggerate, of course. What I mean is that some years previously a directive had come from on high that he might be let out occasionally, for weekends and selected public holidays, on the quiet, and on the understanding that no precedents should be considered set thereby. Stressful outings they proved to be, he would have been better off staying safely inside. Then he was transferred from Anvil Hill, where the hammer of the law falls heavy, to the bosky latitudes of Hirnea House, a place of relaxed incarceration oxymoronically designated an open prison. He had not been happy there; he had much preferred the good old Anvil, where in a roomy but isolated block he had passed some twenty years of a mandatory life sentence contentedly among his mates, his china plates, lifers to a man, like himself.

You understand, the word *contentedly* is employed here in a relative sense; durance vile is durance vile, however plentiful the perks.

Anyway, they, we, the collective we, have sprung him loose at last, and here he is, briskly ascending a gravelled path to where a hackney car awaits him, a big black low-slung old-style petrol-burning model—you won't see many of them on the roads nowadays—with a front as blunt as a dugong's snout, and dented chrome hub caps in which the encircling woods are curvaceously reflected. For we are in the countryside here, among low, sheep-strewn hills which they have the cheek to call mountains, and he savours the birdsong and the breeze, the very emblems of freedom. Hirnea House, an isolated Victorian red-brick many-chimneyed pile, had hardly felt like jug at all, due in part to the fact that until recently it was not a prison proper but a secluded place of detention for the ordinarily insane.

The hackney driver, a gaunt-faced oldster with a smoker's

yellowish pallor, watches him narrowly as he approaches; the fellow knows very well who he is, since the car was ordered in his name—his former name, that's to say—which trails even yet the tatters of notoriety.

Names, names. We could call him Barabbas. But in that case, who is it they are crucifying, over at the Place of the Skull?

He draws open the rear door, slings in his bag and bends low and clambers in after it and slumps with a grunt on to the worn and shiny seat. Must shed some of this flab. No salutation called for, on either side. No apology for being late, either, of course. Drive, my good man. Fuggy odours of stale cigarette smoke, rank sweat, greasy leather, to which medley he supposes he is adding the old lag's tired, greyish reek. His good man regards him in the rear-view mirror with an oyster eye.

"Grand day," he rasps.

And I, where am I? Perched at ease as is my wont up here among the chimney pots, enjoying the panoptic view. We have met already, in one of the intervals of my faltering infinitude. Hello, yes, me again! See how my winged helm gleams in the morning radiance.

He has a friend, name of Billy, a former cellmate from Anvil days. Somewhat more of a mate, when push came to shove, if truth be told, for in the aridity of those lonely reaches the fleshly fires must be fed with whatever fuel comes to hand. But not another word on that score: time has long since quenched in him any lingering wisps of suchlike *feu follet*. Sweet Billy calls himself William now. Went legit and started up a little business, having always been keen on cars. Look here, we have his card here before us:

Hipwell Hire
Wm. Hipwell, esq.—Prop.
Motors for the Driven

And we must have a car: places to go to, visits to pay. Driving licence long expired, but pish to that. His pal Wm. will see him right.

But it turns out his pal has funked it, and he is greeted not by the proprietor in person but by his assistant. This is a decidedly frisky-looking young lady with a ring in her nose—fashions, he notes, have turned feral in the long interval of his incarceration—who from behind her metal desk gives him a measuring look and with a fat grey tongue deftly shifts a wad of chewing gum into the hollow of her left cheek preparatory to addressing his politely spoken enquiry. No, she says, the boss has been called away on business. This is plainly a lie, but she tells it with such barefaced aplomb that it doesn't offend. She casts a chary eye at his Dr. Crippen bag where it rests on the floor beside his foot trying its best to look blameless.

A motor has been laid on for him, she says, "and here's your licence, though that photo don't look a bit like you, Mister Mordaunt." He is pleased, and rewards her with one of his rare and only slightly baleful smiles: this is the first time he has heard his new name, or the second half of it anyway, spoken aloud, and he approves. It has a suitably lugubrious ring. I am thinking not of mort or daunt, not at all, nothing so swankily allusive. What I see is, let's say, some great lumbering moth-eaten beast, a moose, or an elk—is there a difference?—huge of head and scant of haunch, destined to end up on a plaque on a wall in the hallway of a baroque baronial hunting lodge deep in the depths of some forgotten forest in, in, oh, in I don't know where. You get my drift.

Before pocketing the licence he cannot but glance at the mugshot. Faugh! When, where, was it taken? He can't remember. The girl is wrong, it does look like him. It's true, the physical resemblance is poor, but the camera in its merciless way has caught something essential of him, in the menacing set of the chin, in the soiled expression of the eyes. We are speaking here of an inner essence, for the outer man is handsome still, in a brawny, blue-jawed sort of way, though he is coarsened noticeably by now, in the springtime of his seventh decade.

The office is cramped and cosily untidy, just like Billy's side of their cell used to be. Although it is many years since they last were together, he fancies he can detect on the air a trace of his prison butty's once familiar scent, mysteriously reminiscent of the salty fragrance of boyhood's sunburnt summers.

He is naturally put out that Billy—I mean, *ahem*! Mr. Hip-well, as the nose-ringed miss insists it must be, firmly correcting him and at the same time biting her lip so as not to laugh—that he should have chosen to absent himself rather than be here to greet him on his first day of liberty. He feels a premonitory chill. Is this to be the pattern? For a quarter of a century he has been as good as lost to the world, and many whom he once knew are no more, and it would go hard with him were he to be cut thus curtly by the few who remain of his former circle, however loosely bound the links of the chain may have been. What he doesn't realise is that the static universe he has stepped into, where properly speaking there is no past, present, or future, only a smooth sort of timeless non-time, is furnished with a whole new cast of characters for him to disport himself amongst. Oh, yes, high jinks and low are hand-rubbingly in prospect. You'll see.

The car Billy chose for him is a Sprite, a nippy little number painted a racy shade of red, with bucket seats upholstered in a matt black synthetic stuff as soft as a baby's skin and so new it is still tacky to the touch, the clinging surface of which squeals in tiny ecstasy when he slides his tweeded backside across it. The be-ringed young woman, preceded by a small metallic jingling, appears at his side, her buffed and lacquered hairstyle juddering in the strongish breeze. "Here's the key," she says, dangling it at him on a ring not much bigger than the one in her nose, "the tank is full, and don't crash it or Mister Hipwell will murder you, and me as well."

Again, His Misterness, and again that ill-suppressed, saucy smirk; he wonders if this fragrant pink little porker is favouring the boss with her favours. He hopes so. Billy chafed for female company, inside; he had always been adaptable, though he favoured the birds over the boys, as he made a special point of pointing out. "It's like the toothache, sometimes," he would say, gazing off wistfully into that powdered, chiffon-soft seraglio temporarily barred to him behind mistily gilded gates, "or a sort of a throb, like, in that thick part at the back of your tongue." This is the way they talked about you-know-what, like lovesick schoolgirls; lifers don't go in much for smut, you'll be surprised to learn.

The young woman tarries while masterful Mr. Mordaunt jiggles the gear-stick and clears his throat determinedly. He wishes she would go back into the office, for he fears making a fool of himself in front of her, since he's not sure he knows how to handle these newfangled motors. And he's out of practice, too. He hasn't driven since, why, not since that long-ago but never to be forgotten summer afternoon when he steered another car, a rental job like this one but much bigger and black as a hearse, down to a marshy place beside a railway line and abandoned it there, along with its bloodied but still breathing cargo. That was in another life, in another world, and yes, the maid is dead. Here now. Crunch the key into the suggestive little slot, vroom-vroom the engine, loose the clutch, and heigh-ho for the open road. But as it happened, he was too impetuous with the clutch and the car bucked like a spooked horse and the engine coughed and died, amidst peals of unheard celestial laughter. A muttered oath, then the key again, then the clutch again, *doucement doucement* this time, and off.

He had gone only a little way out on the road, however, when his foot faltered on the accelerator and the machine veered lazily to the left and rolled to a sighing stop by the kerbside. He sat forward, hunched over the wheel, gazing slack-eyed and unseeing through the windscreen. The sporty car, the swanky clobber, the office girl smelling of hairspray and sticky-sweet scent, even the innocent sunlight sparkling on the moulded panel of glass in front of him: by the stark facticity of all of this he was suddenly overwhelmed. Most sins can be denied, suppressed, forgotten, even, but not the unabsolveable one he nurses perforce within him, like a withered foetus. What's the point of all this overwrought talk, low facetiousness aspiring to the level of high art? It won't afford a moment's reprieve from the awful predicament of being himself. He murdered a fellow mortal, and thereby left a tiny rent in the world, a tiny fissure, that nothing can fix or fill. He took life, and got life.

What about a little weep, as you sit there sunk in the quagmire of your irredeemable self? Bit of a blubber, make you feel better? Ah, but as you told yourself long ago, if you were once to start you'd never stop. So: let's not.

Pulling himself together with an effort now he squares his shoulders and grasps the wheel more firmly in his two furred fists and with manly force directs the car onwards. No going back. The poor ape has been released into the wild, and still the awful clang of the cage door shutting behind him is, in his ear, the sound of the sanctuary gates slamming to. No, no going back. See him lope away, his knuckles grazing the ground, gibbering, red-arsed and alone, into the frightening thickets of the world.

He has even yet the homing urge, though, and it is to Coolgrange, the family seat, maryah, as we say in Erse, that he finds himself headed, unaware of the wondrous alterations he will encounter there. For we couldn't have let them leave well enough alone, now could we. Stone thrown upon stone, a lick or two of paint, an adjustment to this or that perspective. Why, he'll hardly know the old place, or himself in it.

You will be curious, if not burningly so, to learn how he filled the unfillable days of his stay in chokey. It was inordinately lengthy, for they simply wouldn't let go of him, not out of vindictiveness, in which he admits they would have been entirely justified, but due solely, so he believes, to bureaucratic inertia. This morning, as he waited at the front door for the hackney, which was late— it amused me, mischievous godlet that I am, to torment him with one final little delay—he totted up precisely how long he had spent inside, and was disconcerted, even a shade aggrieved, to find that, allowing for leap years and stopping on the bong of midnight last night, the sum came to a measly eight thousand, nine hundred, and ninety-four days, thirteen hours, twenty-seven minutes, and a sprinkle of seconds. Pah! it was hardly any time at all, when he broke it down like that, though it had seemed to him the very prototype of eternity; what has he been making such a thing about, all these years? How much he has to learn, as he ventures into this deceptively familiar-seeming corner of the multiverse, how much he has to be taught, about the true nature of time.

In the first months of his term, an era that seems by now almost beyond recollection, he experienced duration on two levels. There was firstly the cosmic aspect of the thing. Around him the great arc of existence turned with a barely perceptible motion, while he himself seemed as a squirrel scampering desperately on the rungs of an exercise wheel spinning so fast its spokes appeared a glittering blur. At morning he would wake in a state of panic, exhausted after a night of disorderly dreaming, dash through his day with unabating haste until lights-out came round again, then blunder into what was not so much sleep as a kind of anxiety-stricken paralysis. Yet for all the rushing and racing of his mind, time, in another of its aspects, what we might call individualised time, hung heavy about him, a dampish, clinging stuff, like newly laundered bedsheets on a clothesline, which when he tried to fight his way through them wrapped him round in suffocatingly warm, moist tangles. There was nothing to do, and therefore that was what he did, all day, every day, with fevered application.

Inevitably, and especially in the early passages of his incarceration, he thought of calling a halt to it all by knotting one of those clammy sheets into a noose and stringing himself up from the middle one of the three short iron bars, thick as dumb-bells, set into the small high window of his cell. He was put off this desperate course by the prospect of what it would entail, physical pain and spiritual anguish being not by any means the worst of it. Above all what he could not countenance was the thought of the vulgarity of the spectacle he would make of himself: the goggle eyes, the swollen and protruding, plum-blue tongue, the nether stains and stinks. No, he must hold on, he must endure, there was nothing else for it. All of life is a life term, he told himself, but was not comforted.

By the way, and in the spirit of accuracy, or should I say verisimilitude, the window of his cell on Anvil Hill was not high, was not small, and had no bars. Mesh-reinforced glass, yes, and, outside, a long drop to the uncompromisingly inelastic surface of the exercise yard. Nor was the view anything to write home about. Close to, there was that yard, where in the afternoons the hardier

ones among the lifers played listless games of football, and off to
the side a strip of unreal-looking grass—it might be fake, for all
he knew, a sheet of tufted plastic matting put down to obviate the
need of a mower and his machine—and, down diagonally to the
right, a stunted tree that would neither thrive nor die, but stood
there stubborn, year after year, in springtime putting out grudgingly a few apathetic leaves that seemed to wilt as soon as they
touched the air, and were unceremoniously shed, limp and sallow,
at the first cool breath of autumn. Of the city he could see nothing
save a distant spire, thrusting up out of the smog like the finger of
their God of gods pointing admonishingly in the wrong direction.

How grateful he was for the opulently generous sky, for its
lavish and ever-changing pageant.

We shall not dwell in detail on the strategies for survival and
the maintenance of semi-sanity that he cobbled together out of
the rubble left over after he had arrived, with startling swiftness, at wits' end. Suffice to say that he stuck his nose into many
a book—the library at the Anvil was notably well-stocked, and
was even better so after he had traduced and subsequently wangled
the removal of the prison librarian, an inoffensive child molester,
and got himself enthroned on the departed nonce's still-warm
high-chair—and forswore all hobbies. By day he made up for the
slumber he missed at night, drifting off at any hour and in any spot
he might be in, gently as a leaf sailing out upon a spring freshet;
daytime sleep was a floating state of stupor, blessedly free of nocturnal terrors.

One of his early essays at pretend escape was to imagine, while
lying on his back on his bunk with his hands clasped behind his
head—you can just see him, can't you?—that he was at the home
of friends for a dinner party, and that, sated on fine fare and costly
vintages, and fatigued by the brilliance of the company and dazzled overmuch by the tracer trails of flashing wit whizzing back

and forth across the dining table, he had slipped away to a nearby chamber and disposed himself on a damask-upholstered couch to enjoy a bit of peace and quiet. The fancy of there being others close by and convivially engaged while he reclined in solitude afforded him a crumb of lonely consolation. As the years went on, however, the very idea of being within reaching distance of an occasion of happy social intercourse came to seem more and more implausible, an insupportable dream of otherworldly bonhomie and grace.

His most rewarding means of diversion, in the sweltering stews of his nights—prison, in his experience, is always overheated—was to retrace in fantastically concentrated detail one or other of the rambles in the fields around Coolgrange that he used to take so frequently, so fervently, in the flushed days of his youth. For he was a tireless walker when a boy, and loved nature in all her aspects, the savage no less than the tame. He admired in particular the predators, the skulking fox, the stooping falcon, the domestic cat. Thus he learned at a tender age that violent death is the abiding fact of life. He was not morbid, however, not at all. Indeed, it was the flourishing of things that engrossed him most deeply. For him, everything was animate, especially trees, certain ones of which he held more dear than ever he could hold any human companion. He perceived pure being in all things, in the antics of madness as surely as in the most exacting refinements of religious ritual, in the crudest roisterings of farmers' sons no less than in the action of the sweetest sonnet. And in the being of being he perceived his own. Yes yes, he was a receptive soul, and never failed to spot the flash of the god's polished thigh among the laurel's restless leaves: *et in Arcadia* yours truly, as you see. Why else would we have bothered springing him from captivity, however late in the day we did it? Not much point in his being free if he's not to avail of freedom's abundance.

Yet his desire was not and never had been to sup at the font of the sublime. He cleaved most happily to Beldam Nature at her plainest. Give him a modest urban meadow in the midst of dereliction, sporting groundsel and nettles and a few nodding, lipstick-pink poppies, and he was content. You could keep the plunging chasm and the soaring crag, as far as he was concerned. Nor did he think much of the nightingale's hysterical warblings, or of the much-dithyrambed daffodil, the blossoms of which, as everyone knows but is too embarrassed to admit, are not golden at all, as is pretended, but in plain fact an acid shade of greenish-yellow, the colour of an absinthe-drinker's bile.

The sky, as mentioned, was his loftiest channel of escape; clouds he never tired of, the astonishment of them, in their ever-changing satiny self-absorbed glory.

There was a favourite walk he used to take, or he took it often so he must have favoured it. The official start, official for him, was a short and for some reason permanently muddy lane leading down from the back yard of Coolgrange House, passing through a gateway and straggling off to a small stand of oaks and beyond that to unfettered countryside. The five-barred gate itself, worn by wind and rain to a delicate filigree, the rust reminiscent of a dusting of roughly ground cinnamon, he can this moment picture clearly, with a fleeting pang of inexplicable, sweet sorrow. Sagging on its hinges, it gives, poor old thing, the impression of leaning dejectedly over itself, spent and blear-eyed, defeated by the years. It does open, but he prefers to climb it, enjoying the way it wobbles under him in geriatric panic, clanging and chattering. The action of throwing his leg over the topmost bar causes him to rotate a smart half-turn corkscrew-fashion, so that he finds himself necessarily looking back at the rear wall of the house he has just left, with its untidy rows of tall, sun-dazzled windows that seem to peer down on him with glassy disapproval. Perched there, he imagines himself a dauntless jacky-tar breezily aloft in the swaying crow's nest of a square-rigged man-o'-war out on the bounding main. A boy will be a boy, you see, even this one. And it's true, he was just your normal nipper, harbouring no thoughts of malice and murder. That all came later, and who knows why, or whence?

Immediately beyond the gate was a slanted field traversed by a broad flat grassy bank, immemorially man-made though to no known purpose. On it stood three noble beeches, I think they were, are, beeches, set in a line and spaced an equal distance from each other, evidence again of human agency. Perhaps it was the site of some rustic ritual of yore, featuring porter and music, and maidens and may blossom, and gay gossoons with ribbons in their hats capering the clumsy steps of an old-time dance and lustily clashing together their brandished ashplants. Or, less fancifully, they may have been planted there by some long-forgotten land-grabbing farmer to establish a boundary to which he had no legitimate claim.

In those trees he was privileged one day to spy a cuckoo, that shyest of birds, the minstrel of monotony. An unprepossessing thing it was, to look at, slate-grey with a sharp little bad-tempered beak and a shiny black oval stud for an eye. At his approach, it interrupted itself mid-call and peeped down at him through the leaves, and he could have sworn he heard it give a small gulp, of surprise, or fright, or both. For fully half a minute they contemplated each other, bird and boy, aware the two of them of being caught in a somehow compromising situation and not knowing quite how to extricate themselves from it, like a gentleman and his valet brought face-to-face by ill-chance in the front parlour of a back-street brothel. At length however the bird gave a sort of decisive flounce, seeming to gather up its skirts, and flew off into the second tree, and, when he followed it, off to the third, and then darted away at last and was gone over the brow of the hill.

When in his mind he took one of these meandering strolls down Mnemosyne Lane he was struck anew each time by how much of the far past he was able to retrieve, and how richly detailed in his mind's eye were the landscapes through which his phantom self strayed. However, proud though he was of his powers of recall, he was dubious, too. So clear and convincing were his recollections of that sighting of the cuckoo, and many another encounter like it—such as with the owl that flew low over his head one violet-tinted twilight in the midst of the fields, seeming on its great wings to suck a moving cavity out of the darkening air behind it—that he had to suspect he wasn't remembering at all, but imagining, and that what he was indulging in, huddled in the fug of himself under prison-issue blankets, was but a form of nocturnal daydreaming. And yet so intense seemed the reality, the—what is the word?—the haecceity, of the places and objects he encountered, and so palpable his presence among them, that it seemed to him he was there again, actually there, a big strapping hobbledehoy—again, I exaggerate—as alive as life itself, out stravaging the freedom of the fields, not swaddled in this blood-warm oubliette like a zygote lodged in the wall of the womb, so that, freed at last, he will not be surprised if, when he comes to encounter those happy fields again in so-called reality, both they and he should vanish, with no more than a ploppy little pop, like the non-sound of a soap bubble bursting, for assuredly they must cancel each other out on the instant, the matter of the world as he had known it, and he its anti-matter.

It seemed strange that not once on one of those winked-at weekends of freedom that had been granted him over the years had he thought to return to Coolgrange and have a gander at the scenes of his youth. Not that he held the place in any high regard. He cared nothing for his forebears and their doings—he supposes them to have been scoundrels to a man, and trollops to a woman, if he, their latter-day issue, is anything to go by—and besides he had never done much in the way of stamping on those old stamping grounds. No, it must have been a sort of shyness that kept him away, though what there was for him to be shy of he wasn't sure. Something of himself, perhaps, that might still be lingering there, something of what he had once been, the fresh-faced original that later would become so knocked about and sullied. When his mother died the house had been sold, to provide, it was hoped, a mite for her son's wife—widow, I almost wrote—and her son, his son, their son, to live on. The sum it fetched at auction was disappointing, though hardly a surprise, for the land had been worked out long ago, and the outbuildings were falling down while the house itself was barely standing up. He had thought his gaudy notoriety might fetch a few quid above the going rate, but even the prospect of sleeping in the bloody chamber where the beast himself had slept as a boy was not sufficient inducement for prospective buyers to delve any deeper into their miserly pockets. It didn't make much difference, anyway, since in the end, for all the vigorous efforts in the courts by his sad captain Maolseachlainn Mac Giolla Gunna, SC, RIP, neither he nor his missus saw a penny of the proceeds, the entirety of which was seized for the state coffers, under the terms of some ancient statute of the law of torts which stipulated that being a convicted felon the said appellant had no right of subvention over so on and so forth. In the intervening years the property had changed hands again, and was occupied now by the son of a fabulously famous savant, the old man dead though of deathless reputation, whose theories had struck down at a blow the world's and its wise ones' notions of what's what and where's where and how's how. Have I mentioned already that more than distinguished personage? Professor Adam Godley, deviser of the Brahma theory, qq.v. He was another who saw always the animate in the world's seemingly lifeless lumps, though with not much admiration and less delight. Our chap was acquainted with him, a little, in the long ago, as it happens; in fact, as it happens, Godley had once slept with his wife, or more than once, most likely. Little wheels within bigger wheels, all grinding and grinding away.

He wondered if the new lot might have changed the old name of the place—he had changed his, hadn't he?—in the hope thereby of smudging the association between Coolgrange and him and his infamy. The possibility disturbed him, for reasons that remain obscure. He did not doubt there would be other, more tangible, alterations, for repairs and restoration would surely have had to be effected; as said, the house was hardly liveable in when he was there, and that wasn't yesterday or the day before.

As he drove along now he began to have the curious sensation of all before him continually splitting open, like a great inexhaustible yolkless egg. How was he to cope with earth's profligacy? Prison had winnowed out the profusion of things, but now he was to be thrown back into the middle of the muddle. There was simply too much of everything—look at it!—motor cars, houses, shops, traffic lights, plane trees, hospitals, mortuaries, marching bands, monster meetings, earthquakes, famine, fire and flood, disasters natural and unnatural, corpse-strewn battlefields, mass exterminations, imploding stars, expanding galaxies—and always, of course, people; always people. Too much, too many. His heart quailed.

It occurred to him that he might make a diversion and pay a visit to the seaside. What better balm for the sin-sick soul? Yes, he would go and see the sea. But not now, not today. All this bric-à-brac spilling out of that endlessly separating eggshell and bouncing soundlessly off the windscreen in front of him was as much as he could cope with. The watery wastes could wait, for another time.

Being free, albeit on licence, but free for good if he is a good boy, feels strange. He can't quite credit it, and wouldn't be surprised if a length of elastic attached by a hook to the seat of his trousers were to reach its limit any moment now and yank him back—*boing!*—in the way that so often happens to poor rubber-bottomed Sylvester the cartoon cat. For one held so long inside, the outside is a place apart.

It was the middle of the morning when he arrived at Coolgrange, or what he used to know by that name. There are two means of ingress. The main gate opens on to a short drive that runs between two rows of full-grown lime trees straight up to the house. This he avoided—jailbirds do not fly in by the front way—and instead turned and drove on along the road that follows the curve of the old demesne wall. After a distance of a couple of leagues or so he came to an abrupt right-hand bend, in the angle of which, to the left, was a leafy nook where stood a narrow grey-stone arch enclosing something like a lychgate, if I have the term right, hidden from the road in a tangle of brambles and overlapped by a gnarled hawthorn bush. Here he pulled up, and parked on a triangle of grass as smooth and unnaturally green as the surface of a scummed-over woodland pool. He stepped out of the car, then stopped and stood. For him, a certain air of the uncanny had always attached to this spot. There was a sense of dreamy distractedness, of everything looking away, its attention directed elsewhere. A breeze drowsily tousled the spiked and shinily dark leaves of the hawthorn. The sunlight here seemed vaguer, hazier. No bird sang.

He leaned into the cramped back seat and plucked up his bag; it was as light as his life, what has survived of it. In a spirit of irresponsibility resurgent from the old days he left the Sprite unlocked, though pocketing the key. Let hot-wire who will. What did he care? He didn't even own the thing. Or maybe it would live up to its name and trip away into the woods and by some rude mechanical magic transform itself into a forest nymph, a light-winged dryad, and be happy there, haunting the vernal oaks.

As he went under the stone arch—the low, weather-worn gate had a rusted bolt but no lock—he experienced an odd effect. It was a shiver, or a kind of shimmer, as if he were not he but his own reflection passing through a flaw in a windowpane, or better say rippling over a crack in a full-length mirror. And stranger still, what emerged at the other side was not quite him, or was him but changed, being both less and more than he had been, at once diminished and at the same time somehow added to. The thing took no time at all, was over in the space of the blinking of an eye, yet the effect was palpable, and profound. Something had touched him, and left its indelible mark.

How, he wondered, did the prodigal son feel when the feast was over, the fatted calf picked clean and the guests gone home, the tears his fond old dad had shed on the shoulder of his long-lost boy all dried and life started up again? Did everything seem much like before and every bit as dreary, or was it all lit along the edges with a cold, mercurial flame, the brightness of the new, the re-newed?

Emerging from the shadow of the archway he stepped into that remembered narrow lane overhung on both sides by jostling hedges of hawthorn—there's haw again, that's for ill fortune—and wild woodbine, trembling fuchsia, and many other bushes and shrubs and so on I should know the names of but don't, all in blossom or bursting to be. This rear entrance was known as Lady's Way, no one at this remove could remember why. As a boy coming home from school he would sometimes take this route, daring himself to it, in spite or because of the fact of never feeling quite at ease here, nervous as he was of the straitness of the way and the menacing look of the foliage that crowded above him, even in the supposedly leafless depths of winter. Today he was neither suitably suited nor sturdily booted, the swaying briars had their eye on his camel-hair coat, and it would be entirely consonant with the moment were a bird to fly over and shit on his hat. What had he been thinking of, to come back here, here of all places? This was home no longer, if it ever had been. And yet he was drawn on, deeper and deeper, into a familiar world transformed, a transubstantiated world.

Helen Godley it was who spied him, as he approached purposefully along the back lane. She stopped on the first-floor landing, in front of the tall, arched window there, her right hand resting lightly on the banister rail. What caught her attention was the creamy-yellow hue of his overcoat, glimpsed in flashes as he moved along behind the hedge. For a second, at that distance, she didn't know what he was. He might be an animal of some sort, of any sort, a leopard, a llama, a kangaroo—a camel was the one thing she didn't think of—the notion wasn't so far-fetched. Last summer, or a recent one, Adam had rented one of the fields down by the Hunger Road to a circus for a week, and all sorts of exotic creatures were to be seen grazing the water meadows there, a pair of zebras, a tetchy little Shetland pony with a dainty russet fringe overhanging its eyes, and even a giraffe, that walked very slowly as if on stilts and munched the gorse bushes, its fastidious, leathery lips impervious to the thorns.

What was it called, the show? Somebody's Something Circus. More a travelling theatre, it was, with a long rectangular tent and a stage of sorts at one end and chairs and benches set out in rows. She got Adam to take her to a performance one night. He hadn't wanted to go but she had sulked and in the end he gave in, as she knew he would. The circus acts were interspersed with songs and comedy routines and theatrical skits. There was only a handful of performers, though they all took different parts, the juggler, the beefy strongman, the magician in a spangled cloak, the tiny girl contortionist, then the magician again, in a grubby white swallowtail coat this time, doing card tricks and tucking a chicken under his arm and hypnotising the poor thing by laying a finger along its beak and slowly, slowly lifting the digit high so that the bird went cross-eyed following it and he was able to let go his tight hold of it and it didn't stir a feather, just sat there under his oxter with its legs drawn in, looking up, transfixed. In the interval the one who seemed to be the manager, a squat, muscular fellow with a handlebar moustache, wearing shiny leather shorts and a Tyrolean waistcoat, sat on a chair in front of the stage with one chubby pink knee crossed on the other and played old-time tunes on a piano accordion. "Abdul Abulbul Amir" was one of them, she recalled, and "Yes, We Have No Bananas" and "The Boys of Wexford." The glare and the noise and the brassy music made her seem a child again, sitting in the front row rapt and motionless like that hypnotised hen with her face turned up to the thickly moted light falling down upon her from the stage. The strongman, dressed now as a fat clown with the tube of a car tyre suspended around his middle under his costume, tried to get her to come up on stage and take part in his act but she wouldn't, since he was bound to make a fool of her and besides she had always been afraid of clowns. He smelled of greasepaint and sweat and some kind of vinegary food he must have wolfed down before he came on. When she refused to go up to the stage with him he got into a rage, and cursed her under his smelly breath as he was turning away. Adam, needless to say, pretended not to notice.

Prospero! That was the name of it, it came to her at just that moment, just like that. Prospero's Magic Circus. She wondered if it was still touring; she doubted it, that kind of show was a thing of the past, surely. She'd go to see it again, though, if it did come back. The juggler, in a tight black vest and skintight black trousers and black pumps, had a delicate profile and was as slim as a girl or the son of a neck and a nun; she noticed the twin points of his hip bones and his slender wrists. The day after the show had departed, with the tent folded flat and strapped on to the back of a wagon drawn by two cart-horses, Duffy the cowman found a snake that must have escaped from whatever cage it was kept in and slithered into a ditch and died and the circus people hadn't bothered to look for it before they left. A huge thing it was, as thick as a man's upper arm. It was a python, or maybe a boa constrictor, so Duffy said. He had offered to bring her down to the marshes to see it but she had been too squeamish, and anyway she knew better than to let herself be led into a secluded spot by the likes of the bold Mr. Duffy.

She stood now with one foot braced on the bottom step of the staircase and the other flat on the landing. She saw herself posed there, in a splash of tremulous sunlight, admiring the curve of her hand on the curved rail, like one of the leads she used to play, Antony's Cleopatra, say, or Hedda, or Torvald's desperate wife, making an entrance, with the drama all to come, the speeches, the laughter, the shouting and the tears, and at the close the asp, the pistol shot, the slammed door of the doll's house. She missed it still, that old life in which she got to play so many lives.

But who could he be, the fellow in the fancy overcoat, striding along the lane as if he knew exactly where he was going? No one came in by that back way any more, through the Lady's Gate or whatever it was called. He was very sure of himself, she could tell that even from this distance, by the cut of him, thickset but tallish and so determined-looking, as though he owned the place. Maybe he was a relative, maybe her late father-in-law had a long-lost brother or a love child he had never told anyone about, she wouldn't put it past him, who had come back now to claim his share of the inheritance. She felt a tingle of excitement at the thought of everything being violently disrupted, and was shocked at herself for it. She must be even more fed up than she had realised. Or browned off, that was what they used to say when she was at school. *Honestly, girls, I'm seriously browned off,* pressing the back of a slack hand to her forehead and turning up harrowed eyes to the ceiling, a performer already. Well, the stranger in the custard-coloured coat would be bound to liven things up a bit. Though probably he was just a salesman, or a well-to-do cattle dealer, or another one of those scheming land agents, sneaking in by the back lane to waylay Adam and bamboozle him into yet another sure-thing deal that would cost them a packet and never show a return. Why had she got married in the first place and let herself be carried off into the wilds? She didn't belong in the country, she never had and never would. City streets and street lights and traffic going all the time, the rich warm air of restaurants and the soft half-darkness of bars, the smell of cigarette smoke and wine and men, all that, all that forfeited. She had thought because the father was famous that life with the son would be exciting, that there would be other famous people dropping in all the time, and reporters accosting her and begging her to give them exclusive stories about the old boy. She might get her picture in the papers, as she used to in the days when she too had fame. Some hope.

She wasn't dressed yet, for this was one of her increasingly frequent lie-in mornings. She had on her salmon-pink silk pyjamas with floppy sleeves, and Adam's old washed-out blue dressing gown. She was barefoot. In her room she had been painting her toenails and the polish was still not dry. She was sure her hair was all over the place. If she stood up close to the floor-length window would the Man in the Overcoat be able to see her up here behind the glass with the sun on it? She could press herself flat up against the pane, maybe undo a few buttons and give him an eyeful, that would get his attention, yes sirree.

She went back up to the bedroom and took off the pyjama bottoms and pulled on a skirt. Awful, the sweet yet stingy smell that nail polish leaves on the air; there was her own smell, too, flattish, fleshy, cotton-warm, she only noticed it now. She looked at the disordered bed, the glossy magazine lying face down on the sheet, the dent in the pillow where her head had lain all night. She felt like the ghost of herself come back to haunt the place where she had died only a minute or two ago. Dying is so strange a thing, she thought, so strange. She quitted the room again and shut the door and went on down quickly, the dressing gown billowing behind her and out at both sides. She whistled the tune of a song that had been in her head all morning since she woke up though she couldn't think of the name of it, but now suddenly she did: the Merry Widow Waltz, it was. *Daa da da dah, daa da da dah, daa daa daa.* Oh, the dancers, the orchestra, the shimmering chandeliers!

At the foot of the stairs she turned right and passed swiftly along the back hall, a place that always made her shiver, it was so dim and narrow. She shivered too at the chill of the tiles under her bare feet. When she was young she used to be able to pick up things with her toes, not just easy things like corks and ping pong balls, but pencils, and ha'penny pieces, and even spent matches. She wondered if she could do it still. She was sure a thing like that would stay with you, like being able to swim, or ride a bicycle. But she didn't think she should test herself and maybe find out that she had lost the knack, or, worse, that her toes had gone stiff. In a couple of months she would be forty. Forty! Every time she thought of it she got a horrible feeling in the region of her midriff, like the feeling you get when a lift gives a jerk and suddenly starts going down too fast.

The kitchen had the furtive look it always had when she stepped into it. As if the things in it, the table and the chairs, the pots and pans on their racks, that jam jar of wilted tulips on the windowsill, as if they had all been up to something and had stopped the instant she arrived in the doorway. She had expected Ivy Blount to be there, foostering about in her day-dreamy way, but she wasn't.

Ivy was going dotty, there was no doubt about it. She had always been odd, but lately she had got worse. Waiting for Duffy to marry her was driving her to distraction. He had proposed to her years ago, and had even given her a ring, though to Helen's sceptical eye it looked like one he had got out of a Hallowe'en brack.

He was strange, was Duffy, in the way country people are, at least the ones she had encountered, strange and surly and secretive. Helen was afraid of him, or not afraid, not really, but wary, yes, definitely wary. It wasn't love-crazed Ivy herself the fellow was after but her cottage and the few acres that she had got as part of the sale agreement when old Adam, father to young Adam her husband, bought the house and land from the Blounts she can't remember how many scores of years ago.

What age was Ivy? Sixty? A good bit older than Duffy, her reluctant fiancé, anyway. It was sad to think of the two of them, poor Ivy trying her best to be gushy and girlish and Duffy figuring out how to get hold of the land without the spinster attached. *Very tragicall mirth.* What was that from? She used to be able to keep whole scenes, whole characters, in her head, but all that was left now were broken lines and the odd scrap of dialogue.

The kitchen was dim and dank and smelled of gas from the leaky oven. The place was much too big to be a kitchen at all. It was always gloomy, with shadows under the corners of the ceilings even in the height of summer. It made her think of the set of an alchemist's cave—*O moment, stay! you are so fine.* The floor was paved with flagstones, and there was a big black range, and a dresser, also black, a big square scarred and scored deal table, and a sink wide and deep enough to bathe a fair-sized baby in.

She bit her lip so hard she thought it must bleed, and made

a sound that was partly a sigh and partly a sob. A fair-sized baby. When he was born, her Hercules, her darling Clem, had been hardly bigger than her two hands in which he lay curled, so still, his eyelids swollen and his skin still hot but already starting to cool. Ivy Blount had taken him from her and wrapped him in one of Adam's handkerchiefs, he was that small. Ivy was good to her, that day. Ivy had a good heart, even if she was half-mad.

But what had become of Mister Overcoat?

An old pair of wellington boots, as black and shiny as melted tar and cut off close above the ankles, stood beside the back door, the toes turned inwards. She stepped into them, holding on to the jamb of the door to keep her balance. The nail polish on her toes must be dry by now, and if it wasn't, what matter. The boots were Adam's but they weren't all that much too big for her. For such a hulk he had ridiculously dainty little feet; that walk of his, as if he were running up on tiptoe behind someone for a surprise. She noticed the worn round patch on the inner side of each boot, where his ankles rubbed together when he walked. She frowned again. She couldn't but be fond of him, even still, her big soft harmless pigeon-toed husband. It annoyed her, this loving and not loving him. She wanted a different life, had been wanting it for so long that even the dream of it had gone sour.

She opened the back door and walked out into the cobbled yard, the rubber boots slap-slapping like a clown's shoes; she thought again of the Magic Circus and the slim boy juggler with the face of a starving saint. There was a smell of hens, though there hadn't been hens here since the days of Ivy Blount's mother, who used to sell eggs to passers-by from a stall at the back gate, to Ivy's shame and speechless fury. How things change in time: Ivy keeps a few hens herself now, and trades their eggs on the quiet for bags of sweets and bottles of blackcurrant cordial from old Mr. Petit himself in Petit's Grocery in town.

Provincial life! Dr. Anton had the measure of it, all right.

The sun was shining but the morning air had a raw edge to it still, and Helen drew the dressing gown tightly about herself. The skin of her shins, she noticed, was mottled and shiny and greyey-pink. She wasn't used to seeing her bare skin like this, outdoors, in the unforgiving light of day.

The stranger had come in from the lane and was standing at the far corner of the yard. He was motionless, with his back turned to her, and seemed to be looking intently at something off in the distance. He was holding a new-looking and expensive brown hat in his right hand and batting it softly against his thigh. On the ground at his feet was an old-fashioned pigskin bag with buckles. Rex the dog was sitting next to him on the cobbles, and his back was turned too, as if he too were gazing at the same distant thing, whatever it might be. He sat very close up to the man, so that he was almost leaning against his left leg, and the man's left hand was resting on the dog's head and his little finger was slowly scratching the animal behind one ear. Helen was struck by the oddness of the whole arrangement, the burly man and the big old dog motionless beside him there in the stark morning light, gazing off the two of them at an unmakeoutable distant something. Rex, although he was old now and half-blind and lame with arthritis, always went into a fit of barking if someone he didn't know came into the yard. Maybe he did know the man, maybe the man wasn't a stranger, maybe he really was a long-lost relative, an Amphitryon back from the wars—*When you return, who will you be but you?*—for dogs never forget a scent no matter how much time has gone past since they last smelled it. But really, how strange they looked, the two of them, turned away from her and from the house like that. She tried again to see what it could be they were so busy staring at, but there was only the usual trees and stuff. Helen can never understand why people go on about the beauties of nature; to her, nature is just nature, it's just what's there, so what's the point of exclaiming over it all the time.

"Hello?" she said, too loudly; it sounded like a challenge though she hadn't meant it to. Some critics, the friendlier ones, used to comment on how she could project her voice ringingly to the very back of the stalls and yet maintain a soft light tone apparently without the slightest effort. "Is there someone you wanted to see?" she called, but in a milder register. Neither turned, not the man nor the dog, not right away, though after some moments the dog swivelled an eye in her direction and gave her a look of what seemed weary disdain. He had always been a peculiar animal, so sure of himself and independent-minded; Ivy Blount said it was a pity that when he was born no one had thought to tell him he was a dog like the rest of the litter. Having looked at her for a long few seconds he got up from the cobbles with a painful effort and limped out by the gateway into the lane and was gone. Meanwhile the man too now turned his head and looked at her over his shoulder. He smiled, it was a sort of a smile anyway, baring a tooth out of which the sunlight struck a cold white spark. It occurred to her what a sight she must be, in the cut-off rubber boots and crooked skirt and shiny pink pyjama top and a man's frayed dressing gown. Well, what did she care. So much of her life she had spent in costume, and what would this be but another part to play? Yet she drew the dressing gown more closely about herself. She wished she had stopped to put on a pair of stockings. She didn't like the stranger seeing her bare, blotchy legs.

He picked up his bag and came towards her across the yard, taking his time. Oh, he was so sure of himself, she could tell it by the way he walked and by the look in his eye.

So now here he sits, in the cavernous kitchen, a large gold man—that's how she thinks of him, somehow, hard and glowing and hollow inside—head haught, his knees comfortably crossed and his left forearm and left hand resting lightly on the big deal table beside him. She looks at his hand, at the shiny black hairs sprouting on the back of it and speckling the plump pads between the knuckles; like a pale spider, or a frog getting ready to jump. He hasn't taken off his coat, only unknotted the belt. A cufflink winks. He is at his ease, a lordly presence. And why not, he would say, for was not this house once his? Well, his mother's, anyway. Or so he believes; the question of whose or even what property it is will become increasingly moot, as the days and weeks go on, though only for him.

Where is his hat? What has become of his hat? Ah, there it is, on his lap.

Helen hasn't so much as enquired who he might be or why he's here. His coming, however unlooked for, seems to her quite natural. It's almost as if it was—what-you-may-call-it?—ordained. She thinks of how she saw him striding boldly along the lane, appearing flickeringly in the gaps in the hedge like a daytime will-o'-the-wisp. Yes, she finds no incongruity in his presence here, seated at the kitchen table, large as life or larger. He might have been here for hours; for ages; for ever. She wonders what she might offer him by way of refreshment. For it's clear he has come a long and weary way, this half-handsome, grizzled wayfarer. He appears to be—and this is something she is unused to—he appears to be less interested in her than in the surroundings against which she poses. He casts about. He is in search of something he seems to suspect is not to be found, not here, not any more. His heart beats slowly; it feels swollen. He thinks of his father, standing there at that very stove, stooped and wheezing, a red muffler knotted about his throat, engaged in the slow business of dying.

"I used to live in this house," he says, with a distracted frown. "When I was young."

Helen tries to see him as a boy, a child, a snot-nosed scallywag, but cannot.

"Are you a relative?"

"Whose relative?"

"Of the family. A relative of the Godleys."

He seems hardly to be attending.

"The Blounts?" she prompts.

"No."

Then who is he? Ivy Blount's people built this house and lived in it for, why, for centuries, which is a well-known fact, until Adam Godley bought it from them. How can this stranger say he lived here too? Maybe it's Ivy he's related to, a distant cousin, maybe. Oh, please, let him be—the fun!

"Have you been away?" she asks.

This amuses him.

"Oh, yes," he answers. "A long time."

"And now you've come back."

He fixes her with a quizzical eye.

"Have I?" He turns that doubting eye to the big window above the sink. Without, the wild world worlds, as it will. "Yes, yes, everything is changed," he murmurs, more to himself than to her, in a sort of calm amaze. "I don't understand it at all."

"Yes, it must all seem so—so different."

She doesn't know what she meant by this: what must seem different from what? This place has been the same, this kitchen and all the rest of it, the same since before she was born and even before he was, too, probably. She stands beside the range with a finger to her cheek. The range hasn't been lighted yet—where is Ivy, where can the woman be?—but it keeps yet a glimmer of yesterday's warmth.

Did this fellow have a fall, she wonders, or did he get hit on the head by someone or something and it affected his memory? She has heard of people having false memories which they're convinced are real. There's a word for the condition but she can't remember what it is. Not amnesia, but something like it, something-esia. For he's obviously imagining things. He does seem really to believe this was his or at least his family's home while plainly it couldn't have been. This is interesting. She half remembers a story of a person somewhere turning up like this in some place and claiming to have lived there in another, prior, life. Maybe he's a madman? Does he hear voices, and think he's at home in whatever house he happens to find himself in? On the other hand, people said all the time that everything was changing and anything could happen, because of what her father-in-law had shown to be the case, which apparently was completely different from what everybody had all along thought it was. Her husband has tried to explain it to her, in the way he does when he speaks of his father and his father's achievements and fame, at once dreamy and tense, his forehead wrinkled and his eyes bulging and shiny. She only understood bits of it, and anyway she couldn't see what all the fuss was about. Surely things are simply what they are, whatever anyone thinks or says about them. It stands to reason.

"Different, yes," the man is saying, "and at the same time the same." He lifts his hand from the table and turns it over and looks at his palm and sees a faint, cinnamon-coloured smear left there by the rusty gate in the lane. And there is mud on his shoes, from the sodden ground beyond the gate: shoes, Helen notes, that he didn't buy in a bargain basement or anywhere like it. There's something old-fashioned about him, somehow, it shows in that antique tarnished gilt glow he gives off. "It's very strange," he says. "I feel as if—" His voice trails away. "I feel—"

Yes, he's distracted. There's not only the puzzle of the place, but the fact that it's many a year since he was in such close proximity to a woman. He tries to think. In the interval between his being arrested and put away for life, there must have been females he brushed up against, girl solicitors, newspaper reporterettes and the like—in fact, now that I think of it, his first court appearance was before a lady district justice—but this is woman in full flower, the female entire, in all her otherness. He fancies he can smell her: or no, it's not fancy, his nose is as keen as it ever was. There is the must of sleep, the piney scent of soap, the smell of sweat, and cigarette smoke—is it?—and also a faint trace, a very faint trace, hardly a hint, forgive my mentioning it, of the excremental, for she has yet to take her morning bath. He looks at her. All mortals are naked under their clothes but she is nakeder, to his sharply penetrant eye. He detects in her manner a painful something, some old deep wound, the scar tissue hot and tender even yet. As you see, he is capable of a certain empathy. He wasn't always a murderer, though he always will be.

"Tell me," Helen says, for she's determined to have a straight answer from him about something, anything, no matter what, "tell me what it was you were looking at, in the yard."

"Was I looking at something?"

"You were, yourself and Rex."

"Rex?"

"The dog. You might have been in a trance, the two of you, staring off into the distance."

He ponders this for a moment.

"Ah, yes, the moon, it must have been. Did you not notice it? Very pale and thin. It's there still." He points to the window. "Always strange to see, the moon in daylight." She gazes at him unblinking, entranced herself, a little. "The name, by the way, is Mordaunt," he says, feeling the faint thrill of transgression. He does love a lie, even the littlest and whitest ones afford a dark delight.

"Is it, now." Her smile is ironical, disparaging, as if he had ventured a joke and it had fallen flat. "I'm Helen."

"Felix."

"Oh, yes? I've never met a Felix before. Is that how you pronounce it?"

"It's how I do"—a brief pause—"mostly."

Félix, in the French style. He wonders if it's a bit too far. A lie, to be effective, to do its work, requires subtlety, restraint, the measured touch. Which means nix on the fancy pronunciations, for a start. *Infelix ego.*

Helen reaches deep into the pocket of not-her dressing gown—it's her husband's, remember?—and brings up a packet of Gaspers, the untipped kind. So, his nose was right, she does smoke, the naughty girl. But perhaps they all do, now; in his day it was still ever so slightly the mark of the hussy. She crosses to the gas stove—first the range and now a stove, they must do a lot of cooking here—and ignites a ring with a handy thing that rasps a flint against a file to make a spark; how inventive they are, our busy little Prometheuses. The implement makes Mordaunt think of oil lamps and Primus stoves. Again he feels a stab of something—what, nostalgia? him?—for the dead days long gone. Yes yes, he's quite the softie, at times, in his way, though you wouldn't think it, to look at him and know the things he does, and did.

"Did you really live here?" Helen asks; she wants to keep the subject going, it's too interesting to let drop.

She has twirled the tip of her fag in the pretty blue gas flame, and now she takes a hurried draw at it to get it going properly. She tilts her chin and directs a thin fast stream of smoke at a sharp angle upwards. Light from the window gleams on her taut, polished throat. She is barefoot again, having stepped out of not-her boots when she came in ahead of him from the yard. Her handsome feet are long, slender, arched high at the instep. He wonders how she can bear the raw stone floor; women always complain of cold feet, at least the ones he used to consort with did. Crimson lacquer on the nails. Vaguely he thinks of the block, the martyr's blood; what a mind he has, what a mind—but how would he not?

"Yes, I was born in this house," he says, offhand but insistent. He is immediately startled, not by the assertion but by the starkness of the simple fact: the cord was cut so long ago that by now he finds unlikely the notion of having ever been born in the first place. He feels he has always been here; he would like to know if other people feel the same, or if they can recall their very first memory and thereby know the moment when conscious life began. For they live in the past, a luxury unknown to us the deathless ones, for whom the present perfect is the only tense.

"I've never heard of a family of Mordaunts living in this house," Helen says, thoughtfully.

A family, a flock, a gathering of Mordaunts. He wonders again, again uneasily, about the name, the names, if they were wisely chosen. Well, he's stuck with it, them, now. He is Felix Mordaunt, for good or ill. And knowing him as we do, we can easily guess which it will be.

"And yet we did," he says, "we lived here, father, mother, grandparents, all the way back."

He gives her what he judges to be an irreproachable smile, though what she sees is what she saw in the yard, a kind of rictus, stark, the very mark of insanity, as she thinks it must be. Perhaps he really has come here to kill her, or to kill somebody, anybody, this Mordaunt the Mad. She toys with the thought, airily. To be killed, now, there would be a thing. Again for a moment she sees herself on stage, as someone tragic, Cassandra done to death by an ignoble queen, or Iphigenia the same by her dad, the said queen's fated mate. Oh, she does miss her days on the boards. Often her morning make-up smells exactly like slap. Which reminds her now that her face is as unmade as the bed she not so long ago got out of. What must she be like? *Why, lady, thine own self all unadorned.*

She wonders if he knows she's wearing nothing under her skirt. She looks at her left foot and wiggles the painted toes, the sight of which cheers her up, a little, and pushes away a little further the thought of her dead child, her two dead children, or one and a half, since one died before it could get born; as if one wasn't loss enough for any mother, she darkly thinks. She eyes the gilded man sitting by the table. She probably wouldn't mind being killed by him. His presence has unsettled everything, as she hoped it would, though she's not sure now if she really does welcome the unsettling. She feels a prickling in her nostrils high up between her eyes, as if she is about to cry. And yet she feels she might laugh, too.

"Blount was the name of the family that built this house," she says, loudly again, to drive home the point. "Blount. Pronounced Blunt but spelled oh you."

Oh, you? He stares. His attention must have wandered for a moment, there. Oh, me, what?

"I should make tea," she says, turning her head aside, "or something." She doesn't move to do anything, but continues leaning with her hip pressed against the stove, ankles crossed, a palm resting in the crook of a flexed elbow, her cigarette held aloft between two stiff fingers in front of her face where it is busily smoking itself. Dreamy. She wriggles all of her foot now, her long yet blunt, spelled with a you, blood-red-tipped tootsie. She wouldn't cry, of course she wouldn't. There are times when she thinks she has used up her life's allotment of tears. "Are you hungry?" she asks. "Have you come far?"

"Yes, very far," he says, and chuckles. Every question she asks he seems to find amusing. This should annoy her but doesn't.

The moments pass. *Tum-ti tum-ti tum.* Cloud-shadow dims the window a moment, then the sun returns with a swish. I'm such a lazy slob, she thinks complacently. She likes herself, mostly, just as she is. If only it weren't for the tug of that old grief because—

"It's my husband you want to see, then, is it?" she asks. "Is that why you've come?"

At that table, she thinks of telling him, at the very spot where your hand is resting now, my husband's sister slashed a vein in her elbow and let herself bleed to death. How about that, Mister What's-your-real-name?

"Is he here?" he asks, glancing about but obviously thinking it unlikely. "Your husband?"

In his head he is counting, re-counting: eight thousand, nine hundred and ninety-four days, thirteen hours, twenty-seven minutes and he forgets how many seconds. Long enough, though; long enough.

"Yes, he's here," she says, and then: "I will, I'll make tea."

Just above the funny bone in her left arm is where she cut into herself with the razor. Helen couldn't imagine cutting her own flesh, she wouldn't have the courage, even the thought of it makes her shudder and feel she is going to be sick. But how clever of Petra to know just the place where there would be an artery. She knew a lot of things like that, did Petra; she could have been a nurse, or a doctor, even, even a professor in a white coat and horn-rimmed spectacles. After she was dead they found the project everyone knew she had been working at for years supposedly in secret, contained in a bookkeeper's thick ledger with a cardboard cover of a lovely dark duck-egg blue and filled with names and definitions and pasted-in illustrations. *An Alphabetical Register of All Known Diseases that Afflict Mankind,* the title was, she had written it with red ink in fat, inch-high letters on the inside cover of the ledger; she had got only as far as *chancre,* which by definition wasn't even a disease, she must have put it in just because it sounded so awful. What a mess of blood she left here on the table, and what a job it was to clean it up: Ivy Blount, with an oh and a you, was never the same afterwards, as she never tired of telling anyone interested enough to listen. If you lean down and look close you'll see dark stains still there between the ridges in the wood; no shifting them, even with a scrubbing brush, even with bleach. She speaks all this in her head only.

Petra, poor Petra, she is the past.

"Adam insisted it be kept," she said.

"What?" He gazed at her steadily, uncomprehending, incurious.

"The table. I'd have chopped it up, or burnt it." He doesn't know what I'm talking about, she thought, with sly delight. She turned away and dropped the stub of her cigarette into the sink, where it made a tiny hiss, like the sound of a quickly indrawn breath: taking one more quick puff of itself, the last. Everything lapses, in the long run. "But no, it has to be kept. He eats his break-fast off it, at it, every morning," and then in a la-di-dah accent: "it's positively ghoulish, don't you think—?" She broke off, then spoke again, more sharply. "Look, do you want tea or—?" She sounded cross suddenly, as if he had come there on purpose to be a nuisance and waste her time. But she wasn't cross; it was just, oh, it was just something else, it doesn't matter what. It's always like this in the morning, everything disconnected and annoying; she hates this time of the day.

"I'd drink a glass of wine." Mordaunt said.

His hairy hand emerging from the cuff still rested on the table, not like a spider now or frog but some swifter animal at rest after running. Such a stillness in him; he had hardly moved since he arrived and set himself up in the middle of the kitchen here, like a statue to himself erected on the spot. And all at once it came to her, she didn't know how or from where, that he had been shut away, for a long time, and had just this day been set free and emerged at last, blinking in the light. For he gave off something, something flattish, jaded, the staleness of an attic or a locked back room; that took the shine off the fancy shoes, the new and handsome hat, the opera singer's lavish overcoat. Monastery? Madhouse? The Asylum of Charenton?

"What kind of wine?" she enquired archly, putting on again milady's fruited accent. The fact is she is a little shaken now by the thought of him and what he might really be, and a little thrilled, too, more than a little, which is what makes her keep raising her voice and sounding on the brink of hysterics the way poor Ivy does all the time. He alarms her, thrillingly.

"Oh, anything," the man said. "Gin used to be my tipple. And wine"—again the smile, again the flash of an eye tooth—"*or* wine, that is, not both in the same glass, ha ha."

She nodded, scowling, as if he had said something that required her sympathy and she wasn't prepared to give it. What are the rules of etiquette when an ex-convict calls? For she has decided it was prison he was in, definitely. She always had a gift that way, for seeing straight to the heart of things. Clairvoyance, that lovely word. *Au calme clair de lune triste et beau.* She used to sing a bit, too, *L'invitation au voyage, Die schöne* something, *Les Nuits d'été son chant plaintif.* She sighed, and leaned down and snatched cupboard doors open, slammed them shut again, irritably humming. She really doesn't know where things are kept: this is Ivy's domain, her witch's kitchen. But here was a bottle half full of something dark and serious-looking. She examined the label: *1er Grand Cru Classé.* That should be the thing. She knows nothing about wine. The cork had been bunged halfway back in. When she pulled it out, not without difficulty, it gave a pained little squeal and made a pop and she caught a whiff of rot, of clay, and thought of graves, again. She took down a glass, peered into it to make sure it wasn't dusty, poured the wine, and passed it to him across the table, bumping the base over the wood's raised lines of grain, between which lurked deep down the terrible blood-black stains, as only she, of the two of them, knows. He glanced up at her. She fancied he might seize her wrist and crush the bones inside it like a bundle of twigs; he could do it, she had no doubt, with that hand of his.

"Cheers," she said, jaunty and wry, giving him a crooked smile, like the good-time girl in the saloon, holding the bottle lightly by the neck and wagging it from side to side.

He lifted the glass and drank, his hand and arm sliding oilily along a long-disused but never-to-be-filled-in or forgotten groove; he was as a recovering invalid, stretching and flexing the stiffened muscles, cautiously at first and then in a surprise of pleasure at the familiar ease of it all. The wine was too old: too old and too cold. He didn't mind. To sit at a table glass in hand. April light in the window. This woman. And the daytime moon out there, his talisman, he can see it still through a small pane high up at a corner of the big window, a coin of white gold hammered wafer-thin, transparent-seeming, embossed with the face of some drunken emperor. He has the sense that something inside him, a hunched homunculus, is weeping bitter tears and sobbing while he sits dry-eyed. Handy, a little inner man to do his grieving for him. We should have given one to all of them. Or maybe we did?

Helen slouched back to the range and set herself there in a studied pose, as before, on her mark.

"My husband is in bed," she said, loudening her voice again, as if expecting to be contradicted. They have taken to separate beds, in separate rooms, because of the dead children. "He's asleep."

"Is he." Her husband would be Adam, he thought, sole and undistinguished son of his namesake, the fabled shaker of worlds.

"He has to go on a trip to America," she said. "He needs to rest."

"I'm sure he does."

He took another sip of wine. Yes, altogether too old, yet he savoured the inky, acrid tang of it. The bitterness in his mouth, by a mysterious connection, reminded him that he was homeless.

"I need a place to stay," he said.

"What?"

"A place to rent, I mean, and live in."

She was making herself not laugh, he could see, like Billy's office girl; all women consider all men a scream in one way or another, this is a thing he knows.

"What? Here, you mean?" she asked, incredulous, and he did laugh, shortly.

"Anywhere. But here would do, if—"

Someone approached without, a rapid yet weighty tread. At the top of three wooden steps in a far corner of the room a narrow door he hadn't noticed until now drew open inwards and a big blond man ducked in his head.

Well, not blond, perhaps—we do like an effect—but fair, certainly fair. Fair, large and sheepishly maladroit, and, just now, rumpled after his late sleep. He wore a fisherman's blue jumper, no shirt, baggy trousers, big rough sandals. His brow and the saddle of his nose are of a sandy cast, though his cheeks are pink and softly smooth, as if he hasn't started shaving yet though plainly that can't be. Middle forties? More? Vague anxious eyes, milky-blue. There you have him, Adam Godley the younger, a large soft-faced middle-aged man in clumsy rope-soled sandals a mendicant monk would scorn to be seen in.

His eye fell on the stranger at the table and he paused irresolute, his thumb still on the door-latch. Then he looked to his wife, in her bare feet and wearing his old dressing gown and a skirt and not much else, as was plain to see.

Exits and entrances, where would I be without them? No sooner had this man appeared at one end of the room than at the other end the back door opened with a rattle of loose hinges and Ivy Blount came in.

At sight of so many people in the room she gave a tiny cry and swivelled on her heel and would have fled had not Helen, in her stage voice, called to her sharply and ordered her back.

"The range is out," she said accusingly. Ivy from the threshold stared. Who is this strange man seated at the——? "This," Helen said, turning to address her husband where he teetered yet on the wooden step, "is Mr. Morden."

"Mordaunt," *faux*-Mordaunt put in politely, though with emphasis.

"He needs a place to stay," Helen added, unruffled by her mistake.

Adam looked at her warily—he is ever uncertain of her moods, her caprices, the various mobile masks she puts on and takes off at will—then looked again at the man sitting there, the unaccountable man in the dodgy fawn overcoat.

"There's no kindling," said Ivy Blount, cursing in her mind her supposed inamorato, the feckless Duffy. "I'll have to chop it myself, I suppose."

Ivy is too tall and too thin, with a thicket of greying hair a bird could build in. She is a gentle soul but her heart has become a place of drought. She exudes a mingled odour of house dust and dishwater and the cheap cigarettes that her intended, her all-too-tardily intended, persists in smoking in her presence, although, or because, he knows it annoys her; also of something soft and gentle, the scent of love's old sweet something from long ago. She is a creature out of time.

"Mr. Mordaunt," Adam said by way of greeting, picking his dainty, top-heavy way down the steps into the kitchen proper. "Are you from the——?"

"No," Mordaunt said smartly, and smiled his smile. A bead of rubious light shone in the bottom of his drunk-from glass. He is not from anything, he is not from anywhere; he wishes that to be understood at the start. He is a new thing altogether.

"Ah," Adam said, sounding relieved. "I thought you might be Professor Jaybey's agent or"—he faltered—"or something of the sort."

At mention of him this so-far-unheard-of Jaybey becomes for a moment a presence in the room, a flickering, faceless shade, then fades.

Adam advanced, making formless passes with his right hand, as if he would offer a handshake, but did not. Something seemed to tilt violently above the table, everyone felt it, as of a planchette phantomly roused, then seemed to right itself.

Ivy was on her knees in front of the stove, poking at its ashy innards with a charred stick.

"You'll stay to lunch?" Helen asked of Mordaunt. She turned to Ivy down there kneeling. "He'll stay to lunch."

Ivy said nothing. She straightened suddenly and sat back on her heels; she seemed about to sneeze; didn't; then did. She wiped her nose smartly on the sleeve of her thin grey cardigan. She wore what looked like a man's flannel trousers, old and worn and too big for her besides and sagging at the rear. She hasn't much in the way of hips, or of anything much else in the region, for that matter. She was once a sylph: our lily of the valley, her father said, of all the valleys. Ah, how time abrades them, the mortal ones, how the years wear them down, wear them out.

Adam Godley, shying from the stranger, pursed his lips and skimmed with scampering fingers through the morning's post which someone had left neatly stacked and squared on a corner of the table. He yawned violently, his jaw joints crackling. Always yawns when he's tense, it's a thing he has noticed about himself. He doesn't care to have strangers in the house, as his wife is well aware. What is this fellow doing here and why did she let him in?

"I should be going," Mordaunt said, as if sensing the other's thought, yet did not stir from where he complacently sat.

"But you're staying to lunch," Helen reminded him forcefully. "Do you want more wine?"

He didn't reply, and she uncorked the bottle again, and poured again. How particular a thing it is, she thinks, the muggily soft yet rancid smell of wine in the middle of a morning; like a wrong note in a melody. Mind you, she often takes a matutinal sip herself and more than a sip as we'll see.

Mordaunt's bag was set on the floor beside him like a small smooth fat brown pig with its trotters tucked in. He might have a gun in there, Helen idly thought, or a bomb, even. Whoosh! and the whole place blown sky-high, chairs, tables, pots and pans, parts of people, all raining down clatter! bump! splash and spatter. "Ivy has a room she could rent out," she said to no one in particular, and particularly not to Ivy.

Who appeared not to have heard anyway. She rose from her knees with an effort, dusting off her narrow, chapped, once lily-white hands.

"There's the rest of that steak-and-kidney pie left over from last night," she said. Helen turned away from her to Mordaunt and made her face into a comically tragic mask, the mouth down-turned grotesquely in a sausage shape. A director had once told her she could have been one of the great clowns, a Josephine Baker or a Lotta Crabtree. Lotta——? Never heard of her but she could see her, a fat totty with rouged cheeks and ringlets and a bonnet and a big velvet bow. Thanks very much, I'm sure. "I could make a salad to have with it," Ivy, offhand, added. "Or spuds."

Then for a moment no one spoke, but stood or sat and stared at nothing. They sense without recognition my presence moving amongst them, faintly, so faintly, as of a breeze, a sigh, a soft swirl in the air. Mordaunt was studying the wine glass on the table by his elbow, a goblet set on a stem, and thinking how things are their own ideal forms. A wine glass is a wine glass and cannot be more or less, though Godley the Ungodly and his theories disagree.

"My car is parked on the road out at the back," he said, as if it were a matter of some moment. The others, even Ivy, turned their eyes to look at him. He returned their look with a mild look of his own. "Out by the gate into the Lady's Way," he added, helpfully.

Helen thinks: how does he know the names of places here? Maybe he is old Adam's bastard son, after all, or a distant Blount, and did live in this house, though it's plain to see her husband doesn't recognise him and Ivy doesn't suspect. A mystery man, all right. She's glad he'll stay. Who knows?

A sigh, a breeze, the faintest stirring, then all still again, as if the all is ever still. I see the scene enclosed in a vessel of most fragile glass, my busy little creatures confined in a flask, with a curved and intricate image of the kitchen window reflected in miniature on its rounded cheek.

Someone must watch, it is said, someone must be there. Someone.

In recent weeks, not that she has been counting, not that she's capable of counting, the simplest arithmetic being beyond her powers now where she is, adrift in this glimmering eternal nowhere, she has got it into her head that there are people in the house besides herself. The servant woman doesn't count, she's used to her, although she can't recall her name, she thinks it's the name of a plant or a flower, something horticultural, anyway, she's sure of that. This woman brings her meals on a big silver tray, porridge or a boiled egg in the morning, some sort of soup at noon, usually grey and glutinous though clear sometimes, clearish, with bits of things sunk to the bottom and lozenges of fat floating on top, and in the evening a plate of uncertain stuff, mostly of an off-white shade, such as mashed potato, mushed cauliflower, swedes, though she's not sure about the swedes, she's not even sure she knows what a swede is, never having spent much time in the kitchen, but something, anyway, boiled to a lumpy paste, alongside slices of grey meat, chicken or veal or that pale kind of pork, it all looks the same to her, tastes the same, too, steaming a bit and horribly glistening. She never eats any of it, or eats only a little, in case the woman might shout at her, hardly more than a bite, a nibble, a taste. That tray she does remember, though, from the old days, or the young days it should be, why do they call them old, since everyone then was young, or every one of the ones she remembers was? It has a scrolled silver surround, and delicate handles that remind her of Adam's ears, he had such nicely shaped ears, she can see them now, yes, really pretty you could say, which is remarkable since on the whole the ear is not a pretty thing to look at or especially into. The servant is old, not as old as she is but no spring chicken either, that's for sure. She hardly speaks, except to say hello, how are we today, here's your breakfast, lunch, tea, dinner, sleepy-time glass of milk with a nighty-night pill crumbled into it. The woman, the servant woman, is a scarecrow, scrawny and spindle-legged, with hair like steel wool that she must never take a comb to, the way it sticks out straight from her head in all directions, wiry wavy strands of it, as if she had been struck by lightning or got an electric shock. There seems to be something wrong with her, she's sick in some way, dying, maybe, although of course she never mentions it, maybe doesn't know it. The tray needs polishing, silver if it's good shouldn't be allowed to tarnish, the tarnish eats into it, she thinks of mentioning it to the woman, the maid, if you could call someone that old a maid, but she's afraid she might take umbrage and stop coming. She could easily stop coming, there's no one to compel her, so far as she knows, unless the people might, the strangers she thinks are down there in the house. But say she were to stop coming, then what? Then where would she be? Up the creek without a paddle. Tee hee.

Below her in the house there are sounds, she's sure there are, she tries to concentrate on listening for them, to them, but her attention wanders, and she hears them only after they've stopped, if that's possible, so it may be she's imagining them. Footfalls, she thinks there are definitely footfalls, and voices, too, sometimes, very faint and far off, or faint because they're far off, and kitchen noises, someone raking the ashes in the range and rattling saucepans and running water into the sink. Laughter as well, now and then, only now and then, and only in short bursts. Maybe the woman is the housekeeper and the ones making the noises are the servants, the cook, the scullery maid, the cheeky boy who does the boots, larking while they should be working. But she doesn't think there are servants, any more, if there ever were. And she knows the kitchen is far too far away, she couldn't be hearing sounds up here from down there, maybe she's just remembering them, the sounds of life going on in the way it does. She lives in her mind, in her memory, what's left of it. In fact there are times when she herself seems to be only something remembered. She is losing her sight, her hearing is going too, soon she'll be like a little wrinkled nut, lost and forgotten in the hollow husk of the house.

There is a bad smell from the pot under the bed. She should tell the woman, the maid, the housekeeper, whatever to call her, to empty it, but she feels too embarrassed since she's the source of the stink. She'll have to wait until it gets so strong the woman won't be able to go on ignoring it. How awful everything is.

Umbrage, though. To take umbrage. What does it mean? Isn't umbrage something to do with shadows? *Ombra mai* la-la, she hums the tune aloud in a quavery falsetto. All these remembered things, all in a jumble. She will ask Adam about umbrage. Adam will know, he knows everything. Only, Adam is dead. He is her late husband. Never get used to it, never. And why late? Late of

The Larches, Ballymore the Bountiful, as she is, as she used to be. Late of this world.

Once she was young. Once she was a girl. She feels such compassion for the poor pale frightened creature, the image of Petra, that she was then, knowing next to nothing and waiting anxiously for the future to come and change everything and half hoping it wouldn't. How can we live grown up having once been small? They are so brave, she thinks, children, facing into a world we made for them, so frightened and yet fearless, like little soldiers marching into a battle they know they won't survive, or won't still be themselves if they do. We don't deserve them, and they're stuck with us. She wanted to go to boarding school but they wouldn't let her. Too dear, they said, where are we supposed to get that kind of money? Never short when they wanted to go to the races or buy a new car or for a holiday on the Côte d'Azur. The Côte d'Azur. Oh, the blue down there, the white hotels along the promenade and then the blue of the sea and then the blue sky with a tiny, glittering aeroplane creeping across it.

She remembers suddenly that she has a son, also called Adam, goodness, how could she have forgotten that, is she that far gone? It might be he who is making the noises that she thinks she can hear below in the house, not the ones in the kitchen but the other sounds, the footfalls and the hushed voices speaking and sometimes a cry, or a shout, or maybe it's just something on the wireless, a programme on the wireless. He might be here, with his family, with what's-her-name his wife, and their children along with them, they have children, haven't they, little boys, little girls? But if there were children there would be much more of a racket. If there's one thing she knows about children it's how noisy they are. As well as brave. It's a long time since she has seen one. No, Adam hasn't got any, that's right, his wife, her son's wife, what is her name, keeps losing them, no sooner do they pop out of her than they perish. That must be very sad, for her, for him, and for them, too, of course, the children themselves, the non-children. Would an infant know it's dying? Think of it, just out of one darkness and straight into the next. There used to be Limbo, where they were sent to, but that would be worse than being nowhere, wouldn't it?

Beset by stiffness and her old aches she tries turning over in the bed to get relief only to find she's not in a bed, but half sitting half reclining in the sprawly old practically worn-out couch or chair or whatever it is that used to be in the Sky Room and that Adam would throw himself down on when his calculations weren't going right and he got in a rage and had to lie without stirring to calm himself. One time when he was away she got it reupholstered, the chair, in velvet, of a nice deep rich burgundy red that made her think of popes, and he was furious when he came back and saw what she had done, said it looked like something you'd see in a brothel, well, you'd know all about that, she thought but hadn't the courage to say. When the sun shines in through the window on to the fabric, the red of which by now has faded to a dusty whitish-pink, it gives off a warm dry smell that brings back to her the smell of the canvas shades that genteel people used to hang over their front doors in summer to keep the paint from peeling in the sun, when she was a girl, in Ballymore. Or no, they weren't hung, but stretched, somehow, stretched stiff from top to bottom, with something holding them at the bottom, a rod, yes, a brass rod with a brass knob at either end in the shape of a fir cone or the bud of a flower. She remembers the sound the shades made when they flapped in the summer wind, like flags, like sails, or harder, sharper, maybe like whips? no, sails, like sails. Or flags. Strange, the way when one was young one noticed small things like that, noticed them and fixed them and stored them away, as if thinking they were bound to be important or useful or something in the far-off future. She had a stamp collection in those days. What became of it? It would be worth money by now, thousands, maybe tens of thousands, even. Such lovely colours, such tiny intricate designs. Madagascar. Malaya. The Trucial States. Her father used to buy stamps for her when he went abroad and send them to her, little cellophane packages of stamps, delicate as a butterfly's wings, though sometimes it was an envelope with the stamps still on it. But where did he go, abroad? Where did he travel to and why, that he was able to send things back to her? Oh, she can't remember, she can't remember anything, it's so annoying. It must have been odd, to get an envelope with stamps on it in a stamped envelope. A thing inside of a thing the same.

When she opens her eyes she expects the lids to make a little creak, like a pair of tiny wooden shutters opening. That time in where was it, somewhere in the south, in Roussillon, maybe? in the square room with the big black ceiling beams and the single, square window, and Adam pushing open, flinging open, the heavy shutters that were made, he told her, of olive wood, and letting in the morning light, at first a glaring, grainy haze that dazzled her, then the view coming into view like a painting painting itself in one quick go, the rust-coloured earth and the sinuous black cypresses that looked like plumes of oily smoke and the far hills that seemed no more than a flat cool transparent pale-blue wash. He laughed at her, at her oohing and aahing. "Dashed off by the one-eared Dutchman himself, just for you," he said, with his widest, thinnest smile, standing aside and bowing low with his head cocked to one side and his slender-fingered slender hands held up, one above the other, the palm of one and the back of the other, doing the impresario or master of ceremonies, presenting to her the prospect outside that seemed to her smudged now, that seemed to her spoiled, by him, by his teasing her and laughing at her. When she was away somewhere with him like this she always thought of his dead wife, the woman she had never met but felt she had, so much was she a presence in their lives together, hers and Adam's. He stood close behind her at the window, a head taller than she was, and laid his hands lightly on her shoulders. So hot the day, so hot, and the cicadas wreathing the trees with that terrible throbbing sound they make with their back legs isn't it? My little brown bear, he called her, because of the way her skin got tanned so quickly in the southern sun, and because of her name, Ursula, *ursus* meaning bear in Latin, her name which he knew she hated, and of which he made such playful, cruel and relentless sport. Why did they christen her that in the first place? Maybe they didn't know what it meant in Latin, they weren't well educated, for all their grand ways.

He had no mercy. There were two pearls someone had given him that he kept in a little velvet box, and when she fought with him or more often pleaded he would press them into his ears, one in each ear, to shut out the sound of her voice, and lean back and fold his arms and look at her with his thin, wide smile that made his mouth seem as if it had been painted on, like a clown's. Oh, how he delighted to see her in pain.

And that one, that mother of his, the Widow Godley. A blight she was on us, on me, for as long as she lived. I say to her what she would say to me, the curse on you of the seven snotty orphans, you old rip. She tried to get rid of me at the start. I often think he married me only to spite her.

The window in front of her now, here, the window of what she takes to be her room, her living room–cum–bedroom, as if living and not dying were what she's doing, looks along a muddy lane to an old rusty gate and the small oak wood beyond and to one side, which is hardly a wood at all but only, what is the word, a copse. With her sight so bad she has mostly to imagine the world into being there, and so she can't be sure if there really is a lane, a gate, a wood, or just her imaginings of them, her picturings of them. The house must be real, though, this big old ugly house she has always hated. Away with it! Smash it up, knock it down, burn it to the ground! If only she had an axe, a hammer, a match.

Mice, too, they come and go, she hears their tiny, soft patterings. She doesn't care, there's room for all. She used to have a mechanical mouse, when she was little, you wound it up and put it down and it would scurry across the floor on invisible wheels, it looked just like a real mouse. There's a bigger something too, that lollops along with surprising swiftness, furtively, close by the skirting board, and stops suddenly and sits up on its back legs like a fat and rotting pear that has grown fur, showing her its pinkish-white belly, and regards her with frank interest and what seems to her a touch of amusement, twitching its whiskers and wet nostrils and split snout as it snuffles up all the lovely, to it, aromas, from her and from the bed and from what's under the bed. She knows it's a rat but makes herself believe it a big mouse, a monster mouse, the leader of the flock, King Mus Musculus the Mighty.

. . .

Copse. Funny word. As if it had let drop a letter.

What? Someone has come into the room. She tries to turn her
head to see but she can't, really she can't turn it, or not far enough
anyway, her neck is so stiff. It doesn't matter, it will only be Petra.
It's always only Petra, unless it's the maid. Petra usually appears
at this time, about this time. She is my visitor, no my caller, my
constant caller.

Something ripples in the room, something shimmers, as if the
air had developed a vertical, softly running fold, like the fold in a
gauze curtain blown against by a breeze from an open window, a
window open to the south. They went south from Roussillon to
where was it? The big white hotels on the front, looking across the
Baie des Somethings, where? She wanted to go on and see Venice
but he said no. Too many tears shed there, he said, and got angry
when she asked him to tell her why he had wept, what tears? why?
for whom? But he will never tell her, never let her into his past
where among others his first wife lives, the one who died. He had
secrets, so many secrets, he hugged them to him as if they were his
children, maybe they were his children, a child in every port, ha!
And he would tease her, tease her with his secrets, until she wept,
and then he would put the pearls in his ears and gaze at her as if
she were some sort of curious exhibit, something in a freak show.

She's always so cross, Petra is, when she comes, always cross with
her mother, as if she, the mother, were to blame for things being

so dreadful for her, the daughter, when really everything is dreadful for everyone. But it doesn't last, her daughter's being cross, she gets bored and has to be something else, has to be someone else. Everything bores her. She tells her, Petra tells her, tells her mother, about a young man in the nineteenth century, in France, she thinks it was, he was, or maybe London, or Berlin, or Moscow, or the city of Mulligatawny, she can't remember, it doesn't matter, who blew his brains out and left a note to say it was because of the buttoning and unbuttoning, that he was tired of it and couldn't be doing with it any more. All the buttoning and unbuttoning, he wrote in his copperplate hand, no, no, far better a bullet. And Petra laughs, does her shrill mad laugh that she stifles at once, pressing her knuckles so hard against her lips that they turn white.

They talk of things, all sorts of things, the two of them, she and her daughter. Of the old days, the young days, the happy days, but were they happy? Sometimes. Moments. Intervals. Fizzles. Petra hums now, pale lips clamped tight together, a thread of sound coming out between them, a thin thread, thin and silvery like a cobweb, rising and falling, more a wail than a hum. She sits on the floor, leaning on a fist with one shoulder lifted, her skinny legs folded away behind her like a mermaid's tail. Her mother sees the hatching of pearly scars on the underside of her arm from wrist to elbow. Silence between them, long silence. Then they speak again. They speculate about the young man who shot himself out of boredom. They see him as tall, pale, indolent, wearing narrow patent-leather shoes as soft as slippers, trousers ballooning at the hips but tight round the ankles, a bottle-green cutaway and a nankeen waistcoat and a starched stock soiled along the edge where it rubs against his neck which is grimy already though it's still only morning. He paces a gaunt upper room in a dingy lodging house, stops by a low window, leans down to look out, a hand braced against the casement as Petra's hand is braced against the floor. His narrow face and pale broad brow, like Adam's face, and the gaunt cheeks, the weary, inexpressive eyes. Grey wintry day outside, the wind a faint thin moan. He sees a huddle of rooftops, a steeple a long way off. Steeples and spires everywhere in every hamlet and town and city in the land, spires and steeples, how are they different or are they the same, two words for the one thing? No, the spire sits on the steeple. She believes that's the case. She's glad she cleared that up, a thing like that could torment a body for days. A carter goes past in the street, uttering his incomprehensible cry, his horse clops along, its head hanging, its bony flanks asway, poor starveling. A flaw of smoke swoops down into the street, sweeps on a little way and then is torn into tatters by the wind. You see, Petra says, in those days, in those days there would have been so many buttons, on the sides of his shiny shoes, for instance, and at the ends of the tapered legs of his puffy-waisted trousers, on the cuffs of his coat and on the coat itself, on his waistcoat too, and even at the back of the stock, a single one, not a button but a something else, that holds it fastened, think how annoying all that, all those, would have been to do and undo. She sees his face so clearly, the pinched vexacious mouth, the nostrils two flared black tear-shaped pearls, and the arms lifted in the shape of pointed wings as he reaches all the way round to the back of his neck, the fingers fiddling with the stuck steel stud. And then the pistol. A musket, a flintlock? No, later than that. Black, with a long thin barrel and a chamber that spins. The noise in the room, the crash, the flash, the smoke, and him flung against the wall from the force of the blast and then crumpling, crumpling, his buttons neatly done up, every one of them.

· · ·

Yes, her mother says, yes but to do away with yourself just for that. Ah.

She has an itch, one not amenable to scratching. She is done with her nether parts, she wouldn't think of them at all if they didn't itch and do other things, they're so far away they might as well be on the other side of the world. Grotesque, she has always thought, that there should be such ready access to one's insides. Even as a budding girl she was afraid of that part of herself, more so even than of mouth or ear or other holes, afraid of what she might find if she explored in there with a finger, some lurking goblin, ready to jump out of her, at her, waggling its stumpy hands and making chirruping sounds. What do they do with the remains of a still-born child? Bury it? Burn it? This, however, all this is hardly a fit topic on which to engage her daughter, who is dead, anyway, as she well knows, dead like her father.

What season is it, she wonders. She suspects spring, for the day, what of it she can make out, has a look of spring to it, raw and brightly damp. Wintry before, now spring-like. The window below which she huddles is tall, uncurtained, towering over her like the gallows. A distinctly rococo touch to things today, she notes, first the effete young man with his buttons and a pistol ball in his brain, and now the guillotine. What next? A *fête galante*?

What has come over her at all, to be so scattered, so skittish? It must be the thought of there being people in the house that's making her light-headed. She's sure they're there. If there's enough of them they could fetch her down and have a hooley, round the house and mind the dresser, diddly-idle-dee. Oh, she almost laughs. But it's all a show she's making for herself, of herself, she knows it, a caper cut at the cemetery gates.

Who is there here, who can there be, other than herself, her daughter her Petra, her self herself, the two of them, the lost, the lost ones?

She thinks again of the day she ran away, the night, taking Petra with her. She would have taken Adam too, Adam her son, but he wouldn't go, wouldn't come out of his room, he was afraid of the night and the dark and the owl's cry and the gale seething in the trees. Shame on you, she thought, a big lad like you, thought but hadn't the heart to say. What had happened? Some fight, as usual, screams, blows, things flung and smashing against the wall and Adam her husband's face white as bone and the murderous-looking eyes, icy-cold and unblinking. She drove up into the hills, up and up, not caring where she was going, the headlight beams switching this way and that as if frantically in search of something on either side of the narrow, winding hill road that eventually was hardly more than a boreen, the engine grunting and screaming and the windscreen in front of her seemingly smeared with rain that turned out to be tears, her tears, in her eyes. Then she was walking along, stumbling along raggedly like a broken manikin, holding the child by the hand, a solid wall of wind in their faces, under a frightening sky full of stars, full of them, more light than darkness, a cloth-of-gold with tiny black pinpricks all over it and the moon nowhere to be seen, hiding itself off somewhere on the other side of the planet. Then the road straggled to an end and they were wading through ferns as tall as the child, taller, and some animal somewhere lowing, lowing for its lost calf. She huddled down under a crag, where the ground was dry, on a bed of pine needles, clutching the child against her in a mad embrace, clutching her mad daughter Petra, the stone in her heart. It wasn't cold, why wasn't it cold? Petra must have warmed her, children have so much warmth, warmth to spare. Had all this happened or had she dreamt it? the night in the hills, in the dark and the storm, under the rock, looking out at the sky that was a huge cloth of stars, and in the valley below them the scattered lights where the farmsteads were, the lights, the little lights of—

Her bottle! Where is it, where? Oh, if that was lost, now, if that was lost. She plunges her hands into the gaps between the cushion and the chair-arms, first one on one side then the other on the other, the withered old fingers in frenzied search of the precious thing. They're right, she thinks, yes they're right, this is what they mean by the second childhood, a bewhiskered mouth in the depths of a blanket fastened greedily to the neck of its boccie. Adam was wise to go when he did, even if it took so long, so wearyingly long. The nights she sat by his bed as he struggled to die, the days and nights! Though he never moved, not a twitch, not a start, only the big chest rising and falling in that shuddering way. His trim beard had grown bushy, she didn't know how to cut it, how to trim it. She felt like a votary guarding the sacred statue of some old god, faithfully, selflessly, as the sunset light blazed briefly then slowly faded and the advancing night made the windows grey and then blackened them. Her great man, brought low and ticked away at by time. Where is he now? How could a man so alive be dead? How could—

.   .   .

There it is, ah! the little rascal. Her questing fingers have found at last the stubby flat slope-shouldered naggin of Powers. How did it manage to wedge itself so far down there among the dust and the bits of dried food and the coins she can't be bothered to retrieve? She scrabbles at the cork with trembling fingers, outpops it, takes a sup, gives a little gasp followed by a falling sigh, ahh. The heart's ease. Where does the whiskey come from, how is it there's always a supply of it here all the time? The woman, the housekeeper, must bring it, or maybe it's Adam her son, maybe he's her cup-bearer, what was his name, the heavenly cup-bearer, see, she's educated too, better than her parents were, she knows about the gods and their stories, she must have been a fine scholar in her day, though he always looked down on her and laughed at her when she came out with something, said something ill said. Is it a new bottle, are they new bottles, every time, or do they, whoever they are, take the same one away and fill it, refill it, over and over? She tries to read the label, to see if the gilt lettering has lost its shine by being handled over and over. Can't make it out, with her cataracted eye. Or yes she can.

John Power & Son
John's Lane Distillery

and the three swooping swallows. Is that what they're meant to signify, is it done as a joke, as a kind of a pun, a visual pun? For it's true there are only about three swallows in the bottle, it's that scutty. She takes another, longer swig, and smacks her lips. More power to you, John Power, & to your son. She thinks of the steaming copper vats, and the kegs in big pyramid-shaped stacks in the vast yard, the horses and the drays, the men in old-fashioned clothes and cloth caps with pipes in their mouths and the bottoms of their trousers tied with twine for fear of rats getting in and running up their legs and biting them on their privates. Yes, an ancient infant is what she is, clutching her Baby Power, the pap that gives her suck.

Petra, has Petra gone? No, there she is still, sitting pensive on the floor and leaning on her poor scarred arm. The way she droops her cheek like that and lays it along her lifted shoulder, it makes her think of what's it called, oh, what's it called, that flower? Love-lies-bleeding? Yes, love-lies-bleeding. It's so hard to speak Petra's name without first saying the word *poor*. A cutter, is what she says she is, says it proudly. She likes to cut herself, or cuts herself anyway, whether she likes it or not. She uses, used to use, Adam's old ivory-handled razor that she stole after he grew a beard and kept hidden away in her room. Look at the scars on her arms, the waxy whiteness of them. She pinched my kimono, too, my jade-green kimono, to dress herself up in like a geisha, or not a geisha, no, a priestess, a priestess of the pagoda. My child, my lost one, the stone, the jagged stone in my heart, who one day cut herself for good and all, for bad and all.

She unstrapped the watch from his wrist the day he died and has worn it ever since. She puts her ear to it now and listens in breathless wonder to the sound of time itself, the same time that took him from her and that will soon take her in her turn. Think of those Swiss midgets, they must be midgets to be able to do such teeny work, tapping away with their little silver hammers, screwing in screws a fraction of the size of a pinhead, tightening the springs, making the wheels spin, putting in the rubies, fitting the hands. Why hands? They're shaped like arrows. Time's arrow, fly-

ing through the dark, the hiss of it. Fletcher. Midgets and fletch-
ers. Tickety-tock. Time's hands.

And now she slips down into sleep, or up, for it is a kind of floating sleep, she's afloat on the surface of something, some clear cool
stuff that is half liquid and half air. What is the name of that river,
the Greek one, that the dead have to cross? Lethe, is it, or the Styx?
And Lethe-wards had sunk. See there's another thing she remembers from when she was young, she was always a great reader. The
way they stick in your mind, some words, some lines, some and
not others.

She never dreams, or maybe she does, maybe all she does is dream,
that would account for so much that seems to happen.

When now she opens her creaky eyes the sun, yes the sun is there,
the sun has moved in the window and everything has been rear-
ranged, and all around her is a light, light oh so sharp, and blazing
gold as in an icon. Petra has gone. No matter, she'll be back tomorrow. For now, the waiting, the biding, the watching for some
other to come, though she knows it will only be the maid, the
housekeeper, the nurse, whatever to call her, or only Petra again,
only her poor Petra.

And all that fall shall be, shall be, all that fall shall be what? Borne
up? Ah, but who is there that will do the bearing?

. . .

A sound at her back, oh, say it's not the girl returned so soon, dragging her sorrows behind her like that martyred saint his flayed and bloodied pelt. But no, thank goodness, no, it's not Petra but the dog, Rex, his name she never forgets, even though sometimes she forgets her own if only for a second, here he comes slouching, he has four legs but lurches crookedly along as if he had only three, tormented by his joints as she is by hers, his nails clicking on the parquet, and flops down beside her heavily on his sagging hindquarters. In dog years he's older than she is, there's a thought. Together they face the window, their faces illumined by the light of the spring day. She sees afar a bird or what she thinks is one, but maybe it's only a speck in her eye, a floating dark speck. Is it morning, evening, afternoon? Where she dwells now it's always a sort of moveless meridian. So here they are, woman and dog, the two of them, sharing the vast stillness in which the dog pants softly the way car engines used to pant, pant and shudder, when they still ran on petrol, when she was still a girl. It is as if everything everywhere has stopped, as if the earth has been abandoned. She tries to say the dog's name aloud and some sound comes out, some strangled sound that he seems to recognise, and slowly he lifts his big square head and looks at her, with a calm and disenchanted eye, telling her in a silence more eloquent than any words how it is with him, with her, with all the abounding world.

History, now, history identifies the founder of the Irish branch of the Godley family as one Sir Tristram Goodley, or Gudeley, or Gudley, orthography being an uncertain science at the time, who stepped on to these shores, those shores, on the twenty-third day of August in the year eleven hundred and sixty-something—the date, like so much else, is disputed—at the landing place of Passage on the border between the Counties Waterford and Wexford, one of a party of half a hundred knights accompanying Richard fitz Gilbert de Clare, Earl of Pembroke, Lord of Striguil, self-styled Strongbow, who had crossed over from Wales for the purpose of consolidating a decidedly ragged incursion into these lands, those lands, sometime previously, by a rabble of Welsh-Norman mercenaries passing themselves off as noble lords, who had been hired in by Diarmuid MacMurrough, disputed King of Leinster, to aid him in his struggle with Tiernan O'Rourke, undisputed King of Breffny, whose wife he, MacMurrough, had seized from him, O'Rourke, with her, the Lady O'Rourke's, enthusiastic cooperation. Granted, it may all have been otherwise, as is so often the case in these foundational matters.

From Sir Tristram it is but a short step of eight or nine centuries to the days of Adam Godley, FRS, etc., etc., the subject of a projected biography by your humble servant, William Jaybey, FRSL, etc.

Why, I ask myself, why oh why did I take him, it, on? It's quite a job I have before me, quite a job, and I'm not at all sure I've got the stomach for it, or the head, for that matter. What do I know, unregenerate old Newtonian that I am, of the strange netherworld of unimaginably tiny fragments and forces, of massless points and improbable probabilities, wherein Godley made his profoundest discoveries and had his greatest triumphs? Nor can I pretend I wasn't alive to the dubiousness of the commission from the start, because I was; I knew, and I know, that it may well all end in a helpless pratfall. But here I am, and here I must stay, to fulfill my task as best I can. I feel like one of those effete, incurably melancholy, slightly hysterical young-old boobies to be encountered in the Russian drama of the nineteenth century, in exile on a vast estate a thousand versts from the nearest centre of supposed civilisation, tinkering with a never-to-be-completed treatise on land reform, or the serf question, or the use and misuse of the subjunctive in the works of Lermontov, while all the time pining in secret for the dim-witted landowner's young, feyly lovely, heartlessly provocative and utterly unattainable wife. Oh, God.

Here's how it came about. Here's what happened.

But even that, I mean the thought of trying to say how the thing got going in the first place, puts me in a blue funk. At what instant can anything, anything at all, be said actually to have started? The effort of locating the point of initiation becomes a process of infinite regression, as I well know, having dipped a cautious toe into the vasty deeps of the Great Godley's utterly uncommonsensical theories. To arrive at the beginning I could go all the way back to the moment of my conception but even that wouldn't be far enough. I should need to trace my origins and the origins of everything I am and do to a pinch of the primordial dust of some stupendously distant, long-ago disintegrated star, or even further back again, back all the way to the infinitesimal instant when the touchpaper was applied and the originary fireworks show got under way with a cataclysmic bang the reverberations of which can still be detected by astronomically costly instruments developed specially to perform this single and surely nugatory task. What does it profit us to catch the far faint birth cries of the cosmos?

I wonder what a blue funk is, exactly; *funk* I can guess at, but why should it be *blue*? Must look it up.

Wiser men than I have tried to persuade us that everything that was, is, and will be has already happened, is all of a piece, a block of manifold stuff immovably in place, and we mortals do what we do because we've already done it and thus can do no other. Godley in his early days accepted this as the actually existing state of affairs, yet couldn't stop nuzzling and nudging at it, like a starved dog worrying a bare and marrowless bone. How could one so wilful accept that he was preordained, along with the rest of us, to keep upon a course from which not the slightest deviation had been or would ever be allowed? He couldn't. Surely, he said, surely in the endless falling rain of all that is, it's bound to happen that one day a drop will swerve out of true and set the whole shower of stair rods clattering. That was his, was Godley's, starting point, that veering drop; after it came the deluge.

In this instance, as in not many others, I am at one with him. For as I have confessed I am a born ditherer, finical to the point of paralysis, it's a wonder I ever get anything done. When I arrive at the supposed conclusion of something, even the simplest endeavour, the purchasing of a box of matches, say, or the grasping of the nature of Godleyan supra-time, I am not only surprised but immediately suspicious. For just as it's difficult to say when something started, so too, or more so, I not unreasonably reason, is it uncertain that a thing has ended, since the tiniest event ramifies in all directions, in time and in space. Indeed, I ask myself if I can speak at all of an individual event, of a something having happened, distinct and discrete, isolated from all the other happenings and events going on elsewhere in the infinite foundry of however many universes there are? No, I can not. For nothing exists by itself, in isolation; there is only the continuum, in which everything presses into, bites into and extends from, everything else.

Yes, I know that by definition there cannot be more than one universe. I know that. Thank you.

But wait now, wait. What if Godley had been the first to remark the fact that there's no such thing as a thing, whole, unique and indivisible, and so on? Wouldn't that have been the beginning of something, a new something in the world that hadn't been there before? Or is it all just a trick of language, of the way matters are expressed or choose to express themselves?

And then there's the problem of—

Stop! Just stop. Take a breath and make a start, any start. It can't be so difficult, if others do it all the time, and they do, apparently with the greatest ease, unless they're pretending, which I know is perfectly possible, the world being what it is and the people in it being what they are. But still.

So, let's set these scruples to one side and designate as a clear and identifiable starting point the moment when the letter arrived. A letter can always be depended on to get things going, being the kind of device that would have galvanised into action or at least into active cogitation even our imagined old Timofey Timofeyeovich Tovarich, in his distressful exile out there on the snow-swept steppes. This one came—by the white-gloved hand of a Thurn & Taxis courier, in his high-topped hat, tootling his brass bugle—in one of those long narrow envelopes the paper of which was raspy to the touch, as if the filings of some fine and precious metal had been mixed in with the pulp in the process of its manufacture. It was the kind of envelope that prize announcements are dispatched in—*Dear Cher Herr Señor Signore Lärd Professor! It gives us surpassing Pleasure to inform your Esteemed Self that you have been chosen by the Members of our Jury as the Honoured Recipient of this year's Blankety Blank Award for Blinkety Blink*—and I confess I looked at once, with a leap of the heart, I couldn't stop myself, for a Stockholm postmark. Fat chance—or thin, rather, shouldn't it be? You see, there it is again, the inevitable quibble. My life is strewn with such trivial distinctions, the clinkers in my path, forever tripping me up and landing me flat on my fundament.

I was of course familiar with the name Adam Godley. Who isn't? Indeed, when I opened the letter and my eye fell on the signature I was reminded that I had encountered him in person, the signatory's father, that is, long before, at an international conference on the topic of multi-dimensionality, of all outlandish things; why I should have been invited to partake in such a recondite affair I can't think. Godley by then had been showered with all the prizes and honours that there are. Me he snubbed, when we were introduced. He was a notorious snubber, was Godley, he made an art of it.

He had by then settled into the image of his own legend, tall, thin, elegantly stooped, with a smile expressive of tolerant disdain. A spade-shaped beard added markedly to the satanic aspect it pleased him to cultivate. I was impressed, of course, for he was at the pinnacle of his fame, yet at the same time I found him ever so slightly risible, as he moved amongst us majestic in the aura of his burnished and undentable self-regard. The man exuded disagreeableness like a scent, rarefied and sharp as civet. To those, even the most august, who had the temerity to urge themselves forward into his path with a hand extended, he would respond with barely suppressed mirth, lips twitching and an eyebrow quizzically arched, as if he found their even daring to approach him as amusing as it was preposterous.

At the time, I mean the time of this first, no this sole, and less than amiable, encounter, I was a Visiting Fellow at the University of Arcady far out there on that legendarily relaxed western shore, directing a seminar on the painter Vaublin and his dispute with the *philosophes* and their ill-conceived *Encyclopédie*. Wise old Vaublin, though a mere maker of pictures, knew full well whither those gentlemen and their proto-Enlightenment ideas were headed in a handcart, and dragging a good part of the world along with them. Enlightenment? Endarkenment, say I.

This was the same Arcady where the same Adam Godley, earlier in the century, had brought about the great instauration that was to alter everything for good—or for ill, as more than a few with a stake in the matter would assert—and show, along with much else, that the infinite has its limits, and furthermore that our infinity is only one among an infinity of infinities. At least, that was, and is, my understanding of a theory that has been such a curiously abundant blight upon our poor old innocent planet. Godley himself used to say, with playful scorn, that his discoveries and their effects were as much of a mystery to him as they are to the rest of mankind. Yet he was fond of the venerable institution in the bosom of which he had wrought such wonders, as fond as he was capable of being of anything that was not himself, and that day at Arcady he was, despite the haughtiness of his manner, in what in him passed for a benign, even an accommodating, frame of mind. It didn't last, though; it never did.

During a break in the proceedings, I was loitering by a vast window giving on to a vista of sunlit, blue-and-beige Arcadian coastline, when Godley paused in passing and addressed me. I had thought the titan would have forgotten me the second after we were introduced, but not so, it seemed.

"What was the name again?" he drawled, with a depreciatory wrinkling of that lofty, pale-as-paper brow. "Ah, yes. Jaybey. And how do you spell that?" When I told him, he looked even more sceptical. "That's one I've never come across before. Are you sure you didn't make it up?"

I suspect this was his idea of a joke. I was young or at least youngish still, and with the assurance of youth's impenetrable carapace I was able to absorb without injury the fellow's casual effrontery, his jaunty contempt.

"Anglo-Norman," I said brightly. "Like Godley. We both came over with the marauders, I believe."

Godley smiled a chilly smile, pursing his lips, and gave his beard a considering, downwardly caressing stroke with the palm of his right hand, one of his characteristic and, I bet, carefully calculated gestures. I could see him preparing a rejoinder but then deciding he had got all there was to be got out of this exchange—he derived a certain arid entertainment from the sad comedy of other people's paltry lives—and with a shrug and another, colder, smile he moved on, in search of meatier quarry than I among the milling crowd.

I should have been crushed to be thus cursorily dismissed, but I wasn't; who knows, perhaps I had a premonition that the day would come when I would be afforded the opportunity to exact my revenge, even if only posthumously. Godley had descended upon the occasion like a visiting deity requiring the adoration of the multitude, expressed in choric encomia, with libations of blood and the squeals of sacrificial maidens. His walk, I noted, was the stately, unhurryable swagger of the one hundred per-cent self-made celebrity. He was there to receive an honorary degree and be awarded a medal, which tributes he acknowledged with a brief, sarcastic address and, at the close, the regal lifting of a long pale hand. Uncertain applause was followed by a hushed hubbub. The honoured one, it was generally agreed, had proved himself a thoroughgoing shit. The medal in its box he left behind on the rim of a urinal in the gentlemen's lavatory, which those who had conferred it took, rightly, I don't doubt, for a deliberate slight.

I have always been of the conviction that in order to give a true, measured and balanced account of the span of a human life, a biographer must, at a certain essential level, hold himself superior to his subject. By now, Adam Godley's name has been inscribed among the stars—there is that black hole in the galaxy of Canis Major that's named after him, the dog—but his biographer is here to tell you he was no luminary, nor is, in whatever version of infinity his shade may be throwing shapes upon the walls and scaring the daylights out of yet another phantasmal world beyond this one. A speculative genius, yes, I suppose I must grant you that, but in the common run of things a sounding brass and a tinkling cymbal. I must say I'm surprised some coldly ambitious bright young whippersnapper hasn't already had at that particular pair of clay feet and brought down in a swirl of dust Professor Godley's reputation for wisdom, selflessness, and olympian detachment. Instead, the task has fallen to me. I'll do my best, by which I mean my worst. I'm already chipping away with mallet and chisel, though gingerly, for now, and with circumspection. I started on a big toe, and will have got as high as the knee, or higher, come Christmas. Godley's origins were humbler than has been realised heretofore, I'll shine a pitiless light on that aspect of things. Then there's the rest of his life for me to explore, in the desert wastes of which I'll take the measure of his colossal wreck.

And yet, I pause. What has come over me? Why such hostility, why such venom? It can't be because of that snub I got from him in Arcady College's Hermes Hall all those years ago. Can it? I'm not that petty-minded. Am I? No, no. I am a man with a mission. I know my motives are tainted, due in part, and murkily, to my, what shall I say, to my sentimental regard for Godley's daughter-in-law—I'll come to it, I'll come to it—but I'm confident of the rightness of my determination to strip away the myths and misapprehensions that have for so long veiled the figure of Adam Godley in the world's admiring but hoodwinked gaze. Gad, sir, there's such a thing as one's duty to the facts. And let's face it, he was a terrible fellow.

But I was speaking, wasn't I, of the day the post-horn sounded outside my door and I heard the letter land on the hall tiles with that smack of flat finality by which all such communications announce their arrival. *Upon receipt of this demand,* the sound seems to say, *you will be required to effect sweeping changes in your poor excuse for a life.*

Need we go into my personal circumstances at the time? Let's settle for semaphore: dead marriage, no issue, steady creep of age, a few bob in the bank, lanky frame grown scrawny and belly gone to pot, seasonal eczema, ineradicable dandruff, teeth sound or soundish, liver less so. That about sums it, me, up, I should think. That year, the year we're now in, I was myself on a return visit to Arcady, as it happened, though in some splendour this time, my posterior settled magisterially upon the Axel Vander Chair of Deconstruction Studies, no less. Obviously the dents my scholarly reputation had unaccountably sustained in recent times weren't detectable from the far side of that far continent. I had two short classes a week, a handful of conveniently listless students, no administrative duties, and little or no communion with those folk on the faculty who deludedly imagined themselves my colleagues. A cushy number, in other words, and a much-needed relief for my bony old bum. As you will have gathered by now, I am, in my sly and studied way, every bit as arrogant as the man whose life and character I am set to pin out upon a board.

It was April; isn't it always April, somehow, when something happens? I sat in the breakfast nook—yes, my bijou Arcadian hillside residence boasted such a feature, cosy and ever-so-charming, and much vaunted by the extravagantly distraite lady from whom the college was renting the place—not poring over the letter, as might be expected, but regarding it sidelong, with a wary eye. I've always found letters difficult to digest, more difficult than almost any other kind of text, no matter how abstruse or densely composed. This is partly accounted for, I believe, by the abrupt way they arrive, out of the blue and without so much as a by your leave: the postman's coming is not to be resisted, not by the shyest hermit or the bitterest misanthrope. Then there's the impertinent familiarity with which letters address their addressees. How can I be Dear to so many strangers?

Oh, look, I've got a smear of marmalade on a corner of the envelope. Extraordinary stuff, marmalade, the way it goes everywhere, no matter how careful one is with the spoon; there's something otherworldly about it, as if it originated somewhere else, on some other planet, where the laws of mass and viscosity are different from those that hold sway here. I find that's the case with a lot of things. All, with increasing frequency and force, is not what it seems.

The signature, which was what I looked to first, gave me a start: plain Adam Godley, without the discriminating "jnr." For remember, this is the son we're dealing with, let's get that distinction clear at the outset, though some confusion is inevitable. I believe that strictly speaking a son bearing his father's first name can drop the qualifier once the progenitor has passed on. All the same, for a second I felt I had been summoned from above, by one of the immortals, even though in the case of Adam Godley, snr., immortality is unquestionably a figurative term.

I gave the text a quick, nervous scan, touching upon it here and there with the hurry of a first-time fire-walker. Then I had another cup of tea and went through it again, more slowly, with both excitement and a sinking heart. I absorbed the proposition outlined in it, considered my response for something like a second, and decided—as if there were a choice to be made in the matter—to reply at once and say, But of course, yes, certainly! whipping off hat and bowing, scraping, bowing again, thank you thank you thank you! You imagine I wouldn't? That the once briefly celebrated though by now barely remembered biographer of Isaac Newton should decline to write the life of the Newton of the current age? Say no to that? How many kinds of chump would I have shown myself to be. It wasn't a matter of the money, of which the letter made no mention anyhow. Simply, the invitation was not to be turned down, not by me, certainly. Here was the perfect opportunity to buff up my scuffed reputation and restore it to its former shine. Besides, a rumour was going about at the time, and a strong one it was, that Pavel Popov, my ancient but unresting rival, was confidently anticipating delivery of the very invitation that had just come jogging its way post-haste—*tootle tootle!*—up the hill to my secluded nook, and I was damned if I'd let myself be stepped in front of by the likes of a piffling Popov. I was all too aware of the fact that my Polish foe had already penned—blotted, might be the better word—a monograph on Godley's life and work, belittlingly entitled *The Brahman;* it is a snide and shoddy affair riddled with misapprehensions, false conjectures and plain lies. Away with the man!

Yet, as I cautiously fitted on the lid of the marmalade pot, my mood turned glum. I felt embarrassed, I might even say shamed, to be so eagerly, so cravenly, agreeable to young Adam's offer. Oh, I had been noticed, had I, and not only noticed but singled out? What a big baba I am become of late, tugging at the hem of mama's skirt and whining for attention.

Anyway, the die was cast and three times in a row it had come up with a big fat six. That same day I spoke to the deanness of my department, a saturnine spinster, the De Winter Professor of Post-Punk Philology and author, famously, of the seminal essay "Queer Tropes in Webster's *Dictionary,*" to request that she arrange for a substitute to take my classes that afternoon and the following morning, and in a mood of apprehensive adventure prepared to set off eastwards without delay. Why should I not write the Life of Godley? Was I not a man of parts, recipient of countless academic honours, author of *The Force of Gravity: Isaac Newton and His Time,* occupant of the Axel Vander chair at Arcady College and other significant seats of honour?

First thing on the morrow, then, I allowed myself to be shot by vacuum train from the west coast to the east, and well before noon had arrived in recently renamed New Amsterdam. There I found laid on for me a stylised display of spring weather, with sparkling rain showers and scudding clouds and great sweepings of sudden sunlight fleeting across the faces of the *'schrapers,* as the victorious Hollanders have fondly nicknamed those beetling towers so many of which were damaged by rocket fire in the course of the recent invasion and remain in ruins. As always down in the crevasses of that high-built city I imagined myself to be treading the narrow bed of a broad river with the translucent blue undersurface flowing along placidly above my head, a head which, as I emerged from the sooty depths of Stuyvesant Central, felt as if it had been trapped in a vise for the past three and a half frictionless hours of hurtling super-speed travel through the airless dark; I do hate those trains, though they go appreciably faster than the now obsolete and by me unlamented aeroplane. Adam Godley, Adam

Godley the son, that is, as I'm already fed up reminding you, had suggested we should meet in one of those bloatedly grand hotels on the south side of the park. It was, young Mr. G. wrote apologetically, the only place in the city he was at all familiar with, since it had been his father's favourite haunt here in the old days, when Gotham was still Gotham. I, the erstwhile penurious sizar, was impressed, not to say a little awed, to find myself admitted without challenge into such a *paleis* of smartness, elegance and hard graft.

Adam the Second I found to be a large but gentle, shy-eyed fellow, not at all what I had expected and nothing like his father, to look at, and certainly not to deal with. He has the hushed, preoccupied air of one struggling in the toils of an obscure and immemorial sorrow the burden of which a tougher soul would have shrugged off long ago. There had been talk of some trouble or tragedy that had befallen him and his wife, but I couldn't remember the details, if I ever knew them. I asked him how he had come to hear of me, to which he responded with a sweetly disarming smile and the coy assertion that surely there could be few people of any moment in the world who weren't familiar with the name of William Jaybey. This, as we know, is assuredly not the case—is mine a name in your household?—and I subjected the flatterer to sharp and thoughtful scrutiny. What I didn't know but would not be long in learning was that Adam Godley is wholly a stranger to irony. His literal-mindedness drives Helen his wife to distraction, so she says. She, in her air-blue gown and gilded sandals, now there's distraction for you, or for me, anyway, whose all-too-human heart is soon to be in smithereens. I should have been more cautious, should have been more mistrustful of what was being proposed to me, really, I should. But that day my head was so light it was easily turned, for all that it seemed perfectly possible it would end up on a platter.

I had my most serious moment of doubt when I heard that it was Professor Benjamin Grace, Emeritus Fellow of Poststructuralist Studies at the University of Arcady—I know, can't get away from the place—who, speaking *ex cathedra,* or should that be *ex culo,* had proposed me as the ideal person to undertake the authorised biography of Adam Godley, snr. "Professor Grace was a friend of my father's"—as if his father had friends—"and a great admirer of yours," Adam the Son said to me now, his sandy forehead flushing in the glare of his own earnestness. Mind you, I could see from the wandering look in his eye that, kindly disposed though he might be towards the world in general, he had the measure of the ineffable Benny Grace. A "great admirer"? I could hear Benny saying it, with a throb of false sincerity in his voice and in his eye the light of a suppressed snigger.

It's an indication of how flattered I was that even Benny's grotesque shadow figuratively falling across the table didn't cause me to scramble to my feet and flee. At the best of times I'm unaccustomed to being soft-soaped and hearing my accomplishments puffed up; the groves of academe through which I make my hampered way are seldom sunny and often sere. Now I leaned back into the alarmingly warm depths of the low-slung armchair, in which it was hard not to seem to sprawl, put on my spectacles, and examined the drinks menu. Dozens of cocktails, dozens, each one a more elaborate concoction than the last, and not one amongst them that I recognised. I dithered between—there I am, at it again—I dithered between the Haarlem Globetrotter and My Old Dutch, but in the end settled on the old-fashioned Old Fashioned, which sounded just the thing for me. The waiter, in his striped waistcoat and those ridiculous, expanding metal bands that for some reason they wear around their shirt sleeves above the elbow—yes yes, no end to the things that irritate me—smiled his over-familiar smile and pranced away.

The family, young Adam was saying, as if he hadn't already said so in his letter, the family, and he, had decided to commission a biography, the official one, of his father, and they had agreed on engaging me to write it. His tone when he spoke this way of "the family," of its wishes and determinations, made me picture a tiled room with high-set leaded windows and an oak table ranged round by a dozen or so grave-faced worthies in conical black hats and close-fitting bonnets, dressed all in jet with white ruffs, a scene such as one encounters in the canvases of Frans Hals or de Hooch. Mind you, he went on, warming to the task, what was required was an accurate, detailed, and comprehensive account of Adam Godley's life, not a—"what's the word I'm looking for?"

"Hagiography?"

"I was going to say a whitewash, but a hagiography, yes that's it, I mean no it's not, I mean that's what we don't want, definitely not. A portrait of the man warts and all is what we're after. And we believe, I say it again, we believe you're the person to do it for us. Professor Grace speaks very highly of you, very highly."

I nodded, inspecting my fingernails and frowning. Should I believe in this man's laboured sincerity? He had somewhat the air of a conman stricken suddenly by a bad conscience. And what, I wondered, what is Benny up to, exactly? Why hadn't he nabbed this plum commission for himself, when it was going? The Benny Grace I knew of old would not have let pass such a rare opportunity for profit and self-advancement.

The drinks arrived. Young Adam had ordered beer.

"And that's your classic Manhattan, sir," the gartered waiter said to me, applying the base of the glass to a frilled paper coaster on the table before me with a brisk, screw-tightening motion of the wrist. A tawny lock of hair fell athwart his brow; Ganymede, again. We are everywhere, in every form, you just don't think to notice us. The glass had the shape of a crystal chalice; I looked on it warily; what if it was poisoned?

I pointed out with some asperity that I had ordered an Old Fashioned. The waiter gave me a look of pity, all bleached teeth and crinkly grin. "Same thing, sir," he said. That was me put deftly in my place. I harrumphed, and thrashed about a bit, as one does when one's ignorance is exposed, plucking at the knees of my trousers, abashed and blushing, my country mouse's whiskers twitching. Large Master Godley gazed with mild-eyed forbearance upon this little contretemps; he was accustomed to far worse social awkwardnesses, his father having been a regular and terrible maker of noisy public scenes.

All this, my confusion over the cocktail, the fumed fakery of the Oak Room, even those sprung metal armbands, all of it was loured over now by the spirit of Benny Grace, whom I thought of as suspended above the table on leathery black wings, a sort of pentecostal bat. There are certain people, and I've known a few in my time, the very thought of whom brings with it a greyness, musty and meagre, that creeps over everything, like mildew. Their business is, among other things, to remind us of all the past little slips and shames that beset every life and make us squirm anew each time they come irresistibly to mind. Oho, they say, did you really think we had forgotten what you did and where and when you did it, like that time you accidentally farted aloud in the crowded lift and everyone heard and turned to look at you, or the night you were introduced to your fiancée's brother and thought he was her sister and addressed him by the sister's name, or the time—now, this is a good one, are you all listening?—when at a party you turned to the woman behind you and begged her in a hoarse whisper to rescue you from the relentless bore who had been tormenting you for the past twenty minutes, only to be icily informed that he, the bore, was her husband. That's Benny for you, first he throws his arm in friendliest fashion about your neck, then a moment later wrestles you to the floor and leaves you gasping among the fag-ends and the spits.

I sipped my treacly drink and watched young Adam, whose thoughts for the moment had drifted elsewhere. He sat hunched forward on the edge of his armchair, glassy-eyed, his elbows planted on his knees and his hands clasped before him. I couldn't but feel for him, struggling as he seemed to be with an unassuageable inner anguish. He was pale and bloodshot, and exuded a warm, yeasty odour. He had travelled through the night many thousands of miles along the very edge of the stratosphere, and probably in one part of his head he was still giddily aloft in that shiny blue-black zone; those air-powered streamlined dirigibles will never catch on, or at least I hope they won't. I deplore all these gadgets they keep inventing, at once clever and clumsy. Give me my parchment, my quill pen, my tasselled cap and pointy-toed slippers, my lion couchant by my chair and a view of the ideal city, sparkling in miniature, framed in a little square window above my head; for I consider myself not of this brash and steadily corroding new world, that hath such horrors in it.

We talked on, and were all business for a while, but soon faltered and grew vague, and hummed distractedly and drummed our fingers on our chair-arms, and gazed upwards at a loss, frowning, into the uncertain air. It's the general way of things nowadays, in this recessive, Godleyed world. It is a curious phenomenon, though all are subject to it even if we hardly notice it any more. I think of how when we were young a gang of us would race down the incline of a sunlit beach and pitch ourselves headlong into the waves and there at once be brought to a thrashing halt, even the hardiest, or almost a halt, hindered and held by the weight of water and made subject willy-nilly to the sea's sluggish undertow. So it was with us two now, as we drifted dreamily out of our depth in the turbid waters of the Oak Room in the Hotel Grand Plexus on Central Park Zuid.

I came back to myself with a jolt. Adam had been speaking

again, but had I heard him correctly? I thought he had said I was to be put up in the Godley household as a working guest, for as long as the writing of the biography should take. And, yes, that was indeed what he had said. It was advanced not as a suggestion but as a thing already agreed upon and incontrovertibly settled; Adam Godley the younger is not without a touch of his father's imperious resolve after all. It would make the best sense, wouldn't it, he was saying, for me to be there, at Arden House, the family home, where the bulk of the Godley papers are deposited, kept in a steel vault the construction and installation of which was financed out of public monies for the safeguarding of a priceless national treasure. Scholarly institutions in every corner of the world—and the round world has corners, an infinity of them, none of them imagin'd, along with numberless infinities of souls, as the Brahma theory counterintuitively demonstrates—had clamoured to purchase that fabulous trove. However, Adam had been adamant. The papers must stay at Arden. And so, it seemed, would I.

But whoa there, whoa. Everything was going at a frightening gallop, and I told myself I must rein in the plunging steed before it was too late. I should lodge, if not a demurral, then at least a reservation about this commission which I was being, or had already been, corralled into accepting. The proposal itself was worryingly vague. For instance, when I asked which publishers had been approached, the fellow before me took on a look of puzzlement and some alarm. That aspect of the matter hadn't been discussed, he mumbled, smearing the words; he rather thought, he went on, that the family would have the text privately printed and bound. That raised my eyebrows. Such books, I said after a pause, are rarely taken seriously, the assumption being that they had been offered to a great number of publishing houses where the editors had judged them unworthy of commercial publication. Godley pondered this point for some moments, then brightened. Benny

Grace had assured him, he said, that he would play John the Baptist to my Messiah, and Professor Grace, as everyone knew, was not only a man of his word, but also a person of great influence in the world of scholarship and scholarly publishing, and would surely know of other influencers whose support could be called on. And he clasped his hands once more and gazed at me almost pleadingly. Now it was my turn again to ponder. Despite my reservations, I wanted to write this book. It would be bound to perk things up for me professionally, and as I've indicated, things in that quarter were sorely in need of perking. Yet I hesitated. I had come to New Amsterdam in expectation of a prolonged and intricate negotiation, but somehow even the terms seemed already agreed. How had that happened? I hadn't heard myself say yes to anything, yet here I was, pyjamas and toothbrush as good as packed, engaged to billet at the ancestral House of Godley. I felt compromised. I felt like a needy scrivener hired on the spot and about to be bundled off pell-mell to Doughty Hall, there to ghost Sir Digby Doughty's memoirs and fall successively in love with two or three of his romping daughters. It was the damnedest thing and yet it was done. I lowered my upper lip into the smoky-tasting dregs of my drink. The olive on its stick had the look of a tiny head impaled upon a spike.

Did we spit into our palms and shake on the deal? We did not. Though he had got what he came for, Adam the Younger appeared to be more troubled and more weighed down than ever. What was the matter with the fellow? Some people are born to fret—look at me. Adam seemed, he always seems, to be brooding on something other than the matter at hand, like a distraught general devising a strategy for his next battle but one in a war he knows to be already lost. Was he real, or got up? Sore thumbs, the two of us, anyway, I reflected, hapless me with my silly drink, and haggard Godley with his raw pink eyelids and nervous, unhandy hands.

That evening, still jittery from travel fever and elate on the successful outcome of our dealings, the pair of us went on the town together, seeking what diversions we might in the Grote Apfel, as the ruddy-cheeked Dutchmen cheerfully but unimaginatively call the conquered city. We had booze, broads, a barroom fight and a night in the cells, and in the morning a crapulous and shamefaced court appearance, followed by summary deportation and a thunderous warning never to show our faces in this town again—no, of course we didn't; honestly, you'd believe anything. What happened was that when our meeting ended, or better say languished, we shook un-spat-upon hands and parted, Godley shambling off on some unspecified exploit of his own, while I walked east at a meditative pace across the park, misgiving lodged in me like a thorn under a fingernail.

I had booked myself into the shabby splendours of the Pantaloon Club, where in my cavernous and uncomfortable room—the building is nearly as old as the country—I lay down without undressing on the high, majestic bed and dozed fitfully through the afternoon. Then I rose, constricted and sweaty, and made another sombre traversal of the park, and returning took early dinner in a sepulchrally deserted dining room. I wonder if there is anyone who can dine alone and not feel himself to be an object of pity and scorn; the white-jacketed waiter, elderly, flat-footed, served me with an air of commiseration, addressing me in a murmur interspersed with small, whistling sighs. The tall window beside me looked out on an endless herd of rush-hour traffic stampeding past in the lighted dark along Vijfde Avenue. I ordered and drank a consolatory bottle of vintage claret. The bill when it came sent my eyebrows shooting up to near the hairline; would I dare charge a Cheval Blanc '93 to the Godley estate? I didn't, in the end; scrupulous, or cowardly, as ever.

In the middle of the night I woke in the clutches of a nameless dread, or it was nameless until I remembered what it was I had been lured into by Adam Godley not so many hours before, across that low table at the Plexus, where the trembling afterglow of many a disastrous deal floats like ectoplasm on the charred, over-air-conditioned air. I lay on my back with the bedclothes drawn up to my chin, holding on with both hands to the edge of the blanket like a shipwrecked sailor clinging to his spar. A sickly yellow glare from the street lights outside was splashed across the ceiling and down one wall. What have I done? I asked myself. What have I done.

In the morning I took the super-tube back to Arcady; whenever I get into one of those things I feel I am inserting myself into the barrel of an oversized popgun. I was hungover and had the shakes, after the wine at dinner and a subsequent cut-glass goblet of Frapin Fontpinot taken in the club's Harlequin Bar—where the Lithuanian barman, in full livery including a powdered wig and plisséd lace at the wrists, dispatched a scurrying mouse, loudly and juicily, by stamping on it with his heel—prior to my crawling upstairs to bed and oblivion. Or no, not oblivion. In the depths of sleep before that four-in-the-morning jolt into panicky wakefulness I dreamt a dream. In it, I got off a train and was met—

For many years, throughout the greater part of his prison sentence, in fact, Felix Mordaunt had seemed to himself to be a clock. Not a clock of the conventional sort, diligently maintained and regulated and briskly marking off the minutes and the hours, but a clock for all that. His prison day was strictly portioned out, like that of the mechanical figures who make their quarter-hourly round at the top of the cathedral towers in the central squares of carefully preserved medieval cities; he was, as they are, bound upon an unseen archaic mechanism of pins and wheels, of ratchets and levers. He didn't mind, much; he had always prized a pattern. Such freedoms as he had he didn't want—of what use were they to him? The tedium of prison life induced in him a state of only mildly restive torpor, the same that affected everyone inside, not only his fellow prisoners but also the staff and warders, all the way up to the governor himself, a taciturn bachelor with furtive ways and a bad tic in his left cheek. Even visitors felt it, the wives and girlfriends who at the end of their allotted hour would shuffle out through the front gate clutching their handbags tight, their faces washed of all colour, stiff-limbed as automata. The day will come, all muttered to themselves, oh, yes, the day will come when we shall march up here with burning brands and storm the gates and break the locks with our bare hands and fling open the cell doors and lead the inmates stumbling out with eyes and arms uplifted to air and light—*O welche Lust!*—yes, yes, someday. But they knew in their hearts they wouldn't; where would they get the energy, how would they summon the resolve? Theirs is a waning world, as is ours, of course, could we but accept the fact.

Even the inmates, chafe though they would in their chains, did not complain of their plight, not really, not in any heartfelt way. There was an unspoken acknowledgement among them, at least among the more reflective ones, that enervation and inertia made for a natural condition, ordained and proper, suited not only to such as they but to all the others as well, all the heedless others outside, going about their days and nights wilfully deaf to the clink of the unseen fetters that so lightly yet unlockably grip their wrists. Prison is the fallen place that never forgets there was once a paradise, and to be pent is fit punishment for the expulsed, as they well know. This is what all would have said, or something like it, should anyone have felt the need to ask. Yes, the cage, all things considered, is the place for them, for us.

Now Mordaunt is out and moving amongst these long-term inmates who persist in dreaming themselves free and his perplexity deepens daily. There is an effect, a sense as of a general lapsing, of many little turbines trying to start up and failing, that he has encountered repeatedly since his return here—if it is a return, and to here, which everyone and everything keeps blandly assuring him is not the case—especially when it's a question of some particular thing, such as a date, a time, a place. He had felt it happening to himself that first day when he stepped into the Lady's Way and seemed to turn, to have been turned, into a new form of himself. And the others too, all of them, at times they look, it often happens, as if they're not the others who were there just a moment past but other others. This phenomenon, this state they keep falling into, and he keeps falling into along with them, is marked by a kind of, what shall we say, a kind of wistful evasiveness; all enquiries seem to cause in those enquired of an uneasy shying away, a glancing off, a turning aside, as though they had been caught out in some small underhand act they had forgotten about and didn't care to be reminded of. But that's not quite it either. He can't, he just can't fix on it, this effect, it turns fuzzy and won't keep still for long enough for him to get a hold of it. Perhaps he's imagining it, perhaps it's a delusion, a thing that happens in his mind and not in the world. But he knows better than that, he knows it happens, he sees the results. Wrestling with this riddle and others like it, he has begun to wonder if he might be going mad. But if so, he thinks it is a metamadness, the madness of the madman who sees farther and more sharply than the sane ones around him, even if the things he sees baffle him. He has been away so long, you understand, that he brings to everything an innocent or at least an uninformed eye. *We* know all too well what he can only guess at.

He ponders more confusedly than ever the nature of time, not the mysterious entity that doesn't exist and yet bears us kicking and screaming from the cradle to the grave, but the other kind, in all its vicissitudes, the kind that shrinks and stretches and buckles and bends and that Adam Godley tied a knot in that no one can unpick. Consider the moment when, half seas over, you lose your grip on the wine glass and it slips from your fingers and even before it falls you see in a flash the entirety of all that is to come, from the star-burst on the dining room floor to the splinter sticking through your sock and piercing your big toe the day after tomorrow—that kind of time. Mordaunt knows, or knew, his natural philosophy and didn't lack for leisure over the past quarter of a century to keep up, to a fair extent, with the latest tortuosities brought about in that demanding discipline which now, with their rage to invest old things with fatuous new names, they call super-phys, making it sound like a health-giving drink. Except that in those years such advance as there was had taken the form of reces-sion, and showed our universe to be as a diminishing ball of fluff under an empty bed in an uninhabited mansion in a tangled wood on a frozen island on a dying planet floating in retrograde motion amid the illimitable darknesses of the multispace. No progress, then, only regress; no expansion, only shrinkage. And what will be the end? An ape out on the savannah fashioning a flint into an axe-head? Not even that. Not even anything. A set of singu-larities, infinitesimal points of infinite mass getting ready to burst, and us not dreamt of yet.

Oh, he knew his Godley, that wasn't his trouble. He read of the dismayingly deleterious Godley syndromes a new one of which seemed to shoot up every other week and go off like a fire-work and turn the overarching sky a still more bilious shade of sul-phur. He read, and was sceptical. Buffered by prison bars against the endlessly ramifying world, he had taken Godley's radical re-evaluation of all things as a phantasmagoria, a lavish hypothetical light-show put on in a playfully imagined realm. True, he was as fascinated as everyone else when the Godley Interference Effect arising from the field equations of the Brahma theory—that Effect the reality of which is even still hotly contested by the determin-ists, the priests, and the simple-minded, as we all know all too well—showed that every increase in our knowledge of the nature of reality acts directly upon that reality, and that each glowing new discovery we make brings about an equal and opposite dark-ening, the punching of a hole in the wall of the great sphere that is time and space and all besides. As Adam Godley observed, no doubt with a snicker I can almost hear, "Every egghead's every brainwave puts another prick in the shell." Yet Mordaunt in his bleared and stultified isolation assumed this to be no more than the setting out of a principle of universal symmetry, a balancing of x against y with the predicted product z. But it wasn't, and isn't; astounding though it seems, he learned, Godley has shown that just by speculating about it in certain specialised ways we are steadily wearing out the world. And yet, even when the universal ban on Godleyan geometry was declared, and the college departments were shut and the professors pensioned off—rumour had it that the brainier ones among them were to be forced into deep comas in order to quell their catastrophic musings—Mordaunt still insisted it was all a fuss over nothing, the result of another one of humankind's periodic fits of the fidgets, and that it would soon fizzle out. He was, we say it again, mistaken, but stubborn in his mistakenness.

Now a free man, or freeish, he finds it remarkable that as inside, so out. No one complains, no one challenges, no one puts down a parliamentary question. The gradual calamity that is taking place in the substance of the world is hardly remarked. The great vaguening deepens daily, the general mind becomes dull and duller, while all everywhere goes slow and slower. Yet Mordaunt was damned if he would be gulled by what he considered Adam Godley's hifalutin jiggery-pokery; for yes, he had put himself firmly among the ranks of the deniers. He had been set loose from the round of rods and spokes and permitted to clamber down from the bell tower and mingle with the deluded gawpers in the cathedral close, yet he felt he was one among the few who were awake, or perhaps he was the only wakeful one, in this drift of somnambulists. Were he to accost one of them and take him by the shoulders and shake him, no light, he felt sure, would dawn behind the sleeper's glazed-over eye.

And it was this that most dismayed him, this state of inanition all these goings-on had brought about in the realm of human affairs. When first released, he didn't take much notice of it, he who was accustomed to the drowsy pace of life behind bars. Before long, however, he began to understand that something was gravely the matter, though even yet he wasn't sure what the matter was; he was no more sure of anything than was anyone else. He seemed to be abroad in one of those long, luminously clouded days of high summer when the deep glossy light is more like an occlusion, and the figures moving in it take on a metallic glitter that dazzles and deceives the eye.

The place it was, this Arden that used to be Coolgrange, that first shook him. He had thought, as he beetled confidently down the coast in Billy Hipwell's little red motor car, that he was making a homecoming. He knew there would be no one surviving from the days of his youth, but he was confident of encountering the familiar at least in the crumbling old house itself and its environs, in the roads, the companionable trees, the distant views—the things, that is, that endure. And when he arrived there he did find much that he recognised, the arched entrance to the Lady's Way, for instance, and the muddy lane and the rusty gate, the sun-blinded back windows, the yard that smelled still of the hen-run long gone, and, inside the house, known objects, humble ones, it's true, that disposed themselves eagerly before him, pleading to be verified: that hatstand in the hall, a set of fire irons in a grate, the cavernous kitchen with its pots and pans, and the tulips on the table. Yet when he pressed more pressingly upon these talismans even they seemed strangely altered, seemed less themselves than as they would be in a dream. What had happened, what transformation in the texture of things had turned the Coolgrange he had known into this unknown Arden? Is it Godley again, and his infernal meddlings in the essence of our poor planet?

He wishes for illumination, explanation. So much of what he knew having become other has wrought a doubt in him, and a certain dread, however loud his continuing denials. Where has his world gone to? He could set up an investigation, but how frame the questions, how conduct the third degree—how, and on whom to conduct it? He is still on the inside after all, on the inside looking out. Excepting a mirror, how may the eye regard itself?

And so he thought to retrace his steps in hope thereby to rewind time. One morning early he let himself in at the ever-unlocked front door—has thievery been eliminated from the land, along with so much else?—and padded his way through the sleeping house out to, inevitably, the kitchen, that barely revolving vortex into which all are inevitably drawn. There he seated himself with a forearm resting on the table, just as he had done the day when he first arrived and Helen invited him in from the yard. For every groove there is a tongue, for every dove a tail. It seemed to him now the light lay oddly in the window, but he reflected that at this time of the morning everything looks odd, it being the unpeopled hour when the moveless things come into their own. He hadn't had his breakfast yet, and felt hollow, somehow, and a little giddy. Also he seemed on the verge of tears, vague tears, though he knew no cause to weep, or none specific. He rose from the chair, sighing, and opened the rattly back door and crossed the yard and stepped into the leafy lane. Damp sunlight, and the mingled fragrance of loam and lilac, wild honeysuckle, dewy moss. The dog appeared soundlessly from somewhere and limped along beside him on his bockety legs. They seemed, the two of them, already to have come a long and weary way together, from some far-off, fabled region. They arrived at the little wooden gate under the stone arch twined with hawthorn. Here was the spot where only a month or two ago he had stepped through something like his own reflection and entered this otherworld of mirrors and mazes. He should be able to re-step now through that ripple, through that rip in the upholstery of the world, and all would be reversed. He should, but couldn't. Something hindered him, a wall of light, a block of air. The descent to Avernus is easy, as we know, but try getting back up again, then you'll see. And so he stood, with his hand to the low gate and the dog's calm eye upon him, and looked with longing towards the other side of everything, where lay the lost beyond.

Was he wrong, he asked himself, and Godley in the right, all this time?

—I was met, at the railway station, by a large dark heavy-browed man who greeted me with sinister affability and spoke what must be his name but so softly I didn't catch it. Who could he be, or what? He gave no account of himself other than to say he had been sent from Arden House, without specifying in what capacity. He wasn't a member of the Godley family, of that I felt sure, but nor had he the comportment of a retainer. From his dress—tweed jacket and woollen tie, striped shirt, twill trousers with a sharp crease, a brown Borsalino, raffish, broad-brimmed and not as new as when we glimpsed it last—he might be a country solicitor, though one of questionable probity. He was not young but not old either—early sixties, I guessed—and had a curiously humid aura, as though he had recently recovered from a prolonged but only mildly debilitating illness. He relieved me of my bag with the polite adroitness of a master pickpocket. The car, he said, was just outside, and we had but a short drive before us up into the hills. I thought of asking him to repeat his name but didn't, fearing it might be a breach of some rural code of mannerliness; I am a city-slicker, and never wholly at ease without the reassuring solidity of a city pavement under my feet.

I was feeling decidedly shaky. When on my return to Arcady from New Amsterdam I had a second meeting with the glacial Professor Dickinson—known to the faculty as Dictionary Dickinson, or Dic-Dic for short—my announcement that I would be vacating the Vander chair forthwith was met with silence and a tight-lipped, beady stare. Dic-Dic had a way of drawing her brows together and tucking in her chin that never failed to unnerve me. Under the terms of my contract, I was firmly reminded, I still had six weeks of classes to teach this semester. There followed a tense wrangle, couched on both sides in tones of coldest politeness, by the end of which I had succeeded in whittling the six weeks down to three. I packed up my books, including half a dozen borrowed long ago from the college library, and had the janitor, a fellow so fat he did not so much walk as trundle, take them down the hill to the post office in his four-wheel-driven Pelican, of which he is immensely proud.

After that there was nothing to do but look for ways of filling in the time. The days dragged, and the solitary evenings, which I used to find pleasant and restful, were now only irksome. I dined in the Parnassus Club, where on most nights I had the place to myself, the bored staff sashaying dreamily around me on their squeaky soles as if I weren't there. Suspended thus, I became prey to an odd, unattributable melancholy. I felt like an abandoned lover, except that there was no one who loved me for me to be abandoned by. I took solitary walks on the bay shore, in the interminable sunshine, under the gigantic, mantis-like shadow of the great rust-red spindly bridge. One night in the Paris Bar on campus—named not for Paris as in France but Paris as in my half-sister Helen, the daughter of Leda—I was propositioned by a young woman whom I mistook for one of my students; afterwards I wondered if it had indeed been Trudy Tring, got up in fishnet and leather and turning tricks to pay for her tuition.

Then all of a sudden, on one ordinary morning, I was free;

this was a surprise, odd though that may sound, and a relief, too, for in this new epoch of universal decline I always expect the inevitable not to happen, inevitably. I set my students a mind-numbingly extensive reading list, shook the golden dust of Arcady from my winged heels, and here I was, landed back on native soil, with a fluttery pulse and an apprehensive heart. My doubts about the commission Adam Godley had burdened me with steadily deepened the further away I got from Arcady. What if I made a hash of his father's biography? I could see the notices already: *in over his head—singularly ill-equipped—inadequate scientific knowledge—unforgivable gaffes—a shameful travesty.* I wished I had ignored Adam Godley's letter, wished I had torn it up and eaten it. Let Popov have the field, rife with dock and thistle as it is. The westron wave had passed and the halcyon days were o'er, for me. I would sit on no more soft chairs in Arcady, or in any comparable seat of learning, not if Professor Dic-Dic had anything to do with it, and I had no doubt she would.

The car was a surprise. I had expected something old and grand and shabby, a cross, let's say, between a landau and a funeral carriage. I hadn't been in a Sprite before, and felt acutely self-conscious when, after much wriggling and shoving, and having barked both shins, I at last fitted the bony length of myself into the wrap-around passenger seat's unsettlingly intimate yet resolutely unaccommodating embrace. The hood was down. We set off. My driver drove with a debonair touch, steering deftly with just the thumb and two fingers of his right hand, while with his left he plied the knob of the gear-stick like a chess master demonstrating an intricate opening gambit. We skirted the town—twin spires, fish smell, coal smoke—and entered on an unnaturally straight, narrow road that ran ahead for miles and miles, over hill and hollow, without bend or deviation.

"It's called the Hunger Road," the large man beside me confided. "A make-work project from the famine years."

We bowled along fleetly in the eager little car, to the right a steadily narrowing grey-blue estuary, to the left a bog. The wind ransacked my hair and pummelled me about the ears.

"Tell me, Mr. erm——?"

"Mordaunt," the driver murmured.

"Yes, sorry, I didn't hear you before when you——" A vigorous clearing of the throat. "Tell me, why did Adam Godley settle in these parts, do you know?"

Mordaunt raised his eyebrows but kept his eyes on the road. I took the point: was I not the man's putative biographer, and as such should I not be expected to know the answers to such things?

"It's where he was born, I believe," Mordaunt said after a pause, and jerked a thumb over his shoulder. "In the town."

"Yes, but——"

The topic, seeming a dead end, was steered away from and abandoned. Mute miles went liquidly past. A huge, cloud-flecked sky was arched over the body of water on the right, which by now had narrowed itself to a fair-sized river, while the sodden reaches at the left were splashed with watery, slanted sunlight. Bog pools shone like discs of polished pewter.

"The car, I should say, is not mine," Mordaunt informed me, in his oddly hushed and gravely intimate manner; it was as if he were imparting a fact of great import to be shared among only a privileged few. He lowered his voice still further. "Hired."

I was cold in the rushing air; Mordaunt, overcoatless, seemed not to notice the weather. By now that impossibly extended April is long past and we are approaching the start of an unseasonably chilly June. We went up the shallow slope of a low hill, the engine buzzing. There are many such hills in these parts, though in truth they're hardly hills at all but more like grassy mounds, softly moulded, and pudding-shaped, rather like my headgear. They are a more modest species of the genus that encircles Hirnea House.

There's a special word for them, I've forgotten what it is—I am omniscient, yes, but only sometimes. Morains? No, that's rocks and other detritus. Anyway, doesn't matter, this is not a sightseeing tour.

"As it happens, I'm a mathematician myself," Mordaunt suddenly said with unexpected animation, and with the air of one laying down triumphantly a winning card. Then he reconsidered. "Was, that is. Used to be."

"I see," I said, experiencing a spasm of unease. "So that's why—?"

He waited, inclining his head towards me a little way, and when I failed to finish the question, he straightened again and pursed his lips and nodded, as if somehow he had heard what I had not asked.

"No, I'm here by chance, you might say," he said.

Maybe, I thought, he's an out-of-work actor earning a few bob in a stopgap position as driver and general factotum. He had the voice and manner for it.

"Ah, I thought," I said, "I thought you might be doing something on—some project on—"

This faltering sally the man seemed to find funny for some reason.

"On Adam Godley? No no." A pause. "Though I was born here, too, as a matter of fact."

"Yes?"

"That's why I came back."

"So not by chance, then."

"No. But I have stayed by chance, is what I meant."

"Ah."

There once more the conversation, such as it was, lapsed. Mordaunt steadily watched the road, bland of expression, those two fingers hooked nonchalantly on the steering wheel and touching the tip of the encircling thumb. He seemed to me to become more intangible by the moment. It was not that he was without affect, only he seemed to occupy a separated place, a place of motionless, blank detachment. When he had finished saying something he would subside abruptly into stillness, as though within him a motor had shut itself off, to conserve energy and prepare itself for the next run.

But then, and once more to my surprise, indeed to my mild consternation, he launched into an uninterruptible discourse on the subject of his family, of its origins and history in this other-wise unremarkable, wave-washed south-east corner of the land. The Mordaunts had been, and were, no mean people, according to their scion's account of them and their doings. They had fought in wars of conquest and, when it was meet, of rebellion, too; a hardy breed they were, men of the horse, cold steel, and musketry; men of learning and civic energy; the patrons of poets and painters, sages and songsters; masters of craft and husbandry; in short, a noble and distinguished line. All this he delivered in a monotone, the flat and colourless voice at odds with the magniloquent asser-tions it was making, as if it were all a thing he had learned off by rote; yes, maybe he was an actor, in what I had no doubt were his many previous lives.

I was in acute discomfort; the boastful excesses of others always induce in me a state of damp-palmed, anxious constriction that must be embarrassment but feels more like blank terror; it was as if I were being roared at by a ravening lion. If we hadn't been going at a good clip, I believe I would have steeled myself and leapt out of the car, over the low door, and made a desperate getaway across the marsh and into the hills. By now I thought I had fallen into the hands of a dangerous imposter, a clever, polished and cunningly convincing lunatic, perhaps, escaped from some local institution. Who the devil was he? Had he addressed me by my name, when he appeared before me at the railway station? No, he had said only his own, or what I took to be his own, in that breathy undertone, diffidently. Did he even know who his passenger was, or had he picked me out at random? Perhaps it was his way to hang about the railway station, accosting unwary travellers on the pretence of having been sent by Arden House to meet them, and instead of delivering them there, fetching them off into the wilds of the countryside to do them bloodily in. Anything was possible, out here in this barbarous terra incognita.

Mordaunt was silent now; evidently the family saga he had just finished recounting had exhausted his resources, for the moment, at any rate, and the inner engine had switched itself off again. We crested the gentle hill—some say the workings of the Brahma theory are flattening out the very contours of the planet—and presently, to my considerable relief, we arrived at what must be our destination.

"Arden House, they call it now," Mordaunt said, with a hollow, disparaging laugh. "It was Coolgrange in my day. Riddle me that."

He steered the car in from the road and we passed between a pair of weather-worn stone piers. The house stands at the end of a short straight rutted drive. It has the look not of having been built but rather of having accumulated itself haphazard over two or three nondescript centuries. The later Blounts, enfeebled in spirit and increasingly broke, neglected the place badly, and while the Godleys, in sporadic bursts of zeal, had started on successive programmes of renovation, all had lapsed, so that there is an air overall of the gimcrack, of the improvised, of the temporary. The dwelling itself is a straggling, steep-roofed affair with whitewashed walls that with time have turned to a shade of yellow, and somehow cockeyed-looking windows with faded-blue shutters suggestive, incongruously, of the Provençal south. Although it's not apparent from the front, the building is arranged around the four sides of an enclosed quadrilateral that forms a sort of inner courtyard, roofed in with sheets of clear glass at the behest of Adam Godley, snr., years ago. The glazing wasn't a success, and there are leaks in the leading, causing seemingly insoluble problems with damp and mould. Everywhere in the rooms the timbers creak, draughts roam freely like household spirits, and, on rainy nights, a medley of steady, unlocatable drips in the upper storeys are the insomniac's waking nightmare. In the autumn, drifts of dead leaves clog the antediluvian guttering, while in summer the ground floor becomes a sump of unmoving air, heavy and moistly warm.

The most striking feature of the house is a tall wooden tower attached to the left front corner, left as one faces the front, with windows on three sides and a metal roof, cone-shaped and topped by a weathervane, the whole seeming a sort of jerry-built imitation of a feature of one of King Ludwig's less bravura Bavarian excesses. In recent weeks I had studied the place in many a photograph, in sepia sketches and in a reproduction of one remarkably bad oil painting, and I found it uncanny to encounter it now in three dimensions and to scale. I couldn't think what the madman beside me meant by saying it had once been called by another name, for according to my admittedly preliminary researches it was Arden House all the way back to the start. But then, I reflected, there might well be another version of the place, identical in all respects with the original. In the house of Brahma, so capacious, strange, and manifold, there are, as it is told, infinitely many mansions.

Look at those tiny busy flies above that miniature bay tree's neatly barbered globe, what is it they are weaving, weaving?

And there she was, my bright one, to greet me. Although I had never had sight of her before, in life or in imagining or dream, and knew nothing of her in the ordinary way of things, I recognised her at once where she stood atop the front steps in the fresh damp morning light, a forearm lifted to shade her eyes against the sun's glinting arrows. The sight of her made my bookworm's wire-rimmed specs steam up. Sleeveless blue dress, tanned legs—those shapely ankles, delicate as butterflies—her hair the colour of old gold and done in what I believe is called a chignon. And clutching something in her hand, the lifted one, not a branch of laurel though it seemed so, to my already enchanted gaze. Ridiculous, ridiculous to be thus instantly in thrall to a woman of whom I know next to nothing, since there are so very many of them and of such variety. Yet the eye alights on this one or on that and at once all is made radiant. Even we, in our eternal home up there on Olympus, even we don't understand it, and so we never tire of trying to know how it feels to have the experience; think of all the disguises, from swans and bulls to showers of gold coin, that my father Zeus assumed in order to have his way with this or that earthly girl of the moment. It's all beyond reason, yes, but what does reason avail, in matters of the heart? I ask you.

Of course she wasn't there to greet me, not intentionally, not by design. She had come out into the garden to pick that bunch of the somethings she was holding in her hand, and on her way back inside had paused at the approach of the bouncy little lipstick-coloured car.

"I can't understand how any normal-sized person can fit into such a tiny thing," she said, or called down, from where she stood on the high step, framed against the dark depths in the wide-open doorway, indicating the Sprite with an amused lift of her chin. Then she turned her eyes on me and blithely beamed, as if I were just the thing she had been in need of to brighten up her day. "You're the biographer bloke," she said, putting on a cockney accent, "come to do the dirty on my dad-in-law wot's dead."

Years ago she got the notion from somewhere that shaking hands is an insincere gesture, and unhygienic besides, and therefore never does it, so I would quickly learn; she doesn't often stand on principle but in this she does. I had mounted the steps in Mordaunt's ponderous, heavy-limbed wake, and now I stopped and stood grinning, inanely, I've no doubt, before this glowing creature, overcome by shyness and an instant, helpless enthrallment, puffing out my cheeks and making flapping motions with my arms, like a bloody penguin, I told myself, flapping its silly bloody flippers. But oh, I was, I was undone. Somewhere inside me there had been a she-shaped hollow, and now she had stepped forward and fitted herself into it and locked herself there with a click. Love at first sight! The banality of it. Such a thing had never befallen me before, and I couldn't believe it was happening now, just as I had come to an age when Eros, having lost heart, is getting ready to unsling his quiver and unstring his bow.

Mordaunt had carried my suitcase up from the car, and now he set it down, gave a crisp nod, turned and descended the steps, insinuated himself behind the steering wheel and in a puff of briny exhaust fumes was off. Above on the step, nondescript man and resplendent woman stood side by side and watched him go.

"How did you get on with Ivy's Fella?" Helen asked.

"Ivy's—?"

She nodded again towards the little buzzing car as it dwindled down the drive; I heard distinctly in my head Mordaunt softly breathing again the word *hired*.

"It's what we call him," she said. "I'm convinced he's going under a false name anyway. Adam is sure he has seen him or at least an image of him somewhere before. On a wanted poster, I daresay. One morning he just turned up unannounced and my husband in his wisdom let him stay. He denies it, of course, says it was me. I did invite him to lunch with us that first day, mind you.

A mistake. Now we can't get rid of him. He lodges over there"—gesturing splashily in the direction of yet another low hill not far off—"with Ivy our put-upon skivvy, hence our nickname for him, though you mustn't tell him we call him that, or her. I'd have sent him packing, but Adam is a fool and would take in any old stray. How was it when you two met in"—this time she did a nasal Netherlandish whine—"*Noo Ams*? I wanted him to take me with him but he wouldn't. I was only there once, years ago when it was still New York. Playing Rebecca West in that stupid play. A disaster. I was far too young and didn't know anything about anything on or off the stage." She advanced a step and swiftly, with a finger and thumb, plucked something from the lapel of my jacket. "Greenfly," she said, showing a grassy smear on her fingertip. "We're plagued with them this year." She looked past me and glanced about, showing me the line of her jaw, the whorl of her ear, humming softly to herself. "Did he have to twist your arm?" she asked. "Adam, I mean—to do this book thing? He says you're just the chap for the job. He got it into his head his father's life story must be told, and nothing would do but to get you straight off to write it. I think someone else wanted to do it but he'd have you or no one. He's very stubborn, though you wouldn't think it to look at him. I can't wait to read what you write. The skeletons that will come clattering out of that cupboard! Have you found any yet, by the way? Skeletons?"

I shrugged weakly, incapable just then of any firmer form of reply. My voice didn't seem to be in working order; I was sure that if I tried to say something all that would come out would be a mosquito buzz of panic and anguished self-awareness. Locked by now in an agony of shyness, like a heretic clapped into an iron maiden, I stood very stiff and straight with my left arm stretched across behind my back and my left hand clutching my right elbow. What a hopeless dope. Anyway, though my heart was racing, I was

well aware that she had dropped into her mode as the stage hero-
ine, headstrong and highly strung, immured in an old house in the
depths of the countryside with no one to appreciate her beauty,
charm, and keen though veiled intelligence, no one, that is, except
her audience, which for that moment I alone constituted. She gave
me that smile again, bright and glittering, though there was in it,
I saw, a fleck of genuine sorrow that was not part of the part, a
sorrow lodged deep, the same that I had detected in her husband's
eye. I'm not so perceptive in the normal run of things, not when it
comes to the living—history was my first calling, remember—but
sudden love peers deep.

"I'm Helen," she said.

And Helen she was.

I held out a hand, and promptly she put hers behind her back.
It didn't seem at all rude of her. The desperate realisation came to
me, however, that this was likely to be the sole occasion I would
ever have to know the touch of her skin, and she had deprived me
of it. No handshakes. A principle is a principle. But ah, to kiss the
tender inward of thy hand!

I gasped and coughed and in a hoarse murmur enquired if her
husband might be—?

"Oh, he's off doing something with cows." It's obvious she's
vain of her voice, an instrument deep-toned and dark, on which
she likes to practise. "He still fancies himself a farmer, but he's
useless. Are you early? I'm sure he meant to be here when you—"
She trails off and turns from me with an unfocused, fading smile
and steps into the dark of the doorway. Then turns back. "Is that
all you brought, that bag and that measly suitcase?"

"The rest is on the way. My books."

"Right. Your books."

This is the house. Here is the front hall with a hatstand and
a dreaming mirror. The living room: polished parquet, worn

chintz, brass fire irons, a tick-tock clock on a marble mantelpiece. A discarded though still open book is doing the splits face down on the floor beside a baggy armchair which lists due to a missing castor. The parquet under our feet begins ever so slightly to quake. I look to Helen. "There's a train coming," she says. "The line runs beyond that fence. We've got used to it, though it gives people who don't expect it the willies, the way it makes everything rattle."

Then to the kitchen, the heart of the house, as we know by now. The range and so on you have already been introduced to.

"Would you like to have something?" Helen asks, frowning. All this has happened before, she thinks. "Tea, or—" Yes, this exactly.

She drops the bunch of wetly wilting bluebells on to the table. That's what she was holding, outside, while she shaded her eyes—bluebells! Odd, the way things suddenly assert themselves, elbowing forward to have their moment. It is an assertive world, the world we fashioned for them; one day it will assert them out of existence. Ah, the hush that will fall then! And us with nothing left to do but gaze into the looking-glass of our undying selves for all eternity.

There was the usual folderol of arrival, she enquiring if I needed the bathroom and I pretending to be anxious to get unpacked and settled in. I can tell she's glad about the tea, about my not wanting any; the kitchen and its accoutrements is emphatically not her domain.

She says she will show me to my room and leads the way. I bring my bag with me but someone else will carry up my suitcase. We ascend steadily narrowing flights of stairs. The last one allows of single file only. I go ahead, ever careful to show myself the gentleman, my old leather bag stuffed with God knows what clasped to my chest like a big soft brown baby with buckles. Though I must admit I would like to have a look at her from the rear. I can't tell whether the wisp of fragrance I catch is hers or a lingering trace of the bluebells. I think of those flowers expiring where she left them on the table and a breathy bubble of something hot swells inside me; how susceptible I am to these subtleties all of a sudden, raw and susceptible, newer-born than the bag-baby in my arms. Already it has been a long day and I'm all aquiver, nothing to be the same again, my life stirred up as with a stick and made cloudy. She opens a little door flush with the wall and we arrive at the foot of another set of wooden steps, of which there are exactly seven, by my quick count, if the top one is to be considered a step. As before, we climb one after the other into light, it sifts down on us like a drift of luminous dust.

"And this," she says—*she, she*—stepping ahead and opening wider this upper door and pressing her back against it to let me see past her, "this is the Sky Room."

Meanwhile—a word the Brahma theory has made redundant, by the way—*meanwhile,* I say, Mordaunt is steering the Sprite in at Ivy Blount's gateless gateway, and is surprised, not to say taken aback, to behold a sleek black Dolphin parked on the grass in front of the cottage in a glare of incongruity. His startlement lasts only a second, then he knows: who else would come bumping into this bucolic backwater on such a snazzy set of wheels but his old chum Billy Hipwell? Here to reclaim the Sprite, no doubt. But how did he know the place to come to? As far as I can recall, which is quite far, I assure you—a godling forgets only what he doesn't care to remember—we left no address for him at Hipwell Hire. Miss Nose-ring must have nosed him out, the clever thing. The Dolphin is spanking new, and stands ticking faintly in the sun, giving off mingled fumes of scorched salt water, rubber, and scratch-proof paintwork. Mordaunt alights from his own, that is, from Hipwell Hire's, suddenly much diminished motor, and paces slowly all the way round this altogether other, grand, and preposterous machine, walking the fingers of one hand along its warm suave sweltering skin.

He hesitates. He considers. He weighs upon the balance. He could hop back into the Sprite and drive away, away and away, with no one and nothing to stop him, freed man that he is. But why should he? What has he to fear from his Billy Boy? Yet still he hesitates, tarrying beside Billy's sumptuous vehicle, the imposing brightness of which lends an extra, glossy glow to the surrounding sunlight. He will not cut and run. Has he not determined to fashion a new version of himself, to become his own avatar? And does not that require him to slough off as much as he may of the past and its encumbrances? He's well aware of where it is he has come back to, although Coolgrange for him now is not so much the past as a half-imagined place or state of present antiquity. And from it he has been expunged, or as good as, by some trick played upon him by an elusive, ever-branching universe. The change of name in particular galls him. Yet what of it, in the long run? Do we have to remind him again that he invented a new name for himself, so why shouldn't his old home do the same, or have it done for it? And perhaps these transmutations, Coolgrange to Arden House and all the rest, will turn out to his advantage. Old Magwitch can bide here unfettered, unknown and unrecognised, for the present.

From within the cottage comes a streel of antic laughter. He recognises his landlady's tones, unwontedly wild with merriment. He utters an eloquent sigh. He is put upon by many minor irritants, of which Ivy Blount is not the least, and not so minor, at that.

He goes around by the side of the house, with guarded tread, for Ivy's chickens leave their droppings everywhere, zinc-white, emerald, olive-drab, he has often stepped in the stuff. And indeed, here is one of those baroquely comical creatures, scratching in the gravel with a beady mien; it takes fright at his approach—he has been known to aim a kick—and rushes off with a stiff-legged, rolling gait, its petticoats flying. He lets himself in at the back door, which is always left on the latch, for Ivy is a ridiculously trusting soul, like everyone else at Arden, as it seems. Stepping over a threshold always marks, for him, a series of tiny but significant transitions: outdoors to indoors, light to shade, that-he to this-he. Nothing like the slammer to intensify the self's awareness of its self, inexistent or otherwise.

The door, this back door, opens directly into the kitchen. Here he finds a lively scene. A trio of figures is seated at the circular, bare-wood table, which is draped for the occasion in a spotless white tablecloth edged with blue embroidery. Mid-morning tea has been taken—elevenses!—and almost a festive air presides. His entering step falls portentously upon the stone floor. Ivy is giddily in the midst of recounting something—not a joke, surely?—but when she sees his bulky form darkening the doorway she breaks off and her face clouds.

"Oh, you," she says, her voice gone dull.

Billy wears a three-piece dark-brown suit with a badly misjudged broad chalk stripe. In the buttonhole of his lapel there is tucked, most startlingly, a nosegay of dejected primroses.

"Hello, old pal," he says, with one of his guileless winks.

It is a dozen years and more since they last saw each other, but to Mordaunt's eye Billy appears remarkably little altered. This is more of a shock than if his friend had become a bent old man.

"Hello, Billy."

At the table by Billy's side sits his saucy young assistant. Her name, let us say, is Deirdre, pronounced, by her, Dear-dree.

"Mr. Hipwell has come for his car," Ivy says, with a glint of satisfaction. She deeply resents her lodger, foisted on her she can't quite remember how.

"Has he," Mordaunt responds, with a shrouded smile.

He eyes the tea things on the table. There are Ivy's best cups and saucers, and little deckle-edged plates each painted with an identical view of Mount Fuji; a silver sugar bowl and miniature silver tongs; and, mounted on a silver-plated trivet, the teapot itself, like a smooth hot white hen, a frail scroll of steam lazily curling from the tip of its upturned beak; also there is a plum cake, an impressively large wedge of which has already been consumed, and strawberries in a bowl and a silver juglet of cream. Well-born Ivy knows how to put on a spread.

"Pull up a chair," says Billy expansively, as if he owns the place. Mordaunt pretends not to hear, and stands smiling distractedly down on the three of them. He finds it increasingly odd, upsetting, even, to see Billy still much as he had known him and yet changed, sitting here framed in himself unfamiliarly—that unfortunate suit—like a figure at once trapped in and emerging from a block of sculpted stone, though who would want to sculpt Billy Hipwell is a question. On closer view it becomes apparent that the years have blurred him a bit—a pale line of retreat at the hairline, a droop to the eyelids, a sprinkling of marble-dust in the spiv's too long and too narrowly trimmed sideburns—but still he is Billy, our Budd. Mordaunt feels like a statue himself, rocking a little on its plinth in a shivery aftershock from some far quake.

Deirdre smirks at him; she has an impudently knowing air; how much has Billy told her of him and their times together on Anvil Hill? He sees that she has devoted careful thought to what to wear for an excursion into the country. She is clad in a horse-woman's checked tweed jacket with leather patches on the elbows and nipped trimly at the waist, while at her throat there is bunched a loose sort of cravat of creamy silk stuck with an opal pin; he wouldn't be surprised to see, when she stands up, that she's wearing jodhpurs, and riding boots withal. And spurs? No; spurs is too much to hope for. She has set her chair noticeably close to Billy's, which, along with a certain proprietorial smugness in her look, confirms for Mordaunt that what he had surmised, on his initial encounter with her at the offices of Hipwell Hire, is the case, and that she is, to put it bluntly, banging the boss. So far, she hasn't uttered a word. Biding her time, she is. He knows a meddler when he sees one.

He sits down at last, the ends of the chair legs grinding on the stone-flagged floor. This is where he takes his meals, watched over in simmering outrage by Ivy Blount, in her apron and cardigan and man's rough trews. Of Adrian Duffy—that effete first name takes some of the harm out of him, doesn't it—there has not been sight or sound round here since Mordaunt came to lodge, which to Ivy's unremittingly offended eye is another count against this intruder from elsewhere; his simply being on the premises is imposition enough, without his having frightened off her swain.

"You're well set up here," Billy says to Mordaunt, with that familiar, slow smile, at once sweet and sly. The posy of primroses in his lapel is at its last gasp; how brief their day, the flowers of the field.

I could drive him up into the hills and kill him, Mordaunt is thinking—we need to hold on to that car—but what about his girl? Billy he could handle, if he were to take him by surprise, but Deirdre he suspects would be a tougher skull to crack. That merrily mocking eye of hers he finds disquieting. Yet she's just a girl, and didn't he do for one of those already, way, way back?

"Will I pour you a cup of tea?" Ivy grudgingly enquires.

He doesn't answer her, either, behaving as if he hasn't heard; the war between them is for the most part wordless. Now silence drifts above the table like the steam from the teapot's spout. The dog Rex comes in at the door, sees Mordaunt, stops. Mordaunt extends a hand, the animal goes to him, very serious, his tail not wagging. They have reached an understanding, man and dog; they have formed a bond. And to think, Mordaunt before he was Mordaunt used to abhor the brutes, of whatever breed, age, or gender.

Billy, as if performing a conjuring trick, brings out an antique silver cigarette case, clicks it open with a thumb, and presents it flat on the palm of his left hand to the others at the table. It seems he is the only smoker present. "Well, that's handy," he says, with another wink. He selects a cigarette for himself, taps one end of it smartly on the delicately cross-hatched worn lid of the case, and snaps his lighter into flame. All these expensive toys, Mordaunt sourly notes; he has done well for himself, has Billy.

"I'll take a fag," Deirdre says, with an impulsive flounce.

"Right-oh, chickie," her boss indulgently replies, reopening the box and offering it again.

Mordaunt thinks: I could, I could kill the pair of them, him and, yes, his butterball too, who would be the wiser, and scatter those fading primroses on their shallow graves. But he knows it's an idle fancy. His blood-letting days are done with, or so he assumes.

"Are you back from the station?" Ivy airily asks of him. He gives her a nod accompanied by a shrug. It gratifies her that he has had to run an errand, for all his pretensions to grandeur. "So what's he like, this Doctor what's-his-name?"

Mordaunt, scratching the dog behind an ear and frowning, devotes a moment's thought to the question, as though it merits it.

"Dry," he says, judiciously.

Ivy sniffs. "Well, you'd know about that."

"And he's a professor, not a doctor."

Deirdre laughs at this exchange, then gulps and glances quickly sideways at her employer and puts three bunched and pudgy pink fingers to her little scarlet mouth. Nervously she taps the burning tip of her cigarette against the rim of the ashtray. Mordaunt feels sure that misjudged titter will earn her a smack. Billy, though a romantic to the core, by his own account is always strict with his girls—"You don't want to let them get above themselves, it only spoils them rotten."

Ivy rises and brusquely gathers items of crockery and deposits them in the sink, making an aggrieved clatter. She's becoming increasingly cross, for she is, as she would say herself, mortified, by which she means embarrassed, but also, in this case, thwarted. A moment ago all was going swimmingly, now all's awry. Mordaunt might be a ne'er-do-well uncle come back from disgrace and banishment and landed in on her at the most inopportune of moments. She had taken an instant shine to Mr. Hipwell, forgiving him the chalk stripe and even the pug-faced rawsie he brought with him; in fact, they had been getting along very nicely, thank you, the two of them, Mr. H. telling stories from the motor trade—he is quite the raconteur, once one has got over his jackeen accent and can understand most of what he's saying—regarding her the while with a brazenly appraising eye. More's the pity Duffy isn't here, she thinks. If he resents Mordaunt, he should have a look at the more than personable Wm. Hipwell, Esq. Yes, he has given her his calling card, or rather Deirdre has, extracting it at his command like the ace of hearts from a neat, elastic-banded pack she keeps in her purse and tossing it across the table to Ivy with less than good grace. Ivy, poor decent distracted Ivy, how she longs to cling but just can't get a grip. Though she let herself have a little, a very little, brief hope of him, larksome Billy will shortly depart and be gone into the great world where she may not follow. Will he return? Ah, will he. All shall return, down to the moonlight between the trees, the spider at its web.

Deirdre speaks, cocking her head to the side and tipping up her chin, once again the brisk business lady. "I'll take the car key," she says, addressing Mordaunt. Her tone is prim and pointed, though he notes again the hard time she is having of it not to laugh. Either she finds everything risible, or that congested, pop-eyed look is natural to her; he thinks the former the more likely case. After all, she has every cause to be merry, fortunate as she is in having hooked an affluent sugar daddy, even one who in his younger days, though she's unlikely to be aware of it, did time on a broad assortment of charges, including affray, aggravated assault leading to GBH, oh and yes, buggery, the buggeree being a vociferously non-consenting eleven-year-old tough little tyke with two jealously protective and extremely big big brothers. Oh, indeed, Billy's early days were colourful and frequently incarnadined; don't be fooled by the air of youthful puckishness he sports even yet.

Mordaunt is pondering the matter of the key—should he hand it over, or negotiate, with menaces?—when another shadow, far less assertive than his, falls across the threshold.

The years have not dimmed Anna Behrens's beauty, only refined it. Or so it seems to him on his first sight of her after so long. She is tall, slender still, by now a little drawn perhaps, even to say a touch gaunt; her shoulders are sharper, her cheekbones more prominent, and her hair, which used to be the colour of wind-polished wheat, has taken on instead the soft silver hue of wetted ashes. But what poise, what grace, what self-assurance. She leans in the doorway on an ebony cane, and is elegant even in that. She wears a light-blue suit with a narrow skirt, under a navy raincoat with kimono sleeves. She has all over a nacreous sheen, brittle and iridescent. She has stepped in from that other world that Ivy fears, the one of lazy-eyed blondes in blue silk suits wielding costly canes, and the drab kitchen seems to draw back sharply before the fact of her. Mordaunt's swerving glance briefly bares the white at the outer corner of an eye, Billy Hipwell is scrambling to his feet, and Deirdre is already looking daggers. Ivy makes a small pinched circle of her mouth but produces no sound. The dog growls softly.

"I was on the way up to the house," Anna says in a sort of

laughing wonderment, addressing Mordaunt, "and met a rather strange man on the drive who told me I'd find you here."

"And here I am," Mordaunt tonelessly responds. He is thinking a jumble of thoughts, and entertaining not unfond memories. But Anna is the last person he would have expected to track him down. They went to bed together once, more than once, many years ago. Little of all that remains; little, but something, certainly something.

He looks round at the others, at suddenly bashful Billy and Billy's displeased girl, at Ivy and her madcap hair. It's all too much, too—he doesn't know what. A beat of stillness, then everyone starts to speak at once, and immediately stops. There is the sense of an audience unseen in the dark beyond the proscenium arch, packed tight and rolling in their seats in rollicking mirth at this moment of accidental comedy, lines forgotten, scenery toppling, the leading man's wig awry.

"This is Anna Behrens," Mordaunt says; he thinks in passing how odd a thing it is that everyone must have a name, must have two names. "Anna, this is my old friend Billy Hipwell, and—"

"Deirdre," Deirdre says tartly, narrow-eyed, and the shiny tip of her tipped-up nose twitches.

"Deirdre, yes," Mordaunt smoothly echoes. "And—"

Ivy pushes herself forward, asserting a householder's right of address.

"Are you a Behrens of Whitewater House?" she asks of Anna.

"Well, yes." Anna frowns, then carefully smiles. "And you are—?"

"Ivy—"

"Ivy Blount! Goodness, what a—"

"Yes!"

The human concourse, what a thing it is, I've often remarked it. Mordaunt fixes on Anna his strangler's measuring eye. Will he have to kill her, too? What on earth, in earth, will he do with so many cadavers? And how does Ivy come to be acquainted with the money-bags Behrenses of Whitewater House? This is all very disquieting.

"Sorry, but I must sit down," Anna announces. "This blasted knee."

Last week, she informs the table, taking off her gorgeous coat and making a wry face, she displaced the kneecap; something to do with a horse. Billy, who already is well on the way to being thoroughly smitten, brings forward hastily a chair, while offering eagerly that he knows of a man, a bonesetter, who—"People swear by him," he assures her, and smartly advances the chair to receive her neat and tightly skirted bottom. She gives him a brilliant smile of bland dismissiveness.

Ivy points to the teapot where it broods on its stand.

"Will you have—?" Again the tea ceremony. "I could brew a fresh pot."

For answer she receives another flash of that absent smile. Anna always had a queenly presence, Mordaunt reflects. He's worried she will address him by his name, his old name, the only one she knows him by. That would be awkward. He feels at the back of his sinuses a tickle of hilarity. What to do, O god of the crossroads, what to do?

And of course, it's simple, as I shall now demonstrate. Surrender the car key to scowling Deirdre—Anna's coming has altogether wiped away her smirk—shake Billy's hand and mumble something about seeing him soon again, nod to Ivy and get Anna to her feet and propel her, stumping on her stick, through the doorway and out. Unseen, I usher them forward, though they imagine they act under their own steam. The dog, posed sphinx-like under the table, looks after Mordaunt and gives a wounded whine, seeing himself abandoned: to a dog, every action is absolute, every departure final. At me he glares, the only one of them who can see me.

Anna as she goes looks past her shoulder back at Mordaunt and begins to laugh.

"For God's sake, Fre—"

"Ssh!"

How shy and tentative it seems, the seaside, in gauzy weather at the start of summer. Which is to say it seemed so to him on that particular, thinly clouded day when he arrived in the blowsy coastal resort of Ballyless with Anna by his side. For how is he to know what May is like in Madagascar, say, or on the shores of the Caspian, or for that matter on Copacabana Beach, where it's winter and not summer that starts around now and the honey-toned near-naked girls are enjoying their last frolics of the season in the surf? When he had manoeuvred Anna out at the door of Ivy Blount's cottage there was nothing for it but to follow after her, which he did, fairly crowding on her heels. She had come many miles to visit him and whatever her purpose he couldn't turn her away: even a murderer must mind his manners. Anyway, impossible to remain in Ivy's kitchen, after Anna had stepped into it with all the effulgent unlikeliness of an annunciating angel. But what was he to do with her? There was no question of his letting her find her way into the Big House, as the family in their fond yet wryly ironical fashion refer to the mouldering pile that has always been, *pace* Mordaunt's treasured but increasingly disintegrating memories, their home. The very thought of introducing her to

Adam Godley, much less to Adam Godley's wife, was preposterous, was positively grotesque, though he couldn't have said why. Certainly there's no call to bundle Anna hurriedly away, for she's quite the grandee by anybody's standards, if it's a matter not so much of class as of money we're talking about, and it is. But she is an inconvenience, and for all her opulence it's imperative she be got off the premises, and sharpish. She represents some kind of threat of some kind of disruption—again, he can't say which kind of either it is he's thinking of—just when he has got himself unshiftably settled in. And he is quite comfy here, all things considered. He has a nice room upstairs with a nice view over meadows and hills all the way to a gleaming sliver of sea on the horizon, and he can even put up with Ivy, for the time being, while he plans what to do with himself for the remainder of the golden or at any rate gilded autumn of his years; winter will be another matter.

Anna laughed at the dinky little car and refused to get into it. "With this knee?" she said. "And anyway you gave that girl the key." So he did; the Sprite and he would spright no more, so he sadly thought, but told himself it didn't matter, and might even be for the best. The machine was too small for him, he was too big for it. He knew how ridiculous he must look at the wheel, like a grown man, an overgrown man, sedately manoeuvring a child's pedal car.

Thinking thus of childhood things, he recalled thinking as he drove through the splintering world on the day of his release that he should pay a visit to the seaside in search of a crumb of comfort for his uncertain soul. He had put it off then, but why not do it now?

The needle of suspicion again gives him pause. "How did you know to come to the cottage?" he asked, with a touch of truculence.

"I told you, I met a man on the drive and asked him where to find you. And don't growl at me like that."

"What sort of man?"

"Heavy-browed, rough-hewn, a tiller of the soil, I'd judge."

He nodded. "That would be Duffy," he said darkly. "But tell me this, how did you know I was at Coolgrange in the first place"—he gave a bridling laugh—"or Arden House, as they choose to call it now."

She shook her head. "Can't remember." Her eyes, he saw, had become vague, her look blurry, as if in her mind she were detaching herself from him, from herself, from everything, irresistibly. There it is again, that way things have of going blank and seeming to sink.

Perhaps the reason it's familiar, he suddenly thinks, this sense of being dozily adrift in a world gradually, ever so gradually, winding down, according to the first or second or hundred-and-forty-seventh law of something or other, winding down yet never to come quite to a standstill, perhaps the reason he seems to recognise it is that, simply, this is how it was in prison. Could that be it? That simple?

Anna spoke. "What's the matter with you?"

"What?"

"You look like you're about to lay an egg."

Her car was parked in the laneway outside Ivy's gate. It was a Cachalot convertible, a magnificent machine, posher and bigger even than Billy's big posh Dolphin. It had a soot-black hood, and the metalwork was painted a shade of glossy grey like the belly of a freshly caught fish. She opened the door on the driver's side and tossed her walkingstick into the back seat, where it clattered against something.

"Hop aboard," she said, "and we'll go for a spin."

She seemed, he was relieved to see, to have come back to herself, to have regained herself, for here she is again as a moment ago she was, distinct, immediate, Anna and her big gleaming careless car.

"I'd like to see the sea," he said. *La mer, la mer, toujours recommencée!* "I'd like to visit the seaside."

And that was how he came to be in Ballyless, in Ballyless on Sea.

He knew the place, he had spent summers here as a boy, and something of his childhood endures even yet, if only in the smell of the salt air and the quaint look of everything. The village is a straggle of hotels and boarding houses and sun-bleached villas and little shops along one side of a straight mile or so of road, on the other side of which there is an indecisive margin of rushy dunes and beyond that the beach. Anna drove along slowly with the car roof folded back and the windows down, as if her passenger were a hero to be shown off to his public, a commander returned in triumph from a still smouldering Troy, or a poet on the way to Parnassus; all that was lacking was the tickertape, the crown of laurel, the clamorous multitude. He felt a fool.

It surprises him that he has been allowed to come all this way without hindrance, while the other day he couldn't get past the lychgate. That must be somehow the particular entrance from, and exit to, the old world that is lost to him. If that's the case, as well try squeezing back up through the eye of an hourglass.

Ballyless, the village itself, seems all too convincingly unchanged. The two hotels, the Beach and the Golf, are still as they were, and so is Myler's, the grocery-shop-and-pub combined, and the tin-roofed church that inside on summer Sunday mornings gave off an unsanctified, mingled smell of distemper and warm wood and probably still does. He looked bemusedly upon all this, and might have shed a tear if he were someone else. The day was clouded, as we've seen, but the clouds are immensely high and thin, mere scraps of cotton against the blue, and the air is whitely bright, everything stark and sharp-edged as in an overexposed photograph.

"Are you really living with that woman?" Anna asked.

"I'm her lodger."

"Her live-in man! Goodness. Does she bring you bowls of sustaining broth, and rub your chest with liniment of a night?" He glanced at her hands on the steering wheel. Sinews, distended veins, a light spatter of liver spots. He found exciting the spectacle of such a delicately made creature in charge of such an enormous motor car, with its so many dials and gauges, its musky smell, its engine's soft and menacing growl. He nibbled at the plump and velvety inner lining of his lower lip, a thing he has always liked to do, a kind of intimate toying with himself. "And is that where you're going to continue staying?" she further asked. "I mean—?"

He looked away from her, running his fingers over the sun-warmed leather armrest in the door beside him. A fitted ashtray there, under the curved chrome lid of which was stuffed an acrid mash of cigarette butts. Say who, Sherlock? Some polished cad, some country-house rake; she could always pick 'em, could Anna; hadn't she picked him, though she hadn't kept him long?

"Good of you to come and visit me," he said, "uninvited. Want to tell me what it is you're after?"

She laughed, and trod hard on the accelerator and the car sprang forward as if it had been prodded in the rear, with a trident, say.

"Oh, Freddie, you never change."

"My name is Felix," he said severely. He pronounced it this time *fee* not *fay;* he didn't want her laughing at him, trillingly, showing her wet white teeth, in the way that she does. "And people don't change."

"They change their names, Mr."—she twiddled the slender fingers of a lifted hand impatiently—"what is it, again?"

"Mordaunt."

"Mordaunt?"

"Mordaunt."

"Right. Ha. Suits you."

Her lipstick was pale, and when she smiled her lips stretched and turned a glistening grey. A pair of worms, he thought, one draped stickily atop the other, and grinned to himself, liking the fancy. It's the sort of thing that comes into his head. She had told him in that long-ago time that she loved him. She hadn't meant it, he knew it then and knows it now, she had said it only to hear what he would say, to see what he would do. She had been amused by his young man's excitations, his self-love, his desire of the world which she might for that moment embody but couldn't give him, wouldn't. She was the younger by a year or two but she had always seemed to him as old as Eve. Twice they had gone to bed together, and a third time when they were joined by Daphne, his wife. There was a fourth time, too, long afterwards, but that's of no concern to us. In that threefold concumbence it was Daphne whom Anna had desired the more. All this from that time he sees as in an illuminated page in some old tasselled book, with a grave seigneur in a Limbourg-blue robe surrounded by a bevy of ladies with porcelain faces and impossibly high, pointed hats to which gossamer veils are attached at the top, one of whom cradles a unicorn in her lap. His past is set in legend, laughably.

"How well you know me, though," Anna said in her gay and rippling way. "I do have a favour to ask, as it happens."

"As it happens." Here is the up-and-over railway bridge, there is the little station, timeless as a toy. He shot out a hand and seized her arm. "Stop the car, turn it around—"

"Ouch! you're hurting me."

"—turn and go back."

"Why?"

"I want to see it all again."

Grumbling, she did as she was bade and spun the wheel and

the tyres screeched in protest and an oncoming van swerved wildly and plunged past them with an outraged *paarp!*

Mordaunt looked all about more eagerly even than he had before, more puzzled and more beguiled.

"Is it as you remember it?" Anna asked.

"Yes, the same, almost." He brooded in bewilderment. "I don't understand. Some things are just as they were and others are different, unrecognisable."

"Well, you have been gone a long time, *Mr. Mordaunt.*"

He tries to think how he might describe his predicament to her, and don't we feel for him? It's as if he had returned home after long travels through far-off lands and over alien seas to discover all he had known here at Ithaca inexplicably altered, his house remodelled, the locks changed, the housemaids become slatterns, a strange wife in his bed and his changeling children renamed and sullen, and a new cat sitting on the mat, regarding him narrowly with a malevolent green stare. A tabby, it is, on a rattan mat, listening motionless for a mouse. We do like to be specific.

"Ah, well, that's all the doing of our late friend the less than godly Adam, isn't it," Anna said. "He did his fiendish sums and set everything in a spin. It was all chugging along very nicely thank you very much until he stuck his thumb in the works and broke the sprockets."

"Is that all it was?" he murmured wonderingly, in the voice of one peering over the edge of a precipice and seeing clouds far below, as if the world had been turned upside down. "Is that all it took?"

"All?"

"A few equations?"

"A few equations."

How could she be so calm, so casual? Was she not up here beside him, poised on the same brink, with all the others? Look through that gap in the cloud and see how far there is to fall.

Another stretch of road unzipped itself beneath them. Anna locked her elbows and braced both hands against the steering wheel and pressed her back against the back of the seat and sighed. "I should be smoking a cigarette and gaily laughing," she said, "letting my hair fly in the wind, like the girl in the cigarette advertisement. I used to do that, remember? In the days when we were young and lovely."

"I remember."

"You don't."

"I do."

The car slid onwards silkily down the steep of Station Road—there's The Cedars, so much more sadly shabby now than once it was—at the end of which, in a gap between two low buildings, is the beach and then a bulge of indigo-blue sea and then a tall flat chalky sky. All at once he feels light-hearted, as if a door had been thrown open somewhere.

"What about me, have I changed?" he asked.

"You have, you have. You've got—I don't know." She regarded him askance, taking the measure of him. "As if you had turned into your older, gloomier brother. And you look a complete antique in that get-up, by the way."

He drew in his chin and looked down appraisingly along himself.

"The classic style, I would have thought. Tweed never dates, isn't that what they say?"

She inspected him again, more critically, holding in a laugh.

"Fixed in amber," she pronounced.

"Aspic, is what you mean. Get your terms right, if you're going to be offensive."

She gave him a look.

"At least the titfer is new," she said, "thank you, Anna." The hat he had tossed on to the back seat; yes, she it was had ordered it for him, and had it delivered to him on the morning of his release;

a coming-out present, as she wrote on the card before slipping it behind the band. How had she known which size to buy? Another little mystery. "I thought the day should be marked somehow," she said. "I remembered what a shady look a hat always gives you. Though of course you are shady, aren't you. Did they bear it to you in your cell on a silver salver?"

"They admired the pink sash you tied the box with. Or did the hatter do that? Lovely bow, anyhow."

Turn left. The Strand Café. Opposite, a small brown shop that he remembers exactly, unless it's an exact replacement of the original, with fishing nets on delicate bamboo poles and a net bag of striped beach balls and a cluster of whirligigs with pink and white blades propped in a red bucket in the ever-open narrow doorway the narrower glass part of which is fitted inside with a dainty cretonne curtain sallowed by the years. Yes, yes, all there! And in the window, displays of sweets—acid drops, bull's-eyes, bags of sherbet—and a tall jar containing coils of liquorice like glistening fat black shoelaces. People toiled in factories to make these things. As he looked, a small boy, who might have been himself from fifty years ago, came out at the curtained door, eating an ice-cream cone with the diligence and concentration of a potter potting a delicate artefact from a shapeless piece of porcelain.

A shaft of reflected sunlight struck from somewhere and was instantly extinguished. The day had taken on a magnesium glare. How swiftly the light changes beneath that high white skim of cloud. Everything moving, nothing the same from moment to moment, going its heedless headlong way.

"Have you still got my things?" he asked. "Or did you have them taken away and burnt?"

"They're in a trunk in an attic somewhere, or what of them the moths haven't eaten. We must go on a shopping spree and kit you out properly."

"You'll foot the bill, will you? I have no money."

"Go on with you—you must be rolling in it, after all those years living for nothing at the state's pleasure. And don't they pay you for being in prison?"

"Tuppence a mailbag."

"Well, that would build up, over time. I bet you have a big pot of swag stowed away somewhere, the loot you saved up through all the rainy days to spend when a fine one came."

"What notions you have."

"Tell me, were there arrows painted on your clothes? Was there lots of raping? I imagine you had a boy with no front teeth. I read somewhere that's all the rage in—what do you call it? Stirabout?"

"Stir. Porridge."

"Why porridge?"

"Don't know. Something everybody hates?"

She laughed, a gurgle deep in her throat.

"That man back there in the loud suit, back there where you're lodging, he was giving you a queer old eye."

He set his mouth and arched his eyebrows, which always makes him look, he knows, the dead spit of his mother. "That's sharp of you," he said. "He was indeed for a time my catamite. And don't pretend you know the word."

"I don't need to know, I can imagine. His front teeth have grown back, I noticed."

The Golf Hotel again. Myler's again. The field with the chalets in it. This was where he had been, once; this had once been a place for him, a place he knew. Or had it? Wading in the sea here one day when a boy he had trod on a sand dab that squirmed out in terror from under his foot and for a second the universe tilted. Nowhere is home.

"Did you miss me?" Anna asked. "Did you even think of me, even once?"

"You weren't there to miss," he said. "You weren't anywhere."

This was, is, in a certain sense, true. People when they quit his company cease to exist, as far as he's concerned. He hadn't needed to be shut away for this to be so, for so it has ever been, with him. He wonders if it's a matter of a failure of the imagination. It may seem the purest solipsism but it's not. The reality of others he can readily accept, but only in the abstract, and only because it's of no consequence to him if they exist or are a chimera as multifarious as the world. Nor is this indifference, exactly; he isn't Adam Godley. The thing is technical, rather; like, somewhat like, a proposition in logic: I am, in all my amness, therefore they're not, unless they're within sight and sound of me, here and palpable, for me to vivify them. The tree falling in the forest with no one to hear it does or doesn't do something, for the moment he forgets exactly what. He simply cannot conceive of Anna Behrens, to take an immediate example, cannot conceive of her having been somewhere, anywhere, doing things—walking, talking, eating, sleeping, even—during all those years, a quarter of a century, without him by to substantiate her. Nor has this anything to do with love and the hopeless beyondness of *die ferne Geliebte;* he didn't love her, any more than she loved him. He suspects he never loved anyone, if love requires a surrendering of the self, there being in the first place, as he will assert, no self for him to surrender. There is an analogous effect to the one we've been discussing, I've been discussing, which is that when others depart from his company or he departs from theirs, he assumes that he, too, on his side, drops out of existence, for them, to all intents and purposes, to all their purposes, all their intents.

Mind you, that tree in the forest, that old chestnut: there will always be someone or something to mark its fall, if only a fox, a mouse, a nematode, or just the air itself, undulant in waves and particles, in sparkling wavicles.

"What about a drink," he said.

His light mood of a moment ago was gone, and now he was prey to a creeping unease. Anna's suddenly turning up like that had given him a jolt; a soft one, but a jolt nonetheless. He wished she had not sought him out. Before, he had been content, or almost. It had suited him to be at Arden, his halfway house, even if among strangers in an estranged place, Coolgrange as was, Nowhere-upon-Lethe, there's that misted river again. But now out of the past had come this woman, with her provoking humour and playful malice, in whose company he had felt for a while exhilarated, bucked up, on the brink of being the bold old self of the dashing days of his youth. Very disconcerting. He was as the mammoth in the permafrost, the great plates had shifted and the ice had cracked open with an awful grinding and groaning, letting in heady air and light, bright vistas, misty distances, the sound of strenuous winds. This was precisely what he hadn't wanted, is precisely what he doesn't want. What he most sorely wishes for is not to be, or to be and not, both at once. Above all, to be beyond the prattle, the ceaseless, numbing prattle always and everywhere around him, even at Arden, a place sunk though it be in its solitude.

"How do you know Ivy Blount?" he asked. "How does she know you?"

"My father and hers were friends. Well, sort of friends—you know what Daddykins was like. They used to come to Whitewater, the Bounder Blount and his daughter Ivy the Gaunt. Got a painting out of him, out of the Bounder, once, did my old man. A Bonington, pretty as a picture."

"That one of the fisher-boys on the beach?"

"How well you remember."

"How would I not?"

"Poor Bounder, the foolish fellow, he didn't know what he had, sharp though he was about so many things. But that was my pap-pah for you, always on the lookout for someone to rook."

She steered in at the gates of the Golf Hotel. Or is it the Beach?

What was it like to be in prison, she asked him—"I mean really"—as she crept the car up and down aisles of squeaking gravel in search of a place to park. The roofs of the ranked cars shone like the humped backs of so many humpback whales washed up in a row on a beach; the Cachalot, cached, will feel quite at home. Mordaunt was struggling to marshal his thoughts, his thinking. A vestige lingered of the lethargy that had come over him a while back, the state of being stalled somehow between two worlds, between many worlds. Is it prison he's thinking of, again? Every lifer is a hermit, of necessity.

How to describe it to her, how? What he went through was a process of refinement, one that left him much as he was before and yet—well, not shriven, of course, that would be a poor joke indeed, yet stripped and shorn, yes, and to the bone, emaciated in spirit. He prefers himself this way. It is a natural state, his natural state, lean and trim and purged.

"Boredom," he said at last, without knowing he would; the word came out by itself and startled him, and he frowned.

"What?"

Anna is distracted, frowning too, cursing all these cars and their blasted owners.

"You asked me what it was like in prison."

"Yes and—?"

"I'm telling you. Boredom, the essence of it. The quintessence."

"What's the difference?"

"What?"

"Between essence and quintessence."

"Quintessence is the essence of essence. Think of blood as essence and lymph as quintessence. Meister Eckhart—" He broke off, pointing an urgent finger. "There's a place!"

"What? Where?"

"There, there!" the old peevishness breaking out. "Look!"

"All right, keep your hair on." She admired as so often the graceful way the long smooth vehicle dipped its polished nose when the brakes caressingly took hold. "Tell me about Meister What's-his-name and the essence of boredom." He was silent, facing the windscreen. "Oh, go on, Freddie, expound."

But it was no good cajoling him, she knew that pursed, sulky look, the mouth and eyes drawn down at the corners. The moment had passed, he would say no more on the matter. This was a pity. She always enjoyed it when he launched on one of his lectures, his big blue chin set deep into his collar, wedged there like a cobblestone, and his mouth going like a stranded fish's flapping gill. Meister Eckhart, indeed.

She kept one hand on the wheel, placed the other on the back of her seat, half turned and peered over her shoulder, and reversed the car in a wide, swift sweep like a dressage rider backing a thoroughbred into its stable.

He watched her face. She was thinking again of Godley, he knew it; the fellow's fetid reek was thick in the air between them. That was why she had sought him out, he told himself in disgust, not for his sake but to raise an old ghost.

"I take it you did sleep with him, back then?"

"Bingo!" she said, the car deftly stowed. She switched off the engine.

And here they are in the hotel's lounge, seated side by side on a long low sofa with cushions so squashy they might be lolling in warm shallows down at the seashore. The room has markedly the aspect of the parlour in a priest's house: tiny fireplace tiled in beige and inset with a single-bar electric fire, wallpaper the colour of scorched cardboard printed with tumbling, faded roses, a mantelpiece clock with a deliberate, loud and reprehending action. The wall they face, however, is daringly up to date, being a single plate of glass, from floor to ceiling and from wall to wall. Beyond is a swathe of close-cut lawn with croquet hoops, a pitch and putt course, three improbable palm trees, and a disconsolate flag pinned to a tall white pole from which when a breeze goes past the thin white halyard produces a thwack emphatic and flat as a pistol shot. The sun is shining gamely, doing its necessary duty. Weren't there clouds not long ago, whitely flecking the sky? There were, and now they've gone; more of them and more portentous will come rolling along presently. On the lawn outside the window the jet of an unassuming but busy little fountain is aswarm with tiny rainbows that quiver and flit like a hover of hummingbirds. Within, the two friends, the two something-or-others, are drinking gin, inadvisedly, as Mordaunt supposes, yet the part of him still capable of delight delights in the glassy blue glint of it, the teeming fizz, the lemony lemon, and, lo! here's ice again, a cluster of miniature bergs joggling and bumping and cracking in voluptuous agony.

"Do you ever think," Anna said, lifting her unwieldy leg on to a low table in front of her and admiring her expensive shoe, "that it all might mean something?"

"What do you mean, mean something?" he asked suspiciously, unease resurgent in him. But he knew well what she was referring to, the fact of his having done away with a maid, a housemaid, a maid of the house, while going about the tricky business of stealing a painting from Anna's father's stately home, a tale already told elsewhere and in no need of rehearsing here. "What sort of something?"

Anna was absently massaging her knee; it was the left one, or maybe it was the right. He glanced with a frown at the broad tight flesh-coloured elastic bandage she wears under her stocking; it makes him think again of his mother, something he would rather not do, not now or at any time.

"I felt then," she said, "and I still feel, that it was all too, I don't know, too elaborate, not to have been a part of some—what do you say?—some pattern. You know?"

To his mild horror, he did know. Had he not entertained the notion himself, or something like it? Of course he had. Even the nihilist believes in the nothing. Oh, but this was perilous, perilous ground, soft enough to sink in and be stuck fast, if not sucked under entirely. There had been so much of it, the coveted valuable painting and the inconvenient young domestic wallowing in her blood, then capture and trial and prison, the years, the years, and here he was now in a cheerless hotel lounge on a day in summer holding a tall glass between cold fingertips, hearing the bubbles zip and sharply pop, while his mind goggles in dismay at the possibility that what—that what—oh, what does it matter what. For something to mean something it would have to be directed by somebody, like a bad stage play. And then there is the question of a point of view. Considered from a sidereal distance the swiftest scurryings seem a stillness, and the snail keeps pace with the panther.

He felt a little queasy. Should have taken that tea Ivy offered, and a slice of plum cake, to line the stomach. Never drink on an empty bag, his old father used to warn, it was one of his many well-worn apothegms. Goodness me, first his mother, now his father; what further ghoul would lift up its head in the hall of horrors?

"You're talking teleology," he said, "with your patterns and meanings."

"But don't you think—"

"And teleology is theology by other means. Don't tell me you've got religion."

"Always had it," Anna answered cheerfully. "Blasted knee," she said then, pulling a face. He had turned his torso sideways on the sofa to stare at her. She met his deploring eye with a cool one of her own, and laughed. "My Aunt Minnie used to look at me like that," she said. "And you shouldn't pout, as if you're about to say 'par-don *me?*'"

"Do you mean to say," he said, disregarding her banter, "that you believe in it all, death and resurrection, little Lord Jesus and the life to come—"

"Well, yes, most of it."

"—the Holy Ghost? Purgatory? The saints?"

"Oh, the saints definitely," she said, with a show of fervour he hoped wasn't felt. "They're all my friends. I have a particular devotion to Saint Catherine of Siena. She had the stigmata but no one could see it, and was married to Christ, and is buried in Rome in a church built over a shrine to Minerva. Who was Minerva, do you know, you who knows everything, even who Meister Eckhart is?"

Mordaunt took an audibly deep breath and looked about in the manner of one who feels himself cornered. He was in need of another drink. He had forgotten the spell this artful, mischievous, and peculiarly maddening woman could cast, and the way she had of making him feel overborne. Look at him now, in danger of being knocked clear off his pivot, and why, and for what?

"You're laughing at me," he said menacingly.

"I am not," Anna responded with feigned indignation, and laughed.

If Adam Godley's Brahma theory is right, and so far no one has been able to prove it wrong, though not for want of trying, then somewhere in the welter of infinite possibilities the poor

creature whom Mordaunt murdered didn't die and he is an innocent man. This is a dizzying thought, and this is not the first time
he has thought it.

"You used to do that sort of thing yourself, didn't you," Anna
remarked absently, "equations, and so on." It had indeed once
briefly seemed he might have a flair for mathematics—probability
theory was his field, or the field through the gate of which he
aspired to enter—but time and Adam Godley had disabused him
of so fatuous a notion. Godley had gone where no other could follow, taking with him the real sack of swag, the bag bulging with
booty, in short, the entire kit and caboodle. "By the way," Anna
went on, "to answer your question: yes, I did sleep with him, of
course I did. So did your lady wife"—she turned her head and
fixed him with a maliciously eager eye—"didn't you know?"

It was not long after his transfer from Anvil Hill to Hirnea House that he was told one day of the death of his wife and
their son, their only child. The prison governor, that kindly, well-
meaning, and endearingly ineffectual poor man, summoned him
to his office—it had a view of those low, misty hills that for us
have become annoyingly ubiquitous—and broke the news to him
of the double tragedy. Afterwards, all he could remember of the
occasion was a patch of pallid yellow sunlight on the wall behind
the governor's left shoulder, no, the right—how things get turned
around—which brought proustianly to his mind a similar patch
on a similar wall in someone's *Portrait of a Woman with Gloves,*
the picture, the very one, that he had murdered for, or so at any rate
the indictment laid against him said. That, and the governor telling him the pair had both been killed outright, Daphne at the
wheel and their son beside her, and his thinking that the phrase
killed outright sounded oddly judgemental, oddly procedural, as if
the annihilation of his spouse and sole offspring had been carried
out briskly and pursuant to a state directive.

Now he removed a speck of lint from the sleeve of his tweed jacket; must get a lighter one for the palmy days that would soon be here. There is such a jacket among his things that Anna is keeping for him in her attic. He might go over there, one day, and collect it; why not? Nothing to stop him going anywhere he liked, doing anything he wished, supposedly not, anyway.

Yes, he had known that Daphne had slept with Adam Godley, all those ages ago. Anna was still watching him, with her mocking eye. What of it, he asked himself, what of an ancient dalliance? Yet he experienced a small unfamiliar pain in the heart. Or no: it wasn't pain, exactly, but an awareness of pain and its proximity, as when one is in the dentist's chair and the drill jars against the anaesthetised nerve and the body screams soundlessly in terror of the unexperienced agony. Latterly, what he feels is not feeling but the feeling of how feeling feels.

He rarely thinks of his wife, now, or of his son. They seem in a strange way to have joined the ranks of his antecedents. Daphne might be a many-greated-grandmother fabled in the family annals for her beauty, the boy—the man, when he died—a warrior-poet caducously fallen in some archaic battle, at the Siege of Münster, say, or on the salt-sown soil of Carthage. This curious distancing effect he took to be a result of their having died in his absence, behind his back, so to say: recall what we noted above about people being nowhere when they're out of his presence. He hadn't asked to be let out to attend the double funeral—to the shock and muttered disapproval of even the most hardened of the hard old lags in his cell block—and anyway Daphne's parents had made it clear they would regard his presence at the graveside of their daughter and her—*her*—son as the worst of bad taste on his part, a sentiment with which in all conscience he could not find fault.

Anna said now that she must pay a visit to the ladies' room—in fact, what she said was that she needed to do a pee, "damn it"—and with difficulty and a gritted moan hoisted herself aloft with the aid of her stick. To be exact, as Ivy had resentfully noted, it's not a stick but a fine old Malacca cane, slim and supple, with a brass ferrule and a chased silver boss where the handle meets the shaft. It had belonged to her late father. Mordaunt could picture the old tyrant wielding it as he belaboured a loinclothed line of Hottentots as they shuffled unwillingly in single file down the mouth of one or other of the fabulously productive diamond mines he had inherited from his own father and his own father's father. He watched the woman limp away, though she didn't so much limp as lurch, with a forward-plunging motion of one hip, as if she were poling a heavy punt through a reed-choked stretch of shallows. She seemed suddenly much aged; it was as if the mere action of getting to her feet had put years on her. He tried to think what age she would be, but couldn't. It's true, she is still a beauty in her way, bold and bright and fair, as we have observed, and not without grace even at a lurch. But something is definitely amiss with her. Maybe it's only the effect of being with him; he frequently feels himself to be a laming force upon others, and why shouldn't she feel it, too? But no, no, in this case the blight that has so swiftly come over her is not of his doing. She has let go of something; it's as if she had been holding her breath for a very long time and now all at once had released it, in a great gasp that left her slack and stooping. At the door she paused and glanced back at him with what seemed a wearily calculating eye, as if to see if he had seen her sudden transformation.

The clock on the mantelpiece ticked, and time, as bidden, passed. He wondered what kind of pants she was wearing. This he didn't consider in any way unchivalrous, nor should we; as well speculate about her underthings as about her soul. It had always been with him a question of the first order as to how far the onion may be peeled before we are no longer what we would have the world take us to be and become instead our true, unvarnished selves, stripped of protective cover and colouring and shoved out on to the heath to shiver in our drawers.

Our true, unvarnished selves. Softly he chuckled.

A gangling boy with startling red hair and an incandescent case of acne appeared before him, with a tray in his large, freckled, raw-knuckled hands. He ordered two more gin-and-tonics—"My wife," just for the hell of it, "will be back shortly"—and the youth mumbled a word and gangled away. Mordaunt watched him go. He wore a waiter's rusty black jacket and black trousers with a metallic-looking, dark shiny stripe down the outside of each leg. The trousers were much too long, so that the backs of the cuffs were badly frayed. For Mordaunt there is always something affecting about people's clothes, not the fact that they must be worn but that they never quite fit, no matter how carefully tailored; in prison, few things were sadder than the sight of a newly arrived young inmate, all reddened ears and shaved nape, lost inside a bleached-out prison uniform too big for him, or trussed up in one too small.

Anna, he recalled, still sorting among his file of memories, used to favour, in the days when he knew her intimately, a curious undergarment made of heavy grey material, something between a Victorian bather's swimming trunks and a Turkish wrestler's trousers, with legs that came almost to her knees, and, unless he was imagining it, an ingenious fly complete with flap and buttons. Well, in those times the blossoming young wore the oddest things, most of which seemed to have been handed down, to girl and boy alike, by their great-grandfathers. Ah, days of gaiety and shabby glamour, soon over, soon gone, though he was never glamorous and ever far from gay.

He looked at his watch. Anna had been away a long time; their new drinks had been delivered and the ice in them was already melting. He gazed out dully at the pitch and putt course, whereon a pair of sexless oldsters togged out in pastel shades were totteringly playing at tortoise pace a sort-of round of sort-of golf.

Then, underneath our clothes, there is our skin, the largest of the human organs, for yes, an organ it is. Skin for him is a subject of the deepest fascination; how do we not marvel at it endlessly, this sturdy, pliant sheath that holds in our insides so discreetly and for the most part with such efficiency, preserving our modesty and shielding from common view the inner fester? We walk about the world a kind of mandrake-shaped, ill-made sausage packed with organs and ordure, bones and blood, and rarely if ever give a thought to the pink, black, or yellow casing that contains us with so little fuss. And what about the thicker stuff, the flesh, that cushions us against the day's minor assaults? One of those deservedly forgotten *petits maîtres* of the misconceived Cubist era, Braque the house painter and melodeonist, I think, or perhaps that little black-eyed devil Pablo Ruiz, once remarked that a house built of flesh wouldn't last long. And yet the things that are made of flesh do last, do endure, and for far longer, indeed, than common sense would expect or predict.

Anna came back.

If anything she looked worse than she had before. Her face had a greasy pallor and her eyes were sunken in their sockets. There was about her in general the stark and sobered air of one who has peered deep into a looking-glass and seen there a new and incontrovertible truth. This deterioration in her in so short a time was dismaying, but it was an annoyance also. He considered himself as concerned as the next man for the well-being of others—hardly at all, that's to say—but he would think it a bit much if it was the case that Anna had sought him out deliberately, just him and no one else, in order to reveal to him some ghastly and possibly terminal malady. Hasn't he enough afflictions of his own without being expected to share in the bearing of her burden, whatever it is? She sat down, cautiously, and put aside her cane and sought a comfortable position for her bandaged knee. What would she say next? Was she going to—oh, please not!—would she be so crass as to confide in him her awful secret? To forestall the possibility he launched at once into a humorous—it was meant to be humorous—account of Ivy Blount's long and melancholy campaign to coerce the cowman Duffy into converting their wearyingly long engagement into a joyous union. He could see she wasn't listening but he kept on anyway. When he had exhausted the topic of Ivy and her hapless love he passed on quickly to others—the charm of the seaside, what mileage she gets from her gigantic car, *A Treatise of Human Nature,* &c.—like a man on the scaffold discoursing desperately to the impatient executioner on anything and everything that comes into his head in order to put off for just a little while longer the severing of it.

"Freddie," Anna said at last, touching a fingertip to his wrist, "do shut up."

"My name—"

"I know what your fucking name is. Will you listen, please?"

She stopped, and so did he, and they sat for some moments in rancorous silence. Then both reached forward simultaneously and took up their glasses and drank. It's peculiarly unsettling when you and the person you're with both perform the same small action at the same time and with exactly the same motions—why is that? Mortal life is a plague of tiny, unaccountable discomfitures, don't you find?

Anna was massaging her leg above the knee, clasping and unclasping the place that pained and softly grunting.

"Did you really get kicked by a horse?" Mordaunt asked.

"More of a nudge, he would have said—the horse, the talking horse."

"Serves you right. Imagine someone sitting on your back and whacking at you with a whip."

"You've never been a woman, *Felix*."

"Quite true, I have not."

"But you've become an animal-lover. I've got religion and you've turned into Saint Francis of Assisi."

Discreetly he pushed back a cufflinked cuff—sartorial standards are being kept up, as we see—and glanced again at his watch. He sighed. He could feel his spirits once more waning, could feel his mind letting go its grip, as if he were on the way to falling asleep. The goddamned Godley effect, again? He roused himself with an effort. "You said you had something to ask of me?" Best get it over with.

The ancient pair of pitchers-and-putters have sheathed their clubs and departed. An ugly cloud the colour and seemingly even the texture of blue marl is forcing itself upwards from the horizon. The palms rattle their fronds uneasily. Presently we shall have rain, the world's weeping.

"Oh, that's right," Anna said, tapping him with a finger sharply on the knee, "I was almost forgetting."

"Well?" warily.

She faced him and as good as beamed.

"I want you to kill me," she said.

I'm settling in, settling in nicely, you will be pleased to know. I work up here every day, weekends included, in the Sky Room, which for now is my room, seated at old Adam Godley's table in front of a shallow bay window. The table is nothing special but I'm fond of it. It is small and square and old, and its top, inlaid with wine-red leather, is badly scarred and has a particularly deep gouge at one corner to which my eye is frequently drawn, don't know why; its single drawer is warped shut. Also, one of its legs is shorter than the others, and I have had to wedge a folded scrap of cardboard underneath it to keep it steady. It has a matching, lyre-backed swivel chair, with curved arms and splayed legs on castors; its padded seat, also of red leather, is edged all round with rather pretty, domed brass nail heads polished to a deep soft shine by the repeated application of posteriors beyond counting down through the centuries, even unto this one. I'm convinced, on no evidence whatever, that chair and table belonged originally to a sea captain in the days of the great sailing ships. I'm prone to such fancies, when it comes to so-called inanimate objects. I sense their thingness, you see, even as I sense my own. In this I am at one with Adam Godley, and feel a great world spirit moving through all things, so that mountains and mahogany tables alike have hearts that beat and memories that remember. Also, there's a bed, for this is the chamber where I sleep, or try to. The bed, though narrow, takes up more than half the floor space, which doesn't trouble me at all. Why would I need more room than I have? This little round, though it's not round, is sufficient for me, more than sufficient. To think, I think, that I now sit and sigh where once the great man sighed and sat, and toss and turn in the bed where he used turn and toss; the most commonplace life has some remarkable passages in it, to be sure.

You understand, when I speak of him as a great man I do so in a spirit of irony. For there are no great men; ask any woman.

Why is it called the Sky Room, I wonder? It's not particularly skyey, and the bay window, comprised of three tall slender panels, the front-facing one only a little wider than the canted ones to right and left, gives a triple view of Arden's unruly lawn and tree-lined drive and little else. Granted, there is sky to be seen, but not much of it and that much unremarkable, even at sunset and dawn, or when the weather is tempestuous and things get flung about in the bruised blue air, leaves, twigs, rooks. But how would it be remarkable, in what way? The sky is just the sky, as everything else is just everything else. It would take a Tiepolo to make of it an arched empyrean teeming with gods and heroes and lubricious fat pink putti; or, if you prefer, a meteorologist, to read the runes of stratus, cumulus, and cumulonimbus, this last my personal favourite, by the way, I delight in zipping through its mighty ice-white columns, helmed head well tucked in and ankle wings folded and chlamys tight-wrapt, making the sparks fly. I note also that for all its ever-presentness, the sky has a singular and uncanny feature, which its first cousin the sea has not, in that it is depthless. Given the power of vision for it, and the water vapour and stardust and the rest of the celestial rubbish all swept away, you would when you look up be able to see clear off to the bend at the end of infinity. Think on that, now.

The fact is, way up here in my quintagonal tower I'm as contemplative and contented as Saint Simeon perched atop his pillar. True, it has taken me a while to accustom myself to the house and its rituals, and even yet it's likely there are unwelcome surprises in store. Establishing oneself in a new place is a delicate business in the best of circumstances, and consider my position, labouring over the life of a man who for long periods laboured in this very room at that very life, the difference being, the radical difference, I suppose you would say, that Godley was living his life while I'm only writing it.

The house, the edifice itself, so I'm discovering, is even more extensive and rambling than I at first took it to be, and much more so than it seems when viewed from outside. There are rooms that lead on to rooms and then more rooms beyond, not a few of them forgotten about or simply neglected and in a state of dilapidation, extremely so in some cases. In one of them, way up under the attic, the glass in all the windows is gone and squares of sacking have been tacked up to cover the staring holes; when the wind is high, as it often is in these parts, I can hear faintly the jute flapping and slapping up there like the luffing sails of my old sea captain's barquentine.

From the outset it was made clear to me—though I can't say who did the making, or by what means, exactly—that I am to be part of the household only so far and no farther. For instance, I don't eat with the family. I breakfast early, before any of the others are up, if I can manage it, which usually I can, for the Godleys are not early risers and Ivy Blount doesn't come up from her cottage before nine. It is Ivy who brings me lunch and dinner here in my room, not without a grumble, I may say; she's particularly resentful of the six or seven steep steps of the narrow stairway she must manoeuvre, balancing a big silver tray in her less-than-steady hands. I never know the day's menu in advance, and must take what I get. This doesn't offend me either, I've never taken much of an interest in food and regard it only as fuel. After dinner I creep down with a book or a couple of ostentatiously scholarly journals and make a roost for myself in an armchair under a lamp in some unregarded corner. No one bothers me, no one tries to engage me in conversation or talk to me about the weather. I am ever anxious for a glimpse of Helen, of course, but she retires early of an evening, or keeps to her room, anyway, and her own undisclosed pursuits. These twilit intervals are peaceful. When restlessness threatens I help myself to a nip or two of whiskey from the bottle of Jameson that is kept on a shelf of the bog-oak dresser in the kitchen. It seems to be meant for my exclusive use, and when the bottle runs low, which it tends to do with surprising rapidity, an unseen hand replaces it with a full one. O O O, that Jamesohonian rag.

I'm free to poke about as I like at any hour of the day, and of the night, too, I'm sure, if I wished. This is a good thing, since I'm an inveterate snooper. A house in which one is a stranger yet permitted to roam at will gives off an almost erotic hum, at least it does for those, like myself, with the ears to hear or feelers with which to feel. The pleasure for me of rootling among other people's things derives primarily from the stealth and circumspection that it calls for. I defy anyone of any sensibility to go clumping about and whistling in a strange house. One creeps, one quavers, halting at the slightest modulation in the silence, a foot on a stair and the other stilled in mid-air, every follicle bristling and all the tiny hairs erect. What is it that compels such hesitancy, such unease? Is it the effect of being overly self-conscious? Am I overly self-conscious? Whatever the reason, I go about my pryings and pawings all aquiver. Remember in those games of childhood hide-and-seek, as you crouched in an agony of suspense in the wardrobe—was there ever a darkness more dense?—amongst the odours of mothballs and stale sweat and your mother's summer frocks, the hardly containable thrill you felt in anticipation of being pounced on by somebody's bossy sister or overly testosteroned older brother? *Vraiment, c'est comme ça avec moi.*

Arden House feels hollow, yet if I knock a knuckle against it there comes back only a dull sound, dull as stone. Vapours seep out of the atrium, as the glassed-in central courtyard is grandly called, though, again, with wryly smiling irony, and create in the surrounding rooms a dampish, greenish atmosphere. It is like being in a cavern, or no, in a cistern, a great, multi-compartmented cistern resting on the seabed deep, deep down, with the fishes looking in and the air steadily leaking out. This sense of submersion, of watery entombment, suits me almost as well as do the mild elations of the Sky Room. What could be more conducive to the contemplation of the stodgy life of a stultified subject than to be sunk fathoms deep in this sink. Stodgy? Yes. Stultified? Certainly. Adam Godley has the reputation of a swashbuckler among crabbed clerks, but his biographer is here to give the lie to that legend. As I have discovered, my subject, behind all the noise and the bluster, was as tentative and timorous as the rest of us. You think to dispute it? Think again.

Another curious aspect of these aimless indoor rambles that I take is that when I'm on them I feel that I'm as good as invisible—no, I feel that I am invisible, not as good as. It's a peculiar sensation but a strong one, and should render stealth superfluous, since if no one can see me why am I so circumspect? I feel as insubstantial as a ghost, and suspect that if I should chance to encounter one of the living she would pass clear through me and register me not at all. She: yes. For there's only one I'm ever in hope of bumping up against. Oh, I see her all the time, since she's about for most of the day, busy at things, but that's no good to me. What I long for is a full-blown encounter, on the sly—an assignation!—and I know I can hang my hat on the possibility of that coming to pass, in this world or any other. Undaunted, though, I dwell on her, on the thought of her, and devise mad possibilities that I hope happenstance might make happen—if all were to perish and just we two survived!—yet even in the throes of this puffed-up passion I know that a moment will come, sooner rather than later, when a cold blast will blow and knock love's soufflé flat as a pancake.

On the subject of phantom creatures, or semi-phantoms, I must tell you of an exciting, exciting at the time, discovery I made one day on my wanderings in the house. It was a discovery I thought must prove richly rewarding, but it didn't. I had ventured to one of the upper storeys and was mooching about up there without a thought in my head except the thought that I should be at my old salt's desk, hard at work, or at work, anyway; to be idle when I might be writing, or preparing to write, or, as more often, destroying what I have already written, always makes me anxious, sedulous poor drudge that I am. Idleness produces in me an actual physical sensation, at the place where I imagine my diaphragm to be. The feeling is hardly distinguishable from a humble case of heartburn, and, like heartburn, discomforts me sharply, but also, unlike heartburn, buoys me up in a strange way; it is as if the process of combustion going on inside me were producing a gas lighter than air, so that as I go I seem to be bouncing along, like an over-inflated balloon, in balletic, airborne arcs, weightless jetés, my toes barely touching the ground. Isn't it odd, that anxiety should work in me like helium? I am ever a surprise to myself, ever a riddle. I wonder if other people are the same, are their own enigma, as I am mine. Perhaps that was the true source of Godley's genius, that he saw how unlike itself everything is and out of that insight built a new and all-too-valid picture of how things are in the human sphere, if it is a sphere.

Anyway, it was in this obscurely agitated and volatile state that I let myself one morning into a large long high-ceilinged upstairs room, with three sombre off-white walls and a single window occupying most of the fourth. The day was overcast yet bright, or seemed bright in the window, for the air out there had a bluish-grey cast as if it were suffused with a thin, unmoving smoke. The furnishings in the room were markedly sparse. There was a broad double bed with short thick legs, looking more like a raft than a thing to sleep on, across which a dark-red cover was untidily thrown, which at first sight was unnervingly like a great splash of blood. Beside it stood a commode bearing an enamel jug-and-basin set, the enamel chipped here and there along its edges to reveal patches of the Prussian-blue substrate; so many lovely secret things we gave them, the most of which they don't even know are there. The floor was uncarpeted, and the floorboards had been painted at some time long ago with a tacky-looking substance, bronze-brown and gummy, that might be creosote. The air was sour, and there was an unpleasant, cloacal odour the source of which I preferred not to seek for. Skewed at an angle under the smokily refulgent window was another odd item of furniture, more than an armchair but less than a chaise longue, and, like the bed, set noticeably low to the floor—had I stumbled into a dwarf's lair, perhaps, or the chamber of a hidden-away idiot child?—on which were piled blankets and shawls and a thing made of heavy lace, faded to an unhealthy shade of light mustard, that I thought might once have been a large net curtain, the lot all heaped together into a kind of nest. This ominous-seeming arrangement I approached cautiously, crabwise, in the wincing manner, apprehensive yet agog, of a traveller on a lonely road late at night coming upon the still-smoking scene of a glorious smash-up involving multiple vehicles and countless casualties. At what I took to be the business end of the jumble of coverings there was an opening, a swirl, a sort of sinkhole, into which, leaning forward on tiptoe, I peered.

After a moment I made out the shadowy lineaments of a woman's face, or of a part of it. There was the black round of a slackly open mouth, a sagging chin sparsely whiskered, and one sunken eye socket. What a thing it is, the stretched, frail integument of a shut eyelid, seeming to cry out for its penny and at the same time recalling the butterfly kisses of our youth: remember them, the shivery flutterings, the mingled breaths, the searing touch of a taut hot cheek against your own? There was a smell of drink; whiskey, I judged. This was somewhat reassuring. An old woman, then, dead drunk perhaps but not dead. Who could she be, left all alone up here, shut away and heartlessly abandoned? You know already, or should, since a little while ago I dished her up to you in the first person, or should that be the last. It was, is, Adam Godley's widow, the once-fair Ursula, Ursula the Pig Woman as her husband used fondly call her, when he was in a fond mood, or Little Bear or Big Bear or Bare Bear, with what Professor Benny Grace describes in a footnote somewhere as his snarling laugh.

Teetering there, gazing down upon this alarming creature, Queen Tut in her cerecloths, I wondered if something now would be required of me, something in the way of rescue, or of the sounding of an alarm, at the least. But maybe, I thought, maybe she's here by her own choice; maybe she crept up here one day to hide herself away and was forgotten about; this family, as I know by now, is capable of anything. But even if that was the case, would I, having stumbled upon her like this, not be duty-bound to bring word of her and her plight to the forgetful folk downstairs? My heart sank. I could already hear the ambulance siren, could see the stretcher being bumped down successive flights of stairs with the swaddled figure strapped to it under its blood-red blanket, could feel bent on me, the busybody, Helen's angrily accusing glare and her husband's milder yet still reproachful eye. Why, for God's sake, why did I allow myself to be inveigled into this topsy-turvy house and made to dwell among these impossible people, of whom here, now, was yet another?

There was a sound behind me, which of course gave me a wholly disproportionate fright. Whom did I expect it to be, the ghost of Godley the Uxorious come jealously to shield his comatose wife from a publishing scoundrel's prying eye? Having straightened up with a snap I turned and saw it was only the housekeeper, Miss Blount, which is what I know her as—she's Ivy to everyone else around here, but I started out with Miss and now I'm stuck with it, and therefore so is she, where I'm concerned. She was every bit as much taken aback at sight of me as I had been at sound of her; well, I suppose I must have appeared an alarming figure, bending forward there at the window with all the signs of ill intent. She had halted in the doorway with her mouth open, gripping her tray, the same one that she brings me my meals on, and was gaping at me, this Nosferatu of the daylight hours. Did she utter a little cry? I'm sure she did, for she's of a nervous disposition, as we know. I took a step towards her and did that thing we saw me doing when I first encountered Helen on the step outside the front door that first day, the thing I always do when I'm caught off guard and at a loss, putting on a puffy, idiotic grin and patting the side pockets of my dejected linen jacket with palms that seemed to have grown suddenly to the size of paddles.

"Oh, Dr. Jaybey!" she said, in a voice unsteady and shrill—I am Doctor to her as she is Miss to me—"I didn't know it was you, with the light of the window behind you."

She had come to administer luncheon to Mrs. Godley. I felt I should give an account of my being here but I couldn't think how to frame it. Anyway, Miss Blount, after her initial shock and when she had recognised me, appeared to accept my presence as not at all remarkable; after all, I am by now a fixture in the household. She set the tray on a small table with a marquetry top that stood beside the chair thing on which the old woman lay. A small thin voice spoke from out the midden of covers. "The train didn't stop

again today," it said querulously. "It doesn't stop at all, any more."
There followed a listening silence, then a rustle, then the voice
again, become unsure and fearful: "Is someone there?"

I looked to Miss Blount. She made a face, involving a sort
of grin, with mouth and chin downdrawn and eyebrows aloft,
intended to express comic despair. It is a thing she does, and never
fails to startle those to whom she does it. Helen calls it her Bride
of Frankenstein face.

Now she addressed the recumbent figure with almost a shout.
"There's a gentleman here to see you." Pause; attend. She spoke
again, in a softened voice, as if to cajole a resistant child. "Will you
not say hello to him? Say: 'Hello, Dr. Jaybey.'"

More tense moments passed and then at last a limb emerged
from under the blankets, a sloth's slowly unfurling arm, slackly
fleshed, the palm of the hand upturned. Miss Blount delved in the
pocket of her apron and brought out a set of dentures, the upper
plate clenched upon the lower, the two held tight together by an
elastic band, which she snapped off. The hand received the teeth,
closed its fingers on them, and withdrew. "I keep them for her,"
Miss Blount confided to me in a whisper, "in case she might swallow them in her sleep and choke." There was a muffled clackety-
clacking under the covers. Stillness again and the drawing in of a
breath, a moment of scuffling and scrabbling, then a thrash and a
heave and the woman sat up.

"There you are!" Miss Blount cried, with a little clap of her
hands. "Aren't you a great girl, now?"

Wild wisps of grey hair on a dull-pink scalp, an unexpect-
edly smooth pale brow, little quick dark eyes shiny as rained-on
sloes, tiny sliver of a nose, the pointed, whiskery chin. All this,
and yet beauty besides, beauty of almost an archaic cast, as in a
bust carved delicately from fine old faded stone. She looked at me,
the stranger, and bobbed her head and shoulders sideways, bird-

like, making a kind of curtsey. Her look was sharp yet uncertain, and for a second I thought she might dart back under the covers into hiding again. Something about her was faintly familiar; had I encountered her somewhere before? She wasn't as old as the slack mouth and whiskery chin had at first sight made me think her to be, but old enough, undoubtedly. And then all at once such a smile.

I was greatly excited by my discovery, of course I was. I felt like an anthropologist who has stumbled upon a tribe as yet unheard-of by any of his rivals, tame as Galápagos tortoises, their language unique, their rituals pristine. I was confident that Adam Godley's widow, whom I had lazily presumed to be dead, would prove an abundant source of otherwise impossible-to-locate material on her late husband's life and shrouded personality; but I was to be disappointed, and sorely so. Her memory was like a crate of Meissen figurines that a clumsy porter had dropped on to a marble floor: they were all there, familiar Pierrot and Pierrette and their company of crimped and crinolined ladies and exquisite fops, but all smashed to pieces and the pieces in a hopeless jumble.

I stayed with her, after Ivy Blount had departed, for an hour or more, in that long bare room, under the wide, many-paned window that gave me the sense of being in a chapel, or a house of prayer at least, one erected by some stern sect committed to plainness and severity in all its observances. The oddness of the occasion was somehow pointed by the fact that there was no chair for me to sit on. I could have fetched one, even if it meant lugging it up from downstairs, but I didn't. I would have to stand, then, shifting my weight from foot to foot, with one arm folded across my chest and, for want of better, stroking my chin with a thumb and forefinger as if deep in cogitation; else I could pace to and fro, or even get down on my knees, like a needy nephew wangling his way into the good graces of a rich and ailing aunt, but the tacky-looking floorboards did not encourage genuflexion. Having mulled over and rejected these alternatives, I compromised by hunkering down beside the old lady, with my skinny and no longer entirely dependable legs folded awkwardly under me, supporting myself with a fist braced against the floor and my other arm draped, as casually as I could manage, along the front edge of the—oh, let's stop havering, in this one case at least, and call it a divan—along the front edge of the divan while she like a yogi sat before me amidst the mound of blankets, her upturned hands resting at her sides, regarding me attentively, now with puzzlement, now with suspicion, but ever with that ineffably sweet, lost smile.

Have I mentioned what she was wearing? A collarless calico shirt with faded blue stripes, buttoned to the throat, and none too clean. Also a padded bed-jacket of threadbare bottle-green silk and a hand-knitted pair of fingerless woollen gloves. Strapped loosely to her left wrist was a man's chunky watch, a Patek Philippe, we do not fail to note, that must once have belonged to her husband, who as we know had a taste for the sumptuary. It made her arm look a shrivelled stick. The dish of gruel Miss Blount had left for her on the table remained untouched; its gluey aroma persisted long after it had gone cold and developed a skin, grey, glistening and somehow malignant, that I can still see though would rather not. It is remarkable, the things that lodge themselves in the mind beyond dislodging.

Presently, reassured it seemed by my unmenacing demeanour, the woman relaxed and was suddenly eager to talk; what she said, however, came out as a senseless gabble. Now and then she would stop and consult the big black-faced watch and frown and lapse into what was not so much silence as a state of absence, her frail head lifted, as if she were listening with an inner ear for a sound or a signal from deep within the house, or deep within herself, if she can still distinguish between the two. Or she would break off and look at me sharply, her smile turning to a reproving frown, as if she had caught me allowing my attention to stray, or as if I had made a facetious remark. For much of the time she seemed convinced I was her dead daughter, although she also addressed me more than once as Adam, whether she meant the senior one or the junior it wasn't clear. In her way, though, she knew what was what, for she wasn't entirely demented, you see, only, as we nicely have it, not all there.

To my surprise and some dismay, I began to find her maunderings, I began to find *her,* strangely appealing, even alluring, one might say; yes, definitely, I was allured. How, in what way? I pondered the question, sprawled gracelessly there beside the chaise longue, I mean divan—my right leg kept falling asleep, and the arm on which I was quakingly propped had developed a cramp—and it came to me whom it was she reminded me of. For she did have a precursor, a most unlikely one, off in the far past, goodness, I hadn't thought of her in I don't know how long. Mysterious are the ways in which memory works, I've often had cause to remark it, as you know. The precious toy is doted upon for a while, then lovingly wrapped in its crackly tissue paper and put away in a chest in the attic and quickly forgotten about, until the day comes when, crouched in dusty light under a dormer window and rummaging deep in the wood shavings in search of something else, one comes upon it with an Ah! of recognition and out it springs, vivid and shiny as the day Geppetto gave it lovingly its final glaze.

The person I had been put in mind of, Mrs. Godley's forerunner, is one I once wooed by way of algebra.

Indulge me, it won't take long.

What age was I at the time? Nine, ten? For we're speaking here of the long long-ago. She was the visiting cousin of a family who lived three or four doors up from where I lived with my family on a tree-shadowed square in the town of my birth, a place as far off from me now as Nineveh. This family had a daughter, and it was she whom the cousin came to visit, though as I recall there wasn't much love lost between the two little girls. The neighbours' child was a frump, and I retain little of her, though I do remember, oddly, a dress she used to wear, made of a washed-blue material, and sewn all over with limp knots of the same blue stuff twisted into the form of some kind of droopy flower, I can see the thing clearly, off at the end of time's ever narrowing tunnel. The visitor, whose name, lamentably, I have forgotten—let's call her Rosie, why not—was of another order of being from the cousin. She was small and plump, in a fetching way, a little bouncy ball of cheerfulness, excitability, and unflagging, gleeful expectation; the world for her was a box gaily painted bright red and decorated with rainbows and stars and silver sickle moons, the lid of which was bound to fly open at any moment and let the maniacally grinning Jack jump out on his big, lolloping spring.

She stayed at the cousin's house for some weeks, maybe a month or even more, for the idyll I look back on seems to have lasted summer-long. I fell in love with her in the fuzzy, prepubescent way that we did in those more innocent times. What she might feel for me, initially at least, I couldn't imagine, though I had a strong suspicion that she found me hilarious. We used to play in the square, she and I and the frumpy cousin, along with other neighbourhood children of whom I remember nothing. We played games of tig and rounders and hopscotch—our name for which, I suddenly recall, was hecka-beds—arguing over who would be "it" or who had hit a sixer. As evening came on and our little band grew tired of the games or bored by them or both, we would linger for a long time, unwilling of the night, leaning our elbows on the rim of the dried-up horse-trough in the middle of the square, discussing in tones of deepest earnestness the burning topics that were exercising our as yet unformed intellects.

One afternoon I invited Rosie and the cousin—the latter I had tried to get rid of but couldn't—into our back yard. There I set up a toy blackboard left over from my even younger years and sketched out on it in chalk a set of simple algebraic exercises I and my class in school had been recently introduced to. It was clear the girls knew nothing about algebra, had never heard of such a thing, and so, much emboldened, I proceeded to expound upon this abstract branch of mathematics to the point of recklessness; already a pedant, as you see, as well as a poseur.

It was a damp, blue-grey day, much like, as it happens, this day of my first encounter with Mrs. Godley. My pair of play-pupils sat side by side before me on the low step outside my mother's henhouse, their arms wrapped round their shins and their skirts drawn tight over their knees. The cousin, who was by far the larger of the two, thick of limb, raw-skinned and bony-kneed, I see at this remove as one of those life-sized cardboard cut-outs behind which day trippers stand with their faces stuck through a cut-out hole, grinning witlessly for the camera.

Rosie had an unforgettably adorable little face, with those ruddy, rounded cheeks and tiny hook of a nose; her shoulders were rounded too, her neck was short and her chest was plump, so that all in all she resembled nothing so much as a small bright bird, a tomtit, say, or a robin redbreast. She had a bird's quick, tremulous manner, and was all the time fluffing herself up and switching sharply the angle of her head. I can't explain it, but I see her wearing a pillbox-shaped velvet cap, richly embroidered and strung with beads of milky glass, or maybe they were pearls, though not real ones, of course, Professor Finickety feels compelled to add. Her dress too is brightly coloured, sewn all round with alternating bands of brilliant, brittle-looking silk. She wears, in my imagining of her, I mean in my remembering of her, not stout school shoes, as does her clumpy cousin, but a pair of delicate pumps made of woven stuff, silk again, I think, and also gaily patterned, to match her skirt and her cap. All this gives her, for me, gives, that is, the part of me doing the remembering, the look, odd as it may seem, of the last Empress of China, the wily Dowager Cixi, though an uncharacteristically merry version of her Eternal Majesty, unwrinkled, round-eyed, and rubicund.

The cousin resented me and my *stuupid* equations—what was it all supposed to *mean,* for the love of Mike, and anyway who *cares* if $a + b = c$?—and was clearly suspicious of my intentions. Rosie herself, to the contrary, was enchanted that I should know so much about such a marvellously arcane subject. She sat rapt on the low step, wriggling inside her clothes for pleasure and holding her hands straight up in front of her face and clapping them together very very rapidly, giving a little puff of delighted laughter as each new conundrum magically solved itself on the blackboard before her very eyes. Yes, she thought her instructor a prodigy, and loved him for it. If before I had been for her a figure of fun, now she was won over entirely, and readily submitted to a kiss the next time I contrived to get her on her own. Such, we see, is the power of pure mathematics.

By the by, in case you think I don't know better, $a + b$ cannot equal c. Godley *dixit.* Though we didn't need him to tell us something so obvious. An apple plus an orange are equal to an elephant. Sure they are.

Anyway, given all this, it does seem peculiar that I should catch even the faintest echo of my long-ago lost darling in Adam Godley's tiny, distracted, desiccated widow, but I did; the fancy, I suppose, bloweth where it listeth. I was almost as infatuated with her as I had been with my remembered Rosie. Often it seems to me I didn't grow up at all, that the years simply accrued around me, like the rings in the trunk of a tree, and that at the core the original sapling is still there, dewily aquiver and springing with fatuous life.

I took up a blanket from the mound in which the old woman sat and draped it solicitously over her shoulders, for it was chilly in the room and her wax-paper skin had a bluish tinge where it was stretched over her cheekbones and on the knuckles of her half-gloved hands. Again she watched me closely as I performed this little service, following my every movement, frowning, with nostrils distended as if to get a whiff of me, as I was getting an all-too-definite whiff of her. Seeing me up close like this, surely she would know I couldn't be her daughter, or her dead husband, or even her son. Who, then? Someone with whom she was or had been acquainted, certainly, for why else would I be here in her room, fussing about her like this? I could see her searching through the fragments of the past for a trace of me, like a black-bird rummaging for a worm in a mound of leaves.

Outside, small rain began to drift down, weakly fingering the windowpanes and rolling in shivery rivulets over the glass as if searching for a crack to get in through and shelter from itself.

Mrs. Godley was speaking now, if speaking is the word for her disjointed murmurings, about a girl who died, not her daughter but another, died by her own hand somewhere in Italy, if I heard her correctly. She made no sense, but was deep in the midst of her story when her son appeared, abruptly and without a sound. For such a big ungainly fellow he moves with remarkable lightness of tread—one minute he wasn't there and the next he was. He was carrying a book. He comes up every day at this time to read to his mother, so he informed me, with a sheepish frown. The old woman regarded him in angry bewilderment, wondering, obviously, how many more of these annoyingly unrecognisable wraiths could be expected to pop up out of nowhere in her place of seclusion?

"Well, La, have you been entertaining Dr. Jaybey?" Adam asked of her in a tone of forced heartiness. La is what the family call her. "He's come to write Pa's life story, did he tell you?"

At this she shot him a look of displeasure; even the oldest and the dottiest of them, of us, resent being treated as dotty and old. She fumbled for the edges of the blanket I had put over her and pulled it close about her shrunken, knobbly shoulders, which had hardly more substance to them than a coat hanger.

In fact it was she, I've just realised it this moment, she, not Rosie of old, who wore that silken pillbox cap embroidered with beads, perched with accidental jauntiness on one side of her frail old noggin. How could I have got so confused between the two, between sweet young Rosie and this sad old bag of bones?

I had scrambled to my feet, embarrassed to be caught reclining down there in such a compromised position. I glanced at the spine of the book in Adam's hambone-sized hand. Why, look! it's one of mine, one of my very own: *The Invention of the Past,* no less, the monograph I did with the intention of unmasking that mountebank Axel Vander. But wait, I thought, wait, this can't be right. Why would he think to subject his scatterbrained mother to daily doses of the life of that monster, a greater monster even than her late husband? No no, it was a clumsy pretence, the book chosen deliberately to flatter me, I was sure of it. Yet how would he have known I would be here to see it and notice the title? Has he been carrying it up here with him every day, just in case? What a life that little book has had—there was almost a picture made of it, once, with that actor in it, somebody Cleave, I can't remember his name, you know the fellow I mean.

Now Mrs. Godley spoke up, in a small but newly firm and resonant voice. "He has come to give Petra her medicine," she said. It was Adam she was speaking of but she was glaring at me; she seemed to think she had identified me at last and knew me for a shameless imposter and a quack. "I tell him he's wasting his time," she added crisply, still with that glare fixed on me, "but he won't listen." Her son and I stood and looked down on her in silence, he as much amazed as I, I suspect, by this sudden onset of seeming lucidity. Then her look became clouded again and her eyes filled up with the old confusion. "She was here a little while ago," she said, plaintively, "my daughter, but now she's gone." And then she smiled again, as sweetly as ever, but sadly, too, and for an instant was again a girl. "What am I saying? Of course she's gone, because she's dead, my poor Petra."

I am in the Sky Room again, at my table, working, supposedly. Outside, the day wanes; indoors, too. What should disqualify me as a biographer, what should disqualify me as anything at all, really, is that I cannot take this benighted world at its own measure, and likewise, or more so, the people with which this world is infested. They are so little, and so late. Yet I hear the wind in a crack in the casement, a sound so faint it is almost a nothing, a piping barely audible yet sharp, a tiny song such as Josefine the Mouse Singer herself might have sung, behind the wainscot, standing in front of her folk, and I summon up the others, all the successive others who will be here after I am gone, and for whom the air will pipe again, perhaps, like this, of an evening, in the failing light, and I say to myself that despite everything, even on such inconsiderable evidence, it cannot all be for nothing.

II

However, that legendary *anno mirabilia* started off, so he claimed, with a catastrophic spiritual breakdown. He had travelled halfway round the world in a state of the keenest hope and expectation, not only for his work but for the repair of what he described as his "shattered" nerves, but the near total collapse he suffered in the closing days of the previous December brought him, he wrote, to the furthest extreme of anguish and spiritual desolation. "I can see no way forward," he wrote to Dorothy only days after his arrival, "and I am convinced my coming here was a great mistake, for which I shall pay a heavy price." Arcady, he observed bitterly, was as far from pastoral as could be, the very name of the place a cynical and derisive misnomer.

The college had provided him with an apartment on Euclid Street. That name he chose to take as an augury for good, one of the few such granted him at the time. He often said that "the Father of Geometry was the daddy of us all," and the demotic tenor of the quip should not detract from the seriousness of his regard; the Glorious Alexandrian was one of only a handful of world masters he was prepared to accept on an equal footing.

His accommodation consisted of the upper floor of a two-storeyed wood-frame house, modest but not without charm, as photographs attest [plate 3], on half an acre of level ground at the top of Euclid Street where the foothills begin. It had a steep, shingled roof, four small, storm-protected windows and an open front porch on which there stood an old and weather-worn rocking chair draped with a faded Navajo blanket [plate 4]. The window above his work table looked out on to a square of lawn with a single maple tree much frequented by squirrels, the busy and often amusing antics of which he would study in those intervals of restless suspension when, as he put it, "the sums wouldn't solve" and his mind "went into idling mode." The land where the house had stood is now part of the site of Godley Memorial Laboratories at Arcady, or ArcLab. The house itself was destroyed in a fire supposedly caused by a bolt of lightning that struck the day after Godley's tenancy ended and he set off on his homeward journey, "pursued," as he said, "by furious Furies."*

According to his own account of this period, the drive in him to take his own life remained strong through the winter months at the start of his year-long stay. He harped on the theme in letter after letter to Dorothy, although it should be noted that in writing to other correspondents he gives no hint of self-destructive tendencies, and his tone is as usual languid and relaxed. To Dorothy, however, he worked up an image of himself as a soul driven to its limits by despair and the consequent urge to destroy himself; he wrote, echoing Nietzsche, whom he idolised, "I have looked deep into the abyss, and the abyss has looked even deeper into me." Other than the letters of his that Dorothy preserved, the only

---

* Meteorological records show no sign of electrical storm activity in the area at the time. As we have seen in the previous chapter, Godley was a tireless fabricator, who never passed up an opportunity to dramatise himself and the circumstances of his life.

scrap of evidence to support these extravagant claims is a telegram he sent on his thirty-third birthday, on December 25th, a date he famously shared with Sir Isaac Newton, in reply to one from Dorothy carrying birthday greetings and expressions of love. Godley's cable reads: "Unlikely to see my thirty-fourth stop." It is signed, "The Crucified."

Contemplating this stark prediction, one has the suspicion, difficult to dismiss, of a cruel contrivance. Is the message really an expression of despair, or a gesture aimed at posterity? Or is it merely a heartless joke at his wife's expense? The signature would suggest the latter is the case. It is of course another Nietzschean reference, but also one of numerous comparisons he made, not entirely facetiously, between himself and the Son of Man.

The most striking, and strident, account of his state of mind at this time is contained in a long and detailed letter to Dorothy dated 29th February. There had been a blizzard the previous night, he wrote, and he had sat for hours in the open, in the rocking chair on the porch, purposely coatless and spurning the protection of the Indian blanket; his aim in exposing himself to the elements in this fashion was to bring on a fatal dose of pneumonia, he told her. Such an act of desperation, indeed of near-insanity, would be proof that he was bent on self-destruction. Again, however, the records throw doubt on the entire incident. Snowfalls are extremely rare in those latitudes, and blizzards unheard of. Weather reports for the last week of February show nothing more than instances of morning fog and occasional rain showers at night.

Thousands of miles away, Dorothy was racked with worry. "He telephoned me late one night," she said, "or in the early hours of the morning, rather. He was sobbing, and I could hardly make out what he was saying. He was 'going to end it,' he told me. I didn't know what to do. I was on the other side of the world." She was powerless, and her plight was made worse by the fact that she was unrelentingly disapproved of by Godley's mother, "the Widow Godley," as her son with bitter jocularity referred to this formidable person, whom he regarded with a mixture of fondness, exasperation, and shame. Dorothy was not in the habit of confiding in her mother-in-law, and on this occasion as on all others said not a word to her about the contents of Godley's letters and his supposedly deteriorating mental condition. "She would just have told me it was all my fault, as usual," Dorothy sadly noted.

That February night, when supposedly he sat shivering on the porch in Euclid Street while the "blizzard" raged, marked the nadir of his sojourn in Arcady, so he said. He was alone and isolated, his wife was unreachably distant, and he seemed incapable of fending for himself. He hardly bothered to eat, and shed weight to an alarming degree. He let his beard grow, and was surprised when it came out streaked with grey. "I was a thirty-three-year-old dotard," he noted with grim irony. Most debilitating of all was the fact that his work was stalled, and he could not restart it. He felt that it was, as he said, "all up" with him.

These assertions baffled Dorothy. When she saw him off, in the week before Christmas, he had shown no signs of mental distress. Yes, he was "feeling his age," as the saying is. Many of the greatest scientists have done their most inspired work before the age of thirty. Newton was twenty-five when he developed the theory of gravitation, Heisenberg twenty-six when he published the uncertainty principle, and Dirac at the same age devised the Dirac equation. What had Godley produced that would come near to fulfilling the early promise he had displayed in his youth? A handful of papers, one or two of them admittedly brilliant, published in obscure journals, would hardly have ensured him a place in the pantheon of the immortals.

The question remains as to the true state of his mental health in those months. Perhaps he did contemplate the possibility of failure, and did think of ending his life, as he assured Dorothy. But why would he make no mention of any of this to the people around him at the time? It is possible of course that he was in deep mental anguish but determined to "suffer in silence," confiding his plight only to Dorothy and otherwise maintaining his accustomed mask of hauteur and insouciant disdain. But would such a keen-eyed observer as Benjamin Grace, for example, not have seen through the mask, however expertly it was fashioned?

A possible solution to the mystery is that in those letters to Dorothy he was "laying a paper trail," that is, creating a record which would, in the formula of the cosmologists of old, "save the phenomena." Should he fail in his endeavour to develop what was to become the Brahma theory, the correspondence would be there to show that the reason for it was his crippling mental condition. How could a man in the midst of a total nervous collapse and contemplating suicide be expected to concentrate sufficiently to crack the most secret codes of the universe? And by not speaking of his distress to anyone other than his wife, he would earn the added bonus of seeming to be a model of steely reserve, unsparing of himself and saintly in his consideration for the sensibilities of his friends. Of course, this would be to credit him with positively satanic powers of ingenuity and concealment. *Verbum sat.*

Whatever the truth or otherwise of Godley's condition, deliverance was on hand, in the form, unsurprisingly, of a woman, as was to be the case so often throughout his life, even to the end.

The circumstances of his first, or more likely his second, encounter with Anna Behrens are unclear. Both claimed, no doubt for reasons of their own, to have forgotten exactly where in Arcady, or when or how, they met. All that can be said with any certainty is that it took place at or shortly before the beginning of April. In a letter to Dorothy dated the fourth, Godley mentions having had a "spiky exchange the other evening with a rich bitch pretending to run a gallery here who claims to know you." At the time Anna Behrens was managing a small commercial art gallery at the lower end of Paris Street where it straggles to a stop in the marshes at the margin of Hellenic Bay. She had come over the previous year to attend the University of Arcady and complete a doctorate on the Sienese painters of the Quattrocento. Within a short time she had abandoned her studies and begun working, or more likely just "helping," at the Galleria Gannaro, the owner of which was a wealthy but notoriously tight-fisted Roman expatriate of questionable provenance. Eduardo Gannaro, known as "the Bernard Berenson of the Bay Area," dealt in modern art and, more lucratively, in ancient artefacts imported from Europe, Asia, and the Americas via intricate and, as was widely accepted, illicit channels. "He's a greasy wop and patently a crook," Godley wrote of him. There were rumours at the time of a romantic attachment between Gannaro and Anna Behrens, which could account for her suddenly abandoning her studies and going to work for a less-than-reputable art dealer.

By this stage of their life together, Dorothy had learned to spot straight off the first faint gleam of a new light in her husband's frenetic love life. The offhand mention in this letter of an "exchange" with a "rich bitch" glared out at her from the flimsy, pale-blue airmail form. In her careful reply, Dorothy wrote that Miss Behrens must be mistaken, as she knew no one of that name. She waited in agonised suspense for his next letter, but there was to be no more mention of the argumentative gallery keeper. Dorothy could not decide, she confided to me later, whether this should have stilled her suspicions, or increased them. As we have seen, Godley again and again showed himself to be a practised and crafty dissembler, and in the case of Dorothy he took particular delight in scattering clues for her to follow, most of which were false but so cleverly devised that she rarely managed to recognize the ones among them that were genuine. This "Anna Behrens," with whom she was supposed to be acquainted, could be an invention, Dorothy knew, a fantasy figure behind which lay hidden an all-too-real woman with whom Godley had become romantically involved. It is hard to guess why he should have attributed the claim of knowing Dorothy to Anna Behrens, as afterwards she denied ever having made it; probably it was no more than a bit of embroidery, so to speak, meant to confuse and obfuscate. Godley was not only a liar, he also had a genius for embellishing a falsehood.

Some imperceptive observers* have expressed surprise and disapproval at the seemingly calculated cruelty with which Godley treated the succession of women who in the course of his life loved, cared for, tolerated, and nursed him, while bearing uncomplainingly the humiliations he delighted in visiting upon them. Why mention so casually, when writing to Dorothy, the name of a person with whom by that time most likely he had indeed already initiated a love affair? Why refer to her at all? It would be understandable, though no less reprehensible, these commentators suggest, if Godley had felt he had cause to injure or exact revenge upon his already much misused wife, by planting a device that, in the way of all combustible material, was bound to explode sooner or later. But Dorothy Lawless, from all that we know of her, was a gentle, trusting, and loyal soul who would not have dreamt of deceiving Adam Godley in the heartless way that he was deceiving her. Why the malice towards her, we may ask, why the Iagoesque mischief-making made for its own sake, in a spirit, it would seem, of cruel playfulness?

Here we must pause, however, and remind ourselves, once again, that Adam Godley cannot be measured against the ordinary

---

* See, for example, *The Brahman: Notes on the Life of Adam Godley,* by Pavel Popov (Jagiellonian University Press, first, unsanitised, edition, *passim*).

run of men; it is important to keep this fact firmly before us in all our considerations of his character and actions. His was a complex mind in every area of its operations, scientific, social, spiritual. This last is not a word often applied to the man. If he had any spiritual creed it was animism, though a private and characteristically eccentric version of that equivocal doctrine. Since his earliest days, the world and every object in it, from distant galaxies to the simplest molecule, were for him imbued with life, mundane life. He was not a pantheist; he did not believe in God, or any kind of gods. Nor, in his view, does the soul exist. The very concept, he insisted, is, literally, nonsense. We are made of matter, and "no tiny ruby-red lamp burns perpetually within the sanctuary of our breasts." Before we were conceived we existed as pure potential, and when we die, the corporeal material of which we are constituted will crumble into particles and be given back to and distributed in the world, each particle a sharer in the universal principle of life. He liked to quote Schopenhauer, to the effect that after death we shall be "everything and nothing."* Thus the hard, timeless, and still thorny question of how consciousness could have arisen out of mere matter is easily settled. Matter, Godley insisted, is not mere, that is, is not nebulous or inert; on the contrary, it is alive, even at the lowest level, and therefore is immanent with an awareness of itself as existent: is, in other words, conscious.†

---

* "As an individual, with your death there will be an end of you. But your individuality is not your true and final being, indeed it is rather the mere expression of it; it is not the thing-in-itself but only the phenomenon presented in the form of time, and accordingly has both a beginning and an end. Your being-in-itself, on the contrary, knows neither time, nor beginning, nor end, nor the limits of a given individuality; hence no individuality can be without it, but it is there in each and all. So that, in the first sense, after death you become nothing; in the second, you are and remain everything." ("Short Dialogue on the Indestructibility of Our True Being by Death," in *Essays of Schopenhauer,* translated by Mrs. Rudolf Dircks [The Scott Library, London and Newcastle-on-Tyne, n.d., p. 93.])
† ". . . typically confused, if not plain dishonest, thinking." (*Relevant Matter: An Autobiography,* by Benjamin J. Grace [Paragon Press, p. 73].) In his book Professor Grace makes

This belief, if we may so designate it, did not, for its sole adherent, enhance the world or make the people in it seem to be prized the more; rather, it led him to regard things as they are with a mercilessly levelling eye. To Godley, all phenomena, in which he included human beings, even those ones who might have been considered closest to him, were of equal significance, equal worth; or, to put it another way, of equal insignificance, equal worthlessness. Given this radical egalitarianism, behaviour that in others would have been outrageous was, in Adam Godley's case, disinterested and dispassionate; was, in a word, neutral. If he offended, he did so without intent to wound. Indeed, he did so without any intent at all, to do harm or otherwise. It might be said that he brought to his contemplation of the world the benign indifference of the archangels. This self-containedness was easily taken for arrogance, wilfulness, overweening egotism, even rank malignancy. He found it absurd that he should be charged with these and other likewise blameworthy affects. How could he be accused of undervaluing this or that person when he valued all things, including human beings, equally? To point out that he set his valuation at a very low rate is to mistake his position in the matter. Certainly, it can be said that to love all is to love none, and that such generalised love is not love in any real sense. By this view, however, are struck down the teachings of Socrates, of the Buddha, and of Jesus Christ and of his saints, among others.

Anna Behrens was the daughter of Sir Helmut Behrens,

---

a number of wholly spurious claims regarding the role he played in the life and work of Adam Godley. Part at least of the professor's bitterness may be attributed to the loss of his tenured position at the University of Arcady, a loss suffered also by many thousands of others, due to the wholesale closure of mathematics and science departments in academic institutions worldwide following the identification and confirmation of the Godley Interference Effect (GIE) and the catastrophic degradation across all aspects of life, and in the area of technology in particular, that GIE has brought and continues to bring about.

renowned art collector, heir to a vast fortune amassed by his grandfather Hans-Urs von Behrens, from the African and South American trade in the mining of precious stones in the latter years of the nineteenth century.* Some time before, at an unspecified date, Godley had visited Whitewater House, Behrens's eighteenth-century mansion, which after the death of Sir Helmut the State attempted to buy but failed.† Godley had little recollection of the occasion, and could not remember who it was had brought him there, or why, though possibly that was the day when he and Anna met for the first time. Anna was educated in Switzerland and afterwards studied at Princeton, at Oxford, and at the Sorbonne. When Godley encountered, or re-encountered, her that springtime in Arcady, she was in her middle twenties. A tall, slender blonde, cool, laconic, and sophisticated beyond her years, she possessed the kind of poise and beauty that would have impressed, perhaps even intimidated, Adam Godley, who for all his worldly airs often let the mask slip inadvertently to reveal the unpolished and uncertain provincial lurking behind it. At first, Anna was amused by his seeming self-confidence and swagger, but nevertheless she was surprised to find herself attracted to him.‡ If she was to him a new phenomenon, so too was he to her. He had no interest in her interests, and chuckled at the very notion of the Sienese school of the

---

* It was Helmut Behrens who dropped the aristocratic "von," dismissing it as an affectation; it is worth noting the timing of this gesture, made at the outbreak of the Dutch war against America, as it then was, and her allies, among whom Germany was the most prominent.

† Anna Behrens accused the government of "impudence" and said she would burn the house to the ground before she would see it taken over and opened to "vandals." Certainly, she was her father's daughter, as the saying goes.

‡ There is evidence, none of it strong enough to be wholly conclusive, that she became pregnant by him. B. J. Grace in his memoir reports Godley having said to him one day of Anna, no doubt with characteristic facetiousness, "She's up the duff. Mum's the word." The pregnancy, if it happened, did not come to term. Anna Behrens never married, and remained childless.

fifteenth century. Also, the contemporary artworks on display in Eduardo Gannaro's gallery were in his estimation worthless dribbles and formless splodges executed by talentless frauds. Art was a hoax, he told her, and the practice of it should be suppressed. "Read Plato," he said, "there's the boy who'll tell you how to deal with your daubers." The assurance of his opinion on this, and indeed on all matters on which he took it upon himself to pass judgement, provoked in her, in her turn, some amusement. Yet his single-minded intensity, allied to the offhand, glacial gaiety of his manner, was impossible to resist, for a woman of her temperament and tastes. The fact that he was often petty and quick to take offence, and could strike with the suddenness and speed of a raptor, only added to his allure. She knew there was a wife waiting for him at home, but saw no reason to care. Dorothy she spoke of, when she bothered to speak of her at all, as the Dodo, or, even more dismissively, as the Dot, having heard Godley refer to his wife by these and other mocking diminutives. He passed Dorothy's letters on to Anna to read as they arrived, but apparently she found little in them to interest or entertain her.

There was another and perhaps even more significant encounter in the spring of that critical year. If Godley's personality evinced a touch of the barbarian, Gabriel Swan was a pure primitive. Yet he was the only mathematician, if that is what to call so unorthodox a thinker, whom Godley acknowledged as possessing a mind almost as subtle and inventive as his own. This is all the more remarkable in that, despite claims to the contrary, Swan's legacy in their shared field was negligible, as researches have shown.[*] He made, early on, a not insignificant contribution to the physics of temporality and temporal calculation; he was the first to postulate the existence of the "chronotron," the infamously elusive particle of time; and

---

[*] This contentious matter will be dealt with fully in a later chapter.

was among the earliest proponents of the reality of supra-time, a concept which Godley would later develop and make his own. But this work, significant as it seemed in its day, was overtaken, indeed was subsumed, by the tidal wave that was the Brahma theory. Yet Godley would yield to no one in his estimation of the worth of this damaged, daemonic, figure, who cannot really be counted his friend, unless we are to consider Mephistopheles a friend to Faust. In the time when they knew each other at Arcady, Godley was so taken with him that people spoke of the strange little man as Godley's most intimate, and most dangerous, *âme damnée*. "What I admired most in Gabriel Swan as a theoretician," Godley wrote, "was his contempt for applied mathematics. He anathematised technology, which to him was the unforgivable 'democratisation,' the depraved vulgarisation, of pure theory.* His was the least contaminated intellect it has been my privilege to have encountered in my lifetime." These words were written after Swan's death.†

---

* "Technology is to science as kitsch is to art" (Gabriel Swan, *obiter dictum*).

† It has been strongly suggested, by B. J. Grace and others, that one of the primary aims of the Brahma postulate was precisely the regressive effects its application was certain to have in the realm of technology. As Professor Grace writes: "The depleted and irredeemably dingy world that Adam Godley's scientific advances left us with is the fulfilment of his fondest hope and deepest ambition. We have him to thank—or should we say, to execrate?—for the clumsy and defective artefacts of the present day, which of necessity have come to replace the countless fast, bright, gleaming communication devices pre-Godleyan technology made readily and inexpensively available to millions, indeed to billions, of people throughout the world, thereby enriching their lives and illuminating their days. Truly it has been said of Adam Godley that he is the *spiritus perniciosus* of our time, and, it is to be feared, of times to come." (Grace, *op. cit.*, p. 73.) It should be pointed out that in the closing sentence of this passage Professor Grace is being coy, since it was he himself who applied to Adam Godley the Latin epithet he mentions, apparently in passing. The professor has a case to make, however wildly he overstates it. In this respect, the sharp rise in suicides throughout the world in the years following the general acceptance of the Brahma theory and its consequences cannot be ignored. As another commentator has put it, succinctly if somewhat fancifully, "Before Godley, every event necessarily occurred at the exact mid-point of eternity; it was he who fixed a date and set us on the road to universal death and dissolution."

Swan was the older of the two, but seemed the younger. He was markedly short in stature, stocky and bow-legged, with a mop of glistening black curls "tumbling over his forehead like a bunch of grapes about to go off," as it was said,* and eyes of such a deep shade of blue they were almost purple, their lids heavy, and sharply tapered at the outer corners.† There is an unsubstantiated account of how as a child he was caught in a conflagration, supposedly though improbably at an anthracite mine, in which he suffered extensive burns; it is a fact that his face was terribly scarred, the flesh of his brow and cheeks bubbled and doughy, so that he most closely resembled, as Axel Vander was to observe, one of Arcimboldo's vegetable portraits. In those days, before failure, drink and mental decay had reduced Swan to a bloated wreck, he elbowed his way noisily through the world, prankish and mischievous, his behaviour reminiscent of that of a character out of Plautus or of Aristophanes. Godley, no doubt recalling the religious admonitions of his childhood, said of him that he was the perfect example

---

* By Anna Behrens, in a private communication to the author.
† Axel Vander, a luminary of the Arcady Humanities faculty at the time, said of Swan that he had "the ravaged aspect of a particularly dissolute faun." Vander had lately published his controversial opus magnum, *The Alias as Salient Fact: The Nominative Case in the Quest for Identity.* After Vander's death, the deconstructionist critic Fargo de Winter exposed him as an imposter, and uncovered, among other of his deplorable traits, a long history of anti-Semitism, despite the fact that Vander was himself a Jew, a thing he kept hidden to the end of his days. It was de Winter who demonstrated that Vander's "masterwork" is a hotchpotch of faux scholarship, doubtful research and shameless plagiarism. How Gabriel Swan came to be acquainted with Vander remains a question, one of many such in the lives of these two shady and notoriously secretive creatures, one at the least a *brillant savant,* the other an arch opportunist. Vander later departed Arcady hastily and under a particularly dark cloud, following the death in suspicious circumstances of his wife of many years. The Axel Vander Chair of Deconstruction Studies at the University of Arcady was funded by a bequest in Vander's will. A controversial proposal to erect a plaque in Vander's memory on the Arcady campus was abandoned after a series of violent student protests, in one of which an agent of the Arcady Police Department, Officer Orville Blank, tragically lost his life. (See Jaybey, *The Invention of the Past: The Life and Deeds of Axel Vander* [University of Arcady Press, revised edition pending].)

of a bad companion, as well as a welcome occasion of sin. Others, however, saw in him a tragic figure whose early promise had been snuffed out by self-destructive forces acting upon him since the days of his troubled childhood. There is no evidence to support the charge, brought by Pavel Popov among others, that Swan's mental and physical dissolution can be attributed directly to the malign influence of Adam Godley himself, who, according to his scholarly detractors, robbed his *soi-disant* friend of his sanity by the subtle and diabolical undermining of the desperate creature's already shaky belief in himself and in his gifts. It is true that Swan's psychological equilibrium would have been easy to destroy, and true it is also that Godley was a tease of Luciferian dedication and inventiveness; but there can be no doubt of the high regard in which Godley held this wretched, lost soul.

Anna Behrens regarded Swan with profound and undisguised distaste, which seemed only to feed a masochistic strain in the man's complex personality. His way of shielding himself from her scorn was to pretend not to notice it, and to lose no opportunity of treating her with exaggerated displays of mock gallantry, "fawning and bowing and kissing bunched fingertips with salacious, lip-smacking fervour,"[*] which it seemed served only to intensify her loathing of him. An incident which has been recounted in various forms tells how at a late-night party in the autumn of that year in Arcady, Miss Behrens was driven to fling a glass of wine in the man's disfigured face. One must be careful in giving credence to any of the highly coloured versions of the incident, but certain it is that forever afterwards Anna Behrens would not suffer the name of Gabriel Swan to be uttered in her presence.

Reverting for a moment to the question of what part Swan might have played in the formulation of the Brahma theory, we

[*] Grace, *op. cit.*, p. 47.

note that before the publication of his world-shaking paper, Godley was frequently heard to insist, with unwonted and uncharacteristic generosity, that Swan should be considered a co-founder
of the theory, or as good as. Yet when pressed to specify the exact
nature and extent of his friend's contribution to that dazzling re-
statement of the fundamental nature of reality, he remained notably vague. There is a school of opinion which holds, on the basis
of no tangible evidence, it should be said, that the propositions
supporting the Brahma theory, such as the topological field equations, those miracles of elegance and immaculate simplicity; the
laws that govern the "infinite fissuring" of worldlines; and even
the meta-mathematical technique for combining and recombining
the infinities, were all of them, at least in their initial phases, the
work of Gabriel Swan. According to these wise schoolmen, Adam
Godley, supposedly the sole deviser of the Brahma theory, was to
Gabriel Swan, the theory's true progenitor, as Alfred Russel Wallace, regarded as the father of the Theory of Evolution, was to
Charles Darwin, its actual but unacknowledged formulator. This
is far-fetched, to say the least. After the Brahma theory was published and had achieved universal acceptance, Godley dropped all
mention of Swan and the contribution he may or may not have
made to the project. Swan's champions see this as evidence that he
did make a contribution, that it was significant, and that Godley,
his fame and fortune secured, was anxious to claim the masterwork as exclusively his own. They point to the contrast between
his niggardly behaviour towards Swan and the generosity shown
by the acclaimed Wallace to the overlooked and neglected Darwin,
or, indeed, by the astronomer Georg Joachim de Porris, known
as Rheticus, formulator of the sun-centred model of the world,
to the once renowned but now forgotten Nikolaus Kopernikus.
Certainly it is the case that science, like the game of cricket, has its
Gentlemen and its players.

Some of the most profound scientific discoveries have been made in solitude and seclusion. We think of Rheticus's lonely years at Frauenburg on the Baltic coast at a time when Europe was racked by religious turmoil; of Johannes Kepler misunderstood and unappreciated at the court of Rudolf II in Bohemia at the turn of the seventeenth century; of young Isaac Newton rusticated at his mother's house in Woolsthorpe in Lincolnshire during the plague years of the latter half of the 1660s; of Albert Einstein, denied a teaching post and toiling as "Assistant Examiner, level III," in the Patent Office in Bern, at the beginning of the twentieth century. Adam Godley's achievement over the course of that sabbatical year in Arcady is likely to be the last instance of such a complete, all-encompassing, and seemingly undisprovable reinterpretation of the laws of nature being effected by an individual mind working in total isolation. The methods he devised were wholly new and untried; he had to invent an entirely new form of mathematics with which to tackle the arduous computations that went into the making of the theory. Yet he claimed afterwards to remember little from that year of work. "I was there, of course," he said, "at my rickety little table with the maple tree in the window, yet also in some way I wasn't. I often felt I could read a book, or go for a walk, and come back to find the set of sums I had been working on had solved themselves in my absence."* He would hasten to insist that there was nothing magical or mystical in any of this. Only the procedure by which he worked seemed to operate at a level deeper than his conscious mind could reach to. We have scant record of those procedures as they were, or if they

---

* These were the, probably calculatedly, endearing schoolboy terms in which he spoke of his work; as his being presented with a set of "sums" which it was his task to "do" or to "make come out." It was part of his programme to appear homespun and down-to-earth. Some were persuaded.

were, manifest on the page, since so many of Godley's papers were destroyed in the fire at the Euclid Street house.*

When we speak of Godley's isolation at this time we mean intellectual isolation only. Over that spring his supposedly ragged nerves healed, without treatment and, remarkably, without the least enduring trauma. At any rate, he was fully recovered by the time he met Anna Behrens and "was taken in hand by her," as he later put it. Anna, he wrote, "may not have been entirely a good person," but she was good for him; she "drew me out of myself," and for the first time since his arrival in Arcady he began to see people beyond the loose confines of the campus, although even within those confines he had been anything but gregarious. Anna introduced him to Eduardo Gannaro and "his gaggle of rowdy, epicene young men and phthisic, sulkily silent handmaidens."† There was Axel Vander, of course, memorably described by Godley as "massive of frame, one-eyed and crippled in one leg, blasted and blackened like the stump of an ancient tree that had been struck by lightning‡ one long-ago night of storm and tumult on the Brocken." Godley was briefly drawn into Vander's sulphurous ambience, having been introduced to him by Gabriel Swan, "Vander's familiar," as it was said, before he moved on and became a worshipper at the feet of Godley himself.

---

* It would be remiss not to refer to, in passing, and only in order to discount it, the gossip that went about at the time, of which the likely source is the egregious Eduardo Gannaro, suggesting that "it was not an act of God but of Godley" that destroyed the house: Godley himself, it was said, had deliberately left a pan of fat boiling on the kitchen stove that he had known would flare up and catch fire once he had safely departed. It is the case that Godley was secretive in the extreme, but is it conceivable that he would go so far as to burn down a house in order to "cover his tracks"? The police investigation of the blaze was inconclusive, as is the case with so much else in the life of this always elusive person, who greatly enjoyed playing games of catch-me-if-you-can with posterity.

† Axel Vander, in a surviving letter to Gabriel Swan (Vander Archives, University of Arcady).

‡ N.B.: Lightning, again.

Among this expatriate *cénacle* in Arcady that summer, of which Adam Godley was the senior member in age and intellect, was another of his fellow countrymen, the soon-to-be-notorious Frederick (Freddie) Montgomery. Godley later claimed to have spotted Montgomery straight off as a suspect and potentially dangerous figure, so that he was not at all surprised some years later to learn of the apparently senseless murder of a young woman with which Montgomery was subsequently charged and of which he was found guilty and sentenced to life imprisonment. Montgomery's wife, Daphne, described by Benjamin Grace in his autobiography as "curiously intangible," was a tall, dark-eyed young woman of some beauty, with whom for a while Anna Behrens maintained what Godley suspected was an unnatural attachment. Her later, tragic death in a road accident in which her son also died occurred while Montgomery was in prison; he declined to avail of the offer of a day's special parole to attend the double funeral. There were suggestions at the time that Daphne had been seen to try to wrest control of the steering wheel from her son seconds before the accident occurred. However, she had never in her life shown signs of suicidal tendencies, and reports to the contrary have been discounted. Hers is a sad tale indeed, reminiscent in certain ways of that of Godley's first wife, Dorothy.

It is unlikely that any of these Arcadian acquaintances, with the possible exception of Montgomery, the aspirant mathematician and future murderer, were sufficiently advanced intellectually to be capable of grasping the complexity of the work Godley was engaged in, or to appreciate fully the transformation it would bring about in our conception of the world and of the hitherto unguessed-at forces that sustain and drive it. And needless to say he would not have thought to enlighten them. "To speak about one's work to anyone other than professional colleagues would be indefensibly vulgar," he once observed in response to a question from one of his more intrepid interviewers, adding, "and I make sure to have no professional colleagues." By that time, Gabriel Swan was dead.*

Swan it was who first made mention of the Brahma theory by that title, in a letter to the editorial panel of the *Annalen der Mathematik.* In fact, the word he employed was *Theorem,* not *Theory,* but journalists were no doubt more familiar with the latter term, from Einstein's relativity theory and other like instances, and saw no reason to accept a Latinate usage worryingly reminiscent of their schooldays. So the Brahma theory it became, in popular parlance, and so it remained, to Godley's profound, lifelong irritation. The title of the paper that he submitted to the *Annalen,* a venerable and highly specialised quarterly that continues to be published to this day by Universität Leipzig Verlag, was brief and to the point: "On Singularities and the Fissuring of Worldlines." The paper showed the entirely new and untrodden territory Godley had entered upon, and no one on the editorial panel possessed sufficiently advanced mathematical skills, indeed were ignorant of the meta-mathematics, invented by Godley, in which the theory is formulated, to interpret the paper or be fully cognizant of the depth

---

* In the year when Godley was the subject of a hoax which led him to believe, briefly, that he had been awarded the Sobrero Prize—which of course he would go on to win, famously and controversially, some years later—Axel Vander wrote, in a letter the postmark and the return address of which are illegible, to commiserate with him on the cruel prank that had been played on him, saying that he would surely have the prize another year, and went on to speak of the Brahma theory in such a way as to suggest that he had at least some appreciation of its intricacy and implications. The sincerity of the sentiments he expressed in regard to the hoax was called into doubt when more than one member of the Sobrero Prize committee let Adam Godley know, by way of private communication, that the perpetrator of the hoax was considered to be none other than Vander himself, though the thing could not be proved. From what the present biographer knows of Vander's character, it can safely be said that the conception and execution of such a heartless practical joke would be entirely characteristic of the man. It is no wonder he and Gabriel Swan were close, for both were arch tricksters, although the latter possessed a brilliant intellect while the former was a charlatan.

and breadth of its implications. This did not prevent the members from expressing an opinion in the matter, and there was lively discussion as to whether the paper should be accepted for publication at all. Theories making their first appearance in the pages of the *Annalen* were, and are, considered to have received the imprimatur of the scientific world, and the eminent panellists had never heard of Adam Godley, although some of them were as much impressed as baffled by what seemed to them his paper's utterly bizarre yet peculiarly persuasive assertions. Gabriel Swan somehow came to hear that the decision at Leipzig was balanced on a knife-edge,[*] and took it upon himself, without consulting Godley, to write to the panel a letter of enthusiastic support for what he referred to as the "Brahma theory." Godley never forgave him for this impulsive and, as he saw it, impertinent initiative, and there would surely have been an irreparable break between the two had Godley not valued so highly the company of the person he referred to variously as the Goat-Man, the Mad Child, or, simply, Mefisto.[†]

After much hesitation and delay, the paper was at last accepted. The publication of it, at the close of that year, when Godley was preparing to depart Arcady, went for the most part unremarked in scientific circles and wholly so in the world at large. Godley himself would not stoop to promoting it, and neglected even to mention it in quarters where its significance might have been at least to some extent appreciated. "The general must go a-begging for my little pot of caviare,"[‡] he would say to anyone foolhardy enough to remonstrate with him, the rebuff delivered with that

---

[*] In this context it seems not inappropriate to note that Professor Pavel Popov, at the time an energetically active member of the *Annalen* board, was in the vanguard of the faction opposed to the publication of Godley's paper.

[†] "Mefisto," with an *f* instead of *ph,* is a typical example of childlike, if not childish, Godleyan wordplay; the German word for "fist" is *Faust.*

[‡] Popov, *op. cit.,* p. 127.

quick, dismissive sniff through pinched and elevated nostrils that was to become so familiar to foe and friend alike. What was required was a staunch champion such as Gabriel Swan would certainly have been, and which B. J. Grace would later pretend to be. In the case of Swan, he had already entered on the self-destructive downwards spiral that was to end in his premature demise. In that first publication at Leipzig of what Godley himself was to refer to always simply as the "Singularities Paper," the dedication was to "Gabriel Swan, *maiorem magister.*" In subsequent printings the tribute, initially inserted at the foot of the title page, was silently dropped.

Anna Behrens enjoyed a considerable allowance from her father, and it was she who financed the publication of the paper in book form, under the title authorised by its author: *On Singularities and the Fissuring of Worldlines.** It was issued in a limited edition of twenty copies only, commissioned through Eduardo Gannaro from Unbegrenzt Verlag of Basel. It is a handsome volume, though slim, consisting of just eighteen pages—twelve of text and four of notes, with a brief, two-page preface—bound in dark-blue silk and bearing Godley's initials on the cover, stamped in gold leaf within, appropriately, the twin ovoids of a lemniscate [plate 5]. Of the five early copies sent by the printer to Arcady, by way of T&T registered delivery and intended to reach Godley on the eve of his thirty-fourth birthday, one was dispatched immediately by Anna Behrens, again without Godley's consent or knowl-

---

* The version the printers worked from was a typed copy of the handwritten original; the whereabouts of the manuscript itself remains a hotly debated topic among Godley scholars. Various theories have been put forward. It is said by some to have been consumed in the fire at the Euclid Street house, while others hold that it had already been stolen and sold in secret to Eduardo Gannaro. As to the identity of the thief, there are a number of suspects, including Frederick Montgomery; even Axel Vander has been considered a possible culprit. The puzzle is unlikely to be solved until the paper reappears, if indeed it is still in existence.

edge, to her father, at Whitewater House. Having received it, and his daughter's accompanying letter, Helmut Behrens, though he could not make head or tail of the theory, travelled immediately, on his daughter's instructions, to London, where, as the world knows, he summoned the president of the Royal Society and three of the Society's senior members to lunch at the Athenaeum Club and showed them the precious volume. Although many hurdles remained to be surmounted, including the opposition of some eminent figures in the world of science who should have known better, the rest is history.

Isolated and solitary Godley may have been, especially in the early months of his time in Arcady, but, as he insisted, and as we have previously noted, "aloneness is not loneliness." He was never the recluse that newspaper writers claimed him to be. However, strict rules applied as to when it might be permissible for one or other of his small circle of intimates to call on him. Visits to the Euclid Street house were permitted only with clear and advance notice, and on the understanding that the visitor was liable to be requested to leave at any moment, without warning or explanation. Godley did agree occasionally to be taken out to dinner. His favourite restaurant was the Constellation, a multi-starred establishment high up in the Arcady hills, which afforded an uninterrupted view of the valley and its lights "sprinkled gem-like upon the darkness below."* Among his intimate circle, only Anna Behrens could afford the prices at the Constellation, although Eduardo Gannaro brought Godley there once, late in the latter's stay in Arcady, after the Singularities Paper had been published and its author began to look, to the dealer's beadily perspicacious eye, set for great fame and possibly tappable fortune. On Saturday

---

* Grace, *op. cit.,* p. 87; the self-conscious preciousness here is typical of B. J. Grace's florid and excitable prose style.

mornings, Godley breakfasted at Joe's Diner on Academy Avenue [plate 6], an old-fashioned eatery with red-and-white-checked tablecloths and plastic chairs; the heavy, grey-white coffee cups Godley would still recall many decades later. They made a joggling sound when set down in their saucers that reminded him, he said, of the sound of old men with false teeth laughing; his adherence to animism led him frequently to propose such anthropomorphic comparisons. The waiters wore long, white, tubular aprons and made endless wisecracks, and swore loudly and in friendly fashion at each other and as often as not at the customers as well. Here it delighted Godley to order fried eggs "over easy" with potato "hash browns" and rye toast with "jelly," the latter, it had to be explained to him, being not jelly as he knew it but what he would call jam. Again, it was Anna Behrens who introduced him to Joe's; she said it was the spectacle of him, the first morning they went there, seated at the corner table that was to become his favourite spot, under the "rumbling and spluttering" coffee machine, with one of the house's trademark outsized linen napkins tucked inside his collar and draped across his chest like a baby's bib, and streaks of egg yolk and glistening dabs of butter on his chin, that made her imagine, for a brief interval, that she might be in love with him, as he was already insisting it was incumbent upon her to be.

Although he was a tireless worker, he did permit himself some distractions. He had no ear or eye whatsoever for high art, but he appreciated keenly what later would come to be known as "popular culture." His taste ran to the swooniest, most saccharine cheap music from the immediate post-war era. He loved "the movies," too, and frequently attended afternoon showings at the Arcady Arthouse [plate 7], a campus cinema specialising in classic black-and-white pictures from the heyday of Hollywood. He favoured Westerns in particular. He and Gabriel Swan, who shared his enthusiasm for "those morality tales of our time," as Godley described them, would take the middle two seats in the front row, and sit rapt, their faces lifted in childlike bliss to the flickeringly glowing screen. More than one of his commentators, Pavel Popov and B. J. Grace prominent among them, has suggested that this supposed predilection for simple pleasures and humble pastimes was a carefully managed pretence, aimed at promoting the image of a down-to-earth personality with unpretentious tastes, in the line of other masters of masquerade such as the two Alberts, Einstein and Schweitzer, and the philosopher Ludwig Wittgenstein. "I act," Godley used to remark, "therefore I am an actor." Following Swan's death, he never again visited the Arthouse, and gave away, or threw away, his gramophone records.

No one was permitted to see him at work. Just as the sheets of graph paper, which he used up by the boxful, seemed to him sometimes to fill themselves automatically with line after spidery line of minuscule calculations, so too, as suggested earlier, he wished others to believe that the work somehow did itself, and that his presence up there at the table before the window with the view of the maple tree and the squirrels was required only when a pencil needed sharpening or when a fountain pen ran dry. He used to refer jocularly to his workroom as the "black hole" from which nothing emerged, not even light. When he was away from his desk and out in the world people attested to the uncanny sense they had when they were with him of his being there and at the same time not, present and at the same time elsewhere. All this legend-making he greatly enjoyed, actively encouraged, and frequently contributed to on the sly. In later years he delighted in the image of himself as a magus, privy to mysteries, a high priest of the arcanum, the celebrant of ancient rituals in a brotherhood of one, while at the same time he insisted he was just a humble "pusher-around of figgers," a "chisler at his sums." By some he was taken at his word in these disavowals. However, many a one who thought to patronise him found themselves to their surprise drawn irresistibly in at the perihelion of the enchanter's orbit, only to be unceremoniously ejected at the far chillier aphelion.

A master withholder, he managed to seem to give of himself endlessly, in a great and inexhaustible outpouring of light and sustenance, like the sun itself. This was a skill he acquired early, and one he never ceased to refine. People came to him imagining it was of their own volition that they did so, not registering the force of the gravitational attraction he worked on them. He would fix on a new person and decide to be interested in him, or, as more often, her, watching motionless out of those hooded, dark-violet eyes, watching and studying, weighing and judging. He had a place for each of his captives, a fixed orbit around the blazing star that was himself. Appointed planetary transits only were permitted, and none must seek to eclipse the light of another. And there he ruled, at the centre of his little cosmos, *le Roi Soleil* supposedly *malgré lui*. Surely we must agree, whatever our reservations, that there is something impressive, even admirable, in the romance of so violent an extreme of wilfulness, self-regard, and unremitting resolve.

III

I had been at Arden House for the best part of a fortnight, kicking my heels and fretting, before Adam Godley at last saw fit to unveil, with what in that ham-fisted man passed for a ceremonial flourish, the secret vault wherein his father's papers are stored. Vault my eye. It's a most bizarre set-up, consisting of a pair of alcoves or recesses concealed behind false partitions in one of the half-dozen down-stairs rooms that give on to the glassed-in central courtyard on four sides. The room is large and handsomely proportioned, and although, or because, it's cluttered with all sorts of oversized and over-heavy bric-à-brac, the atmosphere is bleak and unwelcom-ing, as is most of the rest of the house—no wonder they spend so much time in the kitchen, where at least it's warm for most of the day. This room is known as the Library, grandly but misleadingly, for there's not a single volume to be seen there, and there's no sign of a bookcase or bookshelves. I must say it's a queer place to store such highly valued material, considering the state of the walls on the outside—that is, the courtyard side—which are damp up to the dado line and above it are cankered with dry rot. The alcoves, one to either side of a tall central window, reach to the ceiling and together stretch the width of the room. So shallow are they that even a normal-sized person is hard put to squeeze through. When Adam opened one of the two concealed doors—they're made to look like the window's slanted embrasures, complete with scrolled beading at ceiling and floor—he had to stand back to allow me to get past him, and even then I was required practically to shimmy in sideways. Within the alcoves, the floors and ceiling and plaster partition walls are reinforced with flame-proof cladding. What sort of a mind can have dreamed up such a tomfool arrangement? Adam is immensely proud of it, of course, and was as pleased as a boy scout when he was demonstrating to me the hidden thing-umajigs on the fake embrasure panels that when pressed release the spring-loaded devices holding them shut. The Godley papers are stored in shallow steel cabinets, filed in dull-red cardboard folders, meticulously if eccentrically catalogued; the task was carried out shortly before her sad self-inflicted death by Godley's daughter Petra, *diese Niemandskind*—need I say more? The temperature within is maintained electronically at a constant level and the air is dry and dead. You wouldn't want to be claustrophobic in here, was my first thought, accompanied by a warming glow of malice that I couldn't and can't quite account for. I wonder if the Godleys realise how uneasy I am amongst them and the shades that haunt their house. And if they do know, do they care?

The papers themselves are not all that mysterious—I try not to dwell on what treasures may have been lost in the Euclid Street conflagration—and I can't see that they warrant these extravagant security measures. I should say that as yet I've made only a cursory examination. Who knows, maybe I'll snuffle out a truffle or two among the dross. In the alcove on the left is kept the scientific stuff, the notebooks and worksheets and so forth, while the one on the right contains the correspondence; of the latter, "voluminous" is the word that comes tritely to mind. Among the letters from his peers—not that he would admit to having peers, not amongst the living—there's an admirably chirpy one from Feignman, whose life-work the Brahma theory set at naught, and a rather pathetic one from Falconer, ditto. Only that surpassing though bloodless master theorist Paul Dirac hails Godley with due regard as a confrère and equal, in a rather stiff but cordial note addressed to him after the scientific world had been compelled to acknowledge, with the illest of ill grace, the significance of his achievements, "most of which," as Dirac wrote with warm approval, "cannot even be explained adequately in words at all." There are reams upon reams of the graph paper Godley used exclusively all his working life, covered with the great man's tiny squiggles, and spattered with blots, too, since he used throwaway fountain pens and wrote everything in heedless haste, his mind running ahead of his hand. Also there are carbon copies of numerous articles by him, most of them lofty-toned but venom-tipped ripostes to the challenges and criticisms of various of his professional rivals—and weren't there plenty of them, I might add. Also, there's an extensive collection of offprints from scientific journals which are of little interest and will be of less help to this poor scribbler in his daunting biographical task.

I could see that young Adam—I shall have to stop calling him that, the fellow is pushing fifty—was somewhat cast down by the muted response, which was as much as I could give to the storehouse of treasures he had thrown open to me. True, even the most jaded researcher will experience a shivery frisson when he first lays hold of a document on to which the heel of his subject's writing hand has sweated; to such a one a smudge of cigarette ash or the mandala print of the base of a tea mug is as a bloodstain to a bloodhound. And speaking of blood, one rainy and otherwise unremarkable afternoon when I was browsing among the correspondence files, I came upon, on a four-times-folded yellowing foolscap sheet of paper—"To the Editor, *Nature:* Sir, I have read with amused forbearance what Professor Popinjay imagines is his rebuttal of my rebuttal of his rebuttal, and"—what at first I took to be just such a tell-tale rusty-brown stain. On closer inspection, however, it turned out to be not blood but, and perhaps more interestingly, a dried-out smear of lipstick. What would I not give to know whose lips they were that pressed upon that piece of paper, and what was the occasion of their doing so.

Adam clicked shut the vault's twin doors and with a disheartened sigh led the way out to the—yes, you've guessed it—the kitchen; I wonder if there is a people somewhere in whose dwellings the lavatory is the place where the clan members gather. He offered me a bottle of beer. I'm not a beer drinker but I drank the stuff anyway, suppressing my burps. Morning sunlight in the window, and, beyond, the invigoratingly youthful green of the summer morning. Adam sat at the table with one leg hooked on the rung of his chair and the other hoisted up with the heel of a sandalled foot tucked under a haunch, which pose made him seem even more the overgrown schoolboy. What a large head he has, like a sandstone orb from off the pillar of a stately gate. He has always the faintly perplexed, faintly pained aspect of one who once was lightsome and gay and can't understand what happened to make him not so now. But then, as I've said, something of the same mood holds throughout the house. This has to be the legacy of Godley *père,* old Vesuvius himself, whose enduring mephitic vapours we surviving Pompeiians must grope our purblind way about in. How can young Adam—there I go again—how can he be son to such an arrogant, vainglorious father? The genes he inherited on his mother's side must have vanquished quite the toxic paternal strain. He was disgruntled still, I saw, and I wished I could think of something to say in praise of his precious vault and thereby lighten even by a little his heavy heart. I wonder how that magnificent wife of his puts up with him.

It was of his mother he spoke now, saying it must seem cruel of the family to leave her all alone in that big bare room upstairs. He has reverted to this matter on more than one occasion, and obviously it pricks his conscience, as so it should. But the fact is, he says, holding wide his hands with meaty palms upturned, the fact is, it's by her own choice that she stays up there. It seems that, foreseeing her own death and perhaps knowing the appointed day and even the hour, Mrs. Godley has been steadily ridding herself of worldly possessions, including a decent room and bed, so as to be as little encumbered as possible at her going hence.

"She made us take everything out except the bed," Adam is saying. "It was *theirs,* you know, hers and my father's, but we had to saw off the legs so she can get in and out of it. Also she insisted on keeping that awful couch thing she dozes on all day."

I nodded politely; as we know, I don't think the old woman half so pathetic as her son is making her out to be. I grant you, she speaks and acts as if she were gaga, but I suspect there's a great deal more going on behind that pale unblemished brow than her son would give her credit for. She puts me in mind of one of those splendid female mystics of the medieval Church, Julian of Norwich, say, or Hildegard of Bingen, the Sibyl of the Rhine; I also think of the Empress Theodora as depicted in those superb mosaics at Ravenna: that stark face, those big dark staring, passionless eyes. I don't know what age she is, but she might live on for years and years, swaddled in her winding sheets like a living mummy.

"All shall be well," I heard myself murmur, pausing to express a beer-belch into a fist, "and all manner of thing shall be well."

Adam looked at me searchingly, wondering, it was plain, if this gnomic utterance might be intended as an obscure joke.

"Do you think so?" he asked, cautiously.

"No, of course I don't," I snapped, and felt my forehead redden. "It's just something silly someone once said."

I don't know how to talk to people, that's the fact of the matter. I get into a tizzy, you see, and blurt out the first thing that comes into my head, hardly knowing what I'm saying. It gives me a sense of precipitate, continuous falling, as in a dream. For me the act of speech is a form of defence, desperate and not effective at all, a burning stick thrust at the muzzle of the pouncing tiger. Julian of Norwich, indeed! Who for years and years I took, not unreasonably, to have been a man. And I a historian!

Adam returned to the topic of his mother. "Poor La," he said, in the tone of one wringing his hands. "She used to be quite lively, when she was young." He paused, frowning. "So Pa always said, anyway."

We were silent then and sat waggling our beer bottles, hearing the soapy suds sloshing about inside them. I was thinking of Adam's wife. I think of her a great deal, as you can imagine. In fact, I suspect I'm always thinking of her, that she's always there, the background radiation of my inner universe, against which now all the grosser events of my life and thought and sensations play themselves clumsily out. I feel a fool, thrashing helplessly in the throes of this absurd passion. Yet I wouldn't be without it; love is a warmer for the cockles of the chilliest heart. Don't mistake me, though. When I say love, I mean, well, not quite love, not in the world's sense. It's her flesh I'm after, not her soul. For this I make no apology. A carnal obsession is no less noble than one of the heart, so-called. To adore the body is to forgive it for being body, and that's much, isn't it? Why ask for more? But of course, there is more, was more. In a way, I think—the thought has just occurred to me—in a way, I wanted to be her. Heavens! Lovestruck indeed.

A blackbird unseen outside the window started up with his delivery boy's whistle. Imagine a world without blackbirds. But then, imagine a world with blackbirds.

Adam, striking off in a new direction, enquired as to the progress of what he described, apparently without the least trace of irony, as the "great work." He dipped his head in that boyish way he does and glanced up at me sideways. "I've been meaning to ask."

I have to confess that for a moment I couldn't think what he was talking about. I have these lapses, pay no heed.

"I've just finished the second chapter," I answered guardedly. "It took a while."

But wouldn't have, I thought of adding, had you given me access before now to the stuff hidden behind the panelling in that damp and frowsty so-called Library where no book lives.

"Really?" Adam looked surprised. "That's quick."

"It always goes fast at the start," I said, "before the misgiving sets in."

"Misgiving?"

"As to one's abilities—as to one's capabilities. About the wisdom of having taken on the task in the first place." Should I be saying these things to my patron and paymaster? Or prospective paymaster, since I haven't seen a penny yet, or had word of one. But I couldn't stop—blabber-mouth, that's me. "And doubts, of course, as to the project itself."

This brought a sombre pause.

"Doubts," Adam murmured, turning the word this way and that and examining it closely, as if it were a coin of uncertain value, in a foreign currency. Then suddenly and with almost a violent movement he released his heel from where it had been jammed under his thigh and turned to me with his arms extended flat along the table and spoke with awful earnestness. "But my father *was* a great man, wasn't he? I mean, a genius, yes?" I had leaned back smartly and withdrawn my own arms for fear he might grab on to me and, oh, who knows, take hold of my hand and press it to his heart, anything is possible in the impossible world of Arden. "You see," he went on, his voice thickening, "he never talked to me about his work—"

"You weren't alone in that."

"—so I can't judge. Not that I could judge if he *had* talked to me"—a plosive little laugh—"since I don't understand much about the things he did, his theories and so on—"

His voice trailed off.

"You're not alone in that, either," I said tartly.

But he wasn't attending, burning as he was in a fever of doubt and neediness.

"You see," he said, "I wonder sometimes, well, I just wonder if—"

He broke off then and gave himself a shake, rueful and exasperated. The situation was positively gruesome. What was I to say to him? We both knew what and how his father was. I felt like a Victorian headmaster being pleaded with by the captain of the School XI to confirm that the chap's famous and much decorated pater stood steadfast against the native horde at the Battle of Blighty Bluff and didn't turn tail and run away as the chaps in his form are saying he did. I can tell fibs with the best of them, the best of you, but on this occasion I knew I must be silent, must stick to the truth, which as we know is not sticky at all but slippery as silk though not so smooth. I could say it was professional honour that forbade me offering him the diplomatic platitudes he was pleading for, but I won't. If Adam Godley was great, where did his greatness lie—don't you love the incorrigible trickiness of words?—beyond the confines of his work? He treated his wives abominably, did who knows what to who knows how many girls—I shall probably find out, as I worm my weevilly way through those wads of paper in the right-hand vault—and comprehensively mistreated his children, making a mess of this so needy, young-old fellow in front of me, and driving the other one to do away with herself. He exploited his friends, or those who aspired to be such, and struck down his rivals without mercy and with much dark delight. The world by now should know him for what he was, and what dirt remains still hidden I'll make it my business to dish. But how could I communicate such matters to his son?

The fact is, my mind was still half, more than half, on Helen, this man's exquisite and, so far as I'm concerned, inviolable wife, though what I might dare expect or hope for from her I'm hard put to say. Few things more laughable than an old man's lust. Though lust is not the word; it's too, well, it's too lusty. What I feel for Helen is a kind of retrospective yearning. Picture me, if you will, with a hand cupped to a burning ear as I strain to catch a lingering note of a lost sweet melancholy music. Oh, don't snigger. I know perfectly well what would happen were I to make one false move against her person, utter one unfalse word into the enchanted cavern of her ear. How can I not be maudlin, castaway that I am? Crusoe fell in love with his goats, didn't he? I too was lost and reported missing, assumed drowned, submerged, and resting calmly in the depths, pearls for eyes and all that, when she reached down one bare arm—see the tiny silver bubbles clinging to each filament of down—and hauled me up, spongy already and dripping a watery gleet, and administered the miraculous kiss of life, and here I am, between blond shore and azure waters, marooned among palms and parrots, before me only a far horizon I'll never get to, nursing a hopeless love as sore as a boil on the bum and no apothecary within a thousand leagues I could apply to for an unguent to cool the sting. My, what a stewpot of metaphors!

In my less agitated moments, my mind leaning back and resting on its elbows, I bask in the glow of this love I fell into the moment I spied her, where she stood atop the front doorstep, in her sleeveless dress, one arm lifted—few things more stirring than the smutch of shadow in a woman's bared armpit—and clutching a spray of damp bluebells, looking down at me, on me, with her hazily self-absorbed smile. All I knew of her that day was her name, which Adam must have mentioned to me in New Amsterdam, but that first sight of her made me stagger inwardly, as if I had been shot clean through the heart with a soft, silent bullet. What was the trigger? The blue of her eye, the shine of her hair, the little swelling of pale flesh at the place where the top of her bare arm joins with her bare shoulder? Was it the April sunlight, or the scent of those heavy-headed flowers? Was it the shape of her ankles? All of it, all of it. She was the completion of a picture which all unaware I had been carrying inside me, a scene as in an old-fashioned postcard or on the lid of a biscuit tin, with a ringlet-ted maiden leaning on a fence in front of a thatched cottage, with hedge and rill and hollyhocks and a dickybird on a bough. Yes, I had been waiting for her, without knowing it. Would another have done as well? Possibly, probably, but I prefer to think not.

I have a fancy, it will give you a chuckle, that at any moment of any day I have only to stop and be still and concentrate and I'll know exactly where she is anywhere in the house. Crouched in my eyrie, up at the level of the treetops, I am a monitoring device calibrated finely enough to detect the trajectory of a Godleyan particle. Below me somewhere she stirs, takes a step, stops, yawns, and the needle twitches. With imagination's feelers I follow the trace of her from room to room, seeing each room smaller than the last, until in the end she ventures all unaware into one of those shallow nooks where her father-in-law's reliquiae are lodged, the secret lock clicks shut behind her, and I, Duke Bluebeard, wraps her in my swirling cloak and—

The high narrow door at the other end of the kitchen opened and she came quickly through and slap-slapped in her sandals down the three shallow steps and stopped. Given what I've just said, had I not known she was coming, had I not been registering her all the way as she approached? I could lie, but I won't: I hadn't. It's all a delusion, I can no more keep mental track of her than I can dance the hornpipe standing on my hands. But delusions are comforting, which surely is why they're universally entertained.

"You two," she said, fixing us with an actorly stare of large surprise and disapproval, "swilling beer and it hardly lunchtime."

She wore shorts today, loose in the leg—my poor heart—and a blue linen blouse. Her sandals were a pair of foot-shaped leather flaps held on by fine leather thongs criss-crossed to halfway up her calves; her feet are barer in them than if they were bare; the lovely curve under her instep makes me catch my breath. Hair pushed back anyhow and tied at the nape with a scrap of ribbon. The broad flat brow, the wide-spaced wide blue eyes, the nose carved in a line falling straight from the forehead to the deep-notched groove in her upper lip, and that's to go no farther south: it was as if a living woman had stepped out of a marble figure by some great Greek. And I, oh, God, who am lower than an insect crawling up her leg.

A thing I treasure in particular, a subtler iteration of the saddle of freckles on the bridge of her nose, are the tiny specks, the colour of dark chocolate, so dark as almost to seem black and almost too tiny to be seen, that are sprinkled on the puffy pads of creamy-white flesh under her eyes. It's an effect I've noticed in heavily pregnant women, which can't be the case in this case because Helen can't be pregnant, even lightly. I grieve for her grieving in her barrenness. I could tell her about my estranged wife Martha and her three or four botched babies—she would keep trying, the poor frantic thing, Martha, I mean—which might console her though I imagine not. I should call her, my wife, we haven't spoken in a very long time. I hear she has taken up with a civil servant, no less. I hope he will be civil to her; I wasn't. As you see, I did have a life, in another version of things.

And yet too with Helen there's a strange effect, I wonder if it's peculiar to me or common to all who have fallen headlong and helpless into love. The thought of her, the idea of her, had been so much on my mind, in my mind, that when the real she appeared, irrupting into the room like light, I hardly knew her. Or no, that's not it, not quite; that's to say, it is and it isn't. The image of her, the conception of her, that I had been holding in my head was so vivid and so strong as to be almost a sufficiency, so that she herself, in the yearned-for flesh, seemed almost superfluous. Does that make sense? It suggests, I know, that for me she wasn't there, not wholly, though what was there was manifestly she, the living, breathing, being. My words are all thumbs today.

It's a rum go, observes the hobgoblin crouched within, this business of love among the mortals.

Anyway, there she stood, at the foot of the kitchen steps, with that handsome, calm, and terrible mask she wears in place of a face. Adam turned to her.

"I was showing Professor Jaybey the vault," he said, with an irresolute smile; it's plain he's a little afraid of her.

"Yes?" She turned to me. "Stifling in there, isn't it. Not that I ever go in. All that bloody paper."

Adam sighed, and it was as if he had put a restraining hand upon her arm. It's plain it pains him to hear the family treasures belittled.

"All that bloody paper," Adam said, his voice too loud and his smile as tight as a fist, "constitutes an invaluable biographical source, Professor Jaybey says."

I had said no such thing. Helen's eye was still on me. She gave a small harsh dry laugh. "I'm sure," she said, and her husband scowled in his chagrin.

She crossed to the refrigerator—an ancient and cantankerous model the size of a sarcophagus, even from on high in the Sky Room at night I faintly hear it groaning and shuddering—and wrenched open the door and peered frowningly in. Adam shot me an odd look, it seemed at once a caution and an entreaty. Something in the tense air turned a notch tighter. Helen took a wine bottle out of the fridge; it had been opened but still had wine in it. She carried it to the table. She set it down on the table. She fetched a glass from a cupboard. She put the glass on the table. She poured wine into the glass. All this with sullen deliberateness. She has the look of a maenad, hard-eyed, heavy-limbed, implacable.

It was Helen herself who had drunk the first half of that bottle she has just taken from the fridge and she means to polish it off before the morning is out. It's a Chablis, crisp and refreshing, just the thing to salve her sorrowing heart. Around this time of year she gets tiddly most days, summoning low moans from Adam and a gratified half-grin from Ivy. Adam dreads a scene, the sobs, the screams, the fists drumming on his chest, he saw enough of that when he was a boy and his drunken mother railed at his heartless father for his betrayals and his mockery. Helen has been a long time in mourning and can't cure herself of it and nor can anyone else. Her lost child's anniversary is imminent, and she is determined to mark the occasion, which as cruel chance would have it falls on the same date as her birthday: birthday and deathday, all in one. Her manner is brittle and gay, she laughs shrilly, stops frequently to strike a pose, her eyes shining and her mouth awry. The house tiptoes around her, holding its breath, wishing the awful occasion had come and safely gone.

The child lived so brief a span he can hardly be said to have lived at all. Have we mentioned that his name was Hercules? Straight off his father diminuted it to Clem. It had come to her in a dream, Helen said, and she would brook no objection to it. Ursula told her the child would never forgive her for burdening him with a name so richly mockable. Her father-in-law was dying, but summoned the strength to laugh at her anyway, saying if she called him by something that heroic the little brute was bound to turn out a milksop. No one was surprised when the poor mite perished. Yes, Helen's husband's chest was hammered on hard that day, the day little Clem suffered a seizure and quickly suffocated. This was the second such loss—there had been a stillbirth, some years previously, have I said that already?—and now Helen is barren—that I do know I have said. Ivy Blount confided all this to me in a hugger-muggery confab we had one day when she had brought me my lunch up to the Sky Room and tarried while I ate it. I felt no sympathy. All I could think of, with my mouth full, was the matter of the lost boys' begetting. I pictured Helen and her top-heavy soft-skinned small-footed husband clasped in one another's arms, heaving and moaning, and I was glad their little runts died on them. I'm terrible, yes; love knows no limits.

But Helen even in her sorrow refuses to give in to gloom. "I'm going to throw a party," she announced now, with offhand defiance. "A great big splash of a party, yes." Adam briefly closed his eyes, as if to ward off the prospect of what was to come. The last party that was held here was on the occasion of Adam Godley's being awarded the Sobrero Prize. A proper hooley it was and went on for days and ended only when Petra went up to her bedroom and hacked all her hair off with a pair of pinking shears and Benny Grace drank a bumper of champagne all by himself and tripped over the dog and fractured a femur. Good dog, Rex.

Helen now took up the wine glass in both hands and lifted it to her lips and drank deep. I watched her smooth sheer throat, thinking of the first Adam and of adam's apples and the impenetrable strangeness of all things. "Don't you think it's a good idea?" she gaily challenged. "A midsummer day's dream." Her eyes swam; she seemed to be crying even as she unsteadily laughed. "We'll invite everybody," she said, "everybody—we'll invite the whole fucking county!"

Mordaunt had not imagined that he had heard, or seen, the last of Anna Behrens, and he had not. For all the languidly laughing façade she presented to the world, Anna was possessed of an irresistible will, and her life was dedicated to the pursuit of selfish ends. After all, she was the daughter of Helmut Behrens. She was spoilt and grasping, two among her qualities which anyone else would surely deplore, but for which Mordaunt admired her, if grudgingly. All the same, he wished she hadn't bobbed up out of the past like this, sudden and startling. It was as if Ophelia were to rise up from the glassy waters under the willow, smiling, and demanding to do things, and to have things done to her. Why couldn't she let him be? Not long out on licence—a life sentence is for life, remember—he is jealous of his solitude. In the prisons in which he had been held, and Hirnea House was no less of a penitentiary than the Anvil, it had required cunning and ingenuity, along with carefully applied bribes, for him to manage to be entirely by himself for fully five minutes of any day, or for that matter of any night, for even at night, stretched rigid on his cot all alone in a corner of a cube of tumultuous dark, he had felt watched and monitored. He could hardly accuse Anna of being a spy, but she was definitely an intrusion. People with time on their hands are a menace, always imagining others as idle and aimless as themselves. How is he to get rid of her? It should be simple, but it isn't. In certain aspects of his character he is, even yet, and contrary to what might be expected, a gentleman, and gentle manners, once inculcated, are as fixed as fingerprints. You or I might simply tell her to go away and leave us alone, but not he, no, not he.

It was not long after their trip to the seaside that the inevitable summons came, disguised as a spur-of-the-moment invitation to spend another jolly day out together. "This time we shall strike off into the interior," Anna wrote, "since you've become a nature lover." The note had been sped to him by T&T express delivery; Anna favoured the delicate but definite gesture, even in something as simple as the sending of a message. The courier, looking unwontedly grubby in his dull gold braid and dented tricorne, had lingered pointedly, angling for a tip, until Mordaunt gave him one of his empty-eyed stares and he took himself off, with a curled lip, insolently whistling. Now Mordaunt sat at the table in Ivy Blount's kitchen and gazed gloomily at the flimsy rectangle of turquoise-tinted telegraph paper propped against the teapot. Ivy was off visiting one of her numerous moribund relatives, and he had been looking forward to spending the rest of the morning going through her things; there were few of her sad secrets he hadn't already unearthed, but this would have been his first opportunity to get into her bedroom and have a leisurely rummage in that final sanctum sanctorum.

He sighed, and drank off the dregs of the tea in his cup—he likes the seaweedy texture of tepid tea leaves—and rose and tramped heavily up the stairs to the bathroom to shave. It was an awful hole of a place, and there was always a dispiriting, flat grey smell. Some days after his arrival Ivy had strung up a makeshift clothesline here by stretching a length of orange binder twine between the knob of the geyser over the bath and a rusty nail in

the wall by the window, so that Mordaunt had to duck underneath it every time to get to the sink. It was another of the ploys,
all equally unsubtle, in Ivy's campaign to irritate him so sorely that
sooner or later he would admit defeat and move out. On the line
this morning there hung a nylon slip, a single woollen stocking,
and a droopy pair of bloomers, elasticated at the legs, that must
have been dark blue originally but through repeated weekly wash-
ings had faded to a peculiarly unpleasant shade of dull mauve. He
stooped and dodged under the twine, baring his teeth, and rose up
in front of the sink, his left eye looming enormously in the shaving mirror propped in a corner of the window.

That afternoon many years ago in Arcady when they went
to bed together, Anna in the midst of things had laid a hand on
his shoulder to stop him doing what he was vigorously doing and
put her mouth to his ear and bade him in a husky whisper to hit
her. It wasn't a smack she wanted, oh, no. He was to hurt her, to
punch her in the chest, to slap her breasts, to thrash her on the bottom with his belt. "Only not the face," she said, pressing a finger
lightly to his lips, "or the legs or arms, the bits that would show
the marks." And she smiled sweetly, making slits of her eyes. He
had as yet never struck a woman, and frankly he was shocked to be
urged to do so now. Nor was he at all sure how to go about it, but
when he demurred she gave a hard pinch to the sensitive part of
the flesh of his side between ribs and hipbone and bade him get on
with it. He obeyed, and did his gallant best, but it was no good, his
heart wasn't in it, and in the end Anna grew impatient and pushed
him away with an angry sigh and turned her back and lay on her
side and muttered that he might as well get dressed and go. He
didn't go, and after a while she relented and they resumed what
they had been doing previously, and all was well, or seemed so.
The matter was never mentioned again, but it stayed there always
between them, lodged in a crevice of memory like a little hard
seed. What puzzled him was not the fact that Anna had asked him

to beat her, but that her asking had caused him such acute and unmanning embarrassment. He would in after-days redden many a proffered bottom with brio and insouciance, but his failure with Anna that afternoon troubled and perplexed him, and continues to do so to this day. All the same, he sometimes wondered if Anna's invitation to indulge in violence against her person might have acted somehow as a licence for a far more momentous and fatal assault later on; it seemed far-fetched, but human motivation is a mystery.

Shaved, he rinsed his face and patted it dry, flicked a fleck of soap from his left earlobe—somehow it always happened, and always like that, on the left lobe—and ducked again under the clothesline, trying and failing to avoid Ivy's flaccid drawers, one leg of which touched the back of his neck with a fishily cold caress. In the kitchen he paused to push a halfpenny piece into the blackcurrant jam in its dish on the table—he in turn had his ways of putting Ivy in a rage—and took up his hat and stepped out at the door into a slick of watery sunlight. He had told Anna not to come to the cottage, but to wait for him at the front gate, in order to lessen the chances of their being observed by someone at the house, though he couldn't think why he should care if they were seen together or not. Now he sauntered down the drive, hands in his pockets and his hat on the back of his head, his shorn cheeks pleasantly smarting. The sun was still doing its best to shine but big swags of livid cloud were bulging in from seawards.

Anna leaned across the front seat to open the passenger door for him. "You look disgustingly pleased with yourself," she said, peering up brightly.

The car inside reeked of hot leather and the sweetish, slightly muddy perfume Anna wore. She put on a pair of sunglasses with tiny circular lenses so dark as to be impenetrable and slewed the Cachalot out of the half-circle of the gateway in a sidewise spray of gravel. He admired again the brusque, no-nonsense way she had with the car; obviously she had long ago made and won her point with the big machine and the matter needed no revisiting. On the road she drove very fast, humming to herself. Mordaunt sat with his hands loose in his lap. His mood was darkening along with the sky. For miles Anna said nothing. He could feel her thinking; Anna thinking always made him uneasy.

They were skimming along a straight stretch of road in the midst of undistinguished countryside—dishevelled fields, sparse stands of spindly, drunk-looking birches, a link of yet more half-hearted hills—when the sagging clouds burst their bellies and released a clattering torrent of hail. So large were the stones and so dense the shower that Anna could hardly see through the wind-screen and was forced to steer the car to the side of the road and bring it to a lopsided stop. They sat in awe and watched the furi-ously falling icy whiteness all round them, and listened to it drum-ming on the canvas hood above their heads. Splatters of waxy slush ran zigzag over the windscreen.

"This is frightening," Anna said in a child's small voice, and hunched her shoulders and shoved her hands into the sleeves of her coat and drew her head into the collar deep down to the level of her nose.

"It's only a summer storm," Mordaunt said, with a dark emphasis, as if the words were meant to mean something other than what they did.

This had happened to him before, once, in Italy, on a road half-way between two of those hill towns, Todi and Terni, was it, were they? A woman sat with him in fright on that occasion also—who? Daphne, he supposed, his since dead wife. Yes, because that morn-ing they had tried to swim in Lake Trasimeno but couldn't find a bathing place. Instead they went to a trattoria on the edge of a cliff above the vast expanse of silver-flecked blue water and sat under a canopy of plaited vines and ate unsalted bread and salty olives and drank a bottle of nauseatingly sweet local wine. He told his wife about the battle of Lake Trasimeno in which Hannibal and his elephants routed the Romans and marched on Rome, where the Senate hurriedly chose for saviour Fabius the Cunctator—"Fabius the *what*?" Daphne exclaimed, and laughed until she choked on her wine and people looked up and frowned—that Fabius who, I warmly note, was friend to the gods and sacrificed the country's riches to them, to us, to the tune of the three hundredth and thirty-third part. Afterwards, in the car, Daphne sulked and said she was sick of him always showing off all the things he knew that she didn't know, and then the hailstorm came on and he had to park the car at a slant at the side of the road just as this car was parked now and Daphne clutched his hand and shivered, and years later, in another car, on another road, she must have reached out like this and clutched their son's hand on the wheel when the lorry had rounded the bend and was hurtling towards them and yawing to one side because its load had shifted—everything here is out of kilter—and mother and son were smashed to death though the lorry driver survived without, as they say, a scratch. Well.

"Well," Anna said, "summer storm or not, I'm frightened by it. Next thing we'll have thunder and lightning."

And what manner of god would I be were I to ignore a cue like that? I lifted a finger and at once a jagged triton skittered down the sky and smote the summit of one of those despondent hills and a moment later came a *craack! thud rumble-rumble thud thud thud* and Anna gave a squeal and wriggled even lower, managing almost to hide herself under the steering wheel.

Mordaunt sighed. What was left of his patience was rapidly running out. You would have thought the years in prison should have been a lesson in forbearance, but he always was irascible and is so still. We might say, indeed, that it was his irascibility, and not any invitation to erotic violence from Anna, that killed that poor young woman, all those years ago. She was the one person too many when she put herself in his path and hindered him, and died of her mistake. Yes yes, let us never forget our Mr. Mordaunt was and is a dangerous fellow and best left unprovoked.

The storm ceased as quickly as it had started, and the world beyond the windscreen seemed to lift its head and look about warily. Anna lit a cigarette with an unsteady hand. Everything dripped.

"The first sign," she said, in a pensive tone, "was a black spot in my left eye. Deep black and shiny like boot polish and the size of a sixpence. I saw it first one morning when I woke up, before I woke up, actually, I mean it was what woke me up. It didn't last long, and I forgot about it. Then my sight in that eye started to fade in a very queer fashion and I went for a test and the doctor shone a very bright light into my eye and I saw it again, the spot, the same size and in the same place as before, down a little to the left, not black this time but a deep dark red like you see on the bottom of a cork when you pull it out of a wine bottle, with the same little squiggly black lines running across it. Quite pretty, really. I was fascinated, couldn't stop looking at it, except that I couldn't look at it because it moved away and kept moving when I tried to follow it. I didn't tell the doctor about it, still not thinking it was anything much."

Mordaunt was trying to open the window beside him; he did not smoke and the fumes from Anna's cigarette were stinging his sinuses and making him cough. Why do things oppose him like this, why do things insist on getting in his way? She watched him fumbling at the window and laughed. "You look like a sailor trying to get out of a sinking ship." She touched a button in the armrest of her seat and his window slid open with a smooth, slicing sound.

"Is there a name for it?" he asked, trying not to sound testy and failing. He was cross at himself for not having known how to open the window.

"Oh, there is," Anna said, "but I've forgotten what it is. Dr. Somebody's syndrome—I hope he's proud of his handiwork."

The cool wet air through the gap in the window was soothing on Mordaunt's brow. As we have noted, it distresses him when people are so inconsiderate as to mention their ailments. He feels ashamed for them, for their soggy misery, for the doleful droop at the corners of their eyes, for their aggrieved and whining boastfulness. It is as if being ill were a state of election they hadn't asked for and are resentful of and at the same time glory in, like the Virgin Mary and her impossible pregnancy.

But there was no avoiding it. Anna had got into her stride, and he knew she would press on to exhaustion, unless tears should intervene: tears can always be depended on to stop in her tracks even the most relentless whinger. He noticed his fists were clenched in his lap, in anger or in dread, he didn't know which, since there wasn't much difference between the two, in his experience. In fraught circumstances such as this he has always a mad urge to laugh, feeling as if a big bladder were swelling and swelling in him while the gas inside it became increasingly compressed. He looked out glumly at the shining road ahead and the drenched fields all round, where unmelted hail was lodged among the grass like scatterings of mothballs; a stab of sunlight sparkled among the birch trees' dripping foliage. Unseasonal weather like this reminds him vaguely of the vague past; why is that? There is a spring-like quality now to the look of this summer day, something raw and oily-smooth as a freshly peeled stick.

He came back to himself with the shuddery jolt of a big old engine starting up. Anna was telling him something about a wasp—could it be a wasp?

"I don't know what kind it is," she snapped impatiently, "just a wasp, some tropical kind—what does it matter? I read about it somewhere, in a magazine in a doctor's waiting room, and God knows I've been in a few of those. It finds a creepie-crawlie, a woodlouse, let's say, that's about ten times its size, and stabs it in the forehead with its poisoned thing, its feeler thing or whatever, and paralyses it, and quickly lays its eggs and inserts them inside the woodlouse's body. Then, before the injection wears off, it covers it with stones—"

"What covers what with stones?"

"The thing, the wasp! It covers the woodlouse all over with stones in the shape of one of those monks' cells so it can't escape when it comes round. Then it goes off and leaves it there, trapped and alive. The ant does. Soon the eggs hatch, and the little white baby wasps inside the woodlouse begin to feed on it, on its living flesh." She paused, and took a deep breath, held it an instant and let it go in a long, falling sigh. She was gazing stark-eyed through the windscreen. "Imagine that," she said, "imagine being eaten alive like that, from the inside out."

He said nothing; he had nothing to say. Anna started the car and bumped it back on to the wet road and they went forward again on fizzing tyres.

"I do want you to do what I asked you to do, the last time I saw you," she said. "I'm perfectly serious."

She said this almost shyly, frowning and tossing back her hair and clearing her throat. Again he recalled her asking him to beat her, that afternoon years and years ago, her fingers digging into his naked shoulder and her breath hot against his ear. He shifted in the seat impatiently. It's not that he doesn't believe her when she says she's ill. She has convinced him—he can almost see the wasps in her skull, the tiny white wasps, feasting on what they find there—and he wishes she hadn't. The thing she's asking of him is absurd, outrageous and absurd. How could she so presume? He feels offended, deeply offended.

"I'd be sent back to prison," he said, reasonably. "And this time they wouldn't let me out."

"No no. I've planned it all." The sun was shining strongly

now on the road before them and each puddle had its lambent wisp of mist. "No one will know it was you."

She launched into another rigmarole; he half listened, trying not to. She would let him know when she was to be in certain places at certain times and he could choose the moment and the method. As far as the world was concerned it would be a random assault by an unknown assailant. He was to do it without notice—"I don't want to see you coming"—and do it cleanly and with dispatch. She would wear something stylish, in scarlet so the blood wouldn't show too starkly; she meant to make a picturesque corpse. Oh, and one more thing: not strangulation, please, which produces a particular effect that is highly unpleasant and shaming, so she has heard. She gave him a meaning look over the top of her glasses that were black and shiny as the eyes of an owl. "Promise?"

He would promise her nothing. It was entirely out of the question—how *could* she ask such a thing of him? For she was serious, he knew that. Flighty and playful as it pleased her to pretend to be, just now she was what she was.

They passed by a farmhouse. In the back yard, garments on a laundry line kicked up their heels in the wind, as full of themselves as corseted chorus-girls. He thought of Ivy's clothesline in the bathroom; he would deal with it as soon as he got back to the cottage. He would run up the stairs and kick open the bathroom door and grasp the twine and snap it off its nail and roll it up and stuff it down the lavatory along with Ivy's knickers and slip and her bedraggled untwinned stocking. That's what he would do.

"First I'll go blind," Anna said, watching the road ahead, "already I can hardly see out of the left one, the one with the spot in it. Then my memory will go and I won't know who anyone is any more and, eventually, who I am, either." She paused, nodding slowly, tight-lipped, confirming it all to herself. "Animals die with their eyes open, did you know that? We're the only ones who can't bear to see what we can't escape. When you creep up behind me and surprise me I'll be gone before I've time to shut my eyes, you'll make sure of that, won't you?"

They had come to the top of a rise in the road and on the other side a valley opened fanwise before them, cradling a checkerboard of fields dotted with farmsteads and huddled woods and grassy rides leading up to tall gates; a river traversed it, a winding seam of mercury; the sky, in the aftermath of its fury, was icy-blue and afloat with small fat fluffy white clouds.

"And anyway," Anna broke out, in a child's aggrieved whine, "it's not much for a girl to ask. And it's not as if you hadn't done it before."

He clasped his fingers tightly together, making the joints crack.

"Once, I should have thought, you should have thought, would be quite enough," he responded in a tone of judgemental sonorousness. My Lord, when you ask me to tell the court—

Down the long slope into the valley; those fields, those farms.

"Do you ever think of her?" Anna asked.

"Who?"

"You know. Her."

He knew. And he does, he thinks of her often, not in remorse and torment as in the early days, but fondly, almost, with a sweet sort of melancholy, as if, as if she were a daughter lost to him long ago. Her eyes, looking out at him between bloodied ropes of hair. Once, in Morocco, another had looked at him in just that way, from behind a bead curtain, inviting him in, murmuring endearments in her exotic soft slurred tongue not a word of which he understood.

"I think of nothing, when I can," he said.

Anna was lighting another cigarette, with one hand on the wheel and one eye shut against the flare of the lighter's flame.

"You don't care what happens to me, do you," she said.

"No."

"Did you ever, really?"

"No."

"No—I know you didn't, don't."

"Then why did you ask?"

"Because I thought you would lie to me. You could do that much. It wouldn't kill you to pretend."

It was like a lovers' quarrel.

"How is your knee?" he asked. "Is it still paining you?"

"My knee is fine."

He is still recalling that evening in the Maghreb, in a villa by the sea, in a room with the shutters shut and the molten sun gone down at last and soft desert rain surreptitiously falling, trying its best not to make a sound, not to disturb the two of them toiling at their pleasures. The girl's enormous, dry, and excitingly raspy brown lips, the tip of her tongue a shiny moist red bead, the palms of her hands a dusty pink, and rough as paper. She embraced him lightly, cradling him as she would a child. Is he now what he was then? The old conundrum.

"My cane back there," Anna said, pointing with her chin, "you could do it with that."

"What?"

"My cane. My walking stick."

"Too light."

"Use extra force."

"Don't be vulgar."

They both laughed, wanly.

"I have something you'd want to get your hands on," Anna said presently. "Something valuable."

"What's that?"

She smiled her cat's-eyed smile. "Wouldn't you like to know."

"Yes, I would."

"Oh, suddenly I have your attention. Short of funds, are we? Strapped for cash?"

"Tell me."

Another farmhouse, another yard, an orchard beyond. To live here and be no one, the birds whistling at dawn, the cattle lowing at dusk. A world apart, set aside, isolate.

"You know the original of Adam's famous paper, his thesis, or whatever it was?"

Waterglass. Why did that word come into his head?

"The manuscript, you mean, of the Brahma theorem? The one he wrote out by hand?" He turned his head slowly and stared at her. "You're not telling me that you—?"

She gave a little eager nod, looking not at him but through the windscreen and smiling with lips pressed tightly together, again like an impish child.

"I kept it, yes," she said. "He didn't care—I think he forgot I was the one who had it." She paused, and narrowed her eyes again, still smiling, still fixed on the road. "It must be worth squillions. Why don't you pop up to Whitewater and have a look at it? Only don't tell me you're coming. Make it a surprise. I'll be dressed in red, and you'll be dressed to kill." Now she too turned, and looked full at him, her eyes shining with a kind of manic mirth. "You did it before, came to steal a precious thing and ended up doing in a girl. Remember?"

He told her to drive him back to Arden House. She stopped at the lychgate. Without another word he got out of the car and slammed the door behind him, pretending not to notice the two fat tears like beads of something trembling at the corners of her failing eyes, while still she smiled and smiled.

Waterglass: like beads of waterglass.

Helen, the woman of the house, was literally run off her feet. Well, not literally, no. Anyway, she doesn't run, much. Nor would she care to hear herself described as the woman of this or any other house, suggestive as it is of the headscarf, the dishcloth, and the slops. Besides, old Mrs. Godley her mother-in-law is still with us, the regnant if doddery dowager, and even Ivy Blount has more of the running of the place than Helen ever did. But this morning she has kitted herself out for the task at hand in workmanlike, in workwomanlike, fashion. The party must be prepared for. She is wearing one of Adam's big white shirts, so loose on her it might be an artist's smock, and a pair of denim trousers, or overalls, I suppose they're called, or is it dungarees, wide at the waist and roomy in the seat, with broad straps over the shoulders and a buckled bib. This unflattering get-up makes her agonisingly desirable, to my ogling eye. The very shapelessness of the garments, inside which the outlines of her form can only be guessed at, sets my imagination going like a steam engine, pistons plunging and the pipes red-hot. She has tied back her hair and wears no make-up, which tells me that for her I am a comfortable old thing, the palace eunuch, harmless to the point of anility and certainly not anyone it would be worth her while getting herself dolled up for. I look at her feet in her thonged sandals and note the chipped polish on the toe-nails; this hint of negligence, along with the loose shirt and denim what's-its, puts me in mind of a tomboy on a raft: my Huckleberry Helen. How widely and far the desirous fancy ranges.

But so busy she is today, so busy and dizzily bright! Since first thing she has been on the telephone, to the butcher, the baker, the man who brings the vegetables in a van. She first wheedled and then bullied Ivy Blount into agreeing to bake a cake, while Adam she dispatched to town to buy a cascade of wine, wine red, white, pink, and sparkling. Everything, she thinks, is going swimmingly. Everything.

The weather is warm, and a big airy cage of sunlight is suspended in the window of what it pleases her to call her office. It is a low brown room, the kind that in olden times a country parson might have composed his sermons in of a Sabbath eve. This is her private place and I am privileged to be here. I am seated at a small round table, shelling peas into a copper bowl, while she is at her untidy roll-top desk, bathed in a gauzy, green-tinged light coming in through that window from the garden. She plies the phone receiver like a barbell. At the end of each call she copies her order into a school jotter, leaning close to the page and squinting, for her eyesight is poor, like mine; the first time I noticed it my heart, my lover's heart, was flooded anew, this time, with a great hot wave of tenderness and pity. She's too vain to wear glasses, of course. Now and then she looks up and glances at me and smiles her lopsided smile. I am her love-slave, as I know she complacently knows and thinks wonderfully droll. Needless to say I have not declared my passion—I'd die first, and may anyway—but she can plainly see how it is with me, by the dejected slope of my shoulders, by the way my hands tremble when she is near, by the moony look in my lovelorn eye. I wonder if the others in the house have twigged how deeply I'm in thrall to her. Has her husband spotted it? Has

Ivy Blount's sinister lodger tumbled to my secret? I have the awful
fear that it may not be a secret at all, to anyone. I may be the laughing stock of the place, for all I know. Well, what do I care.

Through the window I can see a small luminous pure-white
cottony cloud, afloat all alone in the blue, and think it to be the
lingering last breath of some spectre-thin youth, a child of poesy,
who one minute past lay down upon a couch and gave into the
air his quiet breath. A fly alights on the table and stands facing
me, braced on four bandy legs and rubbing its front paws vigorously together in a washing motion. Pretty creatures they are, the
houseflies, their armoured flanks not black, as to the lazy observer
they will seem, but a shiny brittle stained-glass blue, their wings
like ink in water and their eyes as red as rose-hips; always active,
they are, always at themselves, rubbing and scratching and licking.
Flies, that we so casually swat, careless of the intricate webs of
being we thus undo.

Helen rises and replenishes her glass from the wine bottle on
the windowsill and with her loose-limbed slouch comes and sits
herself down across from me at the table. I smell the wine on her
breath, sharp and sour with a citrusy tang. She hasn't offered me
any. She thinks I disapprove of her drinking this early in the day,
which I do.

That cloud is still there, look, hasn't moved at all, only softened its contours, plumped itself up, so that it's more like a pillow
now than a dying breath. There are certain summer mornings,
calm, with a diffuse, grainy brightness and a sense somehow of
glowing heights and far chasms trembling in air, that contrive
to conjure up childhood for me, not the real one I first toddled
around in and then stumbled out of, but the other, prelapsarian,
version that we imagine for ourselves, or that I imagine, for my
self, in which all that was to come hovered before me in the hazy
distance, a floating cotton-coloured miasma of ungainsayable possibility and potential.

Helen was lighting a cigarette.

"You do know he was a terrible old lecher, don't you?" she said. We had been speaking of her father-in-law, in the intervals between her sessions on the phone. "I used to catch him eyeing me, trying to see up my skirt, even when I was expecting and the size of a barrage balloon. He was still at it on his deathbed—he was supposed to be in a coma but I swear I could see him peeping. The lids would be the tiniest bit open and there would be this awful slimy glint between them as if a snail had crawled across his eyeballs." She shuddered, drawing in her shoulders and compressing her lips and making her head quiver in shivery disgust. "He was notorious for it," she said then, with a dismissive sigh, and took a slurp of her wine. "Dirty old brute." She held up the glass and glared at it in disgust. "This stuff has gone tepid."

I ran my thumbnail along the seam of a pod and split it open and the peas splurged into the bowl, rattling like buckshot. I do not like to hear her speak of Adam Godley in this fashion, brash and loud, her eyes aglitter. It's not that I care what she says about him, but the manner in which she says it doesn't suit her. She has a way of showing the crescent of sharp little teeth jostling close together at the front of her lower jaw that makes her mouth seem more muzzle than mouth. Forgive me, I say as I see.

"When he was on his last legs he had a fling with a girl a quarter his age, did you know that? No?" She tapped the barrel of her cigarette with the tip of a forefinger and sent an inch of ash tumbling soundlessly to the carpet at her feet. She can be a proper sloven, sometimes, I note indulgently. Those Gaspers she smokes are as fat as sticks of chalk, and must be bad for her. She gave a small bright nasty laugh. "You mean to say you didn't know about the girl in Venice who killed herself, like his daughter Petra, only she made a bigger splash?—the other girl, I mean." She formed a hand into the shape of a diver and dove it in a curve from high up at her shoulder down into the swallowing depths past the rim of the table. She looked at me and clicked her tongue and shook her head slowly from side to side. "Some biographer you are." She took a deep draw at her cigarette, making a squinched-up face against a curling tendril of smoke. She sat forward until her ribcage was pressed against the edge of the table and leaned heavily on her elbows. "Well, let me tell you," she said. And she did.

Peas freshly shelled give off a soft scent that reminds me of the smell of lilac, wet lilac, at evening, after rain. The world has its secret concordances, not all of them accidental. How little we understand of things, animal migration, the sheepdog's mimicked wide-open eyes above its real ones, murmurations of starlings, the Japanese puffer fish's circular love-blossom lovingly inscribed in the sand of the seabed. Adam Godley himself would be the first to own to the breathtaking breadth of our ignorance, he who was supposed to know everything.

"—and that was her," Helen concluded, "the very last of the old goat's little birdies." She beamed at me; her gaze had slipped somewhat out of focus; it's true, she shouldn't drink in the daytime like this, really she shouldn't. "Isn't it gas?"

Don't you find when someone tells you something of great moment, a thing you had known nothing of before now, you're all agog and at the same time think you'd just as well not have heard it. I had already mapped out a chapter on Adam Godley's multitudinous loves, each one of which I thought I had tracked down and tabulated, and now here was news of a late-flowering passion I hadn't heard a hint of, and which I would have to investigate. Bloody hell; more cause for vacillation. Helen had turned on me a tipsily mischievous eye. Could I trust her story of the girl in Venice and Godley's doomed infatuation? Helen used to be an actress, and must know something of how stories are fashioned, how plots are made up.

I was feeling a little dizzy, sitting within smelling distance of this overwhelming creature. I thought of the two of us as seated at either end of a swing boat—remember them, from the fairgrounds of our youth?—that rose higher at each swing, the force of its arc pressing me back and pinioning me, so that, near to her as I was, I couldn't so much as hope to reach out and touch the sleeve of her shirt, never mind get an arm around her—as if she'd let me even if I were able. Don't mistake me, I know I'm only at play here, amplifying the hour, as no doubt Godley played with his girl in Venice. Soar high, sweet swinging-boat!

From the kitchen, which is a little way down on the other side of the hall, I heard the back door rattle as someone entered from the yard. We went very still, Helen and I, looking at each other in wordless surmise. Whoever was out there had to be someone we knew, someone familiar to us, yet by our look it might have been that we thought ourselves about to be set on by footpad or felon. I could hear my heart's rapid beating. A tiny sunburst on the rim of the bowl before me on the table was shooting out filaments of copper-coloured light in all directions around a seething central core, a galaxy within a galaxy. We heard a cupboard opening, a tap being turned on, heard the water splashing. Something pinged deep in my gut, or maybe it was in Helen's, impossible to tell which. What was there for us to be in fear of? Nothing, nothing at all. We were a pair of children frightening ourselves for the thrill of it. You've known such moments of harkening back even beyond childhood, all the way to the cave and the rumour of ravening beasts beyond the firelight. Something stretched between us, stretched and stretched, and it seemed to me I would never again be so close to her, my dad's daughter, in this life or any possible other. What creatures we are. Helen Helen Helen, Helen the many-voiced, the ship-launcher, the unmanner of men.

Rapid footsteps approached across the hall and Adam appeared in the doorway, with a chipped white mug in his hand.

He was wearing his blue gansey, brown corduroy bags balding at the knees, thick wool socks, and the accustomed desert father's sandals. Seeing me, he frowned. I fear the poor chap lives in a permanent tizzy of anxiety for his impulsive and playful wife, tormented by the jealous thoughts he dare not speak or credit the dark insinuations they would pour in at his ear. I don't blame him, I'd be the same. But I ask, what threat could I possibly represent to him in his married bliss, dusty old codger that I am, with my little pot-belly and my dewlaps, my tics and tremors? And yet it's true, even the world's Aguecheeks were once adored, and who knows but that this one mightn't be so again? Did I not when a boy win a rosebud girl with nothing to aid me but a few equations squeakily scrawled on a toy blackboard? Verily, there are more things in algebra, Master Adam, than are dreamt of in your et cetera.

Ha!

Helen enquires of Adam as to the wine. He got it, yes, yes, he says with a touch of irritation. He left it outside, in the station-wagon. He will bring it in later. He scowls and says no, he didn't get diddled on the price. He frowns at the mug in his hand as if he had forgotten it was there, lifts it, drinks from the water in it. He stares at a wall, a muscle twitching in his jaw. His look is sullen and uncertain. He could be a hulking boy in his first pair of long trousers. Helen winks at me merrily. Her eyes are thoroughly hazed by now—the bottle of Chablis on the windowsill is two-thirds empty—yet at the same time they retain a woozy sparkle. How would it be if I were to begin all subsequent sentences, every one, right to the end, with the magical letter *H* for Helen?

Ha.

"I was telling him about your dear daddy's last great fling," my beloved said to her husband in a tone of airy raillery. "He didn't know about it at all—isn't that rich?"

Adam cast in my direction one of his doggily aggrieved, doleful glances. I suppose he thinks it's I who contrived to get his wife half-drunk, though as he knows she can do it perfectly well by herself. I feel for him, I do, honestly, however much I may seem not to. Helen's lost children were his, too, and he's married to her. Yes, and she is married to him. There's a stark fact to munch on.

He went out. We heard the fridge door opening, and again the sound of something, not water this time, being poured, glug glug. He returned, carrying a glass of milk, most of which he drank off in one go—how thirsty he is today—tossing his head back with a curious vehemence, as if to make a point about something. He turned to speak to Helen but she gave a delighted whoop and clapped her hands. "Look at you," she cried, "you've got a moustache!" She laughed unsteadily and put a hand over her mouth and spluttered through her fingers. Adam wiped the crescent of milk from his upper lip with the sleeve of his pullover. Helen sees how downcast and annoyed he is and in a show of mock contrition she slumps her shoulders and puts on her clown's sorrowing grimace.

I know I should get up from the table and tiptoe away; I make it a rule to avoid all scenes of marital discord, however muted. Helen sees me having the thought and widens her eyes at me menacingly, silently commanding me to stay. Adam drank the rest of his milk. I suspect that, like me, he's prone to boredom, or to the fear of it, rather, which is just as bad if not worse. It would account in part at least for the air of dreamy distress that surrounds him always. Or maybe he's not so much bored but just melancholy by nature; I am too, so I should know.

"I heard a funny thing about Ivy's Fella," he said, coming forward to the table.

He has a curious gait today, seeming at every step forward he takes to be on the point of turning back, as if in response to something someone behind him is saying. His bulk is a burden to him, he tries out ways the better to cope with it, ducking his head, dipping a hip, flexing his large round soft-looking shoulders, like a coalman shifting a too-heavy sack. He is defenceless against himself and the obscure torments that afflict him; I imagine his sister, the suicide, was the same, a purer distillation of him and his pains. I have seen photographs of her, of Petra, and of him with her, and in them brother and sister look nothing alike. She would have been in life more like the ghost of herself than she is now in death. Which I saw the other day, her ghost, I'll tell you about it presently.

Adam dips his fingers into the bowl before me and takes a pinch of peas and crowds them into his mouth and crunches them. He considers the table and the empty chair standing by it. I pause to ask, never mind the irrelevance, if you have ever thought what a life a chair is forced to lead. Look at it, crouched down there all day on all fours, as if paying obeisance, and in constant awareness of the inevitability of being sat on at any moment by any bottom, lean or fat, clean or otherwise, that thinks to stop and plonk itself unceremoniously down. There should be a ritual to be performed before one sits, a little curtsey, say, or some sort of arsy-versy genuflexion. We owe it to those long-suffering beasts of burden who bear us up with nary a protest save an occasional squeak or, once in a way, a rare way, a collapse.

"Go on, then, tell us," Helen urges her husband.

He has stopped thinking about chairs—was he thinking about chairs?—and now sits down on one of them at the table between Helen and me. He looks from her to me and back again. He wears a perplexed, a wondering, frown.

"They were talking about him in Walker's," he said, "when I was getting the wine."

"Who's 'they'?"

"Oh, women. Housewives. They know he's lodging here."

"Yes? And?"

Helen is never more the actress than when she has drink taken. She holds her spine very straight and extends her already long neck and even manages to seem to dilate the pupils of her eyes. A spent matchstick on the floor now catches her eye, and deftly she seizes it in the crease under her big toe and picks it up, hoop-la! the clever monkey-girl.

"It seems," Adam said, speaking slowly, worrying with a fingernail at a hard speck of something adhering to the side of his mug, "it seems he is from these parts, but he's not who he says he is, and his name is not Mordaunt."

"I knew it!" Helen crowed, giving the table top such a slap that her wine glass jumped.

"—and he was in prison."

"I knew that too! The very first day he arrived here I—"

She breaks off and turns to me in delighted triumph. And I seem to hear, at a great distance, something faintly chime. I would think it's just a ringing in my ears except that it's so far away, a far-off tocsin. Something is assembling itself, something is about to be divulged. You know when you stand before an unlighted shop window at nightfall and the forms of the people passing to and fro behind you on the pavement as they are reflected in the darkly lustrous glass in front of you merge with each other and fade into a moveless, depthless plane of shadow. That's how it is with me now, as I wait to hear what more Adam has to tell us.

"Go on," Helen urged again, "go on go on."

Adam shrugged.

"They saw me listening, the women, and stopped," he said. "You know what they're like." He paused, and looked at us both again. "I suppose I'll have to tell him to go." He sighed. He does hate a confrontation.

And I? What am I to make of this? I thought I had it all fixed, now threads are loosening all round the edges, and if I pull on one of them what unravelling will follow? It makes me tired to think of it.

In the course of his years behind bars, Felix Mordaunt had been cured, or had cured himself, of the desire for possessions. Billy's side of the cell might have been the interior of a cargo cultist's hut, with an ever-accumulating jumble of his precious objects, which included a leatherette-bound album containing snaps, faded to ghostliness, of his family and of himself as a youth, also the grass-green, sleek, and wonderfully detailed engine from a Hornby model train set of the Flying Scotsman, and, twined around the bars at the head of his bed, a set of rosary beads with a greenish-white crucified Christ who glowed in the dark. Also, the wall beside his bed was papered to the ceiling with pin-ups, the largest of which and holding pride of place was a glossy black-and-white portrait photograph of Ingemar Johansson, the Hammer of Thor, handsomest of all the heavyweight world champions, to Billy's admiring eye. Mordaunt had no choice but to tolerate this clutter, not wishing to wound his cellmate's sensibilities, or, more to the point, not caring to provoke him, for Billy was a dangerous lad when roused. Mordaunt's own half of the cell was as featureless as the prison's visiting hall. The only things of his on show were a small electric clock, and a calendar, the former to measure time, the latter, durance. In the early days of his term he had kept hidden under his mattress a postcard reproduction of the *Portrait of a Lady with Gloves,* sent to him at the start of his sentence by Anna Behrens. Why he felt the need to hide it he didn't know. Anna had written on the back of it, "Greetings from your old flame," which he considered an uncharacteristic show of poor taste on her part, until it struck him that she was referring not to herself but to the paltry woman in Vaublin's picture. He tore up the card and flushed it down the lavatory. It took four flushes, since the scraps of pasteboard kept bobbing back up, and when they were all gone at last he found he was sweating and his hands were shaking. *Don't,* the girl, the woman, the maid, had said, that summer day long ago, in a strangely firm, clear voice, the moment before he, Thor the Terrible, struck her the first hammer blow, above the left eye it was, just at the hairline. He used to hear that voice often in his dreams, calmly speaking that same word, over and over, but no more. Time first dulls, and then silences all things.

Since returning to Coolgrange, or coming here to Arden—by now he has given up cudgelling his brains over the puzzle of where he is supposed to be exactly, and calls the place Coolarden, or Ardgrange, when he calls it anything—he had begun collecting things again, trinkets and trifles which he picked up here and there about the Big House and brought back and stowed in various hiding places in his bedroom above Ivy Blount's kitchen. There is a silver propelling pencil, the antique silver silky to the touch, with the initials A.G. engraved on the barrel, which he had chanced on on a shelf in the dining room, where someone had propped it in a crystal tumbler and forgotten about it. I shouldn't say he chanced on it, since he had been looking out for just something of the sort, personalised and unique and ripe for purloining. He has an apostle spoon, too, very pretty, though so worn from long use that the figure at the end of the handle looks less like an apostle than the mummified remains of a miniature pharaoh, his frail arms folded across his chest; it has three tiny hallmarks stamped on the back of the bowl, one enclosing the number 925, the second a Tudor rose, and the third a stylised leopard flourishing an impossibly long, whip-like tail. To make out these marks had required the use of a magnifying glass, and after a long and frustrating search he had found one, in the upstairs room where Godley's widow is kept. The glass wasn't large but was heavy, with a thick lens and a bone handle. The old woman, huddled under her mound on the divan, had heard him the moment he stepped across the threshold, and had sat up at once, alert and sharp-eyed. She didn't seem startled by the intrusion, nor did she seem to mind it. She watched him with bright attention, her head tilted to one side, as he moved softly about the room, opening cupboards and getting down on one knee to peer under the bed. In the end he found the magnifier wedged at the side of the divan where the woman was perched. He asked her politely if he might borrow it, but she said nothing, only went on gazing at him intently, as if he belonged to some rare and fascinating species she had not encountered before. Afterwards he had resolved to pay her another, more extended, visit, but somehow had never got round to it. She was not spoken of by the Godleys, not in his hearing, anyway. It occurred to him that she might be a spirit his overheated fancy had conjured up from the land of the dead. Why not? It would hardly be stranger than anything else to be met with in this strange dominion.

The most precious items in his collection were contained in a small oval box crafted from burnished wood the colour of dark honey and fitted with a japanned lid that operated on a tiny, finely tooled brass hinge. He found it in a drawer of the writing table in the Sky Room—the drawer was stuck and it took him five frustrating minutes to prise it open with a steel letter-opener, grinding his teeth and swearing under his breath—before Jaybey, its current occupant, had been installed there. He experienced an odd little surge of Christmassy excitement as he opened the lid. Inside the box were two plump pearls set side by side on a black velvet mount. They were not round but tear-shaped, and had a deep, pinkish sheen. He knew nothing about pearls but he judged these to be genuine. They were old, and obviously had been prized. But whose were they, that they had been left at the back of a drawer and forgotten about who knows how long ago? Old Adam Godley had lived out his last months in the Sky Room, comatose and unstirring, but it seemed unlikely they would have belonged to him. Or perhaps they were a keepsake from one of his many love affairs? It didn't really matter; they are Mordaunt's now, and he, for his part, cherishes them.

He chose with care the places about his room in which to conceal his treasures—the pearls in their box he kept on a shallow ledge of a high shelf in the dark at the back of the wardrobe—for it would be one thing to be unmasked as a convicted killer but quite another to be thought a petty thief. Ivy had stayed out of his room since the day when, thinking he was off somewhere, she had put her head in at the door for a quick reconnoitre and discovered him reclining on the bed with his trousers around his knees, engaged in an admittedly indolent bout of self-abuse. She would make certain next time that he was safely out before she sneaked in to check up on him and his doings. If she were to search and find something incriminating she would carry it straight to Adam Godley or his nosey wife. That would be awkward. He knew he should get a lock for the door, but he was shy of hardware shops, for a reason of his own, and besides he was no handyman.

The one precious *trouvaille,* precious to him, that he hadn't bothered to hide was a clay model of a Chinese dragon, he took it to be a dragon, twice as long as it was high, glazed in green and rich red and cyanine blue, with frightful sharp teeth and starting eyes and what appeared to be a six-toed fifth paw grafted on to the end of its stubby, upward curling tail. This fearsome beast stood at a crouch on the mantelpiece above the room's meagre fireplace, from where it glared with fiery malevolence from morn till night, and sometimes even when he woke in the dark and the moon was in the window he would see it there among the shadows, ready to spring, stark-eyed, multi-clawed, unappeasable. He had found it in what he took to be the drawing room, or a drawing room, on the ground floor, a musty, uninviting place, where it lurked in a bookless glass-fronted bookcase among a menagerie of suchlike trophies, all equally exotic, all equally hideous, brought back from foreign parts no doubt by Ivy Blount's explorer forebears. And this it was that Helen Godley, the nosey one herself, recognised, with a hoot of smoky laughter, and told him she had spotted him for a pilferer the first time she laid eyes on him, yes a petty pilferer, and who knows how many other kinds of villain besides.

He was at the draining board in the kitchen polishing his shoes when he heard her approaching across the gravelled yard. He has three pairs of very good shoes, two brown and one black, crafted for him very many years ago by John Lobb, Bootmaker, of London, and paid for by a fond friend of those days by the name of Charlie French; good old Charlie, gentleman and covert queen. He wonders if the original last, the one Mr. Lobb and his master cobblers carved specially for him, is still preserved, in a dusty cubbyhole in the depths of the St. James's Street shop, along with Palmerston's slippers and the Duke of Wellington's boots. The shoes are in fine condition still, since latterly he had worn them only on the weekend furloughs that punctuated the closing years of his term, his having had to make do inside with prison-issue clodhoppers. He polishes the three pairs at three-day intervals, turn and turn about, whether they need polishing or not; you can tell a lifer by the little rituals he keeps. This one he performs always in the kitchen, at the draining board, ignoring Ivy when she shrieks at him, as she does every time, to do it outside, on the back doorstep, or in the potting shed beyond the vegetable garden. When she sees him getting out his brushes and chamois cloths and tins of specially imported shoe cream she springs up, agile as a chamois herself, and has a protective sheet of newspaper slapped down on the draining board before he can get to it. Nevertheless, he is always careful to leave a few broad smears of polish on the front edge of the board on on the rim of the sink. It's yet another of the little vengeful acts by which he goads her, though she suffers it wordlessly, in ashen-faced fury, as she suffers all his provocations. One night after dinner when he had drunk too much claret—he filches it from the house, no one seems to notice—he remarked that they might as well be married, so thoroughly did they detest each other. Her response was startling. Her features became contorted in the oddest way and he thought she might be about to burst into tears. Instead of which she ran out at the back door, her face very red and swollen. Impossible woman. He doesn't have to stay here; he could go and live somewhere else, at Whitewater with Anna Behrens, for instance, he's sure she would take him in, her designated executioner. But driving Ivy to distraction has become a pastime, an intricate game, like solo chess, which he plays with the finesse and inventiveness of a grandmaster. The truth is, he wouldn't be without her.

The back door was open, and when Helen appeared in the doorway he thought at first it must be Ivy, and turned with a frown from the sink, the polish brush in one hand and a large black brogue in the other. Helen, looking at him, knocked a knuckle anyway on the wide-open door. "Anyone home?" Deliberately she let her gaze wander over him. He had on one of Ivy's aprons, short and frilled and shaped like a scallop shell. "The pinny suits you," she said. It had rained earlier, but the sun had come out again, and behind her the day glittered greenly, reminding him sharply of the day he first arrived here, aeons ago. "May I?" she said, and stepped forward, through the doorway, passing him by and brushing her arm against his sleeve as if by accident. She wore a belted white dress of lightweight linen that left her knees and the polished tops of her shoulders exposed, a pair of pumps with a strap that buttoned across the instep, and a string of pearls. Her hair was loose, and with the light behind her it made a glowing aureole about her head. He let fall a silent, weary sigh. Long though he had been out of the world, he still knew trouble when he saw it coming.

Now he sits on the bed naked, with pillows at his back, his arms and ankles crossed. Opposite him is a small square window, the only window in the room, the lower frame of which is propped open on an upright clothes peg. A breeze enters through the gap, carrying with it rich odours of grass and gorse and sun-warmed trees. It reaches the bed and ripples over him, cool and smooth as satin, tickling his toes and stirring the small hairs on his forearms. Summer. He likes the view from just this position, and often lolls here of a morning watching the weather have its way with the landscape. The woolly foliage and gently rolling hills put him in mind of a Samuel Palmer etching, *The Weald of Kent,* say, or *The Timber Wain,* with those lovely leaning trees Samuel was so fond of. Close to can be seen a corner of the roof of one of the old stone stables, and the gate and beyond the gate the little stand of oaks, and off on the horizon a smear of throbbing brightness that is the sea. The chill slime at his lap is something from the past, a token of other bedrooms, other afternoons. When was the last time he—? He can't remember. No, wait, he can. With Anna Behrens, it was, when he was on the run and she tracked him to his lair, or perhaps he got in touch with her, he doesn't know, it's all so long ago. But how did they manage it, where was it they——? So many things he has forgotten, so many things have fallen out of his memory, like coins through a hole in his pocket. Gone, and he didn't even hear the jingle as they fell.

"I'm told some floozie in a fancy car came to visit you," Helen said, as if she had heard his thoughts. "You kept very quiet about it."

"My business, madam," he answered briskly, with a smirk, "and none of yours."

She lay on the bed on her stomach, resting on her elbows, her breasts bunched fatly between her forearms and her face lifted towards him. She was smoking a cigarette. Light from the window beyond her glowed on her bare shoulders, and, farther along, made twin coronas of the soft down on the plump rounds of her behind. She has the look of a big-necked pre-Raphaelite beauty. He hadn't expected how much to his taste she would turn out to be. He knows so little of himself.

"Who told you?" he asked.

"Duffy."

Him, again.

"You're the original dark horse, aren't you," Helen said, cigarette smoke oozing out at either corner of her mouth. "What's your real name, anyhow?"

He chuckled. "And are you a real blonde?"

"Of course I am." She rolled sideways on her belly and lifted up one hip to let him look. "As you must have noticed."

That first day when Anna Behrens asked him to kill her and he refused, she snivelled like a jilted girl. When people get a notion into their heads there's nothing to be done with them, nothing.

"What if my landlady comes back and finds you here?" he said.

"Ivy? She won't. I gave her the money to get her hair done

in town. It will take them half the afternoon just to untangle the knots."

"You had it all planned, then."

"All what?"

He looked at her, and at himself. "This."

"Well, it was obvious you weren't going to make a move."

"Your husband—"

"Leave my husband out of it. Don't mention my husband."

She tapped her cigarette and knocked a worm of ash on to the sheet and puckered her lips and blew at it. The worm rolled to the edge of the mattress and stopped and she blew again, harder, and it rolled again and fell off, disintegrating in a flurry of soft grey flakes.

"I knew a man once," he said musingly, "who sold his daughter. She was a child at the time."

Helen made a pouting face, wrinkling her nose in disgust. "Why did he do that?"

"Needed money, I imagine. He was a drug addict, or a drinker, I can't remember which. Both, perhaps, I wouldn't be surprised. Then years later he was in a brothel and realised the girl he had just consorted with was her."

"The daughter?"

"The daughter."

She drew on her cigarette and thought for some moments in silence. "Nice people you hang around with," she said. "How did he know it was her?"

He shrugged.

"I didn't ask. Recognised a birthmark, or the like, I should say."

"And did she know who he was?—did she recognise him?"

"He didn't say. Pender was his name. Seanie Pender. He died strangled by his cellmate who went mad. I don't know why he has come to mind. Love, squalor, transgression."

She gazed before her in wide-eyed wonder at the horror of the thing.

"That's a terrible story," she said. "You shouldn't have told it to me. What am I doing here? Squalor is right. You're old enough to be my father. Maybe you are my father, and that's why you've come back." She reached out a hand and made a claw of it and drew her fingernails down his chest, through the crackly grey hairs. "You're a bad man. I knew it the minute I saw you in the yard that morning, standing there, you and the dog looking at the moon."

"Yet here you are."

She pouted again.

"You shouldn't do that," she said.

"What."

"You shouldn't smile like that. It gives me the shivers."

Here's prattle to beat the band. I'm only saying.

She rose up on her knees with a soft grunt and stepped off of the bed and flicked the stub of her cigarette out at the gap at the bottom of the window. "I'm cold," she said. She lifted his tweed jacket from where he had hung it on the back of a chair and put it on. It was much too big for her and made her look small suddenly. She drew the lapels close against her cheeks at either side and breathed deeply in. "Smells of you."

"And how do I smell?"

"Of meat."

"Meat?"

"Sort of. Meat that's gone off." She crossed to the mantelpiece and turned the Chinese dragon to face the wall. "And that thing, glaring at me," she said, with a glare of her own.

He thought of telling her of a thing that had happened to him, on his first day in prison, his first full day, that is, for he had been brought in the previous evening, direct from court. He felt quite calm, surprisingly so in the circumstances, but he supposed now that had been an illusion, and that he wasn't calm at all, but quite the opposite. Prison was a new world, one designed by demons, and how could his spirit be at peace in those dark vertiginous depths. The thing that happened happened on the afternoon of that day, that first, full day, the one he is recalling, an afternoon much like this one, though there were none of Samuel Palmer's homely felicities to be admired from the window of his cell, but only that solitary, drab, unkillable tree. He was sitting on his bunk as he is sitting on this bed, with his legs stretched out before him, not naked then, of course, as he is now, but wearing his threadbare though still scratchy prison uniform, which smelled sharply of carbolic soap and faintly of the sweat of the others like him who had worn it before him, the multiple others. He was thinking of nothing in particular, his mind dulled after the clamour and confusion of the previous day—though his court appearance had been brief since he had lodged a guilty plea and was handed down the mandatory sentence and that was that—and indeed he may have drifted into a waking doze, if such a thing is possible. That's to say he was awake, no doubt of it, but he had that feeling of being about to topple over which comes at the giddy brink of sleep, a feeling which is itself sleep but sleep of a special sort. And he did seem to topple, in a way, in his mind, not forwards, but backwards, back from the brink. The thing was over in an instant, yet it was an instant in which he had been lost to himself entirely, to himself and to the world around him. What marked the experience as singular and strange, strange beyond anything he had known before or since, was that for the sliver of a second it lasted he had ceased to be himself, and everything else had ceased to be itself, along with him. What had happened, he was convinced, and nothing would convince him otherwise, was that for the space of that infinitesimal blink of time, he had somehow crossed over into the non-where of death, had crossed over and returned in the same instant. On that other side, everything had been different, no, everything had been nothing, everything including himself. Nothing. The experience had been, he realised, not an experience in life, and not in death, either, but an absence, an interval, a caesura, whatever to call it, such that the minutest particles fall into, fall out of, when they perform that famously impossible leap from one go-round to another, the riddle of which was solved and so simply by Adam Godley's interference equation. And a mark had been left on him, the indelible mark of Lazarus. The life that up to that moment had been a matter of sprawling possibilities had come suddenly to seem as narrow as the chiselled notch between the two bleak dates on a gravestone, an instant of an instant. He had died, and had lived. Impossible, and yet it had happened.

"How am I going to explain this?" Helen said.

"What?"

"These pearls." In a frenzied passage on the bed one or other of them had somehow snapped the string of her necklace. The pearls had scattered everywhere, and most had fallen to the floor and rolled about. What a time they had spent retrieving them, on hands and knees, naked, picking them up one by one and dropping them into a little carved wooden bowl, which stood now on the mantelpiece, close by the clay dragon. "I'm sure we didn't get half of them," Helen said. "The smallest ones would have fell down in the cracks between the floorboards."

Should he fetch the little ornate box from its hiding place in the wardrobe and show her what it contained? Perhaps he should present it to her, an emblem of the occasion, the two smooth pale ice-white beads glowing in their velvet mount, a diorchic token of the occasion.

Helen was lighting another cigarette. She smokes in an almost vengeful way, as if she were doing it out of spite. Now she shook the match to put it out and hissed a narrow cone of smoke out into the air.

"Adam," she said, " 'my husband,' says you're not who you're pretending to be."

"Who am I pretending to be?"

"He says your name is not Mordaunt, and that you were in jail for a long time, for years and years. I suppose that's where you met the fellow who sold his daughter." Still with his jacket over her shoulders she sat down on the edge of the bed and crossed her legs, and he admired their glowing paleness. The shadow between her breasts was blue like the polished blue of a roof under moonlight. The sleeves of his jacket were so long she had to keep flicking the cuffs back to free her wrists. "What did you do? Did you kill someone? You did, didn't you."

See me, the girl-eater, svelte and dangerous, padding to and fro in my cage. In the moment immediately after the deed was done he had found himself in a new place, and it had come to him that he was no longer human, perhaps never had been human, was a creature apart, hardly even animal, more as a riven stone, a sod of earth, a broken stick. Yes.

"The woman who came here," he said, "the woman you asked me about, she once slept with your father-in-law."

Helen stared.

"Did she, now?"

"In fact, more than once, if I'm not mistaken."

"When?"

"Oh, many years ago. So did my wife."

"Sleep with him?"

"Yes. And with her."

"With your friend the floozie? Your wife? The two of them—?"

"Yes."

Helen set an elbow on her crossed knees and cupped her chin in a hand and lifted an eyebrow sceptically.

"Is all this true, or are you making it up?"

"Why would I make it up? Wives do sleep with other men, you know, my dear."

He regarded her coolly, and she looked away, her forehead pinkening. Moments passed. There was a sudden skirl of birdsong outside, the sound was like something bright flying up into the sunlight, a blade, or a shard of glass.

"Didn't you mind about her sleeping with all those people?" Helen asked.

"My wife? She didn't sleep with all those people."

"Sounds like she did."

"Well, she didn't."

"He did. Old Adam. He slept with everyone."

"Ah." He nodded. By now he too was feeling the chill of the declining day. There was the sense of something subsiding, swaying on the air as it went down. "Matter of fact, I only found out about her and him recently."

"Your wife? I suppose that one told you, when she was here. What's her name?"

"My wife? Daphne. People used to laugh when they heard it, I could never think why."

"I meant the floozie."

"Ah. She's called Anna. You would like her, I think. Or maybe not."

"Huh. All these women. You're as bad as your wife, or the old boy himself." She fiddled with her cigarette, her eyes lowered. "Did she tell you about Daphne?"

"Did she tell me what about Daphne?"

"About sleeping with her herself."

"No. I knew about that. I had guessed it."

"How?"

"We went to bed together, the three of us, one afternoon."

He shrugged. "A chap can tell, you know. I might as well not have been there."

Now a silence. She picked distractedly at the flesh beside a fingernail. "I think I'll get dressed," she said. He watched her. She didn't move, but sat with eyes downcast still, her hair seeming to sag, a drooping aura. She looked smaller again inside the big square jacket, small and young and at a loss, her head propped between the padded tweed shoulders as if it had been severed and re-set in place. He pictured her entrails, the packed purple loops busy fashioning a turd, to be delivered in the morning, prompt as the post or a loaf from the baker's. How startled she would be if she knew what he was thinking. But why? Is she not as cherishable inside as out? Most of what we are is folded away inside us, he thought, the soft engine humbly at its ceaseless labours. I emphasise, these are his musings, not mine. Besides, she might be thinking the same thing about him, or something like it. Never know what's going on in their minds, all the others, never know.

She stood up and took off his jacket and picked up her dress and lifted her arms and shrugged herself into it. She came up through the collar as if through a circle of foam.

"Sunday will be my baby's birthday," she said. "He died, before you ask." She knelt on one knee and slipped her foot into the soft black slipper and did up the button. He knows about her dead children, of whom frequent though only mildly malicious mention is made in Ivy Blount's dinnertime monologues. "Never got born, really." She paused in her buttoning and knelt motionless. "This won't happen again, will it," she said, not looking at him.

"No."

She leaned down and started to button the other strap.

"Will you leave?"

"I imagine I'll have to, now," he said. "Awkward."

"I'm sorry."

"Are you?"

She shook her hanging head from side to side, tight-lipped, heavy-eyed, a bold and sulky child. "Where's the string," she muttered, taking up the bowl of pearls, "it's supposed to have knots in it to keep them from slipping off." Another bird, a cuckoo this time, called afar, as if to mock her, as if to mock everything. Mordaunt sat forward on the bed, his hands linked in his lap. His shins were cold now, he really should get dressed.

Helen with her head bowed looked at him from under her hair.

"You could say you love me," she said. "You could lie, I wouldn't mind."

Again, he thought: they all want to be lied to.

"I love you," he said.

She glittered at him and suddenly flung a fistful of the pearls.

"Liar," she said.

He had ducked too late, and a pearl had struck him at the side of the socket of his left eye, stingingly.

"Pearls before a swine," she said, which only seemed to make her angrier. She straightened up and stood in front of him with her fists at her sides, the knuckles white. "I bet you killed someone," she said. "I bet you did."

People when they are about to weep, he has often remarked it, take on a tense, purposeful expression, as if they are readying themselves to make an announcement.

"Don't cry," he said, trying not to sound impatient, and held out his arms to her. "Come here. Come."

Cuckoo.

But she did cry, not for long, and more out of vexation, it seemed, than sorrow. She blew her nose in the handkerchief he had given her, straightened his jacket where she had hung it on the back of a chair, turned away. However, going out at the back door she halted and threw her arms clumsily about his neck and squashed her mouth against his ear and gasped out something, a plea or a pledge, that he didn't catch. He hated this kind of lavish demonstration. He was barefoot, so that she was on a level with him—she is a big girl, remember—and he felt at a disadvantage, which made him cross. He untangled himself brusquely from her hot embrace and gave her a push which he tried, too late, to disguise as a farewell pat. She looked at him soulfully with wounded eyes and set off unsteadily across the yard, fumbling for her cigarettes.

Back in the kitchen he sat down at the table and remained there for some time, gazing vacantly before him, not minding the chill of the stone floor under his bare soles. He is a man with no strong sense of himself, of his wishes and desires; it was always so, but also certain essential faculties were further thinned out and bleached by the years of incarceration. Indeed, there are times when he forgets himself altogether, when he misplaces himself, as he would his hat, or his door key. It's a not entirely disagreeable sensation. He finds it restful to be released, if only temporarily, from the tyranny of his own surveillance. Is this what death will be like, he wonders, a final lapsing of attention, a distracted letting go? No, it won't. He has seen death, and knows it's a fight to the finish.

He went upstairs and put on his socks and shoes. His jacket smelled faintly of Helen. He stood looking down at the bed and the stains on the sheet that were almost dry by now. What an odd thing it is, he thought, the business that men and women so desperately transact together. Downstairs again, he drank a glass of water—he felt parched, suddenly—then he left the cottage and went out to the road. The day was windless and cool, the sunlight misted, like his thoughts. In his depleted state he feels he is in some way a danger to himself.

Where the road branched he turned left and followed the demesne wall until he came to the grassy patch where he had parked the Sprite that first day. His steps were idle, his way at random, or so it seemed. He entered under the stone arch and walked along the lane and passed through the five-barred gate, catching the sharp tang of rusted iron. It still puzzles him that he's able to come in by the Lady's Way but can't go out. Perhaps, he thinks, it's a form of what long-termers call gate fever, the fear felt at the thought of one day being released into a world they will no longer recognise and which will have forgotten them. He knew of fellows who within a month of being let out had smashed a jeweller's window or knocked someone over in the street just to get themselves sent back safely inside.

He paused to look up at the rear of the house, and for no reason he could think of he found himself recalling the fact that his father could play the musical saw. It was his hobby. He regrets not having asked him how he had come by such a notable skill. Horrible sound it made, a rubbery sort of caterwauling, like a cat at night on a wall. But think of all the days of practice it must have taken before he mastered his instrument. The musical saw. His father.

Now as if on cue Rex the dog came out of his kennel and hobbled at his heels across the yard. The back door was on the latch, as usual, and the pair entered the house and walked about freely in the downstairs rooms. A watchful stillness reigned. Mordaunt feels uneasy in these subdued surroundings. Prison was like a cemetery in which the dead keep up a raucous clamour day and night; within the vast cage, every disembodied bang and clang, every shout and sob, had its metallic echo and made a mingled buzzing in the ear. Whereas the quiet in this house is a scandal. People going about their day should make a decent din, not keep this conspiratorial hush. He imagines whispered conferences, stealthy arrangements being put in place behind closed doors.

At the head of a narrow corridor of black-and-white tiles the dog suddenly got dog-tired and flopped down on his haunches with a muffled clatter of bones and sat and watched the man as he walked on.

Here was a large shabby room, to where over the years many of the uglier items of furniture in the house had found their way, by their own powers, it might be, to form an ill-assorted assemblage. This clutter of blued mahogany, dulled brassware, and dusty brocade is familiar to him. He had known the country-house life, had been in his day quite the swell, in a rakish, down-at-heel fashion, before he went to the bad and fled to the Costa del Dolor to loll and swill, then home again to become a malefactor and consequently a convict: loafer to lifer in three moves.

At the far end of the room an arched window, tall and narrow and quaintly suggestive of an apothecary's cell, with six narrow panes and a cracked lunette, gave not on to the outdoors but into the green-tinged gloom of what they call the conservatory. He stood in the deep embrasure and looked dully into that chill square space, bleak in its bareness. There wasn't so much as a wrought-iron chair or a potted palm to punctuate the wide expanse of floor out there. Between the yellowish sandstone flags, sooty-green pads of moss had shouldered their way up and established a stubborn purchase. He sighed. In these past weeks his heart had languished. His life for so long had been a negative state, constituted of all he wasn't and hadn't, that he no longer knew quite how to have or be, or even if being and having were on offer. And somehow he was, somehow he had become, the obverse of himself. He stood at this window in this unhandsome room as if he were standing inside his own head, peering out emptily into emptiness. He was as a room within a room.

What to do, how to live, or more simply, how to exist. For he long ago gave up on life, no, on living, the vital thing itself.

He stepped away from the window and began to poke about the room moodily, one fist thrust into a pocket of his jacket and his lower lip stuck out. There are moments, aren't there, when one might drift clear of things altogether and cease to be and hardly notice, or not notice at all; that is, not to die but to be lost nonetheless. A wicker basket by the fireplace was piled high with what it took him some moments to recognise, with a sharp stab of remembrance, as the remains of a dozen or more tennis racquets. They were the old-fashioned kind, hardly heavier than badminton bats, the frames moulded in a slender oval shape. They were all broken up, for kindling, he presumed. At sight of them he seemed to hear a faint twock-thwocking from a distant court and the voices of languorously exclaimant girls in white.

A sound at his back made him start. It was the click of what could be a cupboard door shutting, followed immediately by the guttural clearing of a throat. He turned sharply and saw a figure standing at the window, just as he had stood a minute ago, and for an instant, a sublime instant of mingled terror and elation, he took it to be somehow himself, his doublegoer, his living ghost. But it was only Adam Godley. How had he managed to materialise like that, as if he had oozed up through a crack in the floorboards or dropped from the ceiling in a soundless bound? He had a furtive look, the look of a fellow from a senior class caught doing something naughty in the junior boys' latrine. In his hands he held a bundle of yellowed sheets, graph paper, as it seemed to be.

"Oh," Godley said, with a breathy little laugh. "It's you."

Mordaunt frowned. "You gave me a fright. I didn't hear you come in."

"No."

Then a silence such that the churning world might have stumbled to a halt. Godley cleared his throat again.

"I was just," he said, "I was just looking for something."

Mordaunt is aware of his own uncanny aura—he is a revenant, remember—and plays it up to amuse himself and disquiet others. This large person here, with his hare's starting eye and thick, twitchy thumbs, is plainly nervous of him. Human beings. Their orbits do not intersect, their surfaces do not touch. They are as remote from each other as from the farthest nebulae. They live their lives in the lock-up, hearing the gaudy cavalcade passing by beyond the barbed-wired wall and imagining themselves in the midst of it. He knows all about that, oh, he does.

"Found it, then?" he said.

"What?"

"What you were looking for."

"Oh, this," Godley said, again with that gasping laugh, and pressing the papers to his breast under the splayed fingers of both hands, "yes."

"Good."

And with a parting mumble he was gone.

Mordaunt stood a moment pensive, still absently savouring the fragrance of the smashed-up racquets. Might the woman have told her husband of what an hour since had ended in a brief tempest of tears beside that narrow bed in the cramped room above Ivy Blount's unsuspecting kitchen? He wouldn't put it past her. That would certainly account for Godley's queasy look, his abrupt flight. Hmm. Could be deuced awkward. But truth to tell he was experiencing a twinge of queasiness himself. To consort with Helen was to consort with her consort, necessarily, if only to an extent, a tiny extent, and that by proxy, and the thought of any form of intercourse, even at the farthest remove, with the likes of that big bumbling freckled fellow would be enough to turn the stomach of the most undiscriminating debauchee.

He picked up the headless handle of a racquet and hefted it in his hand, thinking. Then he broke wind, producing a sustained and satisfyingly reverberant deep bass note, and made a comical grimace. To be oneself, in all the ambiguity of selfness, that's the hard thing.

Now he went back to the window and stood as before, himself himself. Why, pray, is the embrasure so deep here, why is the angled wall on either side so thick? Run a hand along this edge, stop, tap smartly with the tip of a rigid middle finger, tap tap tappity tap. Auscultate. Comes back a hollow sound. And here's a something—what is it? He pressed upon a shallow indent in the panel and produced a click, the same as the one he had heard before he turned and saw—

But what have we here, by the powers of sesame?

Callooh! Callay! cooed I, and may even have skipped a gleeful step or two in jig time. What has happened, you ask, that has me in such a transport? Wait till I tell you. From out the airless defile of the right, that is, the correspondence, side of the double vault that houses Adam Godley's papers, his son the second Adam has extracted a nugget of the purest gold—you witnessed him making his stealthy exit a moment ago—and handed it into my care. I have dubbed it the Venetian Testament. Has a ring to it, don't you think? Thirteen loose sheets of slightly foxed graph paper inscribed on both sides with a close-set text in that eye-wateringly minuscule hand which by now is as familiar to me as is my own. The pages are punched with a neat eyelet at the top left corner and strung together floppily on a loop of faded blue string. There is no indication of when it was composed; a long time ago, the foxing would suggest, but from the fresh look of the ink it's possible the paper was already old when it was written on. I could have it chemically dated but I won't. It's a letter, of a sort, in draft form, though if it was ever finished it's hard to believe even Adam Godley would have dared to send it. His son can offer no help in the matter of provenance, says he knows nothing of its origins. Yet I wonder: how was he able to put his hands on it so smartly? And how, anyway, did he know it was there in the first place? Once again I have the distinct sense that I am not being told all there is to tell.

What can Petra have made of it? For she's bound to have read it, since on her insistence and against official mutterings—I would remind you that the construction of the vault was paid for out of the public purse—it was she alone who catalogued her father's papers, with selfless application and spurning all offers of professional assistance or advice. Was she shocked by what she read? No doubt she had already read the same or worse in the course of her labours—but no, there could be no same, this one is one of a kind, I'm sure of it. Children find both preposterous and repugnant the notion that their parents could once have loved, wooed, desired as they do, but it's a question if Petra was ever a child, in the commonly accepted sense of that supposedly unambiguous word. She may have been tolerant of, may even, for all I know, have been moved by, this anguished record of her father's final *amour fou*. She may have been jealous, too. From what I've heard of that singular young woman I think it more than likely she was a little in love herself with her unlovable papa. And did she think herself displaced when she learned from this document I am holding, atremble in my trembling hands, that in the girl in Venice he had found, or believed he had found, or yearned to think he had found, one who was possessed of a sensibility as congenial to him as that of his daughter?

Which reminds me, I promised to tell you of the sighting I had of her, of Petra, the other day. Yes, really. She appeared on the main staircase, the one with the exquisitely carved and curved twin banister rails that lead up from the front hall to the first-floor landing. One moment there was nothing, the next she was suddenly there, descending in a flurry of quick little soundless steps. But wait, I must go carefully here. When I say she appeared, I'm

using the word in a special sense, hard to define. There was nothing otherworldly in her aspect—I wasn't Hamlet and she wasn't
Hamlet's father's ghost. All I know of Petra is her image in a few
blurred photographs, in every one of which she shies from the
camera with a harried, pained, and pitiable grimace, yet when I
saw her hurrying down those steps there was no mistaking her.
It was twilight, that dimmening yet delicately lustrous hour so
favoured by ghosts and goblins of all hues and none. I was on my
way up to visit the Dowager Godley—I live in expectation of the
day when the fog will clear from her frenzied brain and she will
spill at last the bushel of beans I know she must be hoarding—and
had placed my foot on the first step when I happened to glance
upwards and—

And what? There is a term for the state between being and not-
being. Liminal? That's not quite it, but it will have to do. Think of
a moment at morning offshore when a calm white sea merges at
its limit with a whitening sky and the horizon fades and the world
becomes the seamless inside of the shell of a great pale featureless
sphere. Think of a thought lying upon a thought like a wolf on
the string of a viol. Think of a figure seen, unseen, and seen again
and then again unseen amid flying shreds of smoke. Think of a
pure white bird suspended against a looming thunder-head then
drifting across a rip in the clouds and merging into light and van-
ishing. Or think how strangers appear in your dreams, unsurprised
and quite at home as they go about their unfathomable business.
There she was, halfway down, a presence and yet not, a girl in
black, so slight, so frail, with her white face and white hands, and
her arms the white undersides of which were criss-crossed with
scars like glistening smears of candle grease. She didn't look at me
or acknowledge me as she went by, in fact I don't think she was
aware of me at all—surely to the dead we would be as insubstantial as they are to us. She seemed preoccupied yet purposeful, as

though she were on her way to somewhere particular, to do some particular thing. I turned to watch her. She passed fleetly along the hall to the front door—why was it wide open?—and stepped out into the evening, a shadow merging into shadows, and was gone. Oh, I know, I know, she was only there because I conjured her, yet how real she seemed, a quick plain presence summoned into life by the force of my imagining.

I can't but wonder if Petra wasn't in Adam Godley's mind when he drafted this cry of love and loss to the person he addresses only as Cissy. I don't claim he harboured carnal longings for his daughter—a possibility from which the speculating mind quickly averts itself—but what is grief if not a form of desire? And he must have grieved for his poor mooncalf in her madness. Anyway, who's to know the nature of his relations with the girl in Venice. There may have been no relations at all, not to speak of, or speculate upon, I mean relations of the flesh. But he couldn't be so blind as not to see an echo, nay, a very replica, of Petra, his own wounded girl, blood of his blood, in the poor lost waif in whose faltering wake he trailed for days and nights through the city's stagnant and deserted labyrinth. Petra was for him his own image in a splintered glass. For all that she was mad, he claimed she was the only one, perhaps the one in all the world, who understood him completely, who understood, that is, not only what he was—his character, his personality, if he could be said to have been possessed of such a thing—but also the profoundest implications of his work. It is unlikely, to be sure. But what did he mean, exactly, when he said she understood him? It may be that he believed she had, not an understanding proper, but a deep intuitive grasp of what he was and the weight and moment of all he had achieved. He acknowledged the rôle intuition had played in the formulation of his most daring hypotheses—"First I dream, then I think," as he famously said, with one eye, no, with both eyes, fixed, and firmly, on posterity—and may have seen in his daughter a damaged prodigy capable of grasping at a glance concepts that even yet are beyond the ken of many of what I am assured are the great minds of the age. Or maybe he imagined her afflictions would abate in time and that one day she would rise up and be the true keeper of the flame, the guardian of the shrine. No limit to the illusions a fond father will indulge in. Good thing he didn't live to see her die.

That wide-open doorway through which she passed, it troubles me, don't ask me why. Something from somewhere else, some echo. Can't think what.

Now here is a strange, not to say a shocking, thing. When I began to read his testament, my eyes out on stalks, for all I tried I couldn't fend off the thought that the man who wrote it might have been human after all, and as capable as any of us of love and suffering and heartfelt lament. You remember how in my early delvings in the vault I came upon another sheet of graph paper with a stain on it which I mistakenly took for a spot of Godley's blood? Well, here was a haemorrhage, the copiousness of which might well require me, the biographer, to re-evaluate him, my subject, at the most radical levels. It was a dismaying prospect. Could I have been wrong about him from the start? Had my prejudice against him deceived me into making him into a monster? For I know there are no monsters. In even the worst of us there's a chink through which the blameless and frightened child peeps out, I know that.

So I must examine my conscience, I must make a reckoning. When was it I began to think him entirely a base rascal, a straw man, a pack of lies? I could say he had the reputation for scoundrelry, known to all. But I had been commissioned by his son to recount faithfully his life story and celebrate his triumphs with moderation—warts and all, remember? Was I to take hearsay for my source, form my judgements on tittle-tattle? Whatever I have said already, let me say this now, that I knew next to nothing of the man, had cared little for or held little against him except my prejudices, until the morning I arrived at Arden and beheld his daughter-in-law up there on the front step in her blue dress with bluebells in her hand, and became at once as a fine-spun glass on the rim of which a wetted fingertip—hers!—would produce sustained upon sustained, exquisitely agonised notes. But why must he be hateful, for her to be loved? On what amatory scales was he to be weighed and found wanting? It makes no sense, no sense at all. And yet for me she was the light that cast him into shadow.

What would he think, I wonder, if he could know that I've read his tormented screed, that I hold it here in my hands, that I have it, so to say, at my mercy. Yet what did he expect when he sat down to write it? Words are stubborn, and will insist on having their say, and on saying it again and again, until the ink fades and the paper and the hand that wrote on it have crumbled to dust. He wanted it read, he must have. And he must have known someone just like me would light on it one day and rush out into the street waving it above his head and shouting.

Yes, I'm troubled. These elaborate coincidences in which I find myself entangled in these apocalyptic yet increasingly inertial post-Godley days, they make me suspicious. They give me at times the fearful sense that what I and everyone else take to be reality is in reality no more than the jumbled fragments of a shattered frieze behind which an altogether other order of things is serenely and immovably fixed, and of which on occasion the world, the metaworld, slyly grants a tantalising glimpse. But no, no, I dismiss all such trite Platonic formulations. Despite the assurances of those who are said to know about these things, in my heart I've never been wholly persuaded—have you?—that a handful of equations dreamed up in a sweat of one man's speculations can have begotten the phenomena that are eating away at the fabric of the world. Things, I am convinced, things are infinitely simpler than Godley's nonsensical premises would have them be. I am, I say it stoutly, an unregenerate stone-kicker.

But come here to me now and listen to this.

My dearest Girl, why should I not be mad? The devil knows I have the disposition for it, and years enough, tho' already in my younger time they told me I was mad, with my fantastical fancies of how the world works, in the great measure and the small, that ran against all sense. But I knew better, and so did you, that snowy afternoon we stood together on the little bridge over the scarab-green canal, you sheltering warm as a linnet under the wing of my great cloak and I lost in love for you, and through you for all things in creation. The Giudecca, was it, or Dorsoduro? I forget. Ah, my brain is addled, sunk as I am in the mire of old age and dull decrepitude. Though I knew nothing of you, not so much as your name, in some magic way it was your call I clearly heard when the postman's bugle sounded its clarion note below the Sky Room here at Arden, and your tone I recognised when they carried your letter to me up the winding stair of the tower on a little silver tray and it spoke to me in a voice like the voice of the wind. All lovers lying in one another's arms are dwellers in two states, his and hers, hers and his, the same and yet unlike as are even the likest twins. I never was your lover nor you mine, not in the common way, yet I held you somehow, and hold you still, in an indissoluble embrace. What a mismatch we were, you hardly more than a child and I a fond old fool. It was between us a thing of the mind, of the heart, of the blood. And why were you set on Venice, of all places, in that harsh season of plague? You had been in the Low Countries, why did you not summon me there? I would have gone to you wherever you were. The doctors bade me not to travel, but when have I ever bent to the bidding of a sawbones? And I was guilty of an untruth for your sake, I who on principle will not lie, no, not even to spare another's pain. What matter was it to me if the woman should feel the hurt of my absence? She has felt that lash often enough, and her hide should be well hardened to it by now. But I did not tell her of you, and therein lay the falsehood, the one I fear was to taint all that followed.

So the opening canticle of Adam Godley's *testamentum de profundis*. You can imagine the tumult of mind it set up in me when I read it first.

Don't you like the man's panache, though, his sheer brazenness, in saying so airily that he wouldn't lie to spare the pain of another, and on principle, at that. Principle! Why, the paragraph in which he makes the claim is crawling with falsehoods, to use his high-sounding term. Let me say at once I'm not averse to the lie, when it serves to oil the grinding wheels of life's machinery. But that kind of lie has a practical aim, whereas, so far as I can see, Godley lied to no purpose other than his own amusement. Item: it was he, and not "Cissy," who suggested they should meet in Venice, as he lets slip later on in a moment of inattention. Why the needless fib, which even for one with his warped idea of fun can hardly have been high in entertainment value? Aren't we reminded of how he lied to his first wife about his encounter in Arcady with Anna Behrens, needlessly and to no purpose? Well, one must just think of it, I suppose, as a grace note on a smoothly flowing melody, executed with a twiddle of the virtuoso's agile little finger.

Note that candour in him was a mode of obfuscation. By admitting at the outset to having lied by omission to his wife about the girl in Venice, he aimed to neutralise the tissue of lies that was to follow. Oh, he was a past master in the art of duplicity, there's no doubt of that. Yes yes, see how I've thrown off my doubts of a moment past and once again contemn him heartily as a fibber and a fraud. That's a relief.

As it happened, he had been contemplating a visit, the final one, surely, to La Serenissima, as its smug inhabitants like to call their city, which pet name every time he heard it made him curl his lip in contempt. He hadn't been there for many years. The last time was towards the end of the aimless wanderings he had embarked on following the death of his first wife, and given that circumstance, it was a less than happy stay. Wintertime then, too, with snow in St. Mark's Square and hoarfrost glittering on the dome of the basilica of Santa Maria della Salute and the canals aswarm with chill and pestilential fumes and fogs. Why would he think to go back there now, at the close of his days? He couldn't properly have said, he says, only there was the general sense of lapsing, of things ending up, and some primordial part of him yearned for the waters of oblivion, and where better to take them than in the sinking city on the lagoon.

Then, fortuitously, came the letter. If it existed and Cissy did write it, as he says she did, it hasn't survived, though that proves nothing. He would have thrown it away, having no use for keepsakes and despising those who did. She was

I pause. I falter. I take a deep breath, another, and another, each one feels like a step, a deep step I must effortfully climb. Dear me. I'm not myself, that's a fact, I'm not myself at all just at the minute. Mind you, when am I ever myself? When has anyone ever been anyone's self?

I must stop. Or no I mustn't, I must keep on. But I have such an ache in my heaving chest—breathing will be the death of me. Flaubert's mother said of her son that he had squandered his life on a mania for phrases. Or words to that effect. *Flaubert, c'est moi.* Except in my case it's not phrases but facts, or facts set in phrases. What else could I have done with my allotted time? Facts, so described, are the tintacks that hold a life in place, the shape of it I mean. Godley's life; my life; yours. But still I ask, what is a fact, exactly? A thing to nail down truth? Ah, truth, now. Bring me jug and basin that I may wash my hands of it.

I say again, I shouldn't have replied to Godley's son, shouldn't have answered his summons to New Ams, above all I should never have let myself come and live here and be foolishly ardent in Arden.

My heart, poor overworked ticker, has been delivered an awful shock.

She will not have me but would another, it seems, or no seems about it, she has had, did have, was had by. And what an other. I might have expected it, it or something like it—though what like of it could there be?

My love for her at first was made in her own image, a big rangy girl with a casque of blonde hair and a sulky mouth, smelling of summer and sweat. And now? Now all is changed, at one blow. Now it's shrivelled and small, what's left of my love, small and shrivelled like a tiny saint miraculously preserved with gloved hands joined and laid behind glass under an Italian altar. Well, a love embalmed is still love, and still can cause the heart to ache. But who'd have imagined I would prove so fickle, I who thought to have found at last the love of my life? I don't know myself, I don't know what I feel; only it hurts.

It was Duffy who spied her, coming out at the back door of the cottage and hurrying off to the Big House. Bold as brass, she was, according to Ivy, and smoking a cigarette, if you don't mind. Poor Ivy, she had to tell me what Duffy told her, when she came up with my lunch, she couldn't keep it to herself a second longer. I don't blame her, how could she not blab. I'm sure my face gave me away, it always does. Dear me, here's a new way to be in pain.

Boohoo, O, boohoo.

I knew it, there is some nasty little god hanging about in these parts, toying with his wand and whistling out of the side of his mouth, delighted at my undoing. They can't bear things to go well for us, can't abide even our most muted jubilations, and so we suffer at their meddling hands.

Think of something else. Dwell on facts, Gustave, *mon semblable,* facts, the best diverters, best sustainers. Doesn't matter a damn what they are or aren't, they'll do, for now. And if they're not the facts themselves but only interpretations? Well, what if they are, or aren't.

Oh, the jaws that bite, the claws that catch!

Go on, go on, steadfast in the face of all calamity.

Why him, of all people? Why him. Foul usurper!

Back to work, back to work.

Here's my nose, there's the grindstone.

I have been through this wretched, what to call it, this wretched "letter" of Godley's three times by now, or is it four, interrogating it more closely at each go-round, and I am bound to report my misgivings, my more than misgivings, as to its authenticity. There is for a start the eerie familiarity of the tale it tells, both in the lines and between them. It really is very strange, and I can't explain it. I'm like a traveller on a high Alpine pass emerging suddenly from the mist and seeing in the valley below, to his surprise and consternation, not another but the same village he set out from a few hours previously, the same or improbably similar, with the same little church quaint as a cuckoo clock, and the rutted snow on the same steep main street, and the same skiers zipping at a crouch between identical black pines down the mountain slopes behind. I feel tricked and betrayed, but I'm not sure how, or why, or by whom, exactly. It seems I am myself part of the charade, and in some way a guilty party, if only by association, or do I mean example. For it's plain that Adam Godley was familiar with my monograph on Axel Vander and his exploits, knew a particular section of it inside out, and took it as a model for his own—what? his own what? How am I to characterise this overheated screed, this so-called Venetian Testament? So-called by me, I'm embarrassed to remind you; that title, at once portentous and vapid, now makes me blush.

But how to begin to say, with any conviction, any assurance, what the thing is? Is it a fiction, a fantasy, the record of a dream? Was it written for the writer's own diversion, to tickle his perverse fondness for the incongruous and the inappropriate, or had he a darker purpose in mind? It smells of contrivance, and I have to wonder if it is not part of a conspiracy against me—yes, me—the dimensions of which I can't begin to guess at. Could it be a forgery? It seems to be Godley's handwriting, but handwriting can be faked, and I'm no graphologist. Do I detect the mark of B. J. Grace, or the lamentable Pavel Popov, or some other, unknown, deceitful fox? But no, Popov would be too timid to involve himself in such a bold deception, and too dim-witted besides; Benny Grace, though—it's just the kind of spiteful jape the egregious Benny would delight in. I've had the feeling, ever since I came here to Arden, that there are forces at work behind the scenes to thwart and deceive me and lure me into making a fool of myself and appearing a public disgrace. Am I being toyed with? Am I the fall guy, the patsy, the mark? Is it all a hoax, a booby trap that will explode under my feet and send me shooting into the air like a skyrocket, arms flailing and my hair on fire? If so, who is the joker, and why the joke?

I felt the first stab of doubt when Adam Godley told me of the driver fellow being there in the Library when he came out of the vault with the bundle of graph paper in his hands. It wasn't that I cared that the security of the vault might be compromised—as if I would—but the thought of that fellow looming there cast a shadow on the thing, made a smudge on its pages, impressed a blurry watermark that would not be washed out. But I ignored my suspicions, and let the excitement of the moment smother them. Strange, these premonitory shivers I am prone to. I must be extra susceptible to the hidden human strain in the run of things. My first glimpse of Helen turned me instantly and inexplicably against old Godley, and the mere presence of Mordaunt the Maniac now seems the forewarning which had I heeded it would have dashed the scales from my eyes long before now. I would be wise to attend more sharply to my inner divining rod. But that's me all over, rash and impulsive to the last. And fearful as well, of course, mustn't overlook the *pusillanimitas*.

If it was Godley and not some interfering imp who drew up this document, he brought extraordinary effort and energy to the project. He devised for it a style, archaic, ornate, declamatory, that is utterly unlike the ironical, icy-cool voice he speaks in elsewhere in his writings, and that sounds throughout like a broad parody of itself. *Tho' in my younger time? My great cloak? Its clarion note? An indissoluble embrace?* Can't you just see the glister of a fool's golden and utterly false dawn?

The narrative he forges—now there's a suggestive word—reflects certain passages of my Vander monograph so closely as to be their mirror image. But how can this be? and why? Is it possible he knew I was the one his son would commission to write his biography? Maybe I was his own choice, maybe he directed in his will that I alone of all the other possible and possibly better equipped candidates should be engaged for the task. But why would he have chosen me? He couldn't have remembered our edgy encounter in

Arcady all those years ago—could he? And even if he had, am I to think the recollection of that moment of passing *froideur* would have swayed him in the choice of a biographer? Above all, why would he go to the trouble of writing, by hand, a thirteen-page text, no, a twenty-six-page double-sided text, on the chance, *primus,* that his son would obey his directive and secure me as his official biographer, and *secundus,* that I would come to Arden and find the letter in the vault and accept it as genuine? No, it's all just too far-fetched, really, it is.

And yet, and yet. In the "Shroud" chapter of *The Invention of the Past* I relate the circumstances of Axel Vander's highly questionable involvement in Italy with a young woman in what would turn out to be the last weeks of her life. She, Catherine Cleave, had been in Antwerp, or Ghent, or Bruges, one of those ludicrously picturesque cities invented by the old masters, doing some kind of study of Vander's work—she was a genuine if eccentric scholar, and as crazy on occasion as Godley's daughter was from start to finish—and had written to him requesting an interview, in order to consult him, the original source, in connection with certain aspects of her research. Vander was settled in Turin at the time, lying low after a lifetime of malefaction, and it was to there that she travelled to meet him, and entered with him on a fatal dalliance. They were together in the city for some weeks, she quizzing him on his crackpot deconstructionist theories, we presume, and sleeping with him besides, or being slept with by him. It's a lurid tale, as tragic as it is sordid, and why Adam Godley chose to ape it in his own fanciful *Liebestodlied* is a mystery beyond my solving.

Cass Cleave was a turbulent soul in sore need of guidance through the maze that was her life, though every thread she followed landed her bang in the lap of the Minotaur. She was the daughter of an actor, and this heritage was I imagine part of her trouble; look at my Helen, she's hardly a model of balance and serenity. Vander treated the poor girl, his Cissy, his C.C., appallingly, moving between smiling contempt and a kind of distracted voraciousness; she felt, she wrote in her journal—there's a testament for you, heartbreaking in its disorder and desolation—that she was being consumed, literally so, that she was being eaten alive by some creature of the jungle. At last she broke free and fled, only to end up smashed to bits at the foot of a rocky promontory in one of those pretty little towns that sit so delightfully along the delightful Ligurian coast.

In Adam Godley's version, which must be, has to be, adapted from mine, his Cissy writes to him in secret, and arranges to come to him in Venice and in her turn be saved by him from her demon lover. Saved? Talk about the frying pan and the fire! All this if we are speaking of the same girl, which we seem to be, he seems to be. Godley and Axel Vander knew each other, they had been in Arcady at the same time and moved in some of the same circles, so why does he not mention him?

Godley had been in Switzerland, saying a not particularly fond farewell to another casualty of the Brahma theory, the Large Hadron Collider—I wonder if previously there was a small one, that grew—before it was shut down and its vast underground network of tunnels and testing rooms flooded with water from Lake Geneva, which famously caused the lake's level to fall by half a foot. He made the side trip to Venice on his way home, whether by a prior plan or in response to Cissy's supposed letter we cannot say; yes, he says he was obeying her summons, but later he contradicts himself, so the question remains open, as do so many others like it. He was installed in a grand hotel on the Canal Grande, hard by St. Mark's. The Palazzo Inverno was the former home and frequent refuge of a northern branch of the Gannaro, the centuries-old Roman family of shady bankers, picture smugglers, and professional assassins, not the least of whose misdeeds was the generation of Eduardo Gannaro, last of his line, of Gannaro Gallery fame and infamy. It was at the Hotel Inverno that my wife Martha and I once stayed, in the time when our marital enshacklement was coming to its messy end. I was drunk for a lot of the time in those days, which I'm sure is why I mixed up the word Inverno with Inferno, and made a fool of myself by complaining to the manager that the establishment was ill-named since our room was hellishly cold. I sometimes think my life in total has been no more than a linked series of mishearings and misapprehensions and the awkward scrapes consequent upon them.

Godley had wired ahead and reserved a luxury suite on the *piano nobile,* overlooking the canal. It was on the same floor that Martha and I had stayed, in a cramped corner room where we were tormented all day and half the night by the avian cries of gondoliers, the slap and chug of the vaporetti toing and froing, and the penitential shuffling of the milliards of tourists' feet along the quayside and in and out of the warren of *calli, callette,* and *calleselle* in the midst of which the hotel squats, at a slight list, like the hulk of a vast and fantastically ornate Venetian man-o'-war. In the "letter"—but I may as well drop the quotation marks, those wings in want of a tiny Fra Angelico angel—he speaks of how on the afternoon of his arrival he stepped out on to the balcony, under a bitter blue sky, and was on the spot transported back to earliest childhood by the sight of a slab of glistening snow on the broad stone parapet. "In the wintertime at my boyish games," he writes, "I would scoop up a wedge of icy snow and put it between two wafers of slate for a make-believe ice cream. I was forever imitating the children of the country folk at their play, you know. There I found the authentic note, the autochthonous real." Aye, he was a great one for the autochthons.

What did they get up to together, he and his girl, in their winter palace on the water, in those enormous cold damp rooms? The letter is rich in detail, at times insanely so, but not in the matter of passions, since as far as that goes it could have been penned by a clergyman's virginal daughter around the time of the Peninsular War. We do hear a lot about the weather. The Inverno's heating system, a misnomer if ever there was one, to which I can personally attest, produced on the days when it was working a fitful glimmer that served only to create a mist that hung in the corridors and reception rooms like so many hanging layers of finely beaded lace. Cissy complained, said she couldn't get warm. She wore gloves and sat on the bed with her arms wrapped round her knees, rocking herself back and forth, back and forth, until Godley lost patience and snapped at her, saying she looked exactly like the plaster saint on one of those collection boxes for the poor that nodded its head in metronomic thanks when a penny was pushed through the slot. Many images like this rise up out of the past, so much so that he accuses her of trying to make him into a child again in his old age. Her passiveness both soothes and infuriates him, until it comes to him that she's not passive at all, but coiled inside herself, waiting. Yet waiting for what?

"You're mad," he shouts at her, "mad as the moon!"

As if that were news to her.

She tells him how she has always liked the idea of entropy, of everything becoming more mixed up and more uncertain until in the end there will be no order to things at all. She would be content in a world at its extreme. He says she knows nothing about these things, nothing! And he utters his cold laugh.

They walk together at twilight through the narrow, echoing streets, under the steep walls with their barred windows set high up; they stroll along the quays, cross and re-cross the humped bridges that look to Cissy, she says, like baroque toys. The city is deserted, emptied of tourists and natives alike by a deadly blight that in the early autumn had swept northwards along the coast and lodged in the moist groin of the Adriatic and spread a poisonous pall over the lagoon; there have been many deaths, how many exactly the authorities refuse to say. She links her arm in his, burrows her gloved hand deep into the pocket of his overcoat. The street lamps are greyly aglow, like rows of dandelion heads. Underfoot the flagstones are slimed with damp, and once, under the arcades in the big square, where it's dim, he stumbled and almost fell, would have fallen, had she not been there for him to hold on to, his saving staff, his staff of life.

"How trite it would be to die here," he says, and laughs again. "The papers would have a field day."

She draws his elbow so tightly to her that he can feel her ribs. She laughs too.

All this laughing, what is it for? So many people strove to know him, he says, so many, pressing forward with their fingers hooked into claws, grinning and spraying him with spittle, while all the time there was nothing to know, nothing to discover. He is as much a cipher to himself as he was and is to them.

They dined at a restaurant on the Rio Carampane. Sea urchins and salt cod, and some sort of red wine chosen at random that turned out to be served chilled, to his annoyance. Cissy ate little, and he ate most of what she left, reaching over with his fork and spearing up choices tidbits from her plate and flicking them into his mouth. He grinned as he chewed, and she could see wet grey wads of the fish's crumbly flesh between his teeth and rolling on his tongue. She fumbled her glass and wine splashed on the tablecloth, and the perfect outline of a man's hand with fingers splayed developed itself, a ghostly pink negative, on the heavy white linen. They sat silent, staring at it; he said it was a good omen, a sign of good fortune, any Italian would tell you that; but she knew better. Godley summoned the waiter, who said with arch dismissiveness that the signore must have pressed his hand there and left a mark with his *sudore*—"your sweat, signore, you understand?"— and demonstrated by placing his own hand over the handprint.

After that, Godley sulked. He did not care to be explained to, by anyone, about anything. She laughed and said he looked exactly like Velázquez's Pope Innocent X, with his cocked demonic eyebrows and scraggly beard and long thick nose. He bet her the price of their meal she couldn't tell him what Pope Innocent's name was before he became pope. "You should know," he said, "you study these things." But she didn't know. "Giovanni Battista Pamphili!" he crowed, sitting back on his chair and smirking. "Pamphili the scourge of the Jansenists. Call yourself a scholar? You're a little ignoramus."

She drew down her head and tucked in her chin and looked up at him solemnly. He folded his arms on the table and leaned on them, his bony shoulders hunched higher than his ears. He looked like a chimpanzee, she told him, a sag-eyed hairy old chimp.

"Pope Pan Pantocrator!" he said, with dark delight.

Silence then in the silent room. He drummed his fingers on the table and looked about at the empty tables. I am become death, destroyer of worlds.

"I knew you'd know a wonderful little place like this," she said disparagingly. "It's so *authentic,* so *exclusive.*" He picked up her hand from where it rested on the table and turned it this way and that, peering at it, as if it were something he was in mind to eat. "You're such a show-off," she said.

"Speaking of show-offs, your father is an actor, didn't you say? Yes. I like actors, their pathos and vulnerability. They do such a good job of protecting us from having to admit we are ourselves, all of us, all acting."

"You should hear yourself, honestly."

The plates were cleared and they drank thimblefuls of coffee black as boots and fiery, straw-coloured grappa from little pot-bellied glasses. There was no one in the place but them. They talked of scabs. In the old and heedless days, when children still played outdoors in places where there were stones and thorns, everyone had scabs, so Godley writes—we're still poring over his letter, remember, sceptical and agog. At first, when the scab has just formed, it's extremely delicate, and will bleed at the slightest exploratory poke or prod. Cuts formed a single scab, but scratches, especially a scratch from a briar, left a long, dark-red ellipsis, like a string of tiny rubies. The bigger scabs, when they had dried and hardened, were the colour of not-quite-ripe blackberries, and had the same dull gleam, and their surface had something of the same bumpy warm firm feel. They were cared for and guarded, and at least once a day were prised up at one edge with a fingernail, gingerly, and only by a fraction, to test the level of resistance still remaining. A little sharp sting was a warning that they weren't mature yet. Came the day, however, when the whole crust could be lifted all the way up, like the lid of a miniature jewel box, slowly and with a held breath. There was always a sticky spot where they stubbornly clung on, or were stubbornly clung on to, necessitating a pause for reflection, after which the operation would be resumed with a firmer, more confident, action, and all at once the carapace would come away, intact and light as a flake of dried blackberry jam, and the last spot of adherence would give way with what felt like a tiny kiss in reverse, and there, exposed at last, would be the patch of unreally new and tender skin, fresh and brittle and shiny as a dragonfly's wing.

It was late when they rose from the table. Godley again had a moment of giddiness, and did a tottery quick little shuffling side-step. This time when she offered to help him he knocked her hand aside angrily and righted himself. They went out into the mist and dark, befuddled, their faces stiff and their foreheads hot. Below the bridges, vague patches of fog moved on the greasy water. From somewhere far off there came a sudden cry, of surprise or fright or both, which from another quarter was answered, it seemed an answer, by a bark of laughter, high-pitched, stridulent, and quickly cut off, as if by a slap. At every corner, in the shadows, rats cavorted freely; it was said the city's cats had proved susceptible to the plague and all had perished, them and their owners alike.

"To be alive in the midst of so much death!" old Adam said gleefully, wheezing, and reached into his pocket for her ungloved fish-cold hand and pressed it hard. "Us two."

At the hotel they went to the bar and sat at a low table in dim lamplight. No one was there except the barman. He was elderly, and bore a marked resemblance to one of the Caesars, with a big unsmiling face that seemed made out of pumice and a bald skull pitted like the moon. He wore a grubby white jacket buttoned tightly all the way up to the Adam's apple. He served them coffee—Godley said he surely would not sleep this night—with little squat tumblers of water on the side. They felt the emptiness of the hotel pressing upon them; now and then the entire building seemed to heave a great soft weary commingled sigh. I should like to know what kind of dress Cissy was wearing, how her hair was arranged, what shoes she had on. I can't see her, and so of course I see instead the ghost of Petra, as she was that day when she hurried down the stairs and flitted past me, all in black, with her stark white face and the scars on her arms and that air of being about some urgent business.

In the lamplight, the water in their glasses had a strange metallic shine, like the shine the air takes on before a thunderstorm.

Did they share a room? More to the point, did they share a bed? He doesn't say. I note that he remarks her legs. They are tapered nicely, and a little bowed, and the two big toes are hooked like thumbs. He likens them to the zinc-white limbs of one of Cranach the Elder's stylised Eves. So perhaps he saw her naked, or nearly so. Or perhaps not. A man can figure a woman's leg entire, all the way up, from no more than the glimpse of an ankle.

They left their coffee undrunk and climbed the broad marble staircase in a tipsy silence, her hand again in his. Her hands are always cold, cold and coldly damp, and so thin he can feel distinctly the shape of each frail bone. They were tired after the long day, and said goodnight in the corridor outside their rooms. What must they have been thinking. They had intended to make a trip next day to Poveglia, but all the ferries had been cancelled, and anyway no ferry served that island of the sick and mad, abandoned now as it is. They would walk over to the Accademia instead, he told her, and see Bellini's painting of the Virgin of the Sidelong Look, disenchanted in her dark-blue mantle and flanked by two small and wonderfully airy trees, her Christ child with sausage curls and sunken eyes leaning against her casual as a corner boy. But Cissy said he could go on his own, that she didn't want to see any pictures. Her mood had turned sullen, or perhaps it just seemed so because she was tired and had drunk too much. She slipped into her room and shut the door in his face, but not with force. No, not with force.

At some late hour he heard a distant sobbing, and went to look for her and found her huddled at the foot of the marble stairs they had ascended earlier. Her arms were folded on her knees and her forehead rested on her arms. He sat beside her and embraced her and said nothing and let her weep. He looked about, wondering, not for the first time, why the steps of these old staircases should be so shallow, so shallow and so deep. Great heights above, Piranesian glooms of stillness and stagnant air; he has a sense of the limitless. His backside is cold from the stone step where he sits. The girl's shoulders shake within his enfolding arm. There there, he murmurs absently. There there. A girl weeping in the night is nothing new to him.

The next day, or the day after, she fell ill. At first there was only a slight feverishness, but within hours she was burning up and shivering, and vomited repeatedly. She had an attack of diarrhoea, too. She was so weak he had to carry her into the bathroom and wait while she voided herself, groaning, with her face in her hands. He had to wipe her bum, too, and cleaned her as best he could and carried her back to her bed. The room with its weak lamp light seemed to expand around him. She wouldn't speak, refusing his increasingly urgent interrogations, shaking her head and turning her face away. She lay under the sheet with her knees bent and her cheek resting on her joined hands, gazing before her out of eyes suddenly grown huge. He sat by her, or else he paced the floor, helpless and annoyed. He had food brought up, soup and bread, and urged her to eat but she turned on to her other side to face the wall. This went on through a morning and an afternoon and into the night. He grew alarmed. He felt what felt like a lover's desperation. What if she were to die?

He went in search of help. The reception desk was deserted. A lamp with a green glass shade, its bulb buzzing, diffused a sinister glow. He had thought of packing his bag and fleeing, or not even packing, of just putting a handful of banknotes on the desk and hurrying off into the night, leaving the girl to recover as best she might, but he knew he couldn't. He banged on the bell with the flat of his hand, once, twice, three times, creating a brassy echo, but no one came. He went into the bar. The barman was there, looking more than ever like Caesar Augustus, seated massively on a stool at the end of the bar, reading the *Gazzetta dello Sport*. He lifted his stony face and regarded with majestic indifference the agitated guest before him.

"The girl is sick," Godley told him, *"molto malata,* you must call a doctor." He used to know Italian, but no more. The man made no reply, only went on gazing up at him without expression, a finger marking his place on the page. *"Un dottore,"* Godley said, floundering, *"un dottore,* for the—for the *puella,* I mean the *signorina.* Please." At last, frowning, the man put the paper aside and rose and walked away with stately tread. After him, the stillness reasserted itself. The only sound to be heard was the faint buzzing of the lamp on the reception desk outside.

After some time the manager came, looking harassed and cross. He had a thin moustache and sharp little eyes as shiny and black as chips of coal. He clutched a table napkin and sucked his teeth at the side; he must have been at his dinner. At first he misunderstood, and thought Godley himself was claiming to be sick, and looked him up and down with a sceptical eye.

"No," Godley, exasperated, said, "no, it's the girl, the girl is sick. *La signorina.* She must have a doctor."

The manager shook his head and muttered something under his breath. He noticed the napkin he was holding, and tried to stuff it into a trouser pocket.

"Is very late," he said.

"She's very sick."

He felt tired, tired and suddenly old. He must have wondered what he was doing there, in an empty hotel in a deserted city on a stagnant lagoon.

The doctor when he arrived was tall and stooped, with a long moist face and a grizzled beard, neatly trimmed. His suit looked to be a size too big for him, and hung about his bony frame like so many drapes of loosened swaddling cloth. He exuded a faint sharp vinegary smell. There was something not right about him, something troubled and illicit. A damaged man, nursing an obscure hurt. Struck off, perhaps, because of drink, or malpractice, working at night here for a pittance, sleeping by day in a room over a shop, cadging drinks and scraps from the counter, gnawing at his failures. Godley saw how alike they must look, the two of them—the same stoop, the same gaunt features, the same pointed beard—and was vaguely dismayed. He felt like a character in a stage farce brought up short in front of his double; he could almost hear the hoots of laughter from beyond the footlights. He saw the doctor too seeing the resemblance. They plodded side by side in awkward silence up the broad staircase, like a pair of long-lost brothers unwillingly reunited by mischance.

In the room with its shaded lamps they stood at the bedside and looked down at the sick girl where she lay on her back with her arms resting on the sheet and her hands clasped on her breast, as if she were at prayer. She gazed back at them in silence, out of her seal's eyes. The doctor leaned forward and felt her forehead, and drew down the lower lids of one of her eyes, and sniffed her breath. Godley had noticed his slender, dark-brown hands, the hands of the man he had once been, long ago. He turned to Godley.

"Non è la peste," he said. "Not the plague—you understand?"

Godley was startled. The possibility hadn't occurred to him.

Now the doctor sat down on the side of the bed and spoke quietly to the girl, asking her something in Italian. She nodded, and he smiled, and he nodded too. Godley stepped back, out of the cocoon of intimacy in which the two had become enveloped. Strange, that thing that happens between doctor and patient. He walked to the window and stood looking out. In the smoky darkness a dull gleam of gold on water. Not a soul. One day soon I shall die, he thought, and felt nothing. Better off, perhaps. Get the whole thing over with, be nowhere—wasn't that what in his heart he had wished for all along? He turned and walked back to the bed.

The girl had a fever only, the doctor said, it wasn't serious, it would be gone in a day, two at most. When Godley tried to pay him he held up both palms and stepped back quickly and shook his head. He seemed to think Godley was the girl's grandfather, and found it nothing odd that the two should be together here, lodged at the Hotel Inverno in a time of plague.

They walked back down the staircase, again side by side, again unspeaking, solemn as undertakers. She would not die; no, she would not die.

When he returned to the room, Cissy was sitting up and

searching for something on the bedside table. She still had a hectic look, but she smiled at him and said she felt better. She said she had liked the doctor. Godley nodded. The community of the afflicted.

"He had been drinking," she said. "Did you notice?"

He told her she should sleep, but she shook her head. Her eyes burned with a fevered light.

That night they did share a bed, but he did not undress, and lay on top of the covers. He dozed fitfully. She talked in her sleep, twitching and sighing. Now and then a kind of ripple ran through her, he felt it, running from the back of her neck all the way down to her toes. She smelled of flowers left too long in a vase.

In the hotel doorway the doctor had paused. *"Lo sai che è incinta, sì?"* he said. "She is pregnant, you know?"

He didn't know. He hadn't known. Whose child? Not his— not his.

The doctor hurried away into the darkness and the fog, he might be a conspirator fleeing a failed coup, lean Cassius, his coat-tails flapping.

Now the night arrived at some significant hour and bells began tolling near and far. To his ear they were as the voices of town criers crying the news that the town was doomed, that its inhabitants must flee, that the Goths were at the gate.

Lying there on the bed in his clothes he drowsed and dozed, and dreamt of death and being dead, which was just darkness, or not even that; a nothing, a no thing, in a no where. *E basta!*

What did she want from him, what was she after? He didn't dare ask for fear she might tell him. Why had he agreed to meet her here in the first place? She had asked that he come, to come to her anywhere, to talk about he didn't know what. Her subject was art and artists, of which he knew little and cared less. Besides, she was so young—what was she, nineteen, twenty? And he was old, so old, with his stooped and scrawny frame, his rope-veined hands, his high forehead with its brownish shine and liver spots scaly and dry as lichen. There were moments when she looked at him and she too seemed old, as old as the city itself, older, but every female of any age was capable of that look, he knew that. And what of the way she turned up her hooded face to him and smiled that unaccountably complicit smile, when they heard the footsteps accompanying them in the little street behind the Salute—what of that?

It was the middle of the afternoon and already the day was fading, though the sky still shone lilac-white in the vaporous atmosphere. This was her first venture outdoors after her recovery, and she went along with careful, mincing steps, keeping close by his side. He had taken her across the canal on some pretext or other. His true aim, which he didn't divulge to her, was to find again the house he had come to on that other occasion after Dorothy died, on an afternoon much like this one. An undistinguished house, as he recalled, faded and shabby, beside a church on an anonymous street that was hardly more than a laneway. He could see in his mind the dirty-yellow stucco on the front wall, and big patches where it had fallen off to reveal the bricks and dusty mortar underneath. In a room in that house, on a high square bed, he had made love to a pale girl, and afterwards had wept in her arms and told her of Dorothy who had drowned herself a fortnight before.

But now of course he couldn't find the house. He was sure this was where it had stood. It must still be here—nothing gets knocked down in Venice—but where was it? He walked with the girl along the narrow street, he scanning the buildings and muttering to himself and the girl saying nothing, only clinging to him for fear of falling, so weak was she still, from the fever and the flux. She tried to link her arm in his but he jerked himself away and glared down at her sidelong, furious and fierce-eyed, and for a second it seemed he might strike her. The child, he was thinking of the child she was carrying. He was—dear God, he was jealous!

It began to snow, lightly and as if absentmindedly, the random flakes not so much falling as faltering in the unsustaining air. It was on their third or fourth go-round that he heard the footsteps. At first it seemed merely that the two of them had fallen out of step and were setting up a sort of syncopation, but no, someone, someone was walking with them, not behind or ahead or to this side or that but as if between them. He halted, and looked all about, but there was no one. It must be because of the snow, he thought, somehow the muffling effect of the snow must have set up an echo. He didn't believe it, but what else was he to think? That was when Cissy turned up her face, bone-grey and drawn in the waning light, and smiled at him in that strangely intimate, knowing way. What was it she was letting him know she knew? He couldn't ask, and wouldn't have asked even if he had been able.

"Come on!" he said roughly, and turned and stamped away, and heard her hurrying steps behind him and, again, also the steps of that ghostly other. His heart was pounding, and sweat ran into the corners of his eyes.

And yet, even as they seemed added to, he wondered, and we can't but wonder with him, if the girl was there at all, or was but another phantom treading at his heels. Was she, we ask again, merely—merely!—a projection of Petra, his daughter whose death did he but know it would follow hard on his own? Of late, his dreams had taken on a newly compelling quality, seemed more hallucination than dream, and he woke from them as if not to the waking world but into another kind of sleep. Was he dreaming the girl, was he dreaming he was with her, were they both dream selves in a dreamt city? Or was she something altogether other. Was she that *angelus novus* who all his life had stood full-square before him, with wide-swept wings, barring his way, the one who would not be struggled past or wrestled with or blessed into submission, the one whose wound he bore and which he would die of—was she that one, or its precursor? The angel it was had hindered him from the start, had made him doubt himself and the things he had to do, the things he knew must be done, the things he would do, and hang the consequences. Always it was there, the angel of failure, of mortality and perdition. The world thought him one of those high, cold heroes riding heedless past death and the devil, but ah, if the world only knew. And yet he did what he did, despite all. How? How in the end did he best the dauntless seraph? Has the girl come here to tell him the answer, or only to ask it in other ways? In other ways.

They stopped together on the humpbacked bridge, above the canal's listless, noisome drain, and she stepped close to him, into his distracted embrace. The snow fell in its hushed fashion. The lights were coming on, the little lights. He held her, and felt her shoulder blades flex under his hand like folded wings.

Afterwards, what everyone remembered was the tablecloths. In the back field, beyond the muddy lane and the rusty gate, on the grassy bank where the three beech trees afforded an expanse of smoke-blue shade, two long narrow trestle tables had been set up, with bolts of linen unrolled along them. The linen's whiteness glowed against the green all round like something remembered, something of happiness lost and never to be found again yet never forgotten. Since the tables were covered with platters of party food—Helen had outdone herself—the tablecloths were really only to be seen in the overhangs at the sides and at either end, reaching almost to the ground, and hiding the ugly metal framework of the trestles. To be admired in particular were the slender conical white flutes, suggestive of cloisters and cathedrals, that the linen formed at each of the four corners of each table. Now and then a warm breeze swooped down the hillside and stirred the cloths in quick succession, for the day was fresh and bright, and when they stirred, stirred and rippled all the way along their length, they seemed to be waltzing, or dreaming of waltzing, by themselves, languorously. They might have been having their own field day, ignoring the noisy guests milling around the place and keeping themselves to themselves, as adults at a picnic will benignly disregard the children in their midst, and fan their throats, and glance about, abstracted, and contentedly sighing. And the guests in their turn seemed oblivious of them, of the tablecloths, yet they all at one time or another found themselves running a hand over the cloth's bright cool crispness, and registering, for no good reason and almost without noticing it, the very texture of the past, the past that is irretrievable but at the same time somehow present, gone yet somehow here and now.

Can there be a genteel bacchanal? Let us see.

A great many people turned up, many more than had been invited, as Helen realised. It didn't matter. She cared little for any of them, invited or not; she had only wanted a crowd, to divert her and take her mind off things. No one had dared wish her a happy birthday.

The gatecrashers, once it was clear that they weren't going to be thrown out, mingled happily enough with the grander guests. These were most notably the fine folk from the other big houses roundabout, tweedy, red-faced men and their lean lady wives in thigh-length cardigans and flower-printed cotton frocks. There were well-to-do farmers, and land agents and auctioneers, and dealers in cattle and grain and farm machinery, and other such uninteresting types; they were Adam's people. Also in attendance were two solicitors, known to be fierce rivals, and two doctors, also rivalrous, Dr. Fortune, who was very old, and Dr. Somebody, whose name no one could remember, who was very young. The local eccentric was there, a wild-haired fellow in a hacking jacket and a clown's checked trousers that flapped comically about his knees as he scurried here and there, buttonholing anyone who seemed likely to listen to his excited jabberings. His face was fascinatingly scarred—shades of Gabriel Swan—for he was an inventor, self-styled, who one day had blown himself up in an experiment involving weedkiller, cane sugar, and hydrochloric acid. He had been seeking to produce a cheap alternative to the expensively processed sea water on which most vehicles run nowadays. Years hence, he will persuade Adam the Younger, no longer young by then, to finance the development and production of a gadget to eliminate the noxious element in the gaseous effusions of cattle; to the amazement of everyone, including both its sponsor and the mad scientist himself, the scheme will prove immensely profitable, so much so that, among other marvellous consequences—even the leaky roof at Arden will at last be fixed—Helen, with a hefty settlement from a judicial separation reluctantly agreed to by Adam the Broken-Hearted, will move to New Amsterdam and transform herself into one of the great hostesses of the age, overseeing a Thursday evening salon attended by the fabulously famous, including poets, painters, and illustrious men of letters, an institution that will become as grand and celebrated as any of its like in the glory days of Old New York. Life's nonsense pierces us with strange relation; doesn't it just.

On arrival at the field, everyone made straight for the tables, and the drink. There was sherry, wine and whiskey for the gentry, kegs of porter and bottles of ale for the others, and lemonade and orange pop for the children. It would be a lovely day, oh, for sure, a lovely day.

Helen, with my assistance, or connivance, if you prefer, had hired in help, a troupe of raucous maidens and larky youths who were, so Ivy Blount opined, more trouble than they were worth. They were reigned over, and reined in, by an Amazon queen, we shall call her Penny, for Penthesilea. Penny is a fine figure of a woman. Her hair is done in heavy ringlets, she has brawny limbs and knees the size of turnips, wears a crooked skirt, and is shod in those zippered black felt bootees I thought had stopped being manufactured a couple of generations ago. She is considered a terror, and will brook no nonsense from anyone, not even from Felix Mordaunt, with his smooth air of old-world authority and menace. Penny it was who with one cold stare put Billy Hipwell in his place, when he had switched to whiskey from Murphy's best pale and begun to shout smut and try to put his hand up the skirt of any girl who wandered into his orbit.

Helen is Penny's one weakness. She is thoroughly infatuated with her, and in her presence becomes as a trembling laurel, fawning and fluttering and tripping over her booteed feet.

Ivy Blount took it as a grievous insult to herself and her privileged position at Arden House that a rip like Penny, with her tinker woman's freckled forearms and a jaw that could chop firewood, should be granted any authority over anyone, even if only for the day. Then there was the high-handed fashion in which she treated Billy, glaring at him with those bug-eyes of hers and hiding the whiskey.

The truth is, Ivy is not well today, and has not been for some time. She suffers increasingly frequent bouts of faintness, while there is a leaden heaviness in her legs. Also, something is the matter with her left eye, it is clouded somehow, and she keeps blinking to try to clear it, but it won't clear. Helen on more than one occasion, sighing, and casting a look to heaven, has offered to have Dr. Fortune look at her, but Ivy insists she is perfectly all right. Ivy will not weaken; she has the honour of the Blounts to uphold. Besides, she considers old Fortune to be a quack.

Queen Penny has her qualities, as even Ivy is compelled to admit, if only to herself. She has a sharp eye, and will manage to curb the worst of the pilfering that is always to be expected on occasions such as this. And sure enough, next day a number of items from the house will be found missing—there it is again, language and its wiles and ways—including a treasured Swan fountain pen that had been young Adam's since his schooldays, also an ingenious bibelot the size of a billiard ball and made of some highly polished metal, which when shaken produced a ghostly tinkling sound, as if two or three very tiny harpsichords were being jostled together inside it. The sly ones among the hired boys, and some of the girls as well, will be suspected of these thefts, but wrongly. Helen alone will guess who the real thief is, and will tell no one.

The Godkin twins, Nell and Nora—a pair of my maenads— live on the next farm up the hill. They are said to be identical, which would provoke a caustic snort from Godley the Elder, for whom the entirety of the world is unidentical with itself. Big-boned and brawny, they swing their hips as they move up and down the tables serving food and drink, their elbows working like knees. Nora is the dominant twin, she being the firstborn, or the second, I never know which it's supposed to be. They had got at the champagne before the guests arrived, and their squeaks and squeals of laughter will punctuate the afternoon like so many squibs going off. At their soberest they are a less-than-gainly pair, and the bubbly has almost entirely undone them. They stumbled about, hilariously shoving each other—"Whoa up there Nellie you nearly had my eye out!"—as glasses slid out of their butter-fingered grasp, and a whole smoked salmon fell into a bowl of trifle and a baked ham shot off its dish and rolled down the grassy bank and disappeared in a tangle of briars. Rex the dog followed closely after them and got to snap up many a juicy tidbit, until at length he had to lie down in the shade under one of the tables, glassy-eyed and panting, his belly swollen and shiny.

Helen, unlike the twins, and unlike herself on many a recent day, as we have seen, was sober. That very morning, she had taken a pledge, returning unopened to the fridge in the kitchen a nicely chilled bottle of Chablis and slamming shut the heavy door and turning smartly on her heel and walking away, her better self behind her, propelling her forward with hands clamped firmly on her shoulders. Now, feeling virtuous but brittle, she attended determinedly to her guests, startling them by her bright manner; such cheeriness was alarming, in one known for her sulks. And indeed, she was faking it, a little, for she was on edge after an upsetting encounter earlier in the day.

She had come down from upstairs and was on her way to the kitchen when she happened to glance into the library and saw that the concealed door to the right-hand side of the vault was ajar. She only noticed it because a strong shaft of sunlight was striking obliquely through the tall window, making a theatrical effect, as if the stage director had asked for a spot just there, to show up where the villain lurked.

And villain there surely was. She walked across the room on tiptoe and with a hooked forefinger drew the door fully open, and found Felix Mordaunt, leaning at ease against the stacked steel drawers with his ankles crossed and a file of papers open in his hands. He let a moment pass before he turned his head and looked at her, with a bold, unflinching eye. He was the last person she would have thought to find here—Jaybey was in and out of the place every day, fussing and sighing—and for a moment she was at a loss. It was strange. She realised that if he offered the slightest excuse for being here, if he made the faintest apology, she would order him out and would call the Guards to see him off the property. It was his boldness, that look of half-amused effrontery, that stayed her—that, and the pang of regret that pierced straight through her, sharp and cold as a splinter of glass, when she thought of their hour together in his room at Ivy Blount's cottage. Just once, she thought, just that one time, and never again.

"I'm forty today," she said.

"Oh, I know," he responded, with a little dip of his head that she supposed was meant to be a bow. "I imagine everyone does."

She straightened her neck and struck an attitude.

"Yes? And why would that be?"

"You're having a party, aren't you?" he said. "Besides, you've been telling everybody for weeks how old you are."

She decided not to be offended, it would only make him smile his frightening smile.

"What are you doing, may I ask?"

"Reading your father-in-law's letters. Why, am I not supposed to?"

"You're not supposed to know they're here. This place is supposed to be secret."

Now he did smile, but faintly, tightening his lips and moving them a little, as though he were biting on some tiny thing with his front teeth. He was wondering if he would have to kill her, too, and the thought almost made him laugh—the body in the library! He closed the file, put it back in its place, and slid shut the heavy metal drawer, then turned and took her lightly by her upper arms and kissed her on the cheek. "Many happy returns," he said. She caught his meaty smell. Just once, and never again.

She knew she shouldn't, she knew it, but she couldn't stop herself. With a sense of falling headlong from a high place she stepped forward, almost barging into him so that he had to retreat, into the narrow, airless space. She linked her arms around his neck and locked her fingers together, as she had done that other, that singular, day when she was leaving Ivy's cottage with his slime still between her legs. She made to kiss him now, as she had done then, but he reared away from her, breaking her embrace, and looked at her with something in his eyes she had not seen there before.

"I'm sorry," she blurted, "I'm sorry, I—"

But she wasn't sorry. Rather, she was furious, it was some kind of fury, and he could see it, she could see him seeing it and being gratified by what he saw. He placed both his hands on her again, his killer's hands, and walked her backwards out of the vault and put her firmly aside, like some dumb creature that had strayed by accident into his path. "Excuse me," he murmured, in a voice indifferent yet faintly menacing, like a policeman's voice, she thought, and stepped past her and strolled across the room, and stopped in the doorway to remove something, a hair, probably, probably one of hers, from the sleeve of his jacket, and was gone.

She stood at the window looking out into the courtyard. Now and then a shiver ran through her, though not because she was cold. The sun was still beating down through the glazed roof out there, but it had moved—could that much time have passed in what had seemed to her so brief an interval?—and its angled beam was broken across the windowsill outside and forming a hot yellow puddle on the floor's sand-coloured flagstones. On this side of the window, at her eye level, a fly was banging itself against the glass in a sort of desperate, hopping dance. She thought of herself barging against the man. She watched the fly's frantic efforts and tried to imagine how it would feel to be trapped like that, what had been air and light suddenly become this invisible cold hard smooth unbreakable barrier. She noticed her right hand, it was clenched into a fist, and must have been, for some time. She was clutching something. She relaxed her fingers. It was a button. She had been holding it so tightly it had stuck itself to her palm. It must be from the man's jacket, and since it was small, it must be from the sleeve. She had read somewhere that someone, Beau Brummell, was it, had started the fashion of sewing buttons on to men's cuffs to stop them wiping their noses on their sleeves. But could that be, since the buttons were sewn along the seam underneath? Maybe they had started out on the top, on the thumb side, and over the years had migrated southwards, as men started using hankies.

But how had she managed to tear a button from his coat? There were strands of thread in the buttonholes. She picked them out with her nails. The button was warm from the warmth of her hand. She put it into her mouth, on to her tongue, and immediately was reminded of the day of her First Holy Communion, she kneeling at the altar rails and the congregation behind her hushed and the priest murmuring the same Latin words over and over as he moved along the line of kneeling girls in their white frocks and white veils, and a beam of sunlight like the one out there in the conservatory coming down from a small high window, and the dust motes slowly swarming in the light and the organ starting up in a sort of whisper, playing the first notes of some hymn, "Tantum Ergo," was it, or "Soul of My Saviour"? Before she knew what she was doing she had closed her lips and swallowed the button, and at once something swelled behind her forehead above the bridge of her nose and she began to sob, loudly, helplessly. It was awful. It was like vomiting. She saw herself as if from outside, as if she were someone else out there looking in at her, as she stood at the window, shuddering, her fingers stiff and thrust into her hair and her palms pressed to her temples, bawling like a baby.

It didn't last long, the weeping fit. When it stopped, she felt better, a little better, but rueful, too, and she glanced quickly over her shoulder in case there might be someone there, watching her with his calm, derisive, dangerous smile. Why had she cried, what was she crying for? Her lost babies, never now to be replaced? The lost years, likewise? The fact that she had made a fool of herself by throwing herself at Mordaunt and was rebuffed? She gave a shivery sigh and wiped her nose on her wrist—Beau Brummell would be scandalised—and sat down on a straight-backed chair and sighed again. What had she been thinking of? Not enough to tear a button off his coat but then to swallow it? They were told that at Communion the Host must not be allowed to touch the teeth, that it must be swallowed whole, in one holy piece, but always it stuck to the roof of her mouth, right up there in the deep hollow that tickled if you put your tongue into it, stuck like a piece of awful, thick tissue paper, and she would have to go back quickly to her place and kneel down and put her hands over her face and pretend to be praying while she worked with the tip of her tongue to dislodge the horrible sticky sickening stuff, which came away in sodden strings and little soft pellets that she could hardly bear to swallow, their no-taste making her stomach turn. The button, however, had gone down as easily as a coin sliding into a slot. It was inside her now, this profane eucharist, and though it wouldn't remain there for long, she was glad to think of it eventually entering the bowels of the earth, or the deeps of the sea, and lodging there, a secret emblem of her moment of mad love.

She went to the kitchen and leaned over the sink and ran the cold tap and dashed water on to her face to cool her cheeks and soothe her swollen eyelids. At least Mordaunt just now hadn't seen her weep, there was that comfort, a grain of it. He was a heartless brute, and most certainly had committed a murder. She should be afraid of him, and she was, but not much, and not always. She braced the heels of her hands on the rim of the sink and stood with her head bent, drops of water dripping from her chin. What did she want, what did she hope for, yearn for? Nothing. Everything.

She dried her face on a tea towel, and crossed the room and drew open the fridge door, looked at the bottle of wine lying on its side on a rack, then shut the door again and turned away.

There were odd sounds in the house, and she went along the corridor to the front hall, to meet her mother-in-law as she was borne down the stairs on some sort of litter with blankets laid over it and under her. Adam had hold of the front end and Ivy was at the rear, with the Godkin twins in anxious attendance fore and aft. They were having a hard time of it, for the litter was wide, and evidently it was heavy. Also, Adam was descending backwards and had to go cautiously, looking behind him frequently for fear of losing his balance and letting his mother tumble down the steps. The frail old woman was half sitting up, leaning on her elbows and monitoring the awkward procession with the keenest interest. Her expression, lively and intent, was that of a child taking part in an improvised game in which she was the central but inactive player.

"Go slow!"

"Mind the wall."

"Jesus, Mary and Joseph."

"Ow!"

The litter, it turned out, was the door from Ursula's room, which Duffy had earlier taken off its hinges, under Adam's instructions, and adapted for the purpose.

"For God's sake," Helen said, "couldn't someone just have carried her?"

Ursula looked at her, the would-be spoilsport, with displeasure, and the twins tittered. Adam said nothing, only grunted. Ivy Blount was panting. What a day!

At that moment, a sleek, moss-green motor car was sweeping in at the front gates with a toothsome grinding of gravel. It was a vintage Alvis, one of the last of the line—those handmade engines could not be adapted to burn brine—smooth-running and handsomely preserved. At the wheel was a blue-jawed, thuggish-looking fellow in a grey tunic buttoned to the throat and a grey cap with a jutting, shiny peak pulled far down. His name is Nockter. His eyes are small and colourless and set close together. He has been to many places, has done many things. Later on, in the evening, when you and I are gone, he will offer the Godkin twins a lift home, which the twins, having exchanged a look, will simperingly accept. Suavely the shining motor will surge along the roads, up hill and down dale. The twins will sit side by side in the back, perched at the very front edge of the seat, their knees pressed tightly together and their hands clasped, not daring now even to glance at each other for fear of bursting out laughing. How thrilled they are, how thrilled and expectant. They will study the bluish line of Nockter's jaw, and catch his flinty eye in the driving mirror and blush. Then Nell, or maybe Nora, will look out at the road and frown and remark, with mild misgiving, that this isn't the way home. And Nockter in his turn will eye them in the glass, and smile, and say nothing. Didn't I promise you low jinks and high?

But it is still early, and so much is yet to come.

In the back seat lolls a fat pale personage in a jacket of loud brown-and-yellow tweed over a striped silk waistcoat. Professor Benjamin J. Grace, onetime Professor of Burble Burble at the University of Babble Babble, is making an entrance.

Well I'll be damned, Bill Jaybey said to himself, a chauffeur, no less, peaked cap and all! He was standing in the front doorway, shading his eyes as he watched the marvellous machine with its following vortex of dust make its stately if bumpy way up the pothole-pitted drive. He sighed. He really couldn't face facing Benny Grace, not just yet. He turned and retreated through the house, displacing air, fleet as a god, for of course he is a god, he is me, as I am he, as they are all me and mine, my made-up creatures, *entheos* briefly, for their brief moment on this patch of earth I've lent them, patches themselves, inspired mechanicals. Here is the timeless kitchen, the back door with its rattly hinge, the yard, the mucky lane and rusty gate, then sunlight and sward, and under the great trees the long tables with their tablecloths, and ranged about, as if scattered at random, my little ones, above them the vast and intricate architecture of a majestically clouded summer sky, and under them the unconsidered grass, with a tousling breeze in it, keeping itself to its grassy self.

He was surprised, was Jaybey, to find so many there already, two score or more by his estimate, and others steadily arriving. Quite a few he recognised, and even those he didn't know somehow seemed not strangers. All were turned housewards and motionless, watching the Dowager Madame Godley being borne forward on her makeshift palanquin, seated upright in a collapse of blankets and regarding them back with a wary though enlivened eye. A chaise longue, upholstered in moth-holed silver satin, had been brought out from the library, with great difficulty— a jutting part of the five-barred gate had caused a long and jagged rip across the stretched material at the back—and on to this she was transferred by her son, who lifted her up with one arm round her shoulders and the other under her knees, and set her down as lightly as a lady's maid laying out her lady's gown.

Silence then, and for a moment it seemed there might be applause, but no one was sufficiently daring, or had taken enough drink, to risk the first clap. Ursula wore a padded green bed jacket and her collarless calico nightshirt, her beaded cap, and a pair of black velvet slippers that had belonged to Petra, the toes of which were bald and shiny; the black-faced watch looked bigger than ever on her shrunken wrist. Ivy and the twins had propped the now disused bedroom door against the trunk of the central one of the three trees, where it stood stark in the unaccustomed light of outdoors, homely and incongruous, its white paint peeling and its porcelain knob chipped.

Felix Mordaunt, a flute of champagne in hand, moved at leisure among the tables, inspecting the comestibles on offer. More than one of the guests regarded him covertly, seeming to know him, or at least to recognise his face, from where or from when they would surely recall if only they could concentrate hard enough. But they couldn't. No one can, in this world that Godley wrought. Something keeps getting in the way, keeps turning their thoughts aside, keeps blunting them, or absorbing them altogether, and soon something else comes along to engage their ever-waning attention.

"Isn't he the fellow who—?"

"Which fellow?"

"The one who—"

"What—?"

"Watch out for the pismires, they're all over that chair."

The Godkin girls were entranced by Mr. Mordaunt, whose stealthy elegance and decayed good looks caused them fairly to swoon. He's a real gentleman, Nell said with a sigh, and yes, Nora agreed, but not like the usual snooty ones you see around here with ramrods stuck up their arses. They admired his double-vented jacket and handmade shoes, his burgundy-coloured silk cravat and sharply pressed twill trousers, the carelessly crumpled hankie sprouting from his breast pocket. He was as old as the hills, of course, Nora observed, but that didn't matter—they preferred a mature man, and besides, this one carried his years with vulpine nonchalance. Throughout the afternoon, they kept finding excuses to drift into his vicinity and smile at him with sly suggestiveness, although, frustratingly, he seemed not to notice, not even when Nora, reaching across for a plate of ham sandwiches on the table he was standing at, let the front of her smock hang out as far as it would go. Well, will you look at him, not batting an eye, Nora exclaimed, and added, "He must be a queer," which shocked her sister. "Oh, no," Nell wailed softly, "no, he couldn't be—didn't Duffy tell Ivy he saw him with her from up the House?"

"The belle of the ball, is it?" Nora said, her cow eyes flashing. "That one would go with Duffy himself, if the mood took her."

In fact, *la belle Hélène* had spotted Nora leaning over shamelessly in front of Mordaunt and showing off her dugs. She should have been angry, or perhaps amused, but she was neither. A wave of what seemed sorrow rose in her like bile and she turned aside.

Poor old Jaybey, loitering at the periphery of the party in his wrinkled linen jacket and despondent corduroys, had been watching her as usual, and saw her now trail away along the grassy path in the direction of the house. He set off after her, going by a cautiously circuitous route. At the end of the muddy lane, instead of keeping on towards the house, she veered to the left. He guessed where she would go, and sure enough a moment later he saw her duck under the arch of tangled brambles and holly that guarded the way in to the holy well. He had thought himself cured of Helen, partially cured, but in truth the malady lingered, and would linger, a chronic affliction. One day, perhaps, when all this was in the past, one day like any other, he would sense a sudden absence, as when at twilight the blackbird's song ceases and the stillness adjusts itself to the new concordance in which yet something has been lost, and he would grope for her name and not find it.

Now he dithered, pressing a finger to a lip. Should he? Did he dare?

If he followed her into the well he could pretend he hadn't known she was there. She would have to grant him a moment of her time, she would not be so hard as to spurn him entirely, greathearted Helen, who did not care to be adored, not by him, anyway. Oh, what to do!

The watchers were watched, for Adam had seen it all, the Godkin girl displaying herself to Mordaunt the Murderer, and Helen turning sadly away, and Jaybey making his circuit of the party guests and around behind the trees yet never losing sight of her. How much, I wonder, is Adam meant to know. Does he know, for instance, that Helen betrayed him with the murderer, and that Jaybey thinks himself besotted with her, and that she longs for another life, far from Arden and from him—does he know these things? I could say, but won't.

I am weary. Even a god flags, sometimes.

Jaybey's nerve failed him, and he went back to the party, and left Helen undisturbed within the sacred grove. See her seated there on the narrow bench, part of an old school desk the legs of which someone long ago cemented into the ground. One elbow rests on a knee, her cheek rests on her hand, the other hand is in her lap, holding something—what is it? a forked twig? She is as mysterious and solid as the androgynous angel in the *Melencolia*. And look, Rex the dog has come and lain down at her feet like the old dog lying by the melancholic angel's side. It makes a picture, doesn't it. Helen weeps a little, since the occasion calls for it, but only a little, and only as if to keep in practice. There are religious mementos all about, strung on the bushes, for believers still come here, by an ancient right of way, and leave behind propitiatory tokens, rosaries and holy medals, statues of the saints, blurred photos of lost loved ones. The water wells up through a patch of vivid green moss and trickles a little way and sinks down again into the soil, forgetful of itself. Nothing will change, she knows, not as she used to wish it would. This seems a kind of ending, for her, who once, did she but know it, was embraced here, this very here, by the god, my doughty, diminishing dad.

In this place of supplication, she thinks not only of her lost children but of Petra, too, and it is Petra who now, up at the trees, approached her mother, enthroned on her ripped chaise longue, and sat down at her side without being asked. Petra? Well, among the uninvited guests there came a young man, or boy, a boy-man, let's say, with a shock of greasy curls and a dead-white face, clad in a suit of mourning black worn to a shine, a quite clean white shirt, and scuffed but dainty shoon. He walks with narrow and not quite steady steps, as if on springs, his hands in the pockets of his suit and his elbows pressed tightly in against his ribs. He smokes without cease, seemingly the same cigarette, and looks about at the others with the rich contempt of the wounded in spirit, smiling a little at one side of a thin-lipped mouth. Although he has somewhat the look of the young Rimbaud—could Rimbaud old have been Rimbaud?—we know who he really is, and so does Petra's mother. Later in the day Benny Grace will make a clumsy pass at him, which he will spurn with a consumptive's sharp, hollow laugh, but we shall be gone by then, so it doesn't matter. What Ursula and this spectral creature talked about we may not know, but Jaybey on his doleful return from the failure of his last hopes at the holy well found them engaged in colloquy, each leaning so far forward their foreheads were almost touching. At his approach both broke off and, though it was plain he had no intention of stopping, turned and stared at him in deepest reprehension as he went past, the young man going so far as to remove the fag from his mouth and twirl it between his fingers in a manner somehow expressive of contempt.

"You," Ursula said suddenly, pointing at Jaybey with a bent and tremulous finger that will not straighten, "I remember you— you once tried to teach me algebra!"

Jaybey, confused and shaken, smiled weakly, said nothing, and moved on. He had noticed the old woman was no longer wearing her big black wristwatch, which disquieted him.

He had been aware for some time of a gnawing sensation within, and now he realised that it was hunger. He had eaten nothing since morning, when Ivy brought his breakfast to him in the Sky Room. She came at the same time every morning, and he made sure to be up and shaved and alert to greet her, and every time he saw how disappointed she was not to find him disgracefully oversleeping, or with a girl he had smuggled in, or sprawled naked in a tangle of sweaty sheets, crapulous and raving after a night of drunken debauchery in one of the town's more disreputable pubs. Hadn't she caught Mordaunt at himself, that day in the upstairs room, so why couldn't she similarly catch him? This morning she had not looked well herself, as Jaybey noticed. Her eyes were sunken, and in the harsh morning light her forehead had an unhealthy, yellowish sheen. This deterioration could not have happened overnight—when was the last time he had looked at her at all closely? Nor was she as talkative as on other, similar, times. Usually she had some snippet of gossip to impart, about Helen's latest misdemeanour or her lodger's furtive and infuriating ways. Poor wilting Ivy. We could tell him what the matter is, but won't, no, we shall keep our peace, on that matter. See how pinched and costive we are becoming, at the end. But ah, it's sad, the poor creatures hardly have time to get the hang of being here before they're fetched away.

Jaybey at each of the two long tables encountered a phalanx of bent backs turned towards him. A great throng had gathered by now, and all it seemed were as hungry as he. Inevitably he thought of piglets at the sow's belly, and of himself as the runt of the litter. And yet how nebulous these people were, not like people at all, really, even though he was familiar with at least some of them. The high full clouds imparted to the air a silvery shine, and the figures moving in it moved vestigially, like wraiths, or like the figures crowding in the background of a dream. Their voices too sounded frail in all that space, and instead of speaking they seemed to make a kind of twittering, as a flock of birds will make, settling upon the darkling trees at eventide. Yes, the day moves on, the sunlight comes and goes, the clouds make their stately, indifferent rearrangements, and the world wanes.

A tall man, grizzled and balding, turned away from the table, leaving behind a gap into which Jaybey darted swiftly before it could close, surprising himself no less by his determination than by his alacrity. Not many minutes had passed since he was bemoaning yet again the fact that Helen wouldn't love him, and now look at him, pushing forward and shoving in his snout with the rest. Were cousin Eros here he'd hitch up his quiver with a pettish shrug of a shoulder and turn away in disgust, but as we know, for poor old Bill that golden lad is a fading glimmer in the zenith.

Hemmed in, he had to stand sideways, with someone's elbow in his back and the warm rump of the woman beside him pressed

against his thigh. He managed to pluck up one of the last of the
paper plates, and surveyed the table. By now all that was left were
the leavings. He managed to seize a chicken drumstick, smeared
with pale glistenings of fat, half of a watery tomato, and a wedge
of soda bread. One of the twins, Nora or Nell, he couldn't tell
which, handed him across the table an inch or two of tepid white
wine in a paper cup.

"Ah, no, the red is all gone," she said, reaching inside her
blouse and hoisting up a fallen shoulder strap, "they lashed into
that first thing."

He nodded, freed himself from the pressing elbow and the
padded behind, and shuffled off morosely with his scraps through
the chirruping crowd. A butterfly fluttered by, he saw it clearly
for a second, saw its translucent, dawn-blue wings with a crescent
of umber spots along the outer margins. The man whose place
he had taken at the table was leaning over a hazy-eyed little girl
who seemed to shrink from him. "In County Clare, my dear," he
said, "there is a town called Quilty, where butterflies abound. But
beware, because—" So that's who he is!

Jaybey moved on, looking for a place where he might sit and
be alone.

But ah, the foolish and unfortunate fellow had quite forgot
the fact of Benny Grace, and now here he was, advancing over the
grass at an eager waddle, smiling in the delighted expectation of
stirring up mischief.

He paused, and looked about.

"Goodness me," he said, hooking his thumbs in the fob pockets of his waistcoat and complacently patting the slope of his big
belly with the fingers of both hands, "look what the Godley Effect
has wrought. How quaint and gay it all is—we're in another part
of the wood entirely."

Below the strident jacket and the fancy waistcoat he wore a
roomy pair of plus-fours, argyle socks, and cream-and-brown

correspondent shoes to conceal his neat little cloven hoofs. He had grown a great deal fatter since Jaybey had seen him last, and by now he was almost perfectly spherical; otherwise he seemed hardly to have aged at all, and his hair was still a shiny shade of black, although when he drew nearer it became obvious that the colour had come out of a bottle. Yet he seemed remarkably vigorous and supple, despite his great girth, while his big round face was as smooth and pink as it had always been, and probably not much altered since he was a baby. "My dear William," he said, advancing and drawing to a halt again and panting a little, "I would not have taken you for the rustic type, but here you are, bonny and burnished and looking as county as could be." He had developed an extraordinary accent, rich and plummy, which along with the tweeds and the absurd socks and shoes gave him the air of an Edwardian swell, though the waistcoat put him at the greenery-yallery end of that spectrum.

They did not shake hands, but Benny bobbed his globular head in a facetious bow, after which they stood a moment taking stock of each other, Benny beaming and Jaybey looking as though he had swallowed something unpleasant which he was trying to disgorge. Then Benny's attention shifted, and his eyes narrowed, and taking Jaybey by the elbow he set off at a surprisingly rapid pace in the direction of a pair of deckchairs set up in the shade of one of the beeches. The chairs had just been vacated, which was what Benny had spotted, and two elderly women in floral frocks were making their beady way towards them. Benny got there first, however, and dropped himself like a sack on to one of the chairs and drew Jaybey quickly down on to the other, uttering a triumphant *Poh!* and ignoring the glares of the two outdistanced ladies.

He set his suety hands on his knees and looked about happily, once more taking in the by now slightly befuddled guests, who were eating the last of the food and drinking the last of the drinks, took in the tables and the tablecloths and the grassy bank on which the tables stood, and the field and on the far side of it the hawthorn hedge, and, rising above the hedge, the numerous and venerable chimneys of Arden House, the bricks glowing darkly in the sun.

"How pleasant it is to be here," he said, "in what I should call the perfect middle of a splendid summer afternoon. So many oldsters, and so many in white. It's like the interval in a cricket match." He glanced at the paper plate that Jaybey was balancing on his knees. "What have you got there? Chicken, is it?"

"You can have it if you want."

"Oh, I wouldn't dream——"

"Here, take it."

Jaybey could not have eaten the meat, or anything else, for Benny's lighting on him had quite taken away his appetite. Benny had the same effect on him as that of a schoolyard bully. Proximity to the fat man put him into a state of subdued yet seething anxiety. On his side, Benny's manner towards his old adversary was one of knowing amusement—derisive laughter always seemed to be bubbling turbidly deep down inside that great gut of his. Benny knew everyone's secrets, or made a convincing show of it. He ate the drumstick with fastidious relish, rolling back his rubbery, purplish lips and extending a delicate stiff little finger. When he had finished, he tossed the bone into the long grass at the base of the tree beside him and dropped the plate on to the grass. From his pocket he produced a large red bandana with white polka dots and wiped his hands carefully, digit by chubby digit.

"Well, William, what's the news?"

"Not much, down here," Jaybey said.

"How goes the *grand projet*? Have you skewered the old mountebank yet?" Jaybey, almost without meaning to, mentioned the Venetian Testament. Benny stared. "The Venetian what?"

"That's my name for it. It's a sort of letter he seems to have written when he——"

"Oh, I know what it is, I know that thing," Benny said with

easy dismissiveness, nodding, which made his multiple chins ripple like the bellows of a miniature accordion. "His suicide note, more like."

"You know it?" Jaybey said, feeling a bleak stirring of alarm. "You've seen it?"

"He told me about it," Benny answered, and gave an elephantine shrug. "All very embarrassing. He went quite dotty at the end, you know, before the Lord smote his self-appointed rival and deprived him of his faculties and took away his will to die." He shifted his shoulders convulsively again. "I told him to tear up the thing, but obviously he ignored my advice." He cast a sidelong glance at his companion and chuckled. "So he's leading you a merry chase, then. And do you anticipate a good clean kill at the end of it?"

At that moment their conversation, if such it could be called, was interrupted by a commotion in the midst of the guests. What had happened? Here is what had happened. Billy Hipwell, drunk and in the mood for romance, had lured Nell Godkin into the clearing by the holy well from which by then Helen had departed. Nell had offered but a token resistance to his advances, and matters were progressing between the dashing motor salesman and the fascinated girl—local lads knew well that Nora was the livelier of the twins and Nell the more gullible—when they heard the sharp crack and slow groan of a branch breaking above them, and at once a figure fell flailing through the dense foliage and landed with a thud and a cry at their feet. "What the—?" Billy exclaimed roughly, like a character in the pictures, raising himself on an elbow, his shirt collar undone and his flies agape, while blushing Nell adjusted her underwear hurriedly. The person scrambling to his feet before them, not without difficulty, for he had sprained an ankle and dislocated a thumb, was, as of course you had already anticipated, the cowman Adrian Duffy, with holly leaves in his hair. Nell, thrilled and in a fluster, fled the grove in search of her sister, who, when she heard all, or almost all, of what had transpired between the two and then suddenly the three beside the holy well, declared that she would send straight away for their brothers to come and give Duffy the Peeping Tom the thrashing of his life. The guests crowding round them sent up a murmur, of approval, as it seemed. She did not need to summon anyone, however, for Billy, our bold Billy, was just then administering to the already wounded Duffy a beating so severe, skilful, and thorough that Dr. Fortune would send the victim to the hospital, where he would stay for a week, moaning and swearing. Helen, told the story later between sobs and hiccups by a distraught Ivy Blount, laughed so hard that her nose bled, and Ivy had to laugh too, poor dying Ivy, laughing even as she wept, and Helen wept, even as she laughed and bled. For by then she had broken her pledge to herself and had drained the bottle of white to the dregs, sitting at the kitchen table, with her legs crossed and swinging one of them.

"What were we talking about?" Benny Grace said, peering up at the silver-grey undersides of the beech leaves above them. He shifted convulsively again in the low chair and rummaged in his crotch—Benny is forever adjusting some intimate part of himself—and dabbed at his eyes with the bandana. "Oh, yes," he said, "yes, our departed colleague whose life and dubious times you are recording. Of course, he never wrote down a single word that wasn't a lie—you do know that, don't you?" He chuckled again, fatly, his jowls quivering. "What did you call it, the Venetian what? the Venetian Testament? Pack of lies, dear boy, a pound-weight packet of untruths. Just like—" He broke off, and sat forward, looking across the field towards the house. "Who is that shady character sloping off there?"

"Where? Oh, him. Name of Mordaunt."

"Mordant, eh? Apt, by the look of him. He seems familiar."

"He's said to have done a murder."

"I shouldn't be at all surprised. What's he up to, skulking along like that? Off to do more killing, I daresay."

But Jaybey wasn't interested in what Mordaunt might be about. He was thinking that, as well as the infliction of pain and humiliation, the bully's project is to extract the texture from things, leaving them engreyed and unlifelike. Until today, until this past quarter-hour, and despite all his misgivings, Jaybey had thought of himself, deep down, deep beyond doubt, as set upon a task at least halfway worthy of himself and his however doubtful talents. Oh, yes, for all we've said to the contrary, he had clung on to a smidgen of faith in the grand project. True, the reconstruction of the life of Adam Godley could be no more than a tattered fiction pierced through by—what did I say?—the tintacks of fact, though as we know there are no facts. Still, even the simulacrum of the life of such a man would be a thing of note, or so he had supposed, until Benny arrived, in his new persona—plus-fours! cricket!— and demonstrated to him, with the flick of a babyishly dimpled wrist, the futility and tawdriness of his endeavour. It wasn't even what Benny was saying, the scoffing denials and offhand dismissals, but his merely being there, pawing at himself and shifting his fat about, that worked the nullifying effect.

"Of course, he filched it all from Gaby Swan," he said now, leaning back in his low-slung chair and making a steeple of his fingers.

"Do you think so?" Jaybey murmured wistfully.

"Yes, and then to cover his tracks he proceeded to erase all mention of his quondam friend. Took the dedication to him off his famous paper, if you remember."

"Hmm," Jaybey said.

He had spent so many long days, so many, from dawn to dark, absorbing the sum of all that he could know of his subject, but what did it signify? The unknown was the greater portion. He saw himself as the cannibal chief sitting alone in the longhouse, the missionary and his missus eaten to the last string of gristle and the tribe in borborygmic slumber after the feast, shaking and re-shaking the Reverend Porkchop's half-hunter, and pressing it to his ear, baffled by the mystery of the tick. He was tired, he wanted it all over and done with. All what? All this, this inexplicable stuff, that cannot be known or understood. I find the world always odd, but odder still, I suppose, is the fact that I find it so, for what are the eternal verities by which I measure these temporal aberrations?

Who speaks here? I do.

"Anyway, he only asked you to write it so that others wouldn't," Benny continued. "Popov, for instance."

"What?"

"This book of yours, I'm sure it will never see the light of day, a way will be found to stop it. His dad didn't want anything like it done at all, you know, and certainly not by Popov, though his pen was poised. Oh, yes, young Adam isn't as slow as he seems. You were the stopgap, old boy, the queerer of the pitch. Ah well. You'll never finish it, anyway. We all know what a slacker you are."

And he smiled.

Mordaunt, crossing the field, pauses to take a last look back. The crowd is thinning, the afternoon has already begun to fail. The clouds, the trees, the grass, the tablecloths. Billy Hipwell, thoroughly soused by now, sits slackly on the ground, leaning against the bole of a beech, talking to Rex the dog.

"Ah, the old bowser, how are you, fella, eh?"

Deirdre stands by, impatiently pouting; she wishes to be away. They came down not in the plunging Dolphin but in the little Sprite, the key to which, as it happens, is snug in Mordaunt's pocket. How did he come by it? How else but by cunning and stealth. He goes on, along the lane, skipping over the muddy patches to mind his shiny shoes. He follows the short way around to the cottage. Ivy Blount is still at the party. He goes upstairs to collect his things. His bag is already packed. He takes his trinkets with him. The collection has been swelled today, for besides the pearls in their japanned box, the apostle spoon, the monogrammed silver propelling pencil, there is added a Swan fountain pen and a little musical silver ball with the charm of which he is greatly taken. Also, there is the Patek Philippe, which slipped so smoothly off the old woman's meagre wrist. The Chinese dragon he will leave on the kitchen table, to frighten Ivy when she sees it, glaring at her with its fiery nostrils flared. In a cardboard file, inside his bag, there rests a choice selection from the Godley papers. He was not greedy, he took only a few good things, the exchange with Dirac on fermions, with Ironmount on matrices, along with some lesser bits and pieces, to make an appendix of sorts to the manuscript of the Singularities Paper, which he will have from Anna Behrens, and which he will sell, privately, through the agency of Guido Gannaro, shady son of the late and even shadier Eduardo of unblessèd memory. He looks about the little room a last time, glances out of the low window—farewell, happy fields!—takes up his bag and hat, and drapes his coat over his shoulders like an old-style opera star. He is on his way.

Helen, sitting with her empty glass at the kitchen table beside the range, sees his shadow in the doorway and scowls. He stops on the threshold, surprised to find her there—shouldn't she be away tending to her guests? Her mouth is slack, her gaze is dulled. Aha.

"You off?" she asks.

"Yes," he answers, coming forward in his looming way. "Things to do, you know."

She snickers.

"Like seeing to your floozie, I suppose?"

"In a manner of speaking, yes."

They are silent for some moments, then with a sweep of his right arm he bids her farewell, turns, and goes out at the door. He had meant to look about for loose cash, but even Helen drunk, as patently she was, would not stand for being stolen from in such a barefaced fashion. He hummed a tuneless tune. The Sprite was parked in the yard. He tossed his bag into the back seat, fitted himself behind the wheel. Helen came and stood in the doorway, leaning against the jamb with her arms folded, her head to one side. Her feet are bare. She remembers his hands on her shoulder blades, dry and cool. She begins to say something but the snarl of the engine starting up drowns out her words entirely.

At the end of the drive he hesitated, then turned left and drove along by the demesne wall. At the triangle of dense green he stopped, stepped over the low car door on to the grass and went in by the lychgate, stopped again, turned, took a deep breath, and sauntered, free as the air, out through the gate he had just come in by, got back into the car, and drove away, with a hard little gratified smile. He would never have been at ease again had he not broken that spell.

He drove over the crest of the hill and pointed the car down the hill's long slope, seeing the town in the distance. On the horizon, a boiling of lead-blue cloud under a low sky of hot peach. They would probably catch him, again. He wouldn't mind much if they did. He might be better off inside, comfy among his old mates. Or maybe they would bring back capital punishment, just for him, a special case. They could hire in some tyrant's hangman to do the job. He grinned into the rushing air.

This thing of darkness I acknowledge mine.

But then he had to slow the car. Some sort of cavalcade was approaching, up the hill. He peered, narrowing his eyes. What was it—? Could it be—?

Helen had walked across the yard and round by the side of

the house. She stopped at the top of the drive. The Sprite was long gone, not even a wisp of salty exhaust remaining on the evening air. She sighed, blowing an involuntary bubble. Her thoughts were all awry. She shouldn't have drunk the whole bottle.

There came some sound, a sort of blaring, as of tinny music from a tannoy, approaching along the road. She put up a hand to shade her eyes. Lorries, was it? And a coloured pole, and a flag. Boom boom boom on the big bass drum. Taddah! It was, yes it was. Prospero's Magic Circus had returned, after all this time, and just for her. She thought of the juggler, his hip bones and exquisite wrists. She set off running down the slope of the garden, barefoot through the warm damp grass. Despite the wine, despite the years, she felt suddenly light and airy, as if a pair of little wings had sprouted at her ankles.

Taddaah!

Komm du, du letzter—

The sun shines, the massed clouds massively move, the hollow music blares, and here the steel tip advances along the line, with a tiny secret sound all of its own, scratch scratch, scratch scratch, and at the last makes a last stab, to mark a full, an infinitely full, stop.